# SOME GO HOME

*A Novel*

## ODIE LINDSEY

A searing debut novel that follows
three generations—fractured by murder, seeking
redemption—in fictional Pitchlynn, Mississippi.

An Iraq war veteran turned small town homemaker, Colleen works hard to keep her deployment behind her—until pregnancy brings her buried trauma to the surface. She hides her mounting anxiety from her husband, Derby, who is in turn preoccupied with the media frenzy surrounding the long-overdue retrial of his father, Hare Hobbs, for a civil rights–era murder.

As Colleen and Derby prepare for the arrival of their twins, they must confront what it will mean to parent children in Pitchlynn, a town whose upscale marketing rebrand will reframe its antebellum estates . . . and erase any legacy of violence. And as the trial draws near, questions of Hare's guilt only magnify these tensions of class and race, tied always to the land and who can call it their own.

Twisting together individual and collective history, *Some Go Home* is a richly textured, explosive depiction of both the American South and our larger cultural legacy.

Nancy Russell

**ODIE LINDSEY** is the author of *We Come to Our Senses: Stories*. He received an NEA-funded fellowship for veterans, holds an MFA from the School of the Art Institute of Chicago, and is writer-in-residence at Vanderbilt University in Nashville, Tennessee.

# SOME GO HOME

*also by* ODIE LINDSEY

*We Come to Our Senses: Stories*

# SOME GO HOME

A NOVEL

ODIE LINDSEY

W. W. NORTON & COMPANY
*Independent Publishers Since 1923*

*for Dana and May*

# CONTENTS

# COLLEEN

# 1

Colleen drove home from the Memphis VA hospital classified as pregnant. She headed southeast for an hour, interstate to state highway, county road onto packed dirt drive, and into her attached double carport. She went in the house, flopped on the bed, and turned on daytime television. Lit a Misty, and nibbled her bottom lip between drags.

She was in love with the idea of having conceived during a recent tornado, a symphony of violence marked by cracked pines and tail clouds, and the pop of the roadside transformer in concussive, blue-white light. Yet Colleen knew she'd been pregnant weeks before the storm, a near-miss, as it were, akin to the funnel cloud itself. She wanted to feel cherished and hip when showing off a debut baby bump, but her condition was seamed to a takeaway of deployment: the inability to protect anyone, let alone a baby.

For a breath, she was yanked under by a riptide of past trauma—but then rolled her eyes and crushed her cigarette out. "You got this," she muttered. "Whatever it is."

She scanned the basic cable lineup for an hour or so, then snapped to and stepped outside. She had promised Derby, again, to get the mess of fallen pine branches off of the roof. After weeks of his griping, and of her dismissing said gripes, things had come to a head that morning. Thus, so, gestation be damned, if Colleen didn't finish the chore today, Derby swore he'd do it for her when he got home from work.

She would not allow that to happen. She grabbed the aluminum ladder from the carport utility shed, then extended it up to the roofline of the small house. The hollow clap of the rung locks clicked like the prize pins on the Wheel of Fortune. Climbing up and onto the low-sloped overhang, she sat down, and brushed the tile grit from her palms.

"*Surprise?*" the VA doctor had asked, glancing at her wedding ring. "*He'll be thrilled.*"

She looked out over the north Mississippi horizon, a rolling green canopy of forest into field, broken now and again by bulbous water towers. Marking tidbit towns she'd known all her life, the vessels were now topped by rings of spiky cell phone antennas, reminding Colleen of the Crown of Thorns. She shut her eyes and listened to the tamped thump of hip-hop in the distance, and knew that just across the county road a group of boys communed around an old car with a new stereo, in a ragweed yard, drinking beer and smoking. Black or White boys, or maybe both, cutting up and ditching school, doing the same thing their fathers had done, beneath the same scab of sun, a different soundtrack on the radio. So went the narrative in rural north Mississippi. For them, for her, for everyone, forever.

The debris pile on the roof—the final claim of that tornadic springtime storm—consisted of leg-thick branches, snapped twigs, and pinecones. Sticky shortleaf needles were scattered everywhere. The late March air was already tight with heat, so Colleen thought about climbing back down for some iced tea. And a hair tie, maybe sunscreen. And her cigarettes, shit. Yet she knew that if she did go back down she'd be done for the day, having failed to complete things, again.

She measured her steps against the slight pitch of the overhang, and began throwing small pine bits to the ground. The more she cleared, the more there seemed to be, so she picked them up faster, cone clumps and branches, slinging all into the yard, catching her balance now and then. She winced when the sweat trickled into her eyes, and her chest felt bruised up from smoking. Still, she cleared the pine trash faster, faster.

"*You know what they call contraception in Miss'ippi?*" the doc had asked. Colleen had shaken her head no.

"*Exactly.*"

A searing pain needled the inside of her forearm. Colleen knew it was a yellow jacket before she swatted it dead. She flicked the wasp away, then slapped at the sting. As a distraction of sorts, she stopped chucking the small bits, and instead gave a go at the large branch undergirding the pile.

The limb was heavy and she dropped it on the first try—then hoisted it right back up. The bark chewed her palms and the wasp sting blossomed, but the bough budged just enough to encourage her. Shoving the pile toward the edge of the roof, Colleen sensed a tipping point. "You're mine," she grunted, her abdomen bricklike as she leveraged her body forward. She threw everything she had in opposition to the weight, and then slipped and slammed down on her ass.

One of her sneaker soles was lacquered with blood. Her eyes darted over to the matted nest of haystick and scrap, and the litter of gray squirrels she'd slid on. Wriggling in the debris was a single spared pup. The inch-long creature bore fuzz as delicate as frost, and its inky eyes were lidded. Colleen got to her knees, leaned in close, and blew. Its head bobbed.

She looked out over the treetops as if seeking counsel, and once more to those crowned-Christ water towers. For the first time in forever, she thought of this nameless grandfatherly type from her childhood, a honey-drawl patriarch who lived in nearby Pitchlynn. He'd been all but installed on a bench in town square, an attraction of sorts, feeding corn kernels to a gray squirrel that sat upright on his shoulder, and astounding any clump-up of passersby kids. Colleen's memory of this time was sunlit. What's more, it carried potential, given the man's explanation of how anyone could raise an orphaned pup, nursing it with an eyedropper, then weaning it on to corn and carrots. Within weeks, he professed, you'd whistle the pet to your side.

She believed this opportunity. She had been that giddy kid.

Colleen closed her eyes and took in the full bore of sun, and she grinned with the feel of its dominance. She stood up, and apologized, and stomped on the nest, then got back to the problem at hand.

# 2

Then it was August. Sweltering, dead-grass August. She was on the couch, in a peach-colored bathrobe, third trimester. Derby had already called four times that morning; Colleen hadn't picked up, but only listened to the answering machine. He wasn't so much checking in on her as he was checking up, exercising his own anxiety. He'd been coiled extra-tight since seeing his father back in the news, as if the old man were anything more than a gust of scorched air (or as if a phone call to Colleen could protect her if he wasn't).

Instead of talking things out, Derby had doubled down on domestic regimen: check-ins, check-ons, grocery lists, chores, and reporting for daily duty at a house-flip gig in Pitchlynn.

Derby Friar, Derby Friar, his jeans forever tucked into his stiff leather ropers. Once a year, he bought a pair of tan, pull-on Red Wing work boots. He spent twelve months scuffing them, wearing them in proper . . . then bought another new pair, and started scuffing again. Every *two* years he bought five pairs of Levi's Shrink-to-Fit 501s. The denim so rigid, so horribly blue. He'd spend a weekend in and out of the tub, soaking and then drying the pants on his body. Derby squished as he walked about, dripping indigo all over everything. Then twenty-four months later, precisely as the jeans got soft and worn, and damn well *perfect* to Colleen, he'd bag them up for the Salvation Army, then start in on five new pairs.

Good ole boy, the best ole boy. His rituals were endearing. Most times, anyway. At first glance, the only thing quirked about Derby was that he had legally switched to using his mother's maiden name. Yet even this was predictable. If Colleen's surname had been Hobbs, she would've buried that shit the instant she turned eighteen. She was particularly thankful for this decision now that Derb's dad was back on radar, and likely headed back to trial.

She'd only met her father-in-law a couple of times, when she and Derby were first married, and when a brief, symbolic effort was made to cross paths. To Colleen, Hare Hobbs seemed like any other old crank. She was lulled by his drawl and easy measure, by his keen questions about herself and her military service, and the way that, well, just the way Hare came across as sort of fragile and empathetic, versus the vile concept she'd been warned about.

Admittedly, it was the only time she'd ever met a murderer. Or, as Hare was so known to point out, an *exonerated* murderer.

Regardless, Derby Hobbs, son of Harold "Hare" Hobbs, was now fully and irrevocably Derby Friar: thirty-two and fit, his eyes fanned by hairline wrinkles. A man who insisted he'd be made whole by a parcel and a small stocked pond, catfish and brim, on the outskirt of Pitchlynn, Mississippi. By a wife to adore and a thirty-year mortgage, a string of journeyman builder gigs, and most of all a brand-new family. Twins, in fact. Goodness gracious.

Colleen loved him, but she ignored his calls. She was bloated and alone in the hot little house, her muscles sore, sleep-deprived, and she didn't have any comfort to give. Hell, even the fact that they needed a landline felt confining. She'd had better cell service in Iraq.

She rubbed a gob of Palmer's Cocoa Butter lotion on her stomach, an attempted arrest of the stretch marks. Knotted up her dull gold hair, then scraped at the freckles of pink polish left on her nails. On the television, a New York celebutante cooked cathead biscuits. Only, to Colleen they didn't look like cathead biscuits, a name that everyone on set only joked about. The show hosts had used no bacon drippings nor buttermilk to prepare them, let alone a cast-iron skillet. She wondered how the celebrity had even landed on TV, doing things that Colleen was more suited to do. It seemed that one simply had to show up on set, be pretty, or rich, or both, and breathe. And feeling fairly certain she could produce three of these four prereqs—show up, be pretty, breathe—Colleen meditated on her ability to parlay such qualities into future success. She swore that after the babies were born, she was gonna . . .

She was gonna what? No matter how often she thought of the future, there was no clarity or specific as to how it would ripen. Rather, Colleen was driven by a shapeless, consuming lack. Made sick by a yearning for some new form of exceptionalism, a feeling that even her pregnancy had failed to quash.

She'd been exceptional, before. Her lungs had ventilated a rich mix of shamal dust storm and South Korean cigs, diesel exhaust and latrine, and toxic, burn pit shit. She'd seen a dead woman laid out on the hydraulic ramp of a Bradley vehicle in a city defined by wailing, foreign gibberish. Her own body had been weaponized, wrapped in MOPP gear and Kevlar and pixelated camo—and it had been combatively unwrapped, too. Exceptional was very, very possible.

Someone knocked on the kitchen door. She hoisted herself up, then waddled over to answer, mumbling, "Jesus Christ," and "Cathead, my ass." The diamond-shaped door window was filled with tendrils of brown hair.

"Hey," Colleen said, beckoning her best friend inside, before turning away to the coffeepot.

"Must be nice to sleep all day," Deana said.

"I wasn't sleeping. I was layin' around."

Deana took a long look at Colleen's belly. "A-*round* is right. Land sakes!"

"Don't even start," Colleen said. "It's hot. My bod's exploding. And I didn't sleep a wink."

"Cry me a Gulf, sister." Deana winked. "Oh hell, did you hear 'bout that missing pilot? The small plane that's gone down in the pines near Holly Springs? They can't find it anywhere. Just heard the distress call for help, and then, *boop!*—nada."

"Sounds about right," Colleen said. "Person tries to flee this place, and even the trees lock 'em down."

Deana grabbed a mug of coffee, then sat down in a wooden kitchen chair. She unbuttoned the top of her blouse to let the air sweep her chest. "My word, get a breeze goin'."

Colleen glared, but then turned on the box fan. She pulled a pack of Mistys from her robe pocket, offering one to Deana.

Deana waved the cig away. "For the record, the pilot wasn't trying to leave Mississippi. He was flyin' *in*."

Colleen huffed in disgust, then lit the smoke.

"Listen, girlfriend. I'm not gonna spend my lunch hour buckin' you up. You invited me over. So you tell *me* something good." Deana snatched the cig from Colleen's fingers, then winked. "I know there's a lump of sugar under all that salt."

"What'd you bring me to read?" Colleen replied, taking the cigarette back.

Deana laughed, then pulled a bundle of magazines from her purse: *Vogue*, *Glamour*, *Entertainment Weekly*, and the like, dated castoffs from the beauty parlor where she worked.

Colleen started thumbing a copy of *Us Weekly* and pointed to a spread of starlets on a red carpet. "She's hot."

"Damn straight. Check those legs," Deana said. "But lord, that's an ugly dress."

"Valentino, though," Colleen countered.

"Valentin-*No* is more like it. That outfit's a felony."

They continued like this over corn salad and sun tea, with Colleen dog-earing any image that made her feel jealous, or inspired, or depressed. Half an hour or so later, an alarm chimed on Deana's phone.

"That's the bell, kid," she said. "Gotta go."

Colleen ignored her and flipped another page.

"I realize that moodiness comes with the hormones," Deana said. "But if I wanted an hour full of mope, I'd go see my husband!"

Colleen glanced up. "You promised it'd get better."

"I still do. You're just feelin' cagey." Deana rapped on the table, then stood up. "As soon as those babies get here, it'll be like your heart's outside your body. Exposed. Alive. Devastated by love. You won't have another want on the planet."

"Right," Colleen said.

Deana helped Colleen to her feet, then beckoned a goodbye hug. Breasts and bellies, their breathing syncopated, things got woozy and still, and safe. Deana ran her chin against Colleen's neck, taking in the scent of that cocoa butter lotion. As their fingers flared on each other's backs, the kitchen fell silent enough to broadcast Colleen's swallow.

"You remember what I was like, Dean?" she asked. "Before Derby and all?"

What came to Deana's mind was a movie scene. A western, or war story. A chick flick, only more. It had taken place four years earlier—or maybe now five—though the memory was crisp. She'd been at work, at the beauty parlor, staring through the plate-glass window, watching an unknown young woman stagger half drunk across the parking lot. The stranger was bloodied to a pulp; a coalition of combat boots, miniskirt, and split lip. She had wobbled through the glass doors, propped up against reception, and cast her one open eye around the room.

Everyone on hand had seen the battered car behind her, and knew that a collision, not some man, had delivered the blows. (This fact had kept things on the savory side of gawk.) A movie. A tragedy. A rock opera. A crime. Nobody in the beauty parlor had known how to react to this . . . this *woman*, clearly whipped, but who seemed brimful of fight. And lost love, somehow. Even at first sight. Lost love.

Deana smiled. "Unfortunately, yes. I remember."

"I'm serious," Colleen said. "I was going somewhere then, you know? I felt like I was still *going*."

Deana wrangled loose from the embrace, and slung her purse over her shoulder. "You were, but in the wrong direction! Getting in your own way, ever' which way."

"Well, I guess you should've let me alone, huh?"

"Probably. And yet . . . here we are."

"Do you realize that I'm 'bout to spend the rest of my life in the same zip code I grew up in?" Colleen asked.

Deana grasped her friend's shoulder, smiled. "This's just hormones. Birth jitters. Believe me, I've been there. Twice."

"But—"

"You'll climb out of this hole, like you always do. Always have." Deana held out an open hand. "Now gimme those cigarettes. I don't know who's selling 'em to you, and I won't tell you not to have one or two. But come on, Colleen. Oh, and the lighter, too. Give it up. *Now*."

# 3

Colleen woke the next day to the bleat of the phone on the stuff-cluttered bedside table. She pawed at the pillows. "Answer that, babe? Derb?"

His side of the bed was empty, meaning that he'd probably left for work. When the phone quit ringing, Colleen sank back into sleep . . . until it rang again. She groaned, reached over, and clicked on the cordless.

"Hello?"

"Speak to Derby?" a woman asked. Her voice was young, yet nicked.

Colleen sat upright.

"Hel-*lo*?" the woman asked again. "You there?"

"Yeah," Colleen answered. "Derb's, uh. He's already gone."

"You know who this is, right?"

Colleen stood up, paced through the house, and looked out the front windows. Derby's pickup was parked at the far edge of the property, where the long dirt drive met the two-lane county road. He was blocked in by a white news van, a TV truck emblazoned with the local affiliate logo. She watched her husband confront a reporter and his cameraman.

"You hear me?" the woman groused.

"Yeah," Colleen said. "I know who you are." She went outside, and began to jog down the dirt driveway, barefoot, her body heaving. She couldn't yell for Derby, lest the caller find out he was still at home. Instead, she waved her free hand in the air to try and get his attention.

He was too busy telling the reporter off. Within seconds the news crew had loaded up and pulled away. Derby hopped in his pickup and peeled out behind them, onto the paved road.

"At least give me his cell number or somethin'!" the woman barked. "Shit."

Colleen stopped in her tracks, all but out of breath. "Winnie?" she heaved. "You know better than to call this house. Derb doesn't want anythin' to do with you, or for sure your daddy."

"Maybe it's mutual, Colleen. But here's the thing. He don't have a choice anymore. Hare's back in jail, and headed back to trial. They booked him this morning. Say they's evidence of jury tamperin', from way back. So now everybody's about to be coming after everybody else. Lawyers, feds, media . . . There are men out there you and I don't even want to think about, Colleen. The type Derby and me grew up around. So he can either deal with me or deal with them. By subpoena, or muscle, he *will* be a part of this deal."

Colleen had not felt threatened since deployment. She blushed. "Tell you what, Winnie. You drag your ass out here, and I'll be happy to—"

The line clicked dead.

Colleen took a deep breath and marched back into the house. She pitched the phone onto the kitchen counter, poured some coffee, and popped a quartet of Tums. Reached deep into the pantry for her grandmother's old metal spice box, and grabbed the pack of Mistys hidden inside. When she couldn't find any matches—Derby had confiscated every last flame in the house—she lit the cigarette on the eye of the electric stove.

A part of her felt awful for Derby. Despite years of effort to earn distance from his father, to ignore the man and try to move forward, a news van had confronted her husband in his own goddamned driveway. Winnie, his sister, would bring nothing but trouble.

Colleen didn't know what Hare Hobbs could or could not do to them. She only knew there was a murder, of a Black man, long before she was born. That Hare had been tried but set free, and that some folks had branded this a sham, while others claimed him a victim-turned-hero, a resistance fighter of sorts. She understood that Derby's childhood had been marked by Hare's public invectives, vile speeches and stunts that some claimed as cover for darker actions.

Over time, the town had ostracized Hare, his family, and by extension their own complicity (though the latter was a long time forgotten). And because Pitchlynn, Mississippi, was a chatty little place, she knew that Derby would now be returned to the front lines of judgment.

So yes, a part of her felt awful for her husband. Yet more so, another part fumed. Fact was, the estate house that Derby had hired on to flip was also the ground zero of his trauma, a space co-defined by Hare Hobbs. The so-called "Wallis House" manor was both historic visual icon and a battlefield of sorts, a site at the dark heart of Pitchlynn itself. Akin to a monument, or burial ground, it was best left undisturbed— lest you stir up a past you never wanted to face.

Derby now flaunted its disassembly. He was all but removing it on behalf of a new owner, an outsider, no less. As if no one would notice. As if no one remembered.

Despite years of refined passivity, her husband had placed himself in the crosshairs of conflict. What's more, he had positioned her and her children there, too. So the vital question for Colleen was whether Derby would fight what was coming, or burrow deeper into denial.

She favored the former tactic.

# 4

Derby went to work, he came home. Kept his head down in between. He skirted the landline, the local news, and the sludge-slow browser on the desktop in the den, locking in only on his wife and his any-day-now twins, and what he could do for all of them. He drove to the store or the gas station only when he had to, and when he had to, he favored places removed from his usual routine.

These off-radar hours had soon cobbled into days, and a week became two put behind him. It was as if the media fire around the Hare Hobbs retrial was somewhat contained, leading Derb to believe he'd been reinstated as a Pitchlynn nobody, at work on a Pitchlynn anyplace.

The folly of his assumption was made clear early one morning, care of a mock invasion of women onto the Wallis House front lawn. They wore antebellum hoop skirts and long gingham dresses. Lacy snoods bundled their hair, and tiny reticule purses hung from their wrists. Their leader, an uncommonly tall woman in a white, high-collared hoop dress, had ordered the lot to the base of a massive magnolia, where they idled for further instruction. Parasols were shouldered and fabric fans held at rest. The tall woman then directed the squad not to flinch, or even *think*, before beckoning a plump young photographer—Hup to!—whose camera straps crisscrossed his chest like bandoliers.

Derby stood at distance, where he'd been prepping for the work ahead. He chuckled at the cliché throwback of the ladies, until he recognized Susan George Wallis—and she caught sight of him. He turned and walked off toward his truck.

"JP!" she called out. "JP, please!"

Derby kept walking. In response, Susan George double-timed across the lawn, calling out his boss's name. The closer she came, the faster she spoke: "I know this is a wild scene to come up on! A babbling legion of old women dressed up as even *older* women, idling on your front lawn. My goodness, I know! I'm sure you must think . . ."

When she finally caught up, Derby turned to face her. "Wrong guy. I'm not JP."

"Well," Susan George replied. "You certainly aren't." She sized him up, from work boots to tool pouch, to the eyes that wouldn't meet her own. "Mr. Hobbs, I wouldn't have expected you here."

"It's 'Friar' now," Derby said. "My mother's maiden name, 'Friar.'"

"How convenient," Susan George replied. Watching the young man fidget while trying to sidestep his kin, she wanted to peel Derby open, to chew on his grotesquerie. Yet she knew better than to press him, especially now that his father's retrial was going forward. There was no Wallis family history without a relationship to Hare Hobbs.

She lifted her chin and cocked her eyebrows. "Did I read in the papers that you married that lady veteran?"

"You did. Been some years back, though."

"Boy, you certainly *love* your complications, don't you?"

"Colleen and I are about as plain as it gets."

She grinned. "You tryin' to tell me that two pair of boots by the bed doesn't add a little *lemon zest* to your relationship? That you aren't up for takin' a few orders?"

"Like I say," Derby replied. "We're the same as everybody else."

"Then aye-aye, Mr. *Friar*." She mock-saluted. "So anyhow, what brings you to our property?"

"I work here. We're 'bout to start renovation. We expect it'll take several—"

"Sorry, but we can't have that, can we? Can't just snap our fingers and change."

"I only do what the boss man asks," Derby replied. "Speaking of which." He motioned toward the guesthouse. His employer, JP, stood idle in the bungalow doorframe, a mug of coffee in his hand. Derby waved him over.

"You and I will have to speak again," she ordered, then turned to greet JP. "What a gift to finally meet you! We weren't sure . . . well, we didn't figure you'd be in town much longer."

"Sorry," JP said, shaking her hand, "I didn't catch your name."

"Susan George. Wallis."

"So," was all he could muster. So this was the woman who'd sent purchase offers for the estate before his wife's body was at rest. The woman whose correspondence had once included the term "future family," as if JP could leapfrog Dru's death. So this was the woman who had raised Dru as much as her own mother had, but who had later shunned the girl, lobbying her parents to send the child off to school.

Susan George pointed to the ladies on the far lawn. "We're generally more on our game about sending advance word of this type of gathering. Marketing the Grandiflora has been such a chore. I'm the mayor, too, you know, so things have been . . ."

So this was Dru's aunt. *His* aunt, by extension, though they'd never even met. Despite the fact that he and Dru had come down from Chicago a near-dozen times before she died, Susan George had never brokered an invitation to visit.

"Grandi-what?" JP asked.

"The Grandiflora. It's a catchphrase we're working with here in town. A lifestyle brand—that's the jargon, anyway—meant to attract tourists and twenty-first century capital." She motioned down to the magnolia. "The title comes from that tree."

Tupelo had Elvis. Tunica had gambling. Oxford had Faulkner and SEC football. In the absence of anything else, Pitchlynn had a handful of stellar antebellum houses, and above all a magnificent *Magnolia grandiflora*. A record-setter, a marvel. And now, should the hired-gun, Atlanta-based PR firm do their job, a tree to be transformed into a registered brand. An image cast nationwide, *Town & Country* to *Travel + Leisure*, AARP to XYZ, to you-name-it; a campaign pitch tailored to "Atlantic and Eastern Seaboarders seeking warm weather, economic bang, and revised, southern charm . . . with a dash of modern whimsy. Duck-fat fried catfish. Kimchi with rib tip, y'all," and so forth.

JP grunted, looked away. He was annoyed by the women who dimpled his fescue, snapped his gardenias.

"My word," Susan George muttered. "Forgive me. I am overwhelmed by the ridiculous, and, given all, a bit nervous about meeting you. So let's back up. Please. We were, are, in disbelief about Dru. I'm devastated. She and my daughter, well. I wasn't just Dru's aunt. I feel like I—"

"I wondered," JP said. "*Why isn't she saying anything about Dru? I wondered.*"

Susan George nodded. "You're right. Again, I fear I am overwhelmed, and—"

"Did you know that she died on a road? My wife? Your niece. That she died walking *into* a road, on purpose?"

"I am aware of everything, JP. And while I can't make excuses for how I mourn, I'm certain I could be better at it." She held a hand out as if to caress him, then let it fall back to her side. "And *Lucy*? Is she here?"

"Where else would she be?"

"Of course. May I see her?"

"No. The sitter just got her down. It was a rough night. Another rough night."

"I see," Susan George said. "Soon, I hope? You know, my own daughter's name was—"

"Lucinda, yes. I'm aware of my child's namesake." He gestured toward the women on his lawn. "So, then?"

"Right," she replied. "I'll get on and finish this photo shoot. But JP, one last thing. This will sound abrupt—I'm afraid it *is* abrupt—but I haven't been able to visit with you, so I have to intrude while I can. You have never so much as acknowledged our offers to purchase this property."

"Correct."

"As you well know, these are above-and-beyond-market-value offers. *Chicago* market value, even. Again, this place is the heart of our town. We've always honored it as such. And we have always had access."

"And?"

"And we *will* of course have access. Though be assured, we'd never change a thing. Wallis House is my father, my daughter, it is Dru.

Even you, JP. Plus, we're spending a whole lot of capital to make it the welcome-home icon for new neighbors."

"This house is a wreck. In fact, Derby and I are about to start——"

"No," she said. "First, you'll have to come by Town Hall. Fill out the historic pres application, then file the associated permit requests. Our bylaws are sticky, and they are ironclad. Yet I am certain the board can look into a reasonable Certificate of Appropriateness for you and Mr. . . . Mr. . . ."

It took Derby a second to realize he'd been cued back into the conversation. "Oh. Friar," he said. "It's Friar now."

"Right. For you and our Mr. *Friar*." She turned to walk back down the lawn. "But that application must be approved before y'all can shave off a splinter. You hear me? Not a splinter."

Mustered beneath the great tree, the ladies tightened their line, standing concave according to height, their backs arched, their lips pursed to within a muscle shy of smile. Susan George strode in front of them, pulling down their breeze-blown flaps of lace, straightening bonnets, and dabbing shine away with her kerchief. She then took her place behind the formation, and cued the doughboy photographer.

JP considered the procedure for a moment, then turned to Derby. "Let's get to work."

Before the last of the women had vacated the property, Derb was taking stock of the scaffold frame, paint tarps, linseed oil, and masks; he checked over the new ladder hooks, extension arm, and the infrared paint scrapers. While doing so, he reiterated to JP that they would get the old paint off of the house with a heat plate, gentle detergent, bristle, and lots of time. They would rely on water blast and patience, but no chemicals whatsoever. This was the old way, the right way, he insisted.

Derby did not bring up the fact that repainting the house *before* structural repair was one hundred percent ass-backward, if not a complete waste of time and money. His boss's decision to kick things off by applying a bright coral-with-pewter-accented, Eichler midcentury palette to a stodgy white manor wasn't just discordant, it was vindictive.

It was supposed to be. This project had nothing to do with restoration. The point was to make an assault.

When the scaffolding was assembled against the back wall of the house, JP called it quits for the day. The men ambled over to Derby's weathered green work truck, grabbing Gatorades from the cooler in the bed.

Derby motioned to the scaffold tower, a visual provocation for any Pitchlynnite of note. "You don't think we need to take a pause here?" he asked. "Get those permits and whatever 'fore we piss the whole town off?"

"We're fine," JP replied. "I've looked over all of it, top to bottom. I even know how long it will take them to litigate. Besides, Derby, their beef isn't over history, or policy. It's about money, plain and simple."

The young man shook his head. "Not here it isn't."

"You'll see." JP rapped on the truck a couple of times, then walked off toward his bungalow.

Derby locked his tools in the truck bed job-box, and set out to trek the perimeter of the house, policing any materials or litter left on site. He'd always been the first to arrive at a job, likewise the last to go home. It was a practice he'd followed even when working for bosses who never noticed or didn't care. First-to-last was a small marker of who you were. It was an identity you could control.

# 5

A few days after the rehab began, JP and Derby stood in the muted morning light, staring into the branches of the giant magnolia. Neither man spoke, but only considered the yellow nylon rope, the bottom end of which was tied to a low horizontal limb. The taut line ran upward, high into the crown of the tree, where something pinkish hung behind a dense clutter of leaves.

*A kite?* JP wondered. *No, and not a balloon. But . . .*

As if triggered, he bolted beneath the tree skirt and to the trunk, hoisting himself onto a bough. He climbed limb to branch, his upward glances blinded by light-breaks between glossed leaves. It was a *thigh*, he had understood. A thigh on a small body.

At sixty feet or so, the stench of spoiled meat mingled with the magnolia oil. At ninety, JP began to gag on the air, and could only sip quick, shallow breaths. Immune to Derby's protests, he moved out on horizontal boughs, one at his chest and the other at his feet, as if inching across a rope bridge. Though the limb he stood on began to creak, to crack, he continued on until he saw her in full: her empty eye sockets, and the jowls rolling over the noose. The jellied blood that trickled her shanks, and the skin flaps that curtained her gutted, pale pink belly.

"Derby!" he yelled. "There's a goddamned sow up here!"

THE MANOR itself was textbook Greek Revival, white on white with pillars and pediment. The property it sat on was parklike, taking up several city blocks, and populated by sugar maple and tupelo, dogwood, elm, and oak. An arcade of towering red cedars lined each side of the long pea-gravel drive. The Pitchlynn Historic Tour bus would idle at the piked iron fence out front, where guides read a script about the elaborate back gardens, "Designed by Vaux, partner of Olmstead," likewise that the site's original, Italianate residence had been razed to bricks when Union forces torched the town.

The tour guides never mentioned that the current house only arrived on site in 1965, having been trucked into Pitchlynn as part of the Civil War Centennial. They gave no dry description of the flatbed rigs that had carted in disassembled hunks of the former Wallis farmhouse, nor the float-like procession complete with Battle Flag bunting. No, the city-approved narrative never detailed the Wallis family notables who had waved from the rolling-by front porch and balcony, nor the scores of Pitchlynnites who had lined the parade route, their own star-and-bar ensigns flying, welcoming some collective return to prominence.

For all the spectacle jubilance of relocating the renamed "Wallis House" into town, scant attention had been paid to the reassembly of the home itself, nor the upkeep to follow. Despite gleaming white paint and seam tin roof, the Greek Revival's temple columns were now cored by rot, and the electrical and plumbing lines corroded. Stress cracks jittered the lime plaster walls of the interior, and the wood flooring was cupped from a buckled foundation. Nobody had lived there for a handful of years, since Dru's parents had passed, within months of each other.

Truth be told, the structural damage was just fine with the townsfolk, as long as the façade of the home was maintained. In fact, truth be told, the giant magnolia out front was far more revered than the manor itself. While the home was in some ways a symbol of who they'd been, the tree was their only true *living* link to history.

"Bel Arbre," as it was now known, had been planted in 1867, by the Ladies' Memorial Association of North Mississippi, a group soon absorbed by the United Daughters of the Confederacy, before reconvening as the "LMA" in the 1960s—so stated the cast-iron marker in front of the estate. A visual record of the tree's planting hung in the lobby of Pitchlynn Town Hall; the large sepia-tone photo featured rows of elderly Confederates in white, pajama-like gowns, bearded and gaunt, many devoid of limbs, as were flanked by younger women in white dresses and nursing caps. The lot were gathered around the just-plotted sapling, as if it were babe-in-manger.

Bel Arbre, now the lynchpin of the Grandiflora campaign, approached 130 feet in height; its base was broad enough to engulf a cabin. The tree had surpassed the life expectancy of any recorded giant southern magnolia, anywhere. Tourists and photographers, historians and dendrologists, had for years gathered on the lawn to take photographs and measurements, or for guided walks. Visitors clamored for genteel portraits with the specimen, their noses buried in bouquets of its saucer-sized flowers. Lecturers went on about the species itself, noting that the *Magnolia grandiflora* even predated the existence of bees, that the toughness of the bloom had evolved to suit beetle-as-pollinator.

The iconic tree and parkscape had served as the Pitchlynn centerpiece for well over a century (though, truth be told, the tree was only christened "Bel Arbre" with the arrival of Wallis House, and that 1965 parade). Generations of marriages and picnics, memorials and outdoor plays, had been hosted on the estate grounds beside the great evergreen. Now and again, when a foreign diplomat or pop icon had come through, they were invariably led to a photo op beneath the tree.

Line drawings of the colossal magnolia were now featured on formal civic objects, from LMA letterhead to the Pitchlynn Board of Tourism logo. One could pick up packets of party napkins embossed with its likeness, likewise bookmarks or decorative plates, bumper stickers or porch flags.

Bel Arbre was what made Pitchlynn special. It was what made them, well, *them*. Even greater, at least for the LMA and invested parties, the tree would now beckon a new generation, and once more restore the town's momentum.

So it was arresting, sickening even, to discover that after the death of the estate's final inheritor——JP's wife, Dru Wallis——the property had been reclaimed as private. Pitchlynn citizens, having grown intimate with her family's de facto donation of the land, couldn't process the fact that the pike iron gates were now shut when not in JP's service.

They were appalled that the floodlights at base of Bel Arbre were now cut off in the evenings, dousing the tree in darkness.

The most prominent among them had at first tried to reason with JP. As a blind offering of faith (and, to be explicit, fortune), the LMA had presented him an inflated purchase offer on the home before he moved down from Chicago. The cover letter detailed their love of the town, their respect for his situation, and their sorrow over the circumstance. It kept mentioning "our tree" and "our house," explaining that though they wished to own the property outright, the offer guaranteed him a say in its use, e.g., memorials and pomp, likewise on-site accommodations for JP and his "future family."

Upon receipt, he slipped their envelope under the silverware tray in his kitchen drawer, then tossed it when packing for the move to Mississippi.

*Future family?*

It wasn't that the money didn't tempt him. Nor did JP want to leave his hometown. Yet selling the estate would have violated his promise to Dru: that they would move back together, and raise their daughter in Pitchlynn.

He had broken this promise, repeatedly, when she was alive. If she had still been alive, he would have broken it again, offering in its place another weekend trip South, or some related geographic panacea. Over the majority of their relationship, he'd been able to tamp down her depression (whether pre- or postpartum, conditions that were never, ever verbalized). Most successfully, he had done so care of a series of homecoming trips South: weekend and three-day visits around the state, which had mollified Dru's insistence that she needed to come home to heal.

The trips had been, JP believed, an earnest compromise. It wasn't as if *he* had any interest in Mississippi. Hell, he'd never even had interest in the region as a whole, save the time he'd considered a college spring break tagalong to Somewhere, Florida. Before he fell for Dru, the South for him had been a one-liner punch line. A banjo lick, or dumbstruck drawl.

Yet there he'd been, in his thirties, with her, in a rental car picked up at Memphis International, cruising through rural spaces he'd not imagined existing in America, in pursuit of what Dru termed only a picnic.

"I hope my being here is a testament to my love," he'd said.

"I believe," she replied. "it's a testament to mine."

They drove past untold numbers of manufactured homes, as were moored on cinder-block slabs; past squat brick ranches with stuck-on carports or cars-in-yards; they passed tractors and chicken-wire trash pens and granaries, and umpteen old pickup trucks parked at the roadside, posted FOR SALE. They moved through verdant fields and treelines, and, for a moment, their car hugged the curved banks of a mud-rich river, the brown water glistening in the spaces between bankside cypress, and with splatters of purple wisteria strangling everything. Now and again, JP had caught sight of chalk-white egrets perched in the shallows. Dru had guided them past kudzu vines that covered the rolling expanses like some green topographical quilt. Kudzu that appeared to be pulled over power pole and barn, blanketing any copse of pine or hardwood that wasn't defended, that had not been chopped back by work crews in orange vests, their ax-like mattocks stabbing the earth in hunt of vine crowns.

All the while there was the sun, the sun, the summer the sheen, the light praising everything into a polarized sort of crispness. That first trip South was about sun, the sun, the sun . . .

The visits had proven an initial success—for Dru's well-being, for them, and for a decent stretch of time. JP trusted the excursions, and he applauded his process. But then one day, back in Chicago, in winter, Dru had walked into the road. Having phoned him a few times, she left a yellow Post-it note on the kitchen table—*Fed Lucy. Going out. Back later*—and was gone.

JP never had the chance to stop breaking his promise, and he never wanted to forget a detail of those trips. So alongside *saudade*, and indulgence, he'd moved down to Pitchlynn for little stabs of lost joy. He was here to understand who Dru would have been, to see what she would've seen, in the flash of her features and her mannerisms in Lucy.

Lucy. Their daughter. He was astounded that the infant had already started to crawl. (Well, she was crawling backward, anyway!) It was an enlightenment to watch her nudge to and fro over Berber carpet, her body a test site of wobble and doggedness. As counterbalance to JP's rifted emotional life, his child now occupied all physical space, care of diapers and onesies and binkies and bibs, and bottles of Dreft detergent; care of nursing nipples that had to be boiled clean, and in burp rags to wash, and in the drums of Earth's Best formula he had to keep on automatic online order, because they didn't carry the stuff anywhere in this dinky-ass town. (Lucy was working through a whey allergy, so she had to have Earth's Best, versus any dairy-based formula. The allergy was a passing, semi-mundane condition, yet try going through *that* diagnosis alone: finding a blood streak in a then-four-month-old's diaper, and navigating the head-on collision of your-just-buried-wife and your-infant-daughter-is-bleeding-internally.) Her plastic bath basin had colonized the kitchen sink. Her putrid, heat-baked diaper disposal defined the air on the back deck. There were the stain sticks, and a car seat, and the banana-flavored Mum-Mum cracker crumbles all over everything. There was the packing of supplies for every single tiny outing: diapers and wipes and rags and spare clothes, and the crying, the howling.

There was the adoration, eclipsing all. JP had experienced, was experiencing, a new-universe-style love for that child. For their child, Lucy, who showcased Dru's single dimple, and who bore the name that Dru had given her, and who was the constant affirmation of her father's redemption, care of the plans Dru had made before the child was even conceived.

Having been too selfish to put his wife's needs above his own, let alone confront her over what he'd known for months before her death—that she was sick, and slipping, not just "moody" or in some "stage"—JP's consequent vow was to live out her expectations. He now swore to provide what she had wanted all along: the restoration of a proper childhood at home, by way of a child, brought home.

JP's arrival to town had been met by an even stronger purchase offer on the house, followed by letters to this effect, and relentless phone calls—none of which he answered or returned. When prominent figures began knocking on his door unannounced, crashing Lucy's naptimes and raking his nerves, he had moved out to the former servants' quarters, an austere beige bungalow at the back of the property. In public, as strangers approached him on the square, or at the grocery or gas station, he walked right past, not a hint of acknowledgment.

The LMA and Pitchlynn elite decided to meet JP on his own terms. He wanted solitude? So be it. They would wait him out, their own silence or influence thrown back twice as hard. At certain restaurants JP was then made to sit without service for as long as he could stand it, or as long as Lucy could stay quiet in the child seat beside him. Boutique store managers often handled every other customer, or vanished altogether, when JP walked in to shop. Now and again, even a lowly grocery clerk closed their aisle just as JP reached the head of the checkout line. In between, everywhere, were the small-town slights, and the turnings-away of service.

He had no family here, nor any prospect of friendship. Pitchlynn, they knew, could be a very lonely place.

Only, they didn't count on his anger, nor the fuel of his regret. The more the Pitchlynnites iced him out, the more determined he became to stay put. To an extent, he even made a game out of things. He realized, for instance, that any restaurant refusing to acknowledge him at a table was entitled to the opera of Lucy's howls. (That child's ability to scream when hungry was profound. And because JP knew precisely when the infant's *want* turned to *need*, he could lift her public crescendo like a maestro.) At the hardware store or grocery, or any place that made him wait in excess, he'd leave a check on the counter and walk out with his items, daring any clerk or shopkeep to test the limits of their passive-aggressiveness.

He was in town now, period. "Future family"? Not a fucking chance.

The tension had played out like a chess match in a room on fire, until late one evening (if you could call a 3:47 a.m. bottle-feeding "evening"), JP envisioned the ultimate affront: he would take control of the thing they valued most, enacting a highly visible, contemporary renovation of the Wallis House itself, with a postmodern rearrangement of the property grounds to follow.

He would gut the place. Cut their hearts out, real slow. From that midcentury paint scheme to a green, leach-field septic; from ab-ex lawn art to a shimmering rooftop field of silicon solar panels. Window frames to wainscoting, every inch of that home would be wrung free of memory, right before their eyes.

Inspired, elated, he had scoured his old rehab plans from back in Chicago, consulting databases of design resource and structural manual, even pop-cultural trend mags and hipster hack websites. His contractor background was reignited to full flare. His creativity was reunited with craft, calculation, even the ability to connive (e.g., he sourced materials from nearby towns, so nobody would get wind of his project). He'd researched both Pitchlynn and Mississippi codes, and had his Chicago property lawyer do the same, just in case. His holdings were shifted and his accounts interlinked. Any legal intrusion on their part would involve motion after motion, year after year.

To keep watch over Lucy during the work hours to come, JP hired a squad of young enrollees in child development and early childhood ed at North Mississippi CC. These young women (for there were only young women in the program) were eager to ply their trade and squirrel away a few bucks. With this caretaking secured, he had at last looked for an assistant.

Interviewing Derby, JP noted the younger man's drive, and his attentive, mindful demeanor. Small-town or not, the guy knew a ton about the materials and process JP planned to employ. What's more, Derby was ravenous for further expertise. And while JP wasn't sure why a local guy with a such a skill set hadn't sustained any clientele, at the end of the day he didn't care. Truth be told, Derby was the only one who applied for the job.

\* \* \*

So NOW, this: flies spattered a lynched sow carcass like raindrops.

JP's arms were locked around the wavering limb. Only after Derby threatened to climb up and fetch his ass did he gather himself and start inching down the tree. Reaching the base of Bel Arbre, JP took a few steps before falling to his knees in the grass.

Derby squatted beside him. "I'll cut that lever rope and get it down now, boss. Take it out to the country and—"

"No." JP said, wondering how close his hired hand was to the LMA, and the rest. How was it, for instance, that the young man brokered no explanation? No shock, nor surprise. Hell, he didn't even offer to call the cops. "Don't you touch it," JP ordered, wondering if what he'd read about Derby's father was true.

# 6

Susan George Wallis sat in a gold silk wing chair and unfolded Dru's letter. Reading it had become almost ritual over the months. Depending on her mood, the process could take on an act of contrition, or catharsis. After crossing JP, however, she'd been struck with a new potential understanding of the document. It was a threat.

The light through the tall windows of her drawing room was dampened by sheeny white curtains. The crisp ticks of her grandfather's regulator wall clock filled the high ceilings of the house.

> *Susan George,*
>
> *You and I know how it works: over time, a secret becomes a lie. A fact becomes lie because of its very keeping. A secret is thus the middle ground: a memory of a fact that dies. Revises. That turns from the truth into lie.*
>
> *Why is this process so hard to explain? It's so strange to write you after all this time. (I can't remember the last time I even wrote a letter.) But I can't not write you, either. You are the only one left who remembers. The only one who might understand that for me, the lie of that tree has turned back on itself, and into memory. It is gravid, flowering again. I know now that the facts of that night will return. I fight this process and try not to obsess. But I can't stop it Susan George: the reversal of time. The remembering of truth is so much just too much.*
>
> *I think this was triggered by my pregnancy. Did this happen to you, when you carried her? Did you remember things? Remember facts buried in lie?*

*In memory: Lucy's legs swayed beside mine that night, in the tree. In Bel Arbre our teenage boyish legs were made thick against the high limb we rocked on. Our feet bumped carelessly as they dangled. I remember her lips: wet from sipping sticky sweet tea. We were newly-minted teens. We could still climb so high. We laughed and she laughs and . . . it was nighttime. It is . . .*

*Only: this is no longer memory Susan George. The lie has turned back on itself, towards fact: we are never away from the tree. Our faces are still shined by humidity. Her mother's car is in the driveway below. The headlights flare the lawn. Her mother calls out for her.*

*You call out for her. She and I are in the tree, again. The ivory blossoms are the perfect mask: our bodies hidden in the leaves. (Do these facts make you uncomfortable, Susan George? Have you moved forever through memory, into lie?) Her smiles: her teeth shining between spread fingers. Her mother yells for her. Car headlights flare the yard.*

*You yell for her. Your headlights flare the yard. We laugh at you and she wipes her mouth. Spits. Giggles. She is bored with us. You and I are lost to her budding adolescence. You scream for her, your headlights beaming. I paw at her to no loving reply. Lost to her attention, we'll do anything to get her back. Below: you scream, while I pull at her, above. She laughs I swat you scream she sways. You call she smiles I pull she . . .*

*She falls. She fell. The truth of this is too much. It was too much for any of us after she fell.*

*I was run off from this fact. Sent away. Banished: my eyes fit to blinders. Run off from her death as if memory were a physical geography. Across years across schools or jobs or loves or cities: run off from that night, pushing fact down to memory, toward lie. As if we could move past her gelled eyes. Past the pulling and screams and the fall.*

*And over years, over jobs, over continents, at long last: things started to revise. For a time, the memory simmered into secret, then cooled down to lie: I had <u>nothing</u> to do with her death. That* *night in the tree became a pastel of sadness that could come but then leave in a breath. It was a shiver at best. I was released.*

*Until one day I looked into a bathroom mirror in Chicago, considering facts: my lips split by winter. My rings under eyes and my belly cast iron. My coming, kicking child. And I saw Lucy's ghost just behind me. And I see her again now: in Bel Arbre. When I sleep when I sit, when I dream. In mirror or window, or still pool of bathwater. Reflection: the lie has turned back into memory, towards fact. The more I fight this process, the more poison floods my body.*

*I am trapped, Susan George. So who else can I ask: did I do it? Did I matter that night? What on earth is the truth?*

*This all sounds crazy. I am sick over writing you with this, but who else can I ask? Who can I tell that she's come back to me? JP? Tell JP that she is just there, outside our window? Floating, her lips parted and glossed? Teeth shattered?*

*No. This is not how it works. You can never confess to an outsider. Never tell someone who stands beyond the map of experience. They can only be permitted to know the lie.*

*Time has reversed itself, Susan George. And this reversal is pulling me down. Lucy is pulling us down . . .*

# 7

Colleen propped up on her elbows, in bed, in her undies and the worn peach bathrobe. Her legs showed as tan against the bleach-white sheets, and her tummy was freakish in protrusion. She snuck the day's first Misty while watching the morning show out of Tupelo.

Derby popped into the doorway. "Hey? I was callin' you."

"Keep callin'," she griped, whistling smoke toward the open window, then, "Sorry, babe. Didn't mean that." She dropped the cigarette in a bedside water glass. "Just half asleep, you know?"

He held his hand out and scowled until she turned over the pack of smokes, which he mashed up and jammed in his pocket.

"And the lighter?" he asked.

She grunted and handed it over.

"And the backup?"

"What?"

He stared at her until she opened the drawer of the bedside table, reached in, and found her hidden cigarette and matches.

"Happy?" she asked, slapping them into Derby's palm.

"Thrilled."

"And?"

"And . . . I was just gonna tell you 'bye, and I love you. So 'bye. I love you."

"Wait. What? Where are you goin' on a Saturday, Derb?"

"No place, really. Just gonna putter outside here. Me and JP, knockin' out a few chores. Isn't my favorite type of Saturday, but someone has to keep the place up, you know? Plus, I wanna stay close to home, in case you need me."

"Wait. Why didn't you ask me to help out? I am capable of help, you know? And I mean, really, Derb? On a *weekend*?"

"Of course you're capable, Colleen. But at this stage, you need to take it real easy. Just 'cause you want to help doesn't mean you need——"

"You have got to stop tellin' me what I need, man. Plus, it's my house. And my Saturday, baby. At least get me into town, so I can see another face."

She turned away, to look at the Tupelo telecast. Reporting live from Maui were Ray and Dottie, a couple from nearby Pontotoc. They'd won the Hawaiian Punch Dog Days of Summer Getaway prize: four nights, five days, all expenses paid, alongside a goofy, on-camera slot to send word about island geography, boat drinks, foreignness . . .

Colleen stared at the surfside scene. "Don't you ever want to be somewhere different, Derb? Be somebody else?"

"You mean, like, *big time* somewhere else? Move away?"

Colleen nodded.

"Did I used to want to run? Hell, yes. Most of my life. But now I want to prove this place wrong. Or prove me right. Shit, I don't know." He stared at her, and smiled, then sat down on the bed. Put one hand around her shoulders and placed the other gently on her stomach. "Besides. Pitchlynn has its fine points."

Colleen scowled.

"Take this one time," he continued. "I was standin' in front of City Hall, when this goddess flowed past me in a red ragtop Corvette."

"Christ, Derby. Just get out of here, okay? I don't wanna hear this story again."

His grin grew even wider. "This was four or five years ago. The whole town had gathered on the square to see the new Strawberry Maiden. And me? At first, I cursed hell for gettin' caught in that parade. I mean, I had things to do, you know?"

"Sure you did," she said. "So *important*."

"Hush." He traced a fingertip over the inside of her thigh. "It was like the whole world filled up with light. You floated by in that spar-kled dress and sash, seated on the trunk of that 'vette. You were like a painting. A masterpiece." He moved his boots onto the bed, and she shifted down onto the mattress. "You were the sun," he whispered. "I couldn't even look at you."

"Stop it."

"Now, that, babe, was the third time I'd ever seen you." He kissed her neck. "And . . ."

She ran a finger over his earlobe. "And what?"

"And though I've lost track of how many times I've seen you since, you *still* knock the breath outta me. So see? You're the reason this town matters. You're the joy of it, the history, the——"

"Now, you hush," she said.

Derby kicked off his boots and scooted down onto the mattress, kissing her breasts and basketball tummy. Colleen leaned back into her pillow, her hands kneading his dark, shower-damp hair, her body undulating and letting him give, accepting kisses as his lips and unshaven chin scribbled over her, the bedsprings weeping in chorus.

Somehow, despite themselves and her condition, her ever-intensified scrutiny of her body, of its betrayal and the post-birth betrayals she knew were to follow, things grew gauzy and trancelike. She melted into the flow and lost everything: where they were, how she got here, and how she would never, ever leave. In other words, she forgot herself——until he giggled.

"What is it?" she asked, propping back up onto her elbows.

"Shhhhh," he whispered, his breath slight over her thigh.

"Seriously. What?"

"It's nothin'."

She looked away from him, and to the white mini-blinds. The plastic slats had been snapped by their old cat, Diva, who'd cracked the blinds while trying to jump out the window. When that cat had finally escaped, it never came home. (Colleen missed having a pet. Derby was the only man she'd ever met who refused to have dogs. He wouldn't even pet a puppy. A *puppy*, for chrissakes.) She looked over to Ray and Dottie: on television, in Hawaii, the plastic leis ringing their necks.

"Go on to work now, giggles," she said.

"I said forget it." He kissed her again.

"Get on to your chores."

"Colleen? It's—"

She palmed his shoulders and pushed him off.

"Fine," he huffed. He sat back up on the edge of the bed and grabbed for his ropers. He stood up, then leaned over and kissed her forehead. "I'll miss you, grumpy. Don't say I didn't try to show affection. I was all set to cancel with JP, and—"

She rolled over to stare at the opposite wall.

He shook his head as he walked out of the room. Seconds later he called out, "I really will miss you. The *nice* you anyway!"

She stared at the rumpled poly bedspread, and at the same old fitted sheets. The latter were chewed to bits by the washing machine agitator; small holes now speckled the fabric, as if the cotton had been flecked by acid. She couldn't even conceive of a time when new sheets or new mini-blinds would hit the top of the need list. There were just too many Band-Aid fixes in front.

On television, Ray and Dottie yammered on about Hawaii. Up Next, Breaking News about the Plane Man Lost in the Pines.

Colleen lurched up, then went to look in the mirror on the back of the bedroom door. She examined her reflection, breasts to thighs, and to the stripe of discolored skin that now stretched south from her used-to-be innie navel, before figuring out what Derby had found so funny down there.

"Oh," she said, her fingers combing the shock of silver hair. She was three months shy of twenty-seven.

She slid into a jersey maternity skirt and stomped outside, hiding in the carport until Derby's truck rounded the bend of the dirt drive. She snuck over to the old barbecue grill, reached under and turned on the propane, and felt around for the hidden pack of Mistys. Lifting the lid of the grill while talking to herself, she held back the translation of her words into tears. The ignitor clicked and clicked when she turned on the knob, its rhythm like yet another metronome of life, or like the stopwatch timer on an action movie bomb. *Click click click click . . .*

Colleen had barely registered the smell of propane when, *click click click . . . Whoomp!*

She leapt back from the fireball, and tumbled into the grass. "Jesus

Christ!" Her eyes darted to her stomach, legs, then to her forearms and the singed patch of hair, wrist-to-elbow. She put a hand to the stove-hot skin of her cheek.

From the base of the grill, the propane hose hissed from a split. Colleen steadied herself, then sprinted over and shut the tank off.

Nothing was secure here. It was all under fire. She leaned against the side of the little house, and hugged her stomach, and wept.

\* \* \*

DERBY AND JP lugged along the dirt pathway in the boxwood green F100. Derb yanked the column shifter into third, and the truck chassis shuddered wildly.

"Someday, somebody'll pay me enough to put a new clutch in," he joked.

"You get paid plenty," JP replied.

They drove over the winding dirt trail, the old truck's engine wheezing like a turbine. Hot air gusted through the triangle side windows and floor vents. Trunks of mature pines whisked by, alongside orphaned hardwood, berry thickets, scrub. Derby spent much of the ride twisting the factory radio dial in an attempt to tune in the Country Gold station out of Tupelo.

This was not work. It was Saturday. Lately, as often than not, weekends meant making the switch from JP's house to Derby's, where the two knocked out chores with beers in hand, before cruising to the catfish pond at the interior of Derby and Colleen's land. There, they determined to pretty much drink more beer, to talk about the work they'd completed on Wallis House, or the workload ahead.

The green and placid pond was at the dead end of the trail. The tree line and sky were mirrored on its surface, and sparse grass grew on the embankments. Beneath the shade of frilled pines were a couple of old metal rockers, a thronelike chair carved of tree trunk, and a rotting bench. They got out of the truck and walked to a wooden bin near the water. JP lifted its top and removed the metal lid of a trash can housed inside. Each man then grabbed one of the large scoops from the reservoir of Sportsman's Choice catfish feed, and slung the pellets in a wide arc over the pond. The feed pocked the water like raindrops.

Within seconds, hundreds of charcoal-gray catfish swarmed the surface, scuttling over each other, their white bellies oily in the sunlight as they gasped for feed. The frenzy made the water look like it was boiling. As a second sling of pellets hit, the fish formed a meta-organism of mouth and fin and whisker. Near the banks a few even breached, their bodies wriggling in the mud, oblong mouths agape, until a minute later, as abruptly as they had appeared, the last of the catfish swam back down to the mud bed.

JP, pleased by the ritual but growing a bit used to it, too, splashed his face with the melting ice water in the cooler. The two then sat and downed their beers, and watched the sun fall against the pond, the atmosphere color. Now and again, a bass cracked the glassy surface. When the silence felt too extended, Derby would mutter on about the ratio of brim fingerling to catfish at stocking, and at what stages each should be introduced to ensure that no species fed off of the other, et cetera, whatever, no matter.

The more they drank, the more the younger man analyzed the mechanics of his anxiety, the gears being his father, the trial, Susan George, Wallis House . . . and the threat that each now posed to his marriage, and his children. With the boil-down of sun, Derby burned to confess his confusion as to why he sometimes even acted despite himself. He wanted to understand how he could sprint from any mention of Hare, yet be brought to heel by the very folks who'd turned the man upside down. How had he gone to work at a place so connected to his pain?

Complicity, it seemed, was on Derby like a bruise, in him like a gene. So when JP recycled their talk back to the house rehab process, he interrupted.

"It not personal, this Wallis House stuff," he said. "Rather, it's *real personal* for the town, but nobody's judging you personally."

JP shrugged, and turned to stare at the lake.

Derby continued, "Place has just meant so much, for so long. Too long for you to occupy it without—"

"See, Derb? You and I are on the same page here. None of this has anything to do with me. I repeat, it has *nothing* to do with me. Besides, is that pig all they've got?"

Derby sipped his beer. "No. There's more."

He could picture the other ones, twisting on ropes. The ones Hare had hung behind the Platz wall. *I was just a little kid*, Derby thought. *I couldn't help but go back there to see.* At the time, the terror had served as both reprisal and warning. He understood now that it was also meant to be a reminder.

He'd never told Colleen about the Platz, the little rally space behind his childhood home, or the militia of men Hare had inspired to build it. Derb was too afraid that if he did talk about it she'd leave him, as had the rest: his mother and sister, friends and girlfriends. The whole town, sort of. Though everybody in Pitchlynn knew the boy had nothing to do with Hare's actions, he'd been stained by association, everywhere he went.

JP spoke up. "Well, they'll have to own every bit of it."

Derby listened to the grind of the crickets and small frogs. He downed his beer, crushed the can, then flung it into the pickup bed. Reached over to fetch another from the cooler, his fingers carving slow channels in the ice water. There was only one left. He held it out to JP.

"Thanks, no. I'd better get home." JP stood up and stretched. "Let that poor babysitter have her Saturday night, you know?"

The truck's headlights soon poured over the darkened trail back, and its bench seat squeaked with every bump. Derby managed to dial in that crackled Country Gold station, though much of the broadcast was devoted to news of the downed plane and its pilot.

Minutes later, they pulled into the carport-slash-workshop, parking the old Ford amid the legion of power and lawn tools, hardware and industrial shelving.

JP said to tell Colleen hello, and to thank her for sharing the weekend. "By the way, are you guys having a baby shower?"

"We haven't even found time to talk about it. At this point, I doubt there *is* time."

"So that means yes. You are." JP grinned. "Or, rather, I'm planning one for you."

"Naw, that's okay, boss. It means that we—"

"We'll have it at my place. You and Colleen come up with a date, and let me know who to invite. I'll tackle the logistics, the invitations, the everything else. It'll be eleventh hour, obviously—we'd better do it next weekend!—but we'll set up in the back gardens and go to town."

"Really, JP, it's not—"

"Like I said, just give me a date, fast, and tell me who to invite."

Derby smiled, and nodded in appreciation. JP got in his car and drove back to town. Though he wasn't sleepy, he was eager to curl up on the pull-out couch in his daughter's room. To lie awake and listen close, as if memorizing her every breath.

COLLEEN WAS startled when Derby came through the kitchen door. She scooted to the sink, and washed the teaspoon of d-Con rat poison down the drain.

"Hey," she said, though she didn't fact him. She'd been so far gone that she hadn't heard the truck pull into the carport, or the men talking outside. So far gone, contemplating the power it took to truly change someone: to steer them off track, to make them *feel* that no matter how much they believed in security, a stranger could show up and take it away.

It was the revelation that even she could take it all from someone, another woman, no less, halfway around the planet, which had taught Colleen not just that life could be snatched from her, but that, in fact, it would. That in a sense, it had.

Coming home to Mississippi, demobbed from active duty, she had understood that nothing—no family, no church, no job, house, or health insurance—could protect you, no matter what you gave up. No matter how hard you believed things were safe. At the end of the day, the only armor against loss were the acute reminders of your own fragility. You could never forget how to die.

She'd been so far gone, staring at a gob of gleaming turquoise putty and strychnine crystals, held just over the large bowl of Hormel Chili,

No Beans. She watched it wash down the drain when Derb walked up behind her.

He kissed her neck, then eyeballed the poison tube on the counter. "We got a mouse or somethin', babe?"

"Somethin'," Colleen replied, scrubbing her hands in the scalding water.

# 8

The Plane Man hung upside down in the fuselage of the crashed Cessna, in the Holly Springs National Forest, in the heat.

"My god, legs, please go numb," he muttered. "My god."

His hands were lacerated, trembling, as he tore off another strip of aeronautical chart. He wadded it between thumb and forefinger and dabbed it into his mouth. His cracked lips pooched as he suckled the pill-ball, the moisture of the gluey paper coating his tongue.

The blood flow had shoved into his head for three sunsets. He'd exhausted the first day trying to pull himself upright, to relieve the pressure in his skull. The effort had required the use of thighs and abdomen in partnership with a shattered femur. The pain of it had thrust him into a limbo of white light.

It was curious now that the three-day migraine had gone away, had ebbed as if bored, as if it were time to step aside for heatstroke. He knew that sepsis was near. He'd been sucking tear-sized drops from the strips of wet aviation map: pea-green-, mustard-, and purple-colored ink; the yellow NAVAID box inside the hatched violet dial marked the Tupelo Regional Airport, TUP.

He baked in the Cessna, his tongue thrush-like with paste. His khaki pants were a tie-dye of blood and urine and sweat, and his limbs were dabbled by bruises and egg-sized clots. Again, he reached up to adjust his right leg, to try and reckon it against the fracture. His screams were fanatical.

He'd spilled his water bottle onto the map that first night. Having spent hours crying out for help, he'd now been silent for what felt like weeks. Greedy for survival, his body was hyperaware. His ears now keyed to every decibel of sound. With the slightest twitter of leaf his lungs seized up and his chest contracted, in an effort to widen the gap between shirt neck and body, to thereby harbor a wisp of airflow.

The map no longer mattered. Despite the intention of the pilot's homecoming, or the years of directed energy and expense—both in service to, and in spite of, his family—the heat now dictated everything.

# 9

*A*fter she appeared I grew obsessed with coming home. JP
and I even traveled down to Mississippi: once a month,
sometimes twice. As often as I could convince him. But you knew
this Susan George. You know everything in Pitchlynn, though you
never dropped by to acknowledge us. No. For years now you have
kept me at distance. Like a fact keeps a lie.

Southwest to Jackson, United to Memphis: I flew home to
reinvest in the state, to amend. (It is such a beautiful space,
Mississippi. We hide how gorgeous it is.) Over road over highway
through Hill Country and Delta, Black Belt and Pine, the car
over asphalt, the finger traces a map. I came home to confront. To
resubject. To remove to . . .

To get back to the wound site. To beg her: leave me be. To save.
Save. Save.

Yes: to amend. No matter how far away you shoved me, I was
stained by home. I can see this now, Susan George. I understand.
The running? The never coming back? It made the most sense
at first: hiding. Escaping the truth that you handed me. Over
years and highways and continents and jobs . . . I believed in the
abandonment of my complicity, my fact.

The more I came back with JP, the more detail was resuscitated:
what happened in Bel Arbre. I could see it. Smell the death of it
everywhere. And I remembered: all the running began with a push:
from me to her, and then from you, to me.

Now, the compulsion to save: my vocation my religion, my
reduction of self. To amend, to outlive, to reparate. To replace:

*houses, people, animals, children. Your daughter: Lucy. For you*
*and for Lucy, I needed to save. To amend: to . . .*

This was as much of the letter as Susan George would read. She folded
the pages back into thirds and stuffed them into the envelope. Held it to
her nose and inhaled, though there was no trace of scent.

She had to decide whether or not to forward it to her lawyers, to
have them contest the Wallis House estate, challenging Dru's capacity
at testament. She knew that the process would be handled in a local
court, by local people. Her people. That the letter itself would serve as
Exhibit A: Dru Wallis, Crazy, and that this, in turn, would bring the
house back to her.

She worried about what this would mean for Dru's child. The infant
had already lost her mother, and had no grandparents or close Pitchlynn
relatives left. Contesting the estate would strip the infant from all connec-
tion to town, to family. This cleaving had already happened, with Dru.

She leaned back into the wing chair and grasped at the armrest. Her
hand quaked as if by muscle memory, as if retracing the jittered application of makeup, years ago—a couple of decades, almost—in an effort
to be composed for the visitation.

Friends and relatives had called on Susan George for days after
Lucy's wake, as had her pastor, and a couple of her father's old associates. The condolences offered by the latter had been fused to the pressing issues of in-town development. (Susan George had by that point
taken over management of the Wallis family holdings.) Between visits,
she had gone back to bed, or gone into the bathroom to vomit. When
alone, she had wandered the waxed wood floors of the house, in the
predawn darkness, in bare feet and mourning dress. Unable to force an
appetite for days, she had opened the refrigerator time and again to the
waft of fetid shrimp under cellophane.

She could still smell the dishes in the days-old sink water. The chain
smoking, the flowers, the phenol of sweat.

Sitting in the gold silk chair, she could still smell all of it.

# 10

In the dim light of Lucy's nursery, JP and Colleen traded in shushes, hand gestures, giggles. As the baby shower guests assembled within earshot of his bungalow, JP watched his daughter fall asleep on Colleen's shoulder, then lifted the infant gently, his breath held—*If she wakes up, we're screwed*—and placed her in the crib. The orange on-light of the humidifier shone like an ember, and a sound machine rumpled the lukewarm air. (JP had experimented with the Rain preset, alongside Crickets-at-Night, Whale Song, and even White Noise; he would never, *ever* dial up Amniotic Heartbeat.) He and Colleen froze when the baby wriggled on the crib mattress, peeping. Seconds later, however, with no further cry or fidget, JP held out his fist, beckoning Colleen's gentle bump.

He beckoned her out into the hallway, then produced a handheld device that looked like a smartphone. "This thing is critical," he whispered, pressing the on button. A night-vision image of Lucy's body popped on-screen.

Colleen gasped.

"Amazing, right?" He showcased the camera settings, Close Up to Wide Angle. The infant's alien body was broadcast in stark white-blue contrast. Framing the monitor image were digital readouts and diagrams: room temperature, Wi-Fi signal, and the like.

Colleen looked away. "That thing freaks me out."

JP slipped the monitor back into his pocket. "Trust me, you'll get addicted to one when the twins get here."

They stepped into the den to bid good night to the sitter, JP offering her a catalog of assurances that he'd be right there, just outside, on the lawn; that the sitter must call or text with anything at all; that he'd check in throughout the evening; that really, she shouldn't worry about bothering him; that . . .

Colleen opened the front door, then hooked her arm around his. The two stepped out into the warm night air.

Taking in the blue-collar horde on the white-collar lawn, she couldn't help but snicker. Colleen still wasn't sure what JP had been thinking, bringing all these county folk to the Wallis House estate.

In lieu of T-shirt and shorts, or any hot-weather staple, the women were outfitted in new or semi-new dresses from the I-55 outlet mall, or maybe the Target over in Tupelo. Some of the men had tucked their plaid and pearl-button shirts into their *good* jeans, while others wore the creased khakis and button-downs generally reserved for Sunday service.

The congregation sat under a wedding-style white tent, under which was a series of tables with white cloths and flowers. Large circular floor fans were stationed at every corner. Foam beer koozies commemorated the event, with *Twice as Nice* scripted above caricatures of twin infants. JP had hired a caterer from the southern fusion restaurant over in Oxford, and while nobody was sure what made "tandoori bbq" tandoori, nor why a pimento cheese wonton was a necessary endeavor, the grub sure was tasty, and its complication cued ample banter.

Somehow, short notice or no, JP had even curated a proper soundtrack—north Mississippi trance blues, old fiddle tunes, and sacred steel gospel—marking a regional authenticity on his part. (*The newbie had paid attention*, they thought. *Good on him.*) A small parquet dance floor had been assembled for the boogie.

"Well?" JP asked Colleen. "Did I pull it off?"

"The question is not did you, but *how* did you? Christ, JP, this spread would take me a year. Thank you. I mean it."

JP held his hand out for her to grasp. "A pleasure. Now let's go charm these people with our refined repartee."

Colleen groused a bit, but let him pull her into the glut of friends and family. This initiated a series of endless hugs and well-wishes, questions about baby-names, and baby-needs, as were woven in to stories of the guests' own baby-based experiences (and/or lack thereof). Such stuff usually taxed Colleen to pieces. On this night, she couldn't kill her smile.

THEY WERE fully immersed in visiting when Susan George showed up. She, too, was appropriately dressed—only more so than the others. Her eyes cut the crowd as if taking in an exhibition, or roadside accident.

JP, Derby, and Deana stood around a centerpiece table, where Colleen sat catching her breath.

"Evening, y'all," Susan George said. "I heard the festivity from all the way over at my house, and figured I'd take a peek. Hope I'm not intruding."

"Well. We did send invitations," JP replied.

Susan George rolled her eyes, then turned to stare at Colleen.

Derby cut in. "This is my wife, Colleen."

"Yes!" Susan George said. "You're the veteran?"

Colleen nodded.

"Wonderful," Susan George said. "You know, we haven't had a baby shower on this land for some time. It's such a fine space for a party, don't you think? A reception, or small concert? Anything that brings the town together."

"It is," JP replied. "Only, *this* party is for the expectant parents. Close friends and family, so . . ."

Susan George stayed focused on Colleen. "You look special."

"Thank you."

"And how lovely you are out of that uniform. No offense, but the look was a bit, well, uncomely. Whereas motherhood . . ."

"Uncomely," Colleen repeated.

"Oh *shit*," Susan George said. "I've offended you. I apologize, I'm just not explaining myself well. I—"

"No worries," Colleen said. "Got used to it years ago."

Deana reached over and squeezed Colleen's forearm. "Need some air, darlin'?"

"Thanks, Dean. I'm cool." She then winked at Susan George. "You know, it can sometimes be an asset to have a female troop on hand."

Colleen had once been lodged inside a Bradley vehicle, in a city, after military curfew. It was so quiet and softly dark; the vehicle sat in silent watch mode, battery-powered. The gentle hiss of manpack radios blended with power line hum, and the scratching of cat paws in the garbage outside. All these low sounds, Colleen remembered now, so low and meditative and droning, nearly secure.

Technically, she was not supposed to have been there. The designated troop, the male who had shared her MOS job qualification, had fallen out with something foodborne. Colleen was the sole, formally-trained alternative in the squad. (Truth be told, nobody really needed her on hand, but regulationwise, the detail couldn't press on without her. Even the vehicle was out of place, since its bulk overwhelmed any reasonable agility. It was parked at remove from the action, on the periphery of the objective.)

"I'm gonna leave," Susan George continued. "Let y'all enjoy your shower."

"Sit tight," Colleen ordered. She and Van Dorn had been the only ones in the Brad. On that night, in that space, Van Dorn had been like some de facto bro minder. A babysitter of sorts, while the squad pursued an extraction, the result of a tip-off, well paid. And this was okay, was procedurally humdrum and calm . . . until the SINCGARS had suddenly lit up with chatter: one frantic operator requesting a medevac, while another answered back for intel.

She and Van Dorn had scrambled for first-aid kits, field dressings. They monitored the tac/nav screen, radio chatter, and the back-and-forth from comm; the sync and squelch, call signs and copy, and the hydraulics of the Brad deck, which had opened like a maw as the squad approached the vehicle.

"I'm picturing this one time . . ." Colleen spoke up, too loud. "This time when my squad brought me an injured hadji woman. She'd been shot up, and they plopped her right down on the ramp of our Bradley. Just there, like you'd plop a shot deer on a tailgate. And——"

"Honey," Derby interrupted. "Stop."

"I'm *fine*, babe." She swatted at him playfully. "Swear to god, I have a point." She patted her tummy and nodded. "Yup, the female was carrying. Was six, seven months along if she was a day. So it was . . . devastating, you know? Because she had, like, a gnarly chest wound. Was done in, no question."

The slain woman's brown eyes had been vacant and dry, though Colleen couldn't help but lean in close, to consider. Behind them, the woman's husband was held at gunpoint, his hands flexicuffed at his back. He screamed so relentlessly that they'd finally jammed him into the back of a Hummer.

"And we all knew what we had to do with the woman," Colleen said, glancing over the rapt faces of the party. " 'Cause everybody knows what to do, right?"

When no one replied, she asked them again, only louder. "I mean, y'all *know*, right? You all grew up the same way I did. You know what we had to do."

The guests' silence held firm, though Colleen was correct: they all knew the answer. The country boys who had been among her squad, whether from northeast Mississippi or northwest Wisconsin, had chosen to do what they'd been taught after shooting rabbits or deer that turned out to be pregnant: they would gut the woman and get the baby out.

Only then did someone remember that a male troop shouldn't mess with a Muz female. So this, then, was the point of Colleen's story—a fact she now decided to keep to herself, given that nobody on hand had the guts to engage it. Since nobody wanted to hear.

She had demanded a field knife, then started in. The woman's belly and body had jiggled on the Brad deck. There was the layer of skin and fat, and entrails that few had seen in humans, but which, yes, were reminiscent of the hunts the lot of them had shared growing up. The guys had stood firm as Colleen reached inside, her hands glistening with blood, searching, seeking, until she'd found it, a bit bigger than a bunny, curled up amid lips of sticky flesh and lining. She had reached in and cupped the infant with both hands, then pulled it to her breast.

The male troops had scrambled to assist her, their hope coalescing into naïve instruction: Water! Snips! Someone get a goddamned bulb syringe! A few of the fathers among them were even flushed by the warm memory of their own children being born, by the terror and miracle of the process. It was glorious. One soldier let slip a soft prayer of relief.

Colleen was the last one to acknowledge the shredding. Against her efforts to cradle the infant, the body seemed to disintegrate, to pour away, until at some point one of the guys—maybe Van Dorn, she couldn't remember—had clenched her shoulder and ordered her to stop, just fucking stop holding it.

She had looked to each squad member, seeking any counter-opinion to the tragedy, before nesting the item back into its mother. Someone had then handed her a brown, standard-issue towel, and another troop poured water over her hands as she wrung them clean. After that, they had put Colleen into the front seat of the Hummer, the male hadji in back, bawling and babbling, and then drove to Charlie Med. En route, when the husband had spit on the back of Colleen's neck, Van Dorn had punched the man and bagged his head, and then punched him again.

At debrief, she could only respond to her CO's questions with name, rank, serial number.

"Anyway," she said, glancing around, "gender protocol ain't always clear-cut, you know? Things aren't always clear."

Derby took her hand, and helped he away from the table.

Susan George called out after. "Forgive me, girl. I'm just an old fool, and I didn't mean to. . ."

"No," Colleen replied. "I shouldn't have said anything. I know better."

JP stepped in front of Susan George, grabbing her by the elbow. "Go."

She yanked free, quick as a viper. "Don't you ever touch me. Don't you touch *any* lady."

"Go," he repeated.

"This is my family home, it is our home. What's more, it'll be our—"

"No," JP said. "I'm erasing the lot of you."

Susan George looked to the party guests, her face equipoised for either support or challenge. Earning neither, she stormed away.

The guests remained stock-still until at last Deana spoke up. "It's all good, y'all. Really. A party ain't a party till some drunk shows up to crash it, right?" She strode out onto the dance floor and cued the DJ into action. "Somebody get out here with me. Let's do this thing!"

# 11

The twins were masterpiece, monument, and renaissance. They were an aria of sticky black hair and gummy, bawling mouths. A bipartite bouquet of smells, and shrills, and crazy thin lips. They appeared as the oldest of elderly men: their eyes confused, and wrinkles profound. Their lack of muscle tone had them trembling with the slightest attempt at autonomy. (What a feat to lift one's chin a mere inch off Colleen's shoulder! Lo, the anguished wiggle!) Each newborn promoted distinct features that were up for familial interpretation: were those Derby's mother's ears on Junior? Was that a left-cheek dimple on Sarah? They had navy-blue eyes and ripe pink skin, and they obliterated Colleen's emotional boundaries. She no longer knew who she was, or wasn't. Most importantly, she didn't care.

Colleen's folks had been on hand in the maternity ward, as had Deana. The latter had fawned over her friend, mouthing an *I told you so* through Colleen's body-busted haze. JP was there, too, the sole actor in Derby's corner, casting off explanation as if he were the first-ever father. Unannounced to all, a reporter from the *North Mississippi Cardinal* had even shown up in advance of a short feature.

Just as Deana had promised her, as had Derby and her folks and everybody else, the twins brought Colleen a new breath of idealism. They delivered to her a clean slate, it seemed, without a hint of narrative complication.

(Truth be told, the birthing process itself was marked by procedural hiccup. Despite the fact that Colleen insisted on the acute rupture of natural childbirth, her delivery was instead defined by Pitocin vs. epidural ministrations, after her water was found to contain excess meconium, necessitating a rapid removal. The doctor had pulled Derby aside to consult on this decision, noting, "Somebody up in there is *stressed*. Couldn't control their bowels." The men had then chosen to flood Colleen with drugs. It was in everyone's best interest, they decided.

*Meconium?* This concept of abundant "uterine stool in amniotic water" was alien, ominous. The already exhausted Colleen had mouthed each component of the term, the chop of the consonants and Latinate vowels, and then muttered her fear of the diagnosis. Yet Derby proved expert at making her feel better; he was strong for her. He was determined to deliver the upside, slamming a door on any darkness. He swore to Colleen that it was going to be fine, and that they and their babies were far tougher than any complication.

He was right. Colleen's thoughts and feelings were a smear of analgesic toil as she shoved, and blasphemed, and sweated to give birth: first to Derby Jr., and then to Sarah Friar. Three weeks early. Expert timing for twins.)

Two days later, having blown past the state's insurance, the pillow-sitting Colleen and flamed-out Derby were sent home to a house packed with gifts. They found scented wipes and diapers from the church, alongside dolls and infant-sized hand-me-downs care of Susan George Wallis and the Pitchlynn LMA. Gift certificates had arrived from friends and coworkers. There were umpteen cards and baby toys bought from that Target in Tupelo. All of this loot had been snuck in by Colleen's parents, who also hung decorations around the house, mostly baby-blue.

Most prescient was JP's gift to Colleen, the "Bresties' Nursing Pillow for Twins." Resembling a flat-topped inner tube, the pillow wrapped around her waist while she sat on the couch. The cushiony platform lay just beneath her breasts, and positioned the twins' bodies to feeding-height. This nursing shelf-of-sorts freed Colleen's fingers to sip tea, or scratch, or to comb the feather-soft wisps of dark hair as the infants suckled. She felt like a barge, but her hands were somewhat free.

Though grateful for everyone's advice, and their affiliated assurances that all would be perfect, the uncertainty of new parenting shoved the couple into panic. Either Derby or Colleen were constantly on the phone, begging counsel. If one of the twins bawled ceaselessly or somehow felt *off*, temperature- or temperament-wise, Derby would call the doctor, then the doctor's receptionist, then the doctor's answering service, and then Colleen's folks. Colleen's own consults were largely provided care of Deana, who knew to wipe a newborn's eyelids clean with a damp cotton ball, or who assured her that the rashes on the back of Sarah's head were just "angel kisses," and that the skin coming off of the babies was simply that: excess skin. Alongside phone-line guidance, Deana was ever ready to rush over and help, porting frozen casseroles or boxes of diapers from the Dollar Store.

History seemed to have surrendered to the moment. For Derby and Colleen, for the first time in forever, everything was focused on the unfolding of new life.

Also, they were exhausted.

They grew united in scorn for the displeasing evolution of bowel movements, and the sour odor of cradle cap (though somehow the stained and crusted umbilical stumps were "cute"). They fretted over the way that Derby Jr.'s off-center nose was mashed against his face . . . then gave praise when it gained proper protrusion, like the rebounding of a soft-rubber toy. The final passage of meconium from each twin was cause for celebration: a couple of beers, alongside some take-out jerk chicken from the reggae-themed restaurant in town.

From the pinhead red bumps on Sarah's sensitive skin to the downy hair covering both of the twins' foreheads, the experience con-joined Colleen and Derby to the breadth of humanity, while simultaneously making them feel as if they were the World's First Parents. Childcare had been done before, sure. But nobody else on the planet knew, or could ever possibly know, the details Colleen and Derby possessed about these particular infants. They felt spiritually enlightened, physically extinguished, and awash in the conceptual promise of opportunity.

When the phone rang one morning, Colleen read aloud the caller ID display:

"Mississippi Department of Corrections. It's Hare."

Derby took in his wife, and now, his children. "Give it here. Let's get this shit over with for good."

Despite years of his skirting, of his denying all confrontation, this sole issuance from Derby seemed to abolish Colleen's frustration. She beamed at him, taking her own, enlightened look around the room. Everything that mattered—*anything* that mattered—was lodged safe between the walls of that cozy, cluttered den. Uncomplicated. Untangled. Untouchable.

"Naw." She smiled. "Let the machine tackle this one. We'll pretend it never rang."

Every cell of those babies was a symphony. Every wiggle and flaw and facial goon, gospel.

# TRIAL

# 1

On the morning that two men found a pig in a tree on the postcard side of Pitchlynn, Mississippi, on the other side of town, the side whose proximal houses were standardized, squat postwar bricks, and whose distal addresses marked tidy, slabbed modulars on oversized yards, a still-youngish man wielding a Bump Fighter razor, towel wrapped around his waist, stared into a bathroom mirror . . . and psyched himself up.

He rinsed the excess shaving cream from his toffee-tone skin. Walked into the small bedroom, and the crosscurrent of ceiling, box, and window-unit fans. (The latter appliance held only a near-memory of coolant, yet it was early enough that the morning air brought a welcome shiver.) He sat on the side of the bed and stared into the mirrored closet doors. Though Doc had thickened a bit since notching his thirtieth birthday, his occupation called for a decent workout regimen. If he flexed, he could still catch a glimpse of high school linebacker physique.

"You got this," Doc told himself. "Not a problem."

He heard his wife come home through the front door, having delivered the kids to the school bus pickup. He stood, pulled his uniform off the clothes rack, and laid it on the made bed. Dressed in anticipation of the gripes and growls to come, as if he had any control of the detail to which he'd been assigned at work.

Sure enough, Jessica walked in grumbling, as much to Doc as to herself. "I can't believe you're goin' to be in the same room with that man. I tell you what, Doc, I wouldn't be able to hold myself back. I just can't believe."

She was coming off of a twelve-hour shift, though her plum-colored scrubs still looked sharp. He admired the way they canvassed her body, conveying her authority, her ability, while contouring her in a way that he dared not acknowledge on this morning. Earnest as he felt about it, she was in no mood for compliments.

"We are not gonna be in the same room, Jess," he said.

She watched him button up his Department of Corrections uniform blouse. "Say, Doc, maybe you and me should switch outfits. You think I could pull it off, impersonating big bad you? Hitch up with your baton, then sneak my way into Hare's cell?"

Doc grinned. "I'm afraid they wouldn't buy it. You're just a little too soft."

"Soft?" she replied.

"I mean *round*. Curved. Perfectly curved."

"You think *I'm* soft, Doc? Give me two minutes, and I'll take care of my business. Of *our* business. In fact, you're such a diplomat, I'm worried you're not gonna—"

"Hold up, I—"

"—not gonna hold fast in the presence of that snake. I'm worried you're not gonna let him know what's up. Make him understand what he did to the family."

"Jess?"

"So tell me, please, are you gonna do that, Doc? You gonna make him know?"

"I can't say a word to the man. I am only there to serve."

"Whatever, Doc." She wiped away a tear. "You have got to make him hurt for what he took."

Doc moved toward the dresser, then clipped his badge onto his breast pocket. "My job is to do my job, okay? To pay strict attention to process and protocol. The more emotional I get, the more mistakes creep up. You know that, babe."

"Fine. Don't get emotional. Get *clinical*, Doc. Get *surgical* on him."

"Jess, the whole point of the retrial is to figure out what's up." Doc paced into the small, carpeted living room to the adjoined kitchen counter, and the coffee. "He wouldn't be locked up if the system weren't at work."

Jessica marched right in behind him. "What do you mean by that? Actually, you know what? It doesn't even matter. The man is vile, and he's guilty—whether he killed Gabe or not. Lord, Doc. Do I have to explain how 'the system' functions?"

"You can't," Doc said. "At least, not now. Besides, I *am* the system. Also . . . I'm late. So I gotta fly, Jess. Love you." He opened the door and started to step out, but froze when he caught Jessica's stare.

"Doc," she said. "I do not like feeling this way."

"I know."

She wiped away a tear. "I am a trained health-care giver. A mother. A gardener, goodness gracious."

"I *know* it, Jess. You're s'posed to be the Steady Eddie."

"But this gets me all kinds of furious. And I don't want it to get me so furious anymore."

"I hear you. I gotta go. Sorry."

"I love you, Doc. But you had better get in there and make that man understand. Make him feel what it's like to be denied."

# 2

Hare Hobbs was slow to rise from his knees, and had to push up from the bunk just to stand. Once righted from genuflection, he let out a wheezy breath and tugged at the waistline of his blaze-orange coveralls.

"You start to pray more at this point," he said.

Doc stared at the polished cement floor, said nothing. He sat alone in the paste-gray hallway, his metal folding chair cocked away from the cell.

"Yeah, buddy," Hare continued. "You spend most of your life not even knowin' you have a body. Never even aware of it, until somethin' breaks or gives out. Or leaks." He snickered. Now, I ain't gonna lie. It takes somethin' out of your manhood and mortality when you start needin' diapers!"

No response.

"I don't piss myself too much or nothin'—yet." He chuckled as he again snapped the orange fabric.

Doc scoffed, though he didn't mean to. He'd been briefed on protocol, and was determined to stare at the floor, at the wall, or at the row of empty cells beside them. Whatever got him through his shift. To do anything more would provoke trouble, reprimand, or both. An entire corridor had been cleared to sequester the inmate, to keep him from riling the gen-pop. For the duration of the workday, and the many to follow before the trial, it was and would be just the two of them, Doc and Hare, their every shuffle and sigh amplified by the hallway cavity of cinder block, steel, and cement.

"You just get to prayin'," Hare repeated. He picked up a fresh bar of soap from the metal sink rim, then sat on his bunk and started to carve it with his long thumbnail. Ivory flakes sprinkled over his hands. He carved with the nail, then rubbed the soap smooth with his thumb pad. Now and again he blew the shavings to the floor.

Soap figurines lined every edge of the cell. White soap rabbits, oak trees, and politicos populated the sink basin and the small window inlet. A platoon of soldiers stood in formation along the floor of the back wall. There were mules and combines and suckling pigs, their fragrance porting the homelike, drowsy scent of fresh laundry. In the month since incarceration, several papers and a national art magazine had inquired about a feature story. Gallerists had already called to offer representation.

"What's my subject here?" Hare asked, motioning to the soap. "An ostrich, maybe? I always wanted to make me an ostrich."

The guard did not reply.

"No. I guess I've never seen an ostrich in real life. And I hate to make a thing I hadn't seen."

Doc pivoted slightly, the chair legs squeaking on cement. He, too, was fascinated with the figurines, and the hypnotic rhythm of the carving: saw then rub, thumbnail to pad; saw then rub, shavings blown to the floor.

Hare glanced up long enough to realize he'd won an audience. "You only wanna carve the things you *know*—you know? Things you've lived. Otherwise, the art ain't real. It's more craft or gimmick than discipline."

At last, Doc looked at the man.

Hare held the soap up. "Picked this habit up in the war."

"Army?"

"Yup."

"Vietnam? Korea?"

"Dubya-Dubya-Two! Lied about my age to enlist. I wadn't yet fifteen at the Battle of the Bulge—you believe that?"

Nothing.

"Crazy, right?" Hare continued. "I started in to whittlin' on bar soap, because I couldn't stand the waitin' around. To die, or to kill—or both." He clapped the soap into his palm. "So, yeah, buddy. This is me, waitin'."

"What kinda soap you find at a war?"

"I'm Hare."

"I know."

The old man stared at Doc for a second, then, "What *kind*? Hell. All these interviews with them art people, and I ain't never been asked that. Good for you. I guess it was always pretty much Fels-Naptha, though you sure can't get that stuff in here."

"Huh?"

"Fels-Naptha?"

Doc shook his head, shrugged.

"Good lord." Hare chuckled. "Ast your grandmamma. Your mama. There wasn't never a better soap. Got a good strong lye base. Yella as butter, but it makes everythin' white."

"And that's the best kind to use? Fels?"

"Naptha. Oh yeah, man. Though your fingers gotta get used to it. It'll give you a rash if you mess with it too long."

"What's the first one you made, anyhow?"

"The first statue?"

Doc nodded in the affirmative.

"Well." Hare grinned. "I'll let you guess. But before you answer, think about it."

The young man didn't need to think. "A woman."

Hare smiled, his teeth rimmed by dull silver. "A woman." He palmed back the thin strands of his gray hair. "Always is, idn'it?"

Doc caught himself grinning, then looked to the floor.

"Yup," Hare said, blowing off the soap splinters. He stood up, walked to the front of the cell, and held out the figurine. It was a sculpture of the Doc, sitting in his chair. Every detail was hairline-precise: white baton dangling off of white belt, against white chair legs. All of him had turned white.

"You kiddin' me?" Doc asked, his eyes wide.

"Go on," Hare said, wagging the figure through the bars.

"Can't."

"Y'all pass all kinds of worse stuff in and out of here. You know it and I know it. Now, come on." Hare stared straight at the other, stared as if looking through him. Doc's eyes cut to the floor, but a moment later he got up from the chair. He stepped over and snatched the figure as if clenching bait from a trap.

Doc traced his fingers over the warm, grease-smooth soap, then groused a bit. "What, you can't make a black one?"

Hare grinned. "Now, wouldn't that be somethin' to give the papers! Say, man. What do folks call you 'round here, anyway?"

" 'Round here," the guard replied, "they call me Doc."

"And what's that short for? Dominic?"

Doc caught himself again, and got his game face back on. "Far as you need to know, it stands for Department of Corrections."

"Copy that," Hare said. " 'Doc' it is."


"You DO it?" Doc asked, toward the end of his shift.

"Do *what?*"

"You know what."

Hare snorted. "Doc, you already have the answer. I was acquitted fair and square, man. In 1965, by a court-appointed jury. So, no. I didn't kill nobody. This retrial ain't nothin' but a show."

"Uh-huh," Doc replied.

"What do you mean, 'uh-huh'?"

"Well, for one thing, you wasn't acquitted. That's just not true. You caught a hung jury, and the prosecutor chose to let it go instead of pursuin' a new trial. You think I don't pay attention? Think I don't read up?"

"The prosecutor let it go because the jury deadlocked at one-to-eleven." Hare stood up from the cot. "I am only here now because some people got nothin' better to do than stir up the past."

"So you sayin' this is all about someone else? You sayin' you never——"

"Think about it, man," Hare interrupted. "Some people—and them people's always either *got* power, or they *want* it—are gonter kick the dust up. Lawyers, politicians, journalists, activists. When they need a lightning rod? When they're runnin' for office, or lookin' for funding, or prestige? They find someone like me to make 'em shine. And there ain't nothin' nastier than an old white trash, uneducated racist. Ain't nothin' easier to point the finger at, neither. Now tell me I'm wrong."

"From what I know, you've earned plenty of it, hadn't you?"

"In the papers, on teevee. Me, and me again. I'm the devil, right? I'm what's wrong with Mississippi. With America. Have mercy! Throw me down and step on my back while you make a sanctified speech about redemption, reconciliation. But the thing is, Doc, I was freed decades ago, by a jury of my peers, one-to-eleven. Ain't nobody wants to broadcast *that* truth, man."

Doc stared back at the floor, considered whether or not to shut the old man up.

"Or, how many times have you read that I'm a *grandfather*? How many times you read about how hard it is to be elderly or *sick* in this state? Or how an eighty-somethin'-year-old veteran has to can veg every year, just to get by? How about that, Doc? You read about that? Nobody wants to read about *neglect*, Doc. The media only crave the takedown. And when somebody needs a lamb for that altar, well."

"You?"

Hare spat on the concrete floor, then ground the saliva under his flip-flop. "Say, Doc, you rich?

"*Me?*" the guard snorted. "Ha!"

"Exactly. I don't know many folks who is. And the ones I do know with money mostly come across't as no-good pieces of puck. Real old families, or pretend like they is. Old houses. Old ways. Know the type?"

"Well."

"Yeah. You know 'em," Hare scoffed. "They's the people that framed me up in the first place. Wallises, and the like." Hare nodded while sizing Doc up. "But you? You obviously ain't one of them!" He walked closer, resting his lank, hairless forearms on the steel crossbar. "And you ain't never gonna be, are you?"

"Nope."

"Nope," Hare echoed. He rattled through a series of conspiracy-minded points, insisting the retrial was a collusion between a Jackson newspaper magnate and the sitting lieutenant governor, in an effort to boost the latter man's election profile. Hare claimed that he was being held illegally, unconstitutionally, asking Doc if he'd ever heard of anyone else, anywhere, who'd been yanked out of his bed, television cameras already cocked and lit in the driveway, decades after he'd already been found innocent.

"I am eighty-some-odd years old now, Doc," he stated. "Do I threaten you?"

Ultimately, Hare even raised the procedural question about how and why it was he could be held in Pitchlynn, and *accused* in Pitchlynn . . . but that the state had worked its ass off to make sure the trial itself would take place in Jackson: the site with the most cameras, most coverage, and most careers to be made.

"This ain't nothin' but a show," he said.

Doc smirked. "Sure. And you and every other inmate in here is innocent. Thing is, your claim's got no *nuance*, man. For one thing, rich people ain't all the same. Hell, back in high school I worked at the club, the Pitchlynn CC. Plenty of those folks were nice. Generous. In fact, I wouldn't mind someday if my wife and me——"

"You was a dishwasher or shitter attendant?"

Doc paused.

"What I thought," Hare said, then spat again on the floor. "Doc, I got a little granddaughter can't even go to school without a camera stuck in her face. Without kids callin' her a racist, or some shit. Tell me she ain't gonna be messed up?"

"Well."

"Thing is, I've already seen this show, with my own kids. It was heartbreaking enough. But my *granddaughter*, man? She idn't yet eight, and the rest of her life's already written. She's gone." Hare paused, and pinched the bridge of his nose. "Retrial, my ass. I didn't kill nobody the first time, and I am not guilty now. It's just that they won't let the memories die. They *cain't*."

"You still here," the guard said. "You the memory."

Hare slipped his arms from the cell grate and turned back to the bunk, limping like a clipped dog. "I guess so."

"It is so," Doc said, wondering if Hare had any idea of how the murder had played out among Jessica's kin, casting them away, scattering them like seeds through the South and Midwest, a few lost forever.

The old man was lank as a ghost and halfway to being one, and Doc needed him to know.

# 3

Hare listened to the approach of footsteps in the empty corridor. Over the many days and rounds of his rotating guards, he'd grown able to discern the rhythm of each man's stride in boot soles, and the corresponding clacks of their utility belts.

"Hey, Doc," he called out. "How you?"

Sure enough, Doc walked into the frame of the cell, newly on shift. The young man sat on the metal folding chair, thumped a newspaper against his knee, said nothing.

"Might as well come on out and tell," Hare said. "We are way past the Code of Silence. It'll be a long-ass shift if you suddenly decide to stop talkin'."

Doc glanced around, as if anyone else were on the bloc. "Look, I ain't gonna bullshit you. Reporters are all over me when I leave here at night. Say they's good money for details about you."

"See there," Hare said. "I told you. How many times I told you? It's all spectacle, Doc. Everybody wants to wring somethin' outta me. A dollar, a rating. Hell, who cares about the truth, anyway?" He paced the cell, his flip-flops dragging the floor. "You know, Doc, the local affiliate won't pay."

"Come again?"

"You heard me," Hare said. "Local networks won't pay shit, 'cause they can't. National media can get away with 'appearance fees' and the like. Point here is . . . well, we're in the fourth quarter now. If you talk to some reporter, it won't change a damn thing about what's gonna happen with me. Know what I mean?"

"Don't be mistaken, old man. I do not need your approval. For anything."

Hare nodded, and glanced to his feet. "My bad. I know you only need to think about you and yours. What'd Miss Jessica say about all this, anyway?"

"She said my ass had *better* take advantage, and make a buck off of you."

"And you said?"

"Told her to mind her business."

Hare tittered. "You did not."

Doc looked down the hallway and, despite himself, smiled. "Well. Okay, I'm lyin'. I told her that if anythin' got out about me leakin' to the press, I'd lose my job."

"What I thought." Hare replied. "And she said?"

"She said I was a chickenshit. That it wouldn't hurt to take a little bit back from you."

"Head on her shoulders. Fire in her heart. That's the kind of woman you got to hold on to—if you can."

Doc raised his eyebrows. "Your wife acts the same, huh?"

"Hell, no!" Hare cackled. "But the *first one did*, for sure."

"And then you quit her for that?"

"Buddy, she ran off and left me on her own. As did the next one, and the next. And my kids did, too. Hell, last time I heard, one of my boys even took on his mama's maiden name. *Friar.*" Hare strung out the syllables. "Sounds like a hen to me. You believe that? *Friar?*"

"Well."

Hare looked back to the floor. "Now, my boy from that first marriage? Sonny? Of all my kids, Sonny was the only one with faith in me. Who knew the truth. He was gonna—"

A buzzer pierced the hallway, and the PA belted instruction. The block froze for a count-off, which was awkward on their corridor, since there was only one inmate to count. When the procedure was completed, Doc stepped close to the cell and shoved the newspaper through the bars.

"I 'preciate you." Hare nodded. He sat on the bunk and laid the newspaper across his thighs. The top fold was defined by another headline about the coming trial. He scanned the weathered black-and-white photo of his younger self, waving from the steps of the courthouse all those decades ago. On the periphery stood a crowd that included Mr. Wallis and his crew, stoic, unconcerned. Hare had grown so tired of this syndicated story line. This picture had eclipsed his entire life to date, and he knew it would likely outlive him.

He flipped the paper over and considered the bottom half. The photo of the downed pilot snatched his breath. The man was middle-aged, and textbook middle management, his photo an obvious crop from a sales-type pamphlet or event. Gazing into the pilot's eyes, which were worn and weathered by anonymity, Hare felt leached of ambition, or hate, or anything, save loss. A second photo detailed the wreckage of the crash and the pilot's critical condition. A medical team declined to issue odds of the man's recovery, confirming only that he was too unstable for LifeFlight transport to Memphis.

"My lord," he said. "What a waste."

"Hey?" Doc asked. "Inmate? I'm talkin' to you!"

Hare's breathing grew as quick and crackled as a trash fire. He looked at Doc, confused, almost childlike. "How'd you do that? How'd you know that this was . . ."

"I'm callin' the medic," Doc said. "Hang on."

Hare's hands quaked, so he clasped them together. "No, no. I'm all right," he said. "Just had a little spell, you know?"

"You sure?"

Hare nodded and cleared his throat, then set the paper down. "Listen to me. Make somethin' out of this nothin'. Talk to a reporter and get paid." He lay down on the bunk and stared at the ceiling. "Everybody leaks, you know that. Just remember: no local papers. You deserve better than you got, Doc. Miss Jessica more than that, I think." He sniffed. "You'll be all right."

"No," Doc said. "I won't."

* * *

Doc PARKED himself in a large leather chair in the corner of the re-fangled Pitchlynn coffee shop. He hadn't yet decompressed from his shift and wasn't ready to go home. So it was either this place, or a bar.

The coffee shop, renovated as the Grandiflora Roasting Co., was yet another broadcast of new, national Pitchlynn. Its fair-trade brew was now too pricey for Doc, and way too strong. There were no longer waitresses or chitchat, let alone a counter and swivel stools. Instead, he was surrounded by screen-bound obsessives, beneath a gale force of air-conditioning from an overhead, exposed duct. The place sold weakly ironic T-shirts, local wall art, and thawed tiramisu. Every minute or so, the sound of a milk steamer scoured the ambience.

Doc picked up a discarded newspaper from the table beside him, the same edition he'd passed off to Hare.

## PLANE MAN IN COMA
## IN NORTH MISSISSIPPI COUNTY HOSPITAL

Rescue teams had spent days scouring the furlongs of national forest for the wreckage. In the interim, the heat trauma the pilot had surely suffered would, at best, cause permanent damage. A quote from a medical first responder indicated cardiac and cerebral edema, and likely kidney failure. By now the plane man's organs had surely inflamed and were shutting down. On the top fold of the paper was that old photo of Hare.

As of late, the reporters had prickled Doc like sweat bees, their relentless come-ons and questions steering him toward cheap conclusions about who, how, and what he was supposed to feel about Hare. The lot of them had brought unwavering judgment. And condescension. Condescension so thick that in some ways it was like a smoke-screen, an easy out. And though Doc didn't want to, and though he hated himself for doing so, this uniform disavowal had made him wonder, well, *maybe?*

"Maybe," Doc said aloud, then withered from guilt. *Maybe Hare hadn't killed Gabe. What if* . . .

He wiped his hand over his mouth and stared around the room again. Even this newfangled coffee shop provoked a what-should-have-been for Doc. It marked the investment of folks who were born with a dollar, or owned a speck of dirt. Investments he could have had. Or, no, opportunities that *Jessica* should have been given, and which might have in turn been provided to his children. Instead, as it was, Pitchlynn was moving forward without them, again.

Doc put the paper down and stepped outside to call Jess. Though she knew his habits, and knew that now and again he needed to burn off a bit of post-work anxiety, on this night she asked him to come on home. She'd had a long, long day at the hospital, one of those shifts where you cleaned up more after physician than patient.

"I got you," he said.

In the background, Doc heard his kids raising Cain, until Jessica threatened to unplug the television. They fell silent as if in shock, and Jess giggled into the phone. She then told Doc she'd keep his supper warmed up. Said she loved him, but that she was overdue for a spot of wine, alongside a British police procedural (a show she'd grown fond of, care of the third-tier cable channels their basic package provided). So, yes, he should please get his ass home, pronto.

# 4

The Plane Man's memory skittered atop time, from five years old to forty-five, twenty-five to seventeen . . .

To being a high school tailback, eighteen years old in '78, ready to take up an offer from the Bear. He had traveled down to Tuscaloosa from Chicago. Rode a bus all the way down South, a Crimson Tide booster having paid the fare. (The prospect's mama couldn't afford a Greyhound, let alone a flight.) The university was made up of huge oaks, red bricks, and white columns. It was a wonderland removed from ice and industry.

He'd thought about seeking out the others then, his daddy and all, just across the state line. He had overheard trickles of phone conversations between his mother and her people back in Mississippi. Heard her insistence that she had to keep running from authorities, and mostly keep hiding from her husband. She'd complained that the man had even made him a whole new family.

In Chicago, Sonny was an outcast, alone; in Mississippi he had siblings. Yet he was not strong enough to seek them out that first time back. It was all he could do to take in Tuscaloosa, to try to impress Coach Bryant, the Bear.

At the end of the recruiting trip he was returned to Chicago, to Austin High and his senior year, intent on playing for 'Bama in fall semester. He vowed to make his name on the Crimson Tide, and he knew that his father and new kin would come sit in the stands on game day. A reconciliation of sorts, a reunion, he would show them that he mattered. Together, they'd suture up the loneliness.

The toss sweep, wishbone, was *his* play, so simple in execution. A stupid play, really. And yet in a stupid scrimmage, some stupid sopho-more lineman had thrown him down well after the whistle had blown. A textbook dial-up, the toss sweep, right; he'd hit the gap and got smashed after the play was blown dead, when his body was unbraced. He had broken his stupid fall with his stupid hand, as he had a thousand times. Only this time, Sonny's ulna had snapped. It spiked out from his forearm like a sundial gnomon.

At first he'd been entranced by the alien injury. He did not under-stood then that his season was over, or that his scholarship would be rescinded. Rather, he had giggled in the delirium, showcasing the bone spike to his gathering teammates . . . before dropping to his backside, screaming.

That pain was now amplified in his split femur, in the Cessna.

"Wasn't even a game," he whispered. "Just a scrimmage. No real yardage."

Having lost his spot with the Crimson Tide, he was recast as a juco tackle dummy in Moline. He'd spent the decades that followed gnawing on life in Chicago—until the day he heard the news of the coming Hare Hobbs retrial.

He now hung in the north Mississippi canopy, in a dated Cessna 152, a twin-seater prop bought on an adrenalized whim, and at the expense of everything owned or saved or credited; a prop mangled, its plexiglass windshield webbed by cracks, and hammocking him. Its wings were snapped like bones.

He only wanted to help his daddy. He had flown down to testify about the man in the chair. Forty-five years later, and Hare Hobbs's innocence had all come down to a man in a chair.

In the boiler-pot fuselage, Sonny was bound to the trickling death of his legs. His sweat glands and bowels having long been evacuated, sharp bursts of white light were now stitched to his pain. He was kept alive, barely, by pill-balls of wet map, his thoughts a queer bricolage of family and football, of Bird Clan Chickasaw and an Indian Head knife, and a ladder-back chair on a porch on Wallis Farm.

Five years old to forty-five, ten to seventeen, his memory slid atop time. He had no idea where the chair had ended up. No idea—nor would he ever learn—that it had been passed off to a thrift store at the edge of Pitchlynn, Mississippi. He would never know that it now existed under a pile of donated, unhung clothes at Annie's Re-Do, a weakly Christian alternative to the heavily Christian Salvation Army. A thrift store housed in a corrugated metal office building, next to the corrugated metal VFW building and a relocated, corrugated CME church.

Back in Chicago, Sonny would picture the chair while gauging the ergonomic plasticities at an office supply chain, or when deciphering knife-scar graffiti on a bus bench. He had checked out from the Harold Washington Library every single book about chair-making, weaving, baskets, Indians, the lot of it.

The man in the chair was the defining image of his childhood, and of Hare's innocence. He had flown down like a dove in command of this revelation.

The Plane Man, Edward Isaac Hobbs, called Ed or Eddie or Hobbs now, but who was still called Sonny by his mama, was prone to spill into obsession while sitting or watching television at home. *Slatted ladder-back interlocking rounds, air-dried, air-tightened. Hand-mortised basket-type river cane—rushes?—woven into herringbone twill. River cane or rushes, as had been picked up from . . . Indians? Basket rushes traded . . . with Indians? Chickasaw, maybe? Bird Clan? Acorn finials. This is how the chair was made. My own family made this. They crafted it, like a story.*

*In a ladder-back rocker, handmade by lathe and chisel, the old man had passed out cold. I saw it.*

*Though in the movies . . . in movies, the Indians never use chairs.*

His mother was still sharp, though her body had wilted. In Chicago, he would go to her apartment on weekends, the one he had been raised in after leaving Mississippi, a rental in West Garfield, the middle floor of a weather-shorn bricked affair, an icon of neglect amid icons of neglect, architectural colossi that had long ago been chopped into multi-units; Sonny would sit with her and visit as she cooked biscuits and grits, and the whole southern business he'd grown up with. Lots of smoky, cheap bacon that required her to flap a dish towel at the fire alarm (or, in winter, required him to stand on a kitchen chair to pop the nine-volt out of the device). Mississippi was all over that house: in the bacon, the biscuits, the drawl, even the tick of the wall clock. In the near-buried stories of the families that lived around them; the relatives left behind, subject to a sometimes vacation north.

Any narrative that had occurred *within* the frame of the state's boundary itself was almost unbearable to Sylvia. They would sit together on Sundays in cheap upholstered recliners across from the flat-screen television he'd given her, talking now and again over a gently dated movie on a gently censored cable channel, he forever brimming to ask her about the chair. About Wallis Farm, and Hare, his daddy.

Until one day, in that small kitchen in West Garfield, the breakfast cooking, cable flick on in the background, he tried to provoke her confession:

"And the chair, Mama?"

She ignored him, or just didn't understand.

"That family chair? The slatted ladder-back?" he continued, having just seen his daddy's photo in the *Tribune*, having only just learned that his elderly father was now back on trial. "*Daddy*'s chair, on Wallis Farm? Where did it come from? Where was it last?"

She crushed the bacon with an iron press shaped like a hog, the sizzle spit pricking her fingers. She did not reply to the question, but rather hummed an old favorite, a Ferlin Husky tune, "Wings of a Dove."

"C'mon," he continued. "At least tell me whose family made that chair. Was it an Indian, maybe? The seat was like a cane-type of weaving. And what do you think happened to it?"

His mama had shrugged, her eyes on the skillet. "Who knows? Ever'body's kin made them things at one point or another. Way, way back, they made everythin' and used everythin'. That chair wasn't special." She had shaken her head, mocking him. "Just some old yeoman-y chair, Sonny. Nothin' more. Let it go."

He was angry, because she was wrong. The chair *was* special. It was a forged family history, dragged along from god knows where. His father had told him this. It was one of those things he could remember. One of the few facts he still believed.

But also, this: it was an alibi. Emancipatory.

"Well then," he'd muttered. "Tell me about Gabe."

Sylvia left the room before he could he could repeat the question. Smoke billowed from the skillet like a ghost in her wake. After a minute, he went and shoved the jammy kitchen window open, and a knife of frozen air slashed Sonny at his gut.

# 5

I t was well past midnight but Doc was awake. Jessica slept beside him, her skin patterned by the silhouette of lace curtains and the dim porch light. He had long ago grown used to his wife's tiny cries—wails of disorientation, forever coupled to her sleep—but he could never get over his inability to heal her.

Jessica, a name given in dialogue with her grandmamma: Jessamine, wife of Gabe.

The old window unit chuffed that last draft of coolant, yet the room remained hot. Doc stared toward the textured ceiling and spinning fan, and tried to calm himself down. He'd been thinking about a long-ago afternoon at the Pitchlynn CC, where he had worked for a time back in high school. He hadn't driven past the club, or through the surrounding suburb, in years. Yet the two recent snippets of conversation had brought it to mind—one with Jessica, the other with Hare.

Doc had been posted to the tepid men's room, where he administered white towels that smelled like blossoms of industrial detergent. He would stack the linens with precision on a chrome wire rack. His other duties were to refill the translucent blue Barbasol jar, the lavender hand soap, and the mints, and to wipe the soiled linen baskets with watered-down cedar oil. Club members were good to him. He was in high school and he was earnest, and he was concerned about the proper execution of every task. They came in stinking and he had helped them to be clean.

He turned a blind eye when he caught them stealing toilet paper, hand towels, and the like, smuggling little freebie caches into their overpriced gym bags. *Toilet paper*, he would think. *How silly.* Why did they do this, given that they didn't need to? When did such a habit develop? Doc's mother would have whipped him to shreds!

The members were good to him, mostly. The men came in tipsy, sometimes, and told him jokes. Man jokes, dirty jokes. Mississippi State jokes that he was allowed in on. A racist joke was sometimes overheard—and, usually, apologized for. (At the least, a "no offense to you" was generally offered.) They flipped him coins often enough, and wished him well. They looted bars of soap and Barbasol, disposable razors and club-monogrammed hand towels . . . and if he saw them do so they winked back in reply, or put finger to mouth, *Shhh*, and he would grin and look away. On his break, Doc ate prime leftovers at the staff table in back of the clubhouse kitchen. Skin-in mashed potatoes. Lamp-warmed roast beef with grilled asparagus. Delicious.

He folded towels in the locker room, holding them to his face now and again, inhaling the detergent and bleach. He had never smelled anything so leached of soil, so fragrant with inhumanity. Once, as he was doing so, a pair of men walked in, their bangs and shirt bellies sweated, their golf cleats pricking the locker room mat. They reeked of whiskey and filth, and seemed very happy. Doc had smiled as they passed en route to their lockers. With this, one of them had stopped, the motion of his gait carrying into a brief, tipsy wobble.

"What?" the man had asked Doc, smiling.

"Sir?" Doc responded. He offered up the towel he'd been sniffing.

"Did you just wipe your face with that one?"

"Nossir."

The man had pointed to the hamper. "Put it in there if you did, right?"

Doc had met the man's eyes and nodded, and he put the towel in the hamper, just in case. The man had then followed his golf partner into the locker area, disrobing for the showers, while Doc went back to tidying up. Moments later, clean and dressed, the two men had again passed the basin area. Doc had looked at them and smiled.

The man's index finger hit Doc's temple like a bolt. "Look at me," he demanded. "Boy, I swear to god if you look at me."

Doc looked only to the reflection in the mirror, at the finger that jabbed into the side of his head.

"I swear," the man had continued. "You ever look me in my eyes again, and I'll . . ."

Doc began to sweat, to shake. He had wished to Christ he *could* look at the man. To stare at him, and through him. Instead, he had only considered his cowed face in the mirror as the man's finger jammed him again and again.

"Don't you never," the man had repeated, now holding his fingertip against Doc's head. "Don't you *never* look at me."

His buddy had admonished him slightly, *Come on, now, Wallis,* and then pulled the man off of Doc and toward the exit. *Let's get us another drink and cool off.*

In the dead-air bedroom of Doc's prefab house, Jessica's sleep was defined by whimpers. Lying beside her, he felt awful for the way she was raised. Dragged place to place, made landless after Gabe's murder, de facto landless anyway, given the fear of rampant slaughter that had consumed Wallis Farm. He thought of her mother's consequent search for kinship, and work, and basic relief; of the driving of her people to and fro over middle America, Pitchlynn to Chicago to Detroit to Greenville, Mississippi, then back to Chicago to Memphis to . . .

Doc's mother-in-law, ambitious for the next rung of stability, availability, had at times left Jessica to a series of surrogates. Over the years, the very definition of *parents* had become mutable for the child, as had *school* or *friend*, or *home*. And although these variables had for the most part inhabited their meaning and position—if you looked at it right, the child's life had been in most ways a bounty of loving kin, both blood and social—one of the stand-ins had not caretaken her as promised. And this betrayal, a nightmare of fractured love and space, had scarred her inside. It now dictated her sleep.

All of this, a legacy of Gabe's murder on Wallis Farm, and the exodus of families that had followed. All of it the doing of Hare Hobbs.

Doc reached over and stroked Jessica's bare shoulder. He knew that, as always, she would wake throughout the night with no idea of where she was. So many years later, and she still had no idea.

"But you're home now, babe," he whispered. "Don't you know?"

Doc lay awake for hours, until the alarm clock screeched.

# 6

"Bring him in!"

Two guards escorted Hare into the visitation corridor as gently as they would have an elder woman to a church pew. The old man's back bowed out in the orange jumpsuit, and his thin legs were fettered. As with his cellblock, the visitation area had been blocked off for Hare alone, to prevent disturbances and to limit further media leaks. The room was silent save for the squeal of shoes on lacquered concrete, and the metallic crumble of Hare's leg chains. The old man was seated, then bolted down to a metal bench at a partitioned desk, a cubicle of sorts, with a perforated fiberglass wall. Once he was in place, a woman and a little girl were escorted to the opposite side of the partition.

Hare's daughter Winnie was dressed in jeans and a shapeless pink T-shirt. Her arms were slim but slack, and one of them bore the crepe-like crinkles of a burn scar. She looked much too old to be the little girl's mother, though she was. The child was seven but small, her blond hair near-white. Her clothes were as frayed as dishrags, yet she beamed with ambition. When she saw Hare, she pulled free of Winnie's grip, then ran up and slapped the partition glass.

"Baba!" she shrieked.

"Ladybug," Hare responded, smiling. "How's my favorite gal? How's them grades, baby?"

"Got A's in everythin'—except maps."

"You mean geography?"

"Yup. Maps."

"Well, what's wrong with geography?" Hare asked.

"Welp . . ." The child sighed. "Them shapes all look the same."

"Maybe. But you can find a Miss'ippi map, cain't you?"

"Sure."

"And you can find America on a globe map?"

"Oh yeah, Baba. That's easy."

"Then you're gonna be all right, Ladybug! Don't fret." Hare turned to his daughter. "None the other family wantin' to come visit?"

"You know." Winnie shrugged.

"Did you call Derby like I told you?"

"Tried. Didn't get him. But it ain't like Derby's gonna call *me* back or anything. If you want to see him, you gonna have to get through to him yourself."

"Oh, I've reached out." Hare snorted. "I've sent a message or more. But he won't respond to me, either, so. However you need to do it, you had better get Derby over here. Come to think of it, get that pregnant vet of his over, too. Folks need to know that I'm a real, live person. A family man, just like everybody else. Problems, successes. Growth. Love. Regret. Redemption."

She nodded. "Colleen ain't gonna let me near their place."

"Change her mind," Hare said. "Carrot or stick—I don't care. Christ, Winnie, get creative. Tell Derby it'll be his last chance to make amends. To ask questions, or say his peace. Or to scream at me— whatever he needs to do. Tell him to do it for Ladybug here, so she can have some kin."

Winnie rolled her eyes. "Check and check, Dad. Okay? Now how 'bout you? You doin' all right?"

"Been worse. You?"

She spoke of bills and property tax due, a busted head gasket and the like. When the child got fidgety, Winnie gave her some paper and a couple of snapped crayons.

"We're gonna have to take her outta class," Winnie said. "Home-school her."

"Now, why on earth would you do that?" Hare replied. "She just said she was earnin' all A's."

"Daddy, you got no idea. A boy shoved her the other day, and the teacher didn't do a thing. The black kids call her names and the white won't have nothin' to do with her."

"But they can't do that. They—"

"Well, they *do* do that, Daddy. In other words, she's already a *Hobbs*."

The child cowed away from her mother's agitation, so Hare tapped the glass. "Ladybug? Hey, girl? You hadn't got anything to worry about at school, okay? Nothin' at all. Just be strong. Keep on earnin' those A's, and it'll be fine. Promise, baby."

When Ladybug nodded an okay, Hare looked back to Winnie. "Don't you dare pull her outta school. We both know how that'll turn out."

"What do you want me to . . ." Her words fell dead against his glare.

Again, Hare changed the subject. "Did I ever tell you that we get the newspapers in here, time to time?"

"Yeah?"

"It's funny how you can read about yourself—only, without ever having talked to any reporter."

Winnie motioned to the guard. "These walls must have ears."

"Naw," Hare said. "I'm talking 'bout things only *family* knows."

She wondered if Hare could still reach out, if there were any men left to pay his retribution. *Six hundred and fifty dollars*, she thought. *Long way. That money goes a long way.*

Winnie had told some Atlanta-based, Black girl reporter about the Platz, the space her father had built behind their house. Fifteen feet high and forty long, cinder-block. Erected between their little place and the near-identical house of the Black family next door. It had featured massive painted images of the Confederate Battle Flag and Mississippi state flag crossed at arms. In the upper corners were smaller versions of the Gadsden and Bonnie Blue. When she and Derby were kids, the Platz had greeted their every glance out of bedroom or kitchen window, and was the framework of every game played in the backyard.

The wall was based on a structure Hare had learned about in a Time Life book on the World War II. It was a thing he had wished to have seen when deployed there. Only, versus the Greek-theater-inspired, German-built amphitheaters he had studied, grand vehicles of nationalist *Volksgemeinschaft*, the Platz was just a backdrop to their flat weedy yard.

This was when Hare still needed to speak, at a time when he still roused the men. Her daddy had been so potent back then. A soldier of sorts, near-legendary to an indulgence of people who winked when they spoke of what he'd done. (Nobody really knew if Hare had murdered that man; they only knew that her daddy had walked out of court in 1965, set free by a jury of his peers, one-to-eleven, a grin on his face, and with an entire state of citizens lauding justice, an entire caste of them positioning Hare as the glorious rebuke to Johnson's Voting Rights Act.) Back when Hare was still an icon to some, despite the water on his knees and his sour breath. When to some he remained both a hero of Wallis Farm, and of the Battle of the Bulge, to boot.

Back at that outskirt-y house she grew up in, the men had brought farm vegetables and venison to aid the family. Winnie remembers watching her mother stab a small knife into the meat, again, again, before stuffing the slits with rolled strips of streak o' lean bacon. Mother had been sixteen when she gave birth to Derby, 1978, the next-to-the-last in a series of spurned, angry girls who had sought Hare out, and who had treated him as landed treasure. His cache. His heroism. Their fathers having all but arranged them as tribute.

Hare's idea had been to erect the Platz as both a barrier and stage. A symbol and physical show of force. Inspired by his vision, the men had come to his house en masse over a series of Saturdays, almost celebratory efforts, and he had fed them whole hog and beer, and they in turn had laid concrete, and metal poles, and cinder block. Winnie and Derby and her mama had watched the structure rise, blocking out the neighboring house, transforming their own backyard into a rally space, a so-called "Mississippi *thingplätze*" where Hare could rail, inspire.

This was 1980, in the wake of Reagan's speech at the Neshoba County Fair, just outside of Philadelphia, Mississippi. Hare had not attended the event, but he, like the rest of them, had seen the frenzy on television: candidate Reagan, August 1980, speaking in front of ten thousand in the swelter, their paper fans wagging, their cheers in

legion when the Republican candidate had proclaimed, *"I believe . . .
in states' rights."*

It was a revolution, a national outcry.

A tribute to be erected in the sunlight.

Reagan's speech had re-radicalized Hare's power, breathing life into
his limp narrative. Hare saw this, and knew that he could rekindle himself, his lust for acceptance—or rather, their lust for him. For days,
they had seen candidate Reagan on television and in the papers. Footage
of ten thousand in the news clips from Neshoba, screaming Reagan's
name. The candidate had issued formal cover fire for their cause, a call
for a return to their massive resistance.

It was genius, this so-called Southern Strategy. Within a week, Hare
had summoned a few men to the house. He drank, and he raved like a
preacher; he claimed that the states' rights speech had turned them all
back into, well, *men*. He waved his arms in revival, and implored them
to consider, to simply *consider* what Reagan's words had meant, and why
every decent White in the South was now ordered to be a Republican.
He challenged them as to why every coon and Jew journalist out of
Washington, D.C., was by then flooding the airwaves with protest of
the phrase.

"I," Hare had repeated, punctuating each word with a clap. "Believe.
In. States'. Rights."

He then called for a toast and they drank. The men teemed with
hope as Hare had promised a homecoming, a crawling back out of the
heaped dirt and disrespect; he swore to a resurgence of state-based
pride, that which the feds had snatched away in the '60s—both 18- and
19-. He cursed the government, the outsiders, the force-fed multicul-
turalism, and the rigged system of leftist revolution and federal redis-
tribution. He quoted candidate Reagan, again, again.

"The signal," Hare had called it. "The return."

The future President's dog-whistle speech had been broadcast
nationwide, as was delivered from right there in Neshoba County. Of
all the places he could go, candidate Reagan had spoken to the South,
the nation, and the world, from Mississippi, 1980.

The men were drunk, their bodies humming with love and promise.

They were baptized in awe when Hare had shared with them his vision: practical yet symbolic. Definitive and strong. He had enlisted them into action, and they in turn recruited neighbors and cousins, coworkers and congregation. And together, they commenced to building the Platz. Steel poles in cement. Cinder block mortared and stacked and painted: Battle Flag and state flag crossed at arms, beneath a single slogan of power: RESIST!

News of the structure had soon spread throughout the region. The monument was photographed for certain pamphlets, or captured on Polaroid. Men drove themselves and their families to Hare's place on the weekend, to see the man and his comrades speak in front of the gleaming, towering Platz. Squads of them began to ride around in search of small actions, late at night, mostly, helping to reestablish old codes of pride and violence.

Soon enough, local and regional candidates were showing up to glad-hand and sing praise, and fund-raise, of course. (Somebody even floated the rumor of an Atwater visit, on behalf of then–President Reagan—thought the appearance was canceled after word had spread too wide for the press secretary's liking.) One year, Old Man Wallis had even dropped by to collect a bundle of small bills for his reelection campaign.

And the Democrats were eradicated on the national ballot. And the years passed and the paint faded, as did the applause. Crowds and candidates stopped paying Hare much mind, as did the bulk of folks in town. Both the Platz and the little house had fallen into neglect, as had the family. Ultimately, their mother had left, not a word, as had the next of Hare's wives, the last of the young women who would take up with him, keep house.

Hare's response to this bleed-out was to stand by the mural in the middle of the night, drunk and slathered in July sweat, babbling about the war, about having been made to mend combat boots like some mascot, some runt coon. He would scream at the Platz, and the family who lived behind it.

Some nights, he dragged his kids out of bed and into the yard, ordering both Winnie and Derby to line up at attention in the moonlight and dead summer air. Bruises had banded their skinny arms from being yanked into formation, from being made to stand drill-parade-still. *Battle of the Bulge!* Hare would scream. *Hero of Wallis Farm!* He had forced the kids to memorize and recite history and edict, rhetoric, and epithet, and when they failed to meet his pleasures, he reminded them that he had a better child and bitch somewhere else; he swore that he was gonna abandon Derb and Winnie, then take back up with these others. And the more the children had cried on those nights, the more Hare had raved about finding his only *real* child, his *good* child, Sonny, the one to save him . . . and then never coming back.

Winnie now stared at her father through the plexiglass partition. *Six hundred and fifty dollars*, she thought. That girl reporter couldn't pay her outright in cash. Instead, the funds had been deemed an "honorarium" by her bureau——as if honor could be found anywhere, ever.

Winnie believed that Derby must have been about seven when he saw the dogs. The painted flags on the Platz were by then half eroded. Even the crabgrass was long dead at the base of the structure, having been starved of sunlight. Rivulets had carved into the rugged rouged earth, and she and Derby would rush outside during rainstorms to float little bits of detritus down the water channels. At that age, Derb had already loved to build things, perhaps as extension of the now-and-again soap figurines his father might carve for them, quarterbacks and ponies, tractors and the like. The boy had made an armada of boat hulls out of split pecan shells, fashioning masts out of toothpicks, with gum-wrapper sails.

Nobody came near their place anymore. The house baked in summer and was clotted with mold. The pantry was a catchall for condiments, dry rice and wheat, and weevils. (Truth be told, though, Hare did sometimes join the children while they played. He would whoop and holler, and chase them around, be the Indian to their Cowboy, or the Kraut to their Joe. He loved them then, they thought. He was *supposed* to love them, they believed, as was proven by these collective bouts of frolic, and fits of joy.) Every drink stripped their father down to the nerves of his recurrent insignificance, pinning him again to implosion, until at some point Hare would yank one of the kids around, or break someone's toy, or, if they were lucky, pick up a stone or cracked brick and just hurl it over the Platz at the house behind. If the latter, he would roar with laughter when the missile plunked off of the neighbor's roof, then dare any one of those sons of bitches to come after him.

The children had learned it was best to laugh with the latter assaults. In contrast to what he might do if they didn't, Hare would wink and maybe clop them on the shoulder, or knead a neck. Most importantly, he would at some point re-disappear, into the house, or into Pitchlynn for more drink.

Now and again, one of the men still left by would come across the kids as they walked home from school, or as they squatted beside some creek beneath the overpass snaring catfish and crawdads for supper. Charity: the man or men might hand off some venison wrapped in foil, or a two-liter, or some candy, and then drive off.

Winnie would take the venison home and stab into it, as her mother had done. Yet there was never any bacon to fill in for succulence. The meat would be gamy and not fresh.

Once, she was alone, cutting across the Piggly Wiggly parking lot, walking home with a plastic sack of ramen noodles, alongside legions of ketchup and mustard packets and saltines snatched from the deli grill, when a man in a huge white pickup had pulled beside her, the diesel engine growling. She'd ignored him at first, but then stopped after he called to her several times, "Hey, girl? You, girl."

The titanium-white pickup was a chrome-gleamed dually whose engine chortled over her like a brimstone sermon. Winnie froze as it pulled alongside.

"Hey," the man had called again, leaning out the car window. He wore a ball cap pulled low over his white hair. Had dark sunglasses. He was familiar to her, though she hadn't placed him at first.

"Need a lift?"

She stared until she had recognized him. "Naw," she replied. "I don't need nothin'." She then turned away, and did her best not to run.

"Stop, goddamn you!" he had yelled, and she did. "Take this," he said, holding out a couple of twenties.

Shaking, she had looked to her feet.

"Jesus Christ," he scoffed, wagging the bills. "You ain't gotta *do* nothin' for it. Just take the money to your daddy. Or, hell, hide it away for yourself. I don't give a shit."

Winnie had pounced like a mouse, snatching the bills from the man's grip. She then darted out of the parking lot and into the litter-filled boxwoods just beyond, crouching there until the truck pulled away. It was the only time she had ever engaged Mr. Wallis.

She and Derby would play hide-and-seek for hours. They played cowboys-and-Indians and tag. They floated pecan-hull boats down the muddy rivulets in their yard. One of the siblings would often duck behind the Platz, then startle the other; they would laugh, and shriek, and chase each other around. Now and again Hare even joined them.

One afternoon, Winnie had refused to play. She told Derby to get on inside the house and stay there.

They had heard her daddy screaming at the Black family that morning, slurring his curses, as was usual. What was not normal was when Hare had actually stormed back behind the Platz to confront the family in person. Winnie remembers watching him disappear, and then hearing the piercing yelps. Yips from the litter of a mixed bitch the neighbors kept. Later, when Hare had taken off and into town, Winnie had crept behind the mural to investigate.

Now, a quarter of a lifetime later, she sat across from her father, and wondered again if he might still be able to hurt her. If any of the men might be swayed to come after her, when Hare found out that she had talked to the press about all this.

The wire story would run within a day, the AP having distributed it to hundreds of news outlets nationwide. Millions of Americans would now learn the truth. The story would destroy any claims Hare had made about his frailty, or his family, or the smear campaign waged against all of them.

*Six hundred and fifty dollars*, Winnie thought. *Maybe a promise of more money to come. Maybe we can get ourselves out of here. Over to Atlanta, or somewhere far-off. Hell, I don't care, maybe someplace like Chicago.* She had told the reporter about the speeches of a twisted drunk, and the lies Hare had fashioned, and the bruises on skinny arms. Of the stabs into turned venison. In a whisper, whimpering almost, she had described the litter of Lab-mix pups strung up in a tree behind the Platz. The litter her kid brother had seen, five or six of them, dangling on thin noose ropes like Christmas ornaments. She swore to the reporter that she had warned Derby not to go back there; Winnie swore that she told him to stay away from that wall.

But he didn't listen, little bitsy kid that he was. And after Derby saw the pups, when he had bolted back to Winnie in hysterics, she struck him to the ground, and told him he deserved it.

The prison visitation room was silent, save for the rub of her child's crayon across paper. Hare stared at Winnie as if to scar her.

"There ain't nothin' to say, Daddy," she muttered.

"That's exactly right," he replied. "There ain't nothin'."

A guard stepped over. Time was up.

Hare nodded, then turned back to his daughter. "Now get Derby on script, you hear? I'll have my lawyers put their calls in, too. We're a family, for heaven's sake. We need the visual."

"Daddy, Derby's not gonna——"

"He'd better," Hare said. He clenched his jaw, and tapped his long fingernail against the glass. "This is my last chance at redemption. So I had better see all y'all in court."

"I guess," Winnie replied.

Hare looked to the child. "I love you, Ladybug. I love you so, so much. As does your mama. So if anybody messes with you at school, you just tell 'em to go to hell, from me, okay?"

"Dammit, Dad," Winnie said.

"But Baba," Ladybug gasped, "I cain't use no dirty words!"

"Okay, okay." He grinned. "I'm just kiddin'. You tell 'em to mind their own beeswax. Now, I want you to keep focused on your lessons, all right? Get smarter than your dumb old Baba, and keep bringin' home those A's—even in maps!"

The girl shrugged. "I'll try, but I'm not promisin'."

Hare chuckled to himself, then held a hand flat against the glass. "You my joy," he said, as the child reached up to match his palm.

# 7

A year or so back, Sonny went to a minor league night game in Scha-
umburg. An office event with his colleagues and clients. They had
sat in a bloc in the party-deck section, high off of the right-field line,
and were provided state-fair-type paper tickets with printed numbers
for a raffle. His boss had handed out vouchers for two hot dogs and one
bev (with anything additional at their personal expense). Chinese-made
headdresses and tomahawks were distributed in support of the team:
the Braves. The office crew had watched the game and cheered appropriately when their company, Praterian Fixtures, was announced over
the ballpark PA. They had nudged on each other, some folks drinking too much. Now and again, the office manager had shushed them to
announce another raffle prize, another dinner for two, or a free spring
cleaning from an affiliated housekeeping service. The Plane Man never
won. He had never won anything.

This was fine. He was a forgotten ex-ballplayer, now middle management, and he had long since gotten used to losing.

As evening took root, the stadium lights turned the ballpark into
a fishbowl, and put a bubble in the sky. At the seventh-inning stretch,
with half the office having slunk back onto the charter bus to nap, their
vouchers long since spent, he'd come face-to-face with a small, hovering eye. A smoked-glass camera eye on a quadricopter drone that had
zipped in, up and down, scanning them all, before stopping pinpoint in
the air in front of his face. Staring.

Hovering. The whir of its propellers. The Plane Man, then called
Eddie, and Ed, and Hobbs, and even Sonny by his mom, had seen
a tiny version of himself in the copter's camera glass—and then, after a

friendly elbow to the ribs from his coworker, had looked over to witness a huge version of himself on the ballpark's diamond big screen. His eyes were glassy, his face leached of want. Still the drone had floated, staring at him, its lens showcasing his age to everyone. He could not stop looking back at it, so he appeared frozen on the screen, as if in a still photo. No smile, no wave, no tomahawk chop. Only a mention of his company as Sonny's mouth began to tremble.

The crowd had applauded, but then bellowed at his non-engagement. To combat the growing awkwardness, the PA announcer started describing the prize, noting something about the Chicago Executive Airport.

Still, he had stared at the fractional version of himself in the glass eye, the quadricopter frozen in front of his face. When the drone had at last zipped away, an usher tapped Sonny on the shoulder and handed over the prize envelope: flying lessons.

* * *

WHITE LIGHT.

He dreamed of Chicago, as seen from above. As if looking down through a camera, or a bird eye, he tracked his own movement through the city. His gaze was fueled by sunlight as he hovered through the stratosphere, coasting like a General Atomics Predator drone, like a great eye staring down, into and through himself, and at the map of his very existence. The chart of his routine had been this for so many years: to bus, to work, to bus, to home, to mother, to grocery store . . . all laid out on a grid. Yardage.

(Back in Illinois, the frigid air and lung crush of winter at his window, he would suit up in his small apartment, and stare into his bathroom mirror, and swear to alter his life, to do something, *anything* different, on the way to the bus, to work, to home, to mother. He swore to inflict some deviation in, for instance, the way he stomped atop the snow to the Jewel-Osco grocery, or at the very least some variation of the groceries he bought there.) (And yet, even now, suspended in what he believed was the Mississippi forest canopy, dislocated, distorted, but in absolute, godlike command of narrative memory, of imagination and creativity, he had *still* followed the same routine. His mind could fly anywhere, any direction, care of any method imaginable . . . yet as he migrated through Chicago, he *still* ducked into the crusted snow and wind, and strode straight to the bus stop; his free imagination still crowded him beneath the humming electrified wire heater inside the knife-scratched plexiglass vestibule. Exactly the same, all his life, his thoughts and body on a landlocked grid, and ruled by little bitty bullshit activities.)

Infection showed him the prism of death, casting him in and out of hallucination, revealing the long-buried memory of his father, and of Wallis Farm, and of the taste of wild blackberries, and the smell of the chinked wood and flashing of the family cabin. Sonny's memory returned him time and again to the leaving, and to the Indian Head knife his daddy had given him. To Gabe, the man who spoke to the mules. To the ladder-back rocker that Hare had slept in, drunk.

He skittered atop time, his vision now and again inhabited by Indians, by things he'd read about and seen on television, and perhaps even heard about, some while back. Their presentations were made on the plastic image wheels of an old View-Master toy stereoscope, a clicking slideshow that showcased the tribe's riverside fields and swidden agriculture; the intricate, densely populated mound-building communities; the global trade routes they had established for beads, and the routes that the Whites had co-established for deerskin; the etchings of long-cleared Mississippi hardwood forest.

The View-Master image wheels illuminated a past that spanned combat and barter, and famine and love and art. From historic petrograph to centralized earthworks and plaza superstructures. Intercontinental trade routes to matrilineal lineage, to . . .

Myth, history, fact, dream. A South before acreage? he wondered. Before race?

* * *

Sonny's mother's West Garfield Park landscape had been decimated for as long as memory allowed. She had rented, forever, an apartment in a row house made of brick and Indiana limestone. It was right across from the elementary school, whose bustle of restless kids and buses and shouts and petty trash had decorated their weekday mornings and afternoons, forever. Over the years, the upper and lower apartments had sandwiched them with families and druggies and squatters, and, for some time, the Dr. Reverend Davie, who they suspected was a fallen sort of pastor, a repentant if not exile who still belted out gospel on every Sunday morning—"Jesus on the Mainline," mostly—warming up for his backup spot at the pulpit. Above them, below, the spaces had trended toward Bedouinism, stop-offs for whomever might proffer first and last months' rent, then sacrifice the latter within a short span of time, having been unable to carry the former in the first place. Pensionless grandmothers or softy poseur pimps. People unafraid to bang on your door and ask you for a dollar, or a dab of jelly, or whatever they might come up needing in a pinch, and who knew to nurture and expect reciprocal requests from you. Friendly people who brought you homemade apple crumble in empty margarine tubs, or who held fundraiser barbecues on the front lawn on summer Saturdays just before rent was due: five bucks a plate, or, hell, four, or, *Hell, gimme two bucks and don't tell anybody.* Even the memory of this delectable food-smoke crushed Sonny with want.

His mother had insisted on growing a small truck garden, at first in pots on the fire escape and rooftop, the idea being they could sell a bushel of veg at some stand or local market. For a few years now, though, she had planted rows in the empty lot next door. The dirt plot was owned by a retired beat cop who had fled their environment the instant he was pensioned. He had kept the property because it was simply too cheap to give up—and he knew that gentrification, his pension, was coming someday soon. Yet as owner, he was also subject to city dumping fines, so he couldn't neglect the property in total. Thus, in exchange for the gardening space, Sonny's mother kept the lot tidy and kept the city fines at bay. She grew good veg, and she shared it, and some folks even helped her for a season, and young kids sometimes tore the crop up as play.

The neighbors who were old enough believed Sylvia was a hippie, her holdover seventies style having arrested somewhere in the eighties. Her long hair and woven sweater, and bulky dress over sticklike frame; it was as if she had left any sartorial aesthetic on the battlefield of her protest days. As if she wore a shroud of that era, the late seventies and early eighties, a reminder of her former agency, of her activism, of her running away from what she had been back in Mississippi.

Chicago, Syl had learned early, was a marcher's town, a picket city, and she had thrown her body in against nukes, against education cuts, against tax breaks for the wealthy, against the mass national release of the mentally ill from institutions. She had exhausted all in order to combat the doctrine of Peace Through Power . . . and, dear lord, above all against the lie of states' rights.

She had fought so hard against Reagan, Reagan, Reagan.

After Sylvia lost that war, the only thing left to document it was the uniform.

Once a week at least, a stout Latino man attached a bright yellow leaflet to her door handle by a rubber band. He did the same up and down the block, dangling flyers off of doorknobs or into the mouths of wall-mount mailboxes. The flyer was an ad on behalf of someone buying "Ugly Houses." It had an email address and a phone number, and it promised the best price, in "Cash Money," for even the worst of dwellings. These were the homes where families lived: *Ugly*. This was the thing nobody had: *Cash Money*. The flyer featured a smiling stick figure with a bouquet of bills in his fist.

She did not own her apartment. She knew nobody on their block who owned their apartment. With exception, perhaps, of the previous couple of years, she could only imagine her village as a ghost area of sorts, a cemetery. A tenant farm without a crop.

The trifolds of bright yellow paper were slipped over her doorknob—and she instantly threw them away. Yet a week later, every week later, the man cycled back 'round, banding new yellow brochures on the worn knobs and handles: *Ugly*. This was agitating to her, because the bright paper often flittered into the yard, the street, the porches, the bushes. *Cash Money*.

The flyer was highlighter-yellow and the wind scattered it, and the rain pasted it to curb and windshield, gummed it to the waist-high chain fence that held her garden. Every week Sylvia cleaned the waddage up. Yet, a week later, more.

ONE SUNDAY, in summer, Sonny had leaned far out of his mother's kitchen window, his face hot from sunlight, his chest and arms teetering in the open air. The bacon smoke clouded out beside him as he stretched farther away, farther on, the gravity nearly taking him down. His eyes had been shut as he contemplated this potential: the falling, the flying, the energy drift of equilibrium, the dive.

"Hey!" a woman's voice had called up to him. "You're scarin' me, man!" Her tone was . . . silk? No. It was butter biscuit, or maybe sacred steel gospel. Each syllable was a glisten on summertime skin. He kept his eyes shut to soak in the thick southernness, and he'd been compelled to stretch even farther out that window, toward her call.

"No, really!" she'd yelled out. "You up there!"

Her whistle pierced his reverie. He opened his eyes and looked down at her: pinkie fingers still angled in her mouth, poised to whistle once more. They stared at each other for a few seconds, until she pulled her fingers from her lips and smiled. Winked. She was perhaps half his age, a twenty-something in a lemon-yellow skirt, and very pregnant.

"Is that streak o' lean fatback?" she'd asked, her hand shielding her eyes from the sun.

He smiled at her, nodded yes.

"Smells divine. So anyway, you okay up there?"

Her voice had been a sort of memory, a fertile rush of kinship that bound them across space, transcending the worn bricks and jammed windows of Chicago.

Sonny had stared at the woman for a few more seconds, considering his answer. "I feel stuck, you know?"

"Ha! I do. I *do* know." She'd smiled again. "Maybe you just need to take off."

"Funny," he said, spreading his arms as wide as wings. "I was just thinking that same thing!" Sonny had stretched even farther out of the window, the frame now hitting his waistline.

"Whoa, man!" she hollered. "I didn't mean 'take off' out of the dang window!"

"No," he'd called back. "I know *that*. I'm only coasting."

"You'd better know it." She laughed. "I mean it. Go easy up there. I've got enough going on without having to worry about you, too."

He'd nodded at her, and mouthed an okay. The young woman winked again, and waved goodbye, stepping to enter the wreckage of a neighboring house.

Sonny's mother had stepped in, and she peered over his shoulder. She recognized the SUV parked at the curb.

"That woman's from back home," Sylvia said. "From Pitchlynn, if you can believe it."

"Did you tell her you'd lived on the farm?"

"Nope. I said I's from West Tennessee."

"But why?"

" 'Why' is because I don't care for Pitchlynn, or Mississippi, Sonny. Besides, her husband's the one behind all this leaflet nonsense. He's the fool who's tryin' to buy the 'ugly houses' out from under everybody. If you ask me, he's as greedy as a Wallis."

Sonny had gazed out the window, hovering almost, as he waited to glimpse the young woman again.

\* \* \*

THERE'D BEEN an exceptional lack of direction in the Cessna. An exceptional range of vision. Sonny had been hooked from that very first flight, the free outing he'd won at the Braves ballgame. Despite the rigidity of the mandatory preflight ritual——conference, weather briefing, chock removal, headset tests; the chatter with Control; the checklist and instrument panel verification—ultimately, piloting had shattered his routine, his map. He could move above time, or story.

The solace and navigability of atmosphere was alien, an opiate. He saw the city by the lake like a dream, as if he were some drifting, lofted Jesus. His instructor, a skinny middle-aged Pole, had provided Sonny disposable wraparound shades as offset to the pilot's own classic gold aviators. Sonny had sensed no boredom in the man, though the pilot admitted to having flown these sky tourism missions throughout the day, every day, for a dozen years.

"Always something new to see," the pilot had said. "The sky, the light, the students. The city. Hell, even the wind!" He'd glanced down at the Gold Coast. "By the way, this is all you, Edward. I am no longer flying this airplane."

There was a hiccup of turbulence as Sonny's hands clenched the yoke. The Polish pilot laughed at the cliché of it all.

And Sonny, Eddie, Ed, or even Hobbs, had heaved with relief as if he had surfaced from the mud. On the wings of a dove, he'd asked the pilot if they could in fact turn *away* from the city, and out over the lake, beyond any marker.

"Roger that," the Pole replied.

Sonny had steered them out, into the sun-buffed horizon. Within weeks, the idea of his mission home would take hold.

# 8

A handful of days after the wire story ran, Derby couldn't help but go track down his sister. As Colleen sat home with the twins, at once delighted and huffing and tense with exhaustion, believing that her husband had had to make an unscheduled run to town to oversee a materials delivery to the Wallis House, Derb was instead cruising his truck over the rust-colored asphalt of Main Street, Marks, Mississippi.

Two-story, mostly brick buildings drifted by like a dirge. The few windows left unboarded showcased FOR RENT and FOR SALE signs and fingertip graffiti in dust. The brick exteriors were pocked like moonscapes, and no scrap of wood—door to banister to window frame—was more than a hash of paint peel and split. The sidewalk plates buckled. Here and there an establishment remained open, a Dollar Store knockoff, or a filling station-cum-grocery that advertised both the usual ("2 Liter, $1.49"), and the extra usual ("Pork Fat, .99/pound").

Though he'd managed to hide the newspaper from Colleen, he felt shot through with anxiety, and compelled to . . . to talk to Winnie? To listen? To scream at her for hounding his wife on the phone? To threaten her for dragging him back into things?

No. He wanted to warn her. To remind her that living an hour away from Pitchlynn was not going to harbor her, or Ladybug, should Hare still be able to mobilize his people. After all, Derby had tracked her down with a couple of calls.

Mostly, he thought, he was there to say goodbye. He was done with her.

Cruising cracked avenues, his hands clammy on the wheel vinyl, Derby thought about the other boy, about Hare's other family, the "better bitch and child" that were mentioned in the story. He wondered if these others were free of themselves, and of the last name they'd been saddled with.

The string of slight houses on Winnie's street were contrivances of warped wood and rust lesion, of blue plastic tarps bleeding over wood-pile and scrap pile, and any pile left to rot. This, in fact, was the poorest slice of the poorest state in the nation. The most illiterate state. The fattest, the highest in teen pregnancy, and the lowest in life expectancy. The most laughed-at and despised and written-off state. Truth be told, it was the dyingest fucking place in America. Nobody cared to save it.

And there he was. And then there was Ladybug, at play behind a saggy chain-link fence. He pulled over, cut the engine, and watched her frolic about with an empty laundry detergent bottle. She threw the orange jug high into the air, then ran under it and caught it—or pouted when she didn't. She then held the makeshift toy on her hip as if it were her baby. The girl cradled the jug in her arm, an act he found tender, if not cute.

But in a shot, Ladybug's eyes grew frantic with fear. She began to sprint around the yard, her open hand thrust out as if to protect the jug-baby from invisible, ongoing assault. She dodged musk thistle and flashing remnant, running away, desperate to fight for the safety of her child.

He put his head down on the steering wheel and he gasped, and wanted to cry. Not for his niece, but for his overarching greed. Fact was, Derby could never introduce this broken element to his own children. Ladybug was lost. Even her imagination had turned against her. No telling how her influence might take root in the twins.

A car horn blared from behind him, followed by the drawled-out holler of the driver. Derby waved the vehicle around, then looked back to his niece. Ladybug now stared at him, her hands grasping the backyard chain link. She struggled to place him, dropping the jug to the ground. He sped away, back toward Pitchlynn.

Half an hour later, Derby mashed the brakes and swerved onto the shoulder. A smile hit his face, and he laughed while slapping the steering wheel. His niece hadn't been using the laundry jug as a doll, protecting it from some unseen terror. Rather, her palm had been held out to stiff-arm defensemen, as would any world-class tailback. That girl had been playing football.

There was so much hope to be reaped from the future, if he could only remember to seek it out. To see it. He threw the truck into gear and headed on home, having decided to contact Winnie when the retrial was over, and Hare was gone for good.

# GABRIEL

AUGUST 6, 1964

# 1

Gabriel strode the calf-high grasses of the glade, his bare shoulders sheened with sweat. Wheatlike brome whisked the pant legs of his overalls. He swung a large club casually, as if he were a batter on deck. Reaching the center of the clearing, he paused and looked around. Stretched. Smiled.

The small meadow, and the wilds that hemmed it into isolation, were his. The parcel had belonged to his father, and his grandfather, and within its unmapped innards he felt a kinship to land and family, and he felt impenetrable.

He set the club down, unfastened the braces of his heavy denim overalls, and stepped into nakedness. The swelter demanded liberation. Gabriel took opportunities.

Across the field, crouched behind a thick brake of blackberry, they watched him.

"Mama," the boy whispered.

"Hush," she said, clenching her child's shoulders, holding him down behind the wall of vines. They had hiked onto Gabe's land to sneak a couple of apron pockets' worth of berries. To snatch a few ripe handfuls for a skillet cobbler for the boy. (She knew that Gabe would have given her the berries had she asked, but the token mischief of the trespass had made the idea fun for Sonny.)

Their presence was now a weapon. "We have to live with that, him," she whispered. "So hush up, and look away."

"But Gabe might see us. He might——"

"Might *nothin'*," she said. "Shh."

"But——"

"He *cain't* see us, if he knows right," she interrupted. "He just cain't. And we cain't tell nobody we've seen him, neither. I mean this, Sonny. Nobody can know."

The woman and child did not face each other. Rather, their gazes were trained on the familiar man whose appearance now favored myth. The boy clasped an Indian Head pocketknife in his left hand, his thumb rubbing the groove in the wood casing. He watched Gabriel swing the club while striding through the meadow. He watched Gabe's stomach, his thighs, his sex.

The cudgel Gabe carried was mesmerizing. Fashioned from a small uprooted sapling whose trunk had been stripped of branches, its gnarled roots were now the killing end of the so-named "tap stick." Clipped to finger-length and sharpened, the roots now twisted from the club head like some arboreal morning star. The grip end of the weapon was wrapped in a strip of worn leather.

A dog bark arrested Gabriel's footsteps. His muscles flared as he scanned the meadow. The bark came again, again, from near where the mother and son were hidden.

"That's June," the boy whispered. "June's gonter tell Gabe we's in here!"

His mother pinched the base of his neck, silencing him. She had known Gabe for six years, since her husband had taken work on Wallis Farm, moving them out of the Delta and back into the hills they'd come from. Gabe was kind and smart. Dutiful. Respectful. A respectful Negro whose interactions thrust just up to (and often beyond) his position, but whose presence seemed welcome nonetheless. She had now and again bartered surplus veg with him, or dry goods; on more days than not they shared a few words in passing. She, in particular, would always ask about his daughter.

Only now, his violence. Gabe focused on the dog, whose barks alerted him to the nearby presence of prey. He trekked toward the blackberry thicket, his steps whisper-light and fast.

Seeing him approach, the boy trembled. This was not the Gabe whose smile had brought comfort, or who had promised to one day teach the boy of the secrets told to mules. No. This was a man alive, muscular and hurtling toward them, bladelike, his bare legs shredding the tall grass, the creases of determination like wounds on his brow.

The speckled feist lunged into the thicket, snapping the air on the far side of the vine-wall.

*Jesus lord*, the woman thought, her nails digging into the boy's arms. She knew only Gabe could call the dog off.

"Say somethin', Mama," the boy whispered. "*Please.*" The blackberry spines nicked his skin as he struggled. His syllables grew soggy with fear, as if he were three years old instead of five. Still, he gripped the wood-paneled knife.

"I cain't, Sonny," she answered. "You don't know what they'll do to him. Gabe can*not* know we's in here."

Just a skillet cobbler for the boy, with a spoonful or three for herself. It would be heaping, sugared, then brown-sugared and buttered, made care of a quick, clandestine jaunt for ripe berries. It had been a nothing idea.

It was now a trial. Was terrorism. For if the boy should tell his father of how he had witnessed Gabe's body? Or no, more specifically, if Hare were to learn that *she'd* been present at the seeing? Retribution would catalyze at the velocity of lightning. No White woman was allowed to see a Black man like this.

Between the serrated leaves they saw the bloody scratches on the dog's snout, and the stab of its tallow-colored fangs.

When Sonny's whispers again rose to words, she clamped her hand over his mouth. The child writhed in an effort to break free of her grasp, his body crushed against her ribs and the blackberries in her apron. His eyesight grew blurry as he fought. Strangely, a piece of him, something beyond even consciousness, thought only of the pocketknife, a dull, Indian Head brand that his father had given him. He determined never to drop it, even as his muscles went limp, and his vision drained to white.

The woman whispered a prayer for silence, constricting her boy ever tighter into the shelter of her body. She quoted scripture as she stared the dog down, her syllables frantic, until suddenly the feist bolted off, flushing a large brown-gray swamp rabbit from the blackberry hedge. She watched as Gabe tracked the rabbit across the clearing, then hurled the club at trajectory, thirty yards or so on a rope, striking it dead. The precision of the kill was astounding.

The woman's trance was snapped by the boy's gasping return to consciousness. Terrified, she smoothed and praised him, shushed his cries, and rocked. "Breathe," she whispered. "Baby? Sonny?"

His small fingers flinched around the Indian Head knife.

Across the field, Gabe ordered the dog, "Bring 'at rabbit here, June!" The feist obeyed him, trotting back with the limp rabbit held soft in her jaw. Gabe was pleased with this. Beyond attack and devotion, June was keenly empathetic: She shadowed him, needed him. Fled him if necessary.

Gabe accepted the hare from the dog, patting it once. "Now go fetch 'at tap stick," he ordered. "Get!" Her tongue flared to one side as she tore through the grass. The dog retrieved the club, cutting a double line in the glade.

With the rabbit dangling from his fist by its ears, Gabe scanned the meadow like a raptor. He stared at the thicket long enough to let on that he'd been aware of the others. Let on, that is, if they could admit it to themselves, confirming their communion with his body, and the assault they could initiate upon it.

Didn't matter. Wasn't nobody going to tell Gabe how to hunt his own land.

# 2

It was August 1964. The mules were all but ghosts, the Delta an army of machines. The atmosphere was a rally space of space flight and microwave, radio and NTSC broadcast. Yet in the northern hills, at least on this particular, singular operation, draft animals still took up the burden of work, lock to dock, first to last light. Given the available technology, the existence of such a throwback space was a perverse bow to nostalgia. A living monument. A snare of lost time.

Fact was, Wallis Farm only brought in heavy machinery every year or so, to stave off an ongoing war with a beaver colony, whose dams and lodges flooded hundreds of working acres. Flatbed rigs would haul in dozers and dumps, dredging the large creek and obliterating the blockages. For a hyphen of time, hydraulics would dominate the pastoral, before making their motorized retreat.

Miss Wallis, or "Miss Beverly," as all were taught to call her, was a funding body of anyone or anything involved with preservation. Fused to her compulsive, obsessive saving of any site deemed appropriately historic, depot to manse to Missionary Baptist church, was a concurrent desire to preserve the natural world. This meant that alongside the aesthetic and production-based sequestration of her farmland, the virtual and relentless encapsulation of the plantation as she had known it during her 1930s childhood, best she could recall, anyway, Miss Beverly did not condone the killing of animals—any wild animals, by any means. She understood of course that hogs had always and would always be slaughtered, gutted, shaved, and boiled (especially at Christmas). But this indulgence, alongside the processing of a necessary few head of cattle, was the extent of the killing on her family land. Period.

She and Mr. Wallis often screamed at each other about this policy. Never in public, though on a breezy day you could hear their clashes drift out of the open windows of the big Wallis farmhouse and all the way down to Gabe's cabin. Mr. Wallis was correct in his assertion that, due to Miss Beverly's mismanagement, the farm had become a coveted animal preserve, one that couldn't be thinned by losing a few head of game. Yet she still forbade her husband the hunt, whether whitetail or bear, turkey or rabbit. Some of the densest and last remaining quail populations in Mississippi even flocked the underbrush. No matter. The farm came from *her* family money, so it was *her* home. And though Mr. Wallis now eclipsed his wife's sociopolitical lineage, and while she took a backseat to him publicly—even letting him rename the farm after himself, Wallis, versus her family surname, George—Miss Beverly would only let him hunt it if she saw the deer turn skinny and sick, a plague threatening the population.

(More than once, Mr. Wallis had hired a couple of boys to capture and hamstring a scrawny buck, then let it loose up by the big house, in hopes she'd determine it wasting. One year, this tactic actually worked, opening a rare, relentless season of killing for Wallis and his colleagues.)

Though it was in fact perverse, Miss Beverly's saving was perhaps benevolent in an adjacent, unintended way. For one thing, versus a labor displacement care of combine or thresher, Gabe remained in charge of the mules, the third generation of eldest males in his family to do so. In turn, her ethic also sustained a relationship to the land, the crop, and the bodies required to operate it all.

For Gabe, Miss Beverly's stubborn, bastard strain of concern served to fortify his ownership of homeplace and land: thirty acres and a cabin, bought outright from Miss Beverly's grandfather by his own.

(Truth be told, everyone who'd been on Wallis Farm long enough knew that Gabe's parcel was the result of a negotiation, a payoff intended to put down lingering interfamily questions. They knew that Grandfather George's offer of landownership had been a condolence, a dividend. A consolation prize to his shadow kin.) (Folks did *not*, however, know that when the deal was first brokered to Gabe's grandfather, the ex-slave had initially vowed to turn the bribe down, and to instead pursue his true birthright at the courthouse in Pitchlynn. Indeed, the eldest Gabe had understood that his body pumped just as much George family blood as did any of the man's other children—his half-siblings, to be clear—so he knew that he was owed far more the paltry land than he'd been given.

(In the end, however, Gabe's grandfather was also a pragmatist. He came to realize that legal protest would only cost his family everything, at best running them off the farm and out of town . . . whereas, conversely, even a stamp of landownership would radicalize them toward independence. Someday. So instead of challenging his birthright at the courthouse, the old man had gone to a bank. He'd hired out a safe-deposit box, and he took the folded paperwork—a little quitclaim deed put together by his former master, and upon which the eldest Gabriel had scrawled his mark in ink—and he placed it in the box, right and proper, right there in town. He had not been treated well by the banking staff, and he held serious mistrust of the institution itself. Yet this was during the time after the War Between the States but before *Plessy v.*; the time that had even been marked by a Black United States senator from Mississippi. When Black lawyers and policemen might even be seen on some streets, when the eldest Gabriel was not alone in his pursuit of stability, and resource, and formal immersion. This was deep into Reconstruction. And like these other men, Gabe's grandfather had chosen to engage the process, to perhaps even *believe*—regardless of whether some squat Pitchlynn bank clerk wished to reciprocate the engagement or not. As such, the entire operation with the bank had felt . . . dignified? No. Not dignified. Not even safe. But *possible*. Yes, that was it: leaving the bank, a participant in trust, Gabriel felt robust in that he felt slightly possible. His investment in the contract, and the bank, and the land, was by default and legal compact their co-investment in him. Though he and his own could still be throttled by terror, deprived of all franchise, he believed that the money and land would make him valuable soon enough.)

The parcel had been sold to Gabriel's namesake for the laughable price of $175. The debt had been cleared within two seasons.

Gabe's father had rebuilt the shotgun cabin years before:

re-chinking the walls, and adding a floor of pine boards, and a second bedroom off of the back, kicking the shape of the shotgun cabin out into a half-T, and then a full-T design as the family expanded. The children had been enlisted early and often to maintain the home, and they were taught every aspect of construction, repair, and sustainability. They had lived off of small truck farms, earning both their own veg and a few dollars at town market, or on the farm store, alongside a share of knowledge passed down care of turned soil and yanked weeds, care of pinching worms from tomato plants, of waiting for the second hard frost before pulling greens. Three generations of Gabe's household understood that peanut vines were the perfect supplement for the paltry head of milk cows kept in a pen out back. The roughage was economical and healthy, and the cows loved it, though you had to plan ahead, had to first throw the plants on the roof flashing to dry them out, to get them good and brittle. These things the children knew. Small things, perhaps. Petty things that might matter to no one else. Yet these processes, these strategies . . . this *precision* was the difference between survival and being starved off.

Though technically the thirty acres belonged to his entire family, Gabriel, the oldest of seven, four of whom were still living, was inheritor and caretaker. His siblings were settled with this, knowing the land was theirs to build on if they chose. By mid-century, the bulk of them had moved on anyway, northward for work, mostly, toward both true and imagined liberation.

Gabe's relationship to the White neighbors who owned nothing—croppers and migrants who, among the Black field hands who still worked the farm, cycled on and off, depending on their ambition or endurance—was a conflux of resentment and situational respect. Never equality with the Whites, but situational respect, it seemed.

His own work was the life chore of teaming and driving and tending the Wallis Farm mules, lock to dock, first light to last. Gabe's family had been on that farm longer than most—including Mr. Wallis—so his legacy, like that of the mules, was hard-wired to the bare function of things.

The main room of his cabin was patched by the faded floral wallpaper his wife had picked out years before. The bedroom walls, too, were a mash of these patterns, on account of either the store holdings, or their money, running erratic. (Mina would buy what remnants she could, when she could, then paste them up like a quilt.) The windows featured sun-faded, sage-colored curtains. He had an old wood-housed radio, though he no longer listened every day. The kitchen now had a small icebox and a rudimentary electric stove. The bathroom, fitted with exposed pipe, was dominated by an honest-to-goodness bathtub, a jubilatory improvement on the outdoor corrugated trough he'd grown up with. On the floor in the front room was a patchwork rug his wife had woven out of linen and rag scraps. Folded and draped over Gabe's iron bed frame was a quilt the elder ladies had given him after she was gone.

Mina's pregnancy had been weak. One afternoon, Gabe came in from the mule barn and found her on the floor, her sack dress soaked below the waist. He had mobilized then as he had not since the war, tending to his wife while spreading word to the neighbors, conscripting everyone in her service. Within an hour the farm's veterinarian had ordered Mina to stay in bed, explaining that she had a thin something-or-other. (The vet's counsel was not owing to an abolishment of Black physicians, but rather to a lack of time to get to the colored hospital way over in Clarksdale.) Per these orders, Mina did nothing for nearly three months: no work, no cooking, no helping anyone out. No money made from laundry or stitching, from engaging the egg trade with the Lebanese peddlers who still came around, their delivery trucks like satellites from their brick-and-mortar stores, loaded with sundry, and who nurtured any available market, with any available race. No, nothing but rest. Though Mina had begged Gabe to let her up, he was relentless, and shrewd in his ability to forfeit his own needs: nourishment or habit, or touch.

Because of this discipline, she had made it through childbirth. Death would not put the family at distance. Instead, it was the fierce protectionism of motherhood that pulled them part.

The newborn was small but loud—deafeningly loud—from the first hour. At the baptism, that baby had bawled like nothing anyone had ever heard. The women on hand had soon bawled right along with her, though their spirited moans proved mere wake to her vessel.

Jessamine, named after her mother.

Life was defined by the child's screaming. Gabe and Mina had soon tried any remedy offered, rubbing dirt on her gums, rubbing sugar and whiskey and starch. Still, the baby would not cease. Jessamine's cries had dwarfed their cabin hour after hour, robbing the family's sleep and their meals, and shattering all tranquility.

It was as if the infant's howls were a facilitator, a relentless, verbal conduit that forced Gabe and Mina to confront an ongoing rift. Over the years, as their neighbors and family had begun to dissipate, leaving Wallis Farm for places north, for those apparent, abundant sites of redemption and autonomy, a lake of murky ambition had formed at the heart of the couple's relationship—with each partner standing on opposite shores. Mina wanted to move on, to thrive among the part of the family who'd left this place a near-generation before, and who would still welcome her in Bronzeville, or Paradise Valley, or Cedar-Central. Gabe, however, was convinced that stewardship of the land, and the reward that this entailed, was close at hand. Like his grandfather and father, he believed with that their children would inherit the mantle of ownership, the land-legacy that had defined Mississippi for so many.

Pushing their divide, baby Jessamine wailed like a siren, exacerbating all, forcing emotion, and action, to the surface. The mobile health nurse even found that the child's throat had scabbed over.

At times, the new parents could only leave the infant on their old tick mattress, writhing on her back, pillows surrounding her like a padded sort of fort, at which point Mina would leave the bedroom and drift to the front room and weep, at which point Gabe would sit in his chair and rock, and drift for a moment into a sort of dulled, dampened space, an emotional landscape first discovered during the war; his feelings were held in a place somehow *beyond*, someplace invulnerable, recognized but removed. Like loving someone through a window.

When Gabe's sister Jeanes finally left the farm, no lingering regard for her homeplace, or her inheritance-in-land, Mina had begged Gabe that they follow suit. When he wouldn't relent, his wife had cursed him, and then asked him, and then promised her partner that movement toward the unknown would deliver a new opportunity. New life. Mina swore to Gabe that Chicago would bring about an armistice between them. Would rehabilitate, would remortise them. That it wasn't too late to change. So many, many others had done so before them.

Assaulted by his love for her, and by the screams of his child, and by the past, and the promise of everything he had known and been raised to know, to do, Gabe couldn't help but *bifurcate*. He broke himself in two, and told Mina to go on ahead. He put up a grin, and asked her to please stake some new ground on the family's behalf, and he promised to follow her, them, as soon as he had secured the next yield, and a little bit of money. (Or better yet, he thought, by the time of the harvest she would return to him, the child a bit older, and they could retain the family course.) He had hated to propose this split, and he hated himself for wanting it, and he swore it was only temporary.

"I just cain't, Lord," Gabe had prayed for forgiveness. "I am so sorry, but I cannot handle this now."

Mina had accepted the plan, though in the buildup to departure she had offered time and again to back out. She knew that Gabe had wanted her to stay, and she would've done so if he had asked, if he had confessed that he couldn't go forward without her.

It was true: He wanted Mina to back out. Was desperate for her to stay. Yet with the agreement, Gabe had witnessed the new flare of life in his wife, care of expectation alone. He could see that she needed the move more than she needed even him. Asking her to stay would only scar things up further. So he didn't. He couldn't.

After the decision was made, the child fell silent. Over their final nights together, Gabe had sat for hours on the floor, watching Jessamine fidget and stretch. He was tickled to discover that her facial features, though chubby and mostly obscure, had also bunched into familial traits: Jessamine's teacup chin, and his own mother's squinchy smile eyes. He flat-out bellowed when the baby put her entire foot in her mouth. And when the child drowsed, he cooed to her, and sang, and whispered to her of her forebears. With her every yawn, he took in the pleasant sweet-sourness of her breath. Gabe would fall asleep next to the baby, Mina stepping around him in the small room, putting the child into the crib, and readying herself for rest. After, she would rouse Gabe from his spot, and the two of them would tiptoe over the wide, creaking floor planks and into bed.

Jessamine was now ten years old. She and Mina still lived on the same block as Jeanes's family in Chicago, as had been arranged before the move. Gabe's daughter had proper schooling, a cobble of proper parentage, and four cousins close as siblings, alongside two generations of kinfolk and extended community. Mina wrote him often, begging him to release himself from the farm, to open up to the world. There was Vietnam and James Bond. Marvin Gaye and Willie Mays and Malcom and . . .

A black-and-white photo Mina had sent was tacked to one wall in his cabin. It showcased his daughter in a long, dark coat, her body cocked against the wind as she waved a mittened hand, the snow and brick apartment houses behind her, and the scaffoldlike Bronzeville rooftops in the distance. Mina never pressed Gabe to send any more money than he could spare, but she always, repeatedly, pressed him to move, or to even just visit them, to see what it was like. She was waiting.

Gabe sensed that an upheaval would soon come to Wallis Farm. He couldn't *not* know that a resolution, a dividend, would soon show itself, rewarding him for having held firm to the land. His best guess was that someone would soon offer to buy him out, though he prepared himself also for the opportunity to buy.

Whatever the case, he needed to see this era through. He had to, for all of them. He would go to his family when it was done.

THE MULES. Gabe thought nothing about shoving the heel of his fist into a sweated latch and cheekbone, or about flaying a haunch with the strap—though he rarely had to. The animals knew him too well for violence. He issued orders and praise into their cathedral-arch ears, driving them as he'd been shown by his father. He shoed and fed and teamed up and cared for them, brushed them down, and cut out their fly bites and festers. Each mule seemed resigned to his authority, in large part because Gabe never, *ever* forgot to maintain the hierarchy. One lapse in posture or placement would beckon a death-kick to the head.

The Wallises had always allowed their workforce to harness and clop a borrowed surrey into Pitchlynn on Saturday afternoon, though unlike his forebears, Gabe took his damned pickup truck (if he even bothered to go at all). Outside of fairs or special events, or perhaps a revival, walking the town square was for upstarts, for young people. In his late thirties now, Gabe had grown tired of looking for whiskey, or companionship, and he was tired of dressing in anything but overalls. Mostly he was tired of the expectation that he change into town mode, aloof and disengaged, so as to avoid judgment or threat. (If he did go to Pitchlynn, he sure as hell wasn't going to fashion himself as some pre-war, darky pilgrim, some barefoot pageant to Wallis nostalgia by riding in on a creaky wagon, a haystick in his mouth as he reined a span of mules. He had driven an Army deuce-and-a-half transport truck across half of Europe, for chrissakes.) Wed to his solitude, Gabe did what he pleased, mostly, while on his own land. He passed the nights with the far-off broadcasts of the radio, or by talking to himself, remembering.

# 3

Gabe wasn't sure whether or not he would salt and hang the rabbit meat in the smoke-shack. Though it was late in the day, his appetite hadn't yet shown itself, on account of his preoccupation with whomever had spied on him from behind the thicket in the glade.

Beneath the olfactory rush of sweat and meadow, of forest, dog, and musk, he was convinced he'd caught the scent of ladies' soap. The thought of it made his insides feel like petals peeling into a whorl.

He stood outside the log-wood shack that housed his salt box and cast-iron kettles, and the rafters where he hung meat to cure. The rabbit lay across the waist-high carving stump. The feist, June, panted heavily as she lay in the dirt near his feet. Gabe issued the dog a quick syllable of praise, then picked up his long knife and began dressing their kill.

Someone shouted his name. He looked up to see three young men approach. One of them, Junior Bates, was a farmhand he'd known since the boy was bug-sized. The other two, also young Black men, were strangers. Gabe ignored them, looking back to the stump as he severed the rabbit's back feet. No good would come of the men wanting anything from him.

"Gabe, hey, Gabe?" Junior called again. "Need to talk with you, man."

The strangers walked up, keeping a respectful distance, eyeballing the knife and the growling dog. "This is Robert and Don," Junior announced. "They's here on account of—"

"I know why," Gabe interrupted, swatting away a congregation of flies. "I know. And I don't hold any strike against you men. Y'all are doin' important work. But I've done fine for a long time on my own, and I have my own mission in process. So y'all need to keep on walkin', and work your campaign out somewhere else."

Gabe threw the rabbit's feet down to the feist, then severed the head and did the same. The dog's eyes stayed locked on the strangers as she gnawed into tendon and bone.

"Mister Gabe," Junior continued. "You're the only one on this farm who owns his house. You a war hero, man. Ain't nobody can tell you what to do. Even if they try, they can't—"

Gabe took his knife to the back of the rabbit, slicing the length of the fur. "Snicks, Kings, and Riders," he mumbled. "COFOs and all? Y'all got some *names*, boy!" He chuckled to himself, then laid the blade on the stump, then started tearing the hide away. Once more he stared at the young civil rights workers. "Like I said. Y'all need to point it in another direction. But good luck to you. God bless."

# 4

Hare Hobbs knocked on the tall wooden door, and was beckoned into the sporting hall. The shadowy, open room was massive enough to swallow his own cabin several times over.

Someone asked if he wanted a drink. He did, so they made one for him, with a handful of ice shards dug from a fogged pewter pitcher. He had never been invited here, though he knew the men gathered at the converted barn on a regular basis. He'd often heard their laughter frill the night.

Now it was him here, inside, with them. No women came into this space, save, he supposed, the servants. This was strictly Mr. Wallis's domain, a large, gutted, A-type barn-turned-sporting-lounge. When not in Jackson, Wallis was here, holding court with his peers. Despite the fact that Miss Beverly wouldn't let him hunt the property, or perhaps as antidote for his desire to do so, the room was outfitted as a sort of refined game camp. Buck and black bear heads were mounted on rough pine paneling, and bunk beds were installed in the spare rooms. Rifles stood upright behind a glass-front antique rack. The central wall of the hunt lodge featured a large stone-mantel fireplace.

And there was whiskey. Good whiskey.

The crew of men on hand were mostly residents of the big houses in Pitchlynn proper, though some were from Holly Springs and Oxford and elsewhere nearby. (Hare guessed that like Mr. Wallis, these were landowner-donors-turned-Jackson-politicians, their last names adorning library and street sign and legislation.) They sat comfortably on the large leather-and-tack couches, or leaned against the rough-hewn wooden bar, packing the ends of their unfiltered cigarettes before light-ing, then exhaling plumes as thick as cream. They were warm toward each other, and, somehow, toward Hare.

He had no idea why he was here, why Mr. Wallis had come down to his cabin to ask if Hare could meet some of the boys who were gather-ing to talk "farm affairs." Even Hare's wife and son had known some-thing was off. As if to ward away her husband's anxious, unspoken thoughts (of debt unpaid, or chore unfinished? of termination on the farm?), his wife, Syl, had offered a terse smile just after Mr. Wallis left their porch.

"Next thing you know you'll be a boss," Syl had assured Hare. "Someday soon we's gonna wake up in our own little house. Own our own little plot."

They both knew she was lying.

Mr. Wallis asked Hare to sit in an emerald-colored armchair of rough cotton and brass tacking. He did. Over long minutes, the men then bantered about Ole Miss football, about the '63 SEC title—the school's sixth—and the prospect of another national championship, only this time undisputed. They vowed that no federal court or social-ist President could, or would, continue to force the school's hand or policy. The cohort then carved out space for Hare to join the conver-sation, but he didn't. Instead, he sat there grinning, terrified that the sweat from his neck and shoulders would stain the deep green chair upholstery. He hunched forward to avoid contact, making him appear touched by disfigurement.

Mr. Wallis had finally cut the clatter by asking if Hare always went by his nickname, or if he ever went by Harold—noting that Harold was an incredibly strong Viking name.

"Mr. Wallis," Hare replied, "you can call me Harold, sure, though nobody's called me anythin' but Hare since I's a boy."

"Fine," Mr. Wallis said. "So, Harold, do you have any idea why you're with us?"

"Nope," Hare answered.

The men chortled lovingly at this bluntness, and smiled as if he were a friend far removed, someone welcomed back into their fold. Hare grinned back briefly, then sipped his whiskey and sucked a fleeting ice shard.

Mr. Wallis continued, "You are here, Harold, because I have *noticed* you. The way you carry yourself. The way you raise your boy—what's his name?"

"Edward. But we call him Sonny."

"Edward," Mr. Wallis repeated. "The way you wrestle your tasks, as if throwing them off, as if fighting for the next prize to be taken. You are not a man easily satisfied, are you?"

Hare was uncertain as to how to respond, so he didn't. If asked the same question forever he would never think of himself as fighting through anything, save hour to hour, row by row, cotton shank by shank. Still, in answer to the silent pause of the group, Hare nodded in the affirmative.

"Exactly," Wallis said. "You are that man. And you're humble about it. A fine trait."

The men grunted their agreement.

Hobbs smelled himself amid the scent of dampened fire and pine and coffee. He wanted to dive his nose close to his armpit, as his ripeness was so out of place. *This ain't real*, he thought, looking around for any authentication. *They think I'm slow, like some heifer or sow. They need somethin' offa me.*

"Now, look, Harold. We ain't here to play poker."

*You won't have it*, he thought. *I ain't no sow.*

Wallis lumbered the floor in his tan quarter-brogues, then set his drink on the jagged stone mantel. "Tell me, friend. What do you know about what the coloreds have going on around the farm? What jungle drums have you heard?"

"Wellsir," Hare muttered, adjusting in the green armchair. "I don't really know. I haven't, really."

"Don't worry, Harold. We're not a lynch mob. Not out to wreak hell. It's simply that our business is to know what's goin' on." He then pointed at Hobbs. "It's your business, too, Harold. Because god love 'em, no matter how good I am to those people, no matter how much food, tack, seed, clothes, what have you—and I promise you I have never, *ever* touched my scales when weighing yield—they don't trust me."

"I reckon that's because——"

"I know why it *is*, Harold. Thank you. And I have to live with it, same as I live with my teenage daughter. But just as I must watch over a child who don't know how to care for herself, I need to know what's goin' on with my coloreds. I need you to tell me what's out there, for ever'body's good."

"Mr. Wallis, I really don't."

"Harold?"

"Yessir."

"How long you been on this farm?"

"I guess we're right up against six years now."

"Is your boy in school?"

"Yup, much's they offer, anyway."

"County schoolhouse?"

"Yessir."

"And your wife? What's her name?"

The volley of questions made Hobbs wriggle in the chair. "Well . . . My wife, Mr. Wallis?"

"Your wife."

"Syl. It's Sylvia."

"Sylvia. Mother of Romulus and Remus."

"Pardon?"

"Nothin'. Sylvia and . . . the boy's name again?"

"Edward Isaac."

"*Isaac?*" Wallis grinned. "That's a *Semite* name, Harold!" The men sniggered at this. "A Semite name if there ever was."

"I don't—— We got it out of the——"

"I'm kidding, Harold. I know, I know. You picked it from the Bible, as well you should. Isaac is a fine name. A strong name."

"From the Bible," Hare echoed. "Anyways, we call him Sonny."

"Yes. Edward Isaac and Sylvia. And your boy, Edward, he's at the county schoolhouse? And your Sylvia." Wallis paused. "Say, does your wife still wear feed clothes, Harold?"

"Sorry?" Hobbs shifted again.

"She still trade eggs? Wear sack print dresses?"

"Well." Hobbs looked to the dark corner of the room. "Not always. 'Pends on how we're doing. What part of the season it is and all."

"How's that feel, Harold? Your dear wife, Syl, is *still* dressed in feed sack, like her mama would've worn? You boy startin' the county school, instead of bein' up to the new Christian academy with his own kind? My Susan George is in class there." He glanced around the room. "She'll do just fine."

"Well, Mr. Wallis—"

"No more 'Mr.,' Harold. I'm askin' you, how does it *feel*? Your wife in coon clothes, your boy in a coon-trash school? All of you working until your back breaks while people like us, like me and the boys here, sit up in this lodge and drink whiskey?"

"Mr. Wallis, I guess—"

"I said no more goddamn 'Mr.' Harold! Just answer me."

"Well . . . it *feels* like that's our lot right now. My daddy raised us to believe that hard work and—"

"Don't patronize me, man." Wallis stepped forward to lean over Hare, speaking at the short edge of shout. "Your home a slapdash of splintered pine and bricked newspaper? Your meals of cornbread and hog fat? How, Harold? You're a veteran, right?"

"Battle of the Bulge, yessir, I—"

"So how do you *stand it*, man? My whiskey? My warmth?" Wallis paused. "My simply bein' born rich as the only reason why I am here—and why you are down there, in the shacks?"

"Well, it don't feel so goddamn—" Hare caught himself, and stared at his shoes.

Wallis smiled, stepped back, and looked around to his chorus. "Yes," he said. "It's not fair, is it?"

Hare finished his whiskey, calming himself. "I guess sometimes it's not. But the work 'round here ain't bad or—"

"Right, right. Calm down, we're just talkin'. Nobody's throwing you off the farm for speaking your mind, *friend*."

"I just wouldn't want you to think that—"

"Quite the opposite, Harold. Like I said, I've noticed you. We've noticed you. A soldier. And when we notice leaders, we bring them together. Help each other out, see? Now, first off, your boy should be in a proper school. A private, Christian school. And your wife? Sylvia? She should have a dress befitting a woman of her race."

"All due respect," Hare said, "we's just fine here. We want to work hard and——"

"Don't get me wrong, Harold. Your work *is* your value. Your honesty and toil, your virtue. I'm not proposing pageantry, man. I'm suggesting you be awarded a bit more stake, for a bit more work. For instance, the ability to obtain some of your own land?"

"Sir?" Hare said.

"Over time, of course. Ownership takes time, Harold. But a little bit of something yours, maybe? Sound good?"

*They will not have me*, Hare thought, though he could not restrain his swallow. *Battle of the Bulge.*

He felt like they could see inside his history, as if they could see him at sixteen, mending boots and binding blisters. A runt. A platoon runt filling canteens like some mascot, some toy held back from combat.

He'd been pinched by the other soldiers, had been goosed and kicked. Tickled, even touched. Hare had fetched their coffee and bullets, and soap, always soap; he became a washerwoman of sorts. The platoon had repeatedly hidden his gun and bayonet, the only two things a troop was never, ever permitted to lose. *Army even let those black bastards fight at the Bulge*, Hare thought. *While I got treated like some Christy poster pinup.*

"You are a leader among us, Harold. A sergeant, taking charge." Wallis raised his glass. "And we need your leadership. Your eyes, your ears. Your fists."

Hare felt stripped naked as Wallis and the men bunched around him, smiling, enacting his manhood. Fact was, he had come home from the war still a runt. Had redeployed to no inheritance, save the ready-made narrative of a war hero, a title that defined him despite of what he really was: less than nobody; a mascot; a washerwoman, likened to the wobble-legged Black maids who trudged the roadsides at early morning toward the proper White homes they tended in Pitchlynn proper.

These men now stood too close to that truth. They could see inside Hare. Could take his story away.

Wallis continued, "And in exchange, there could be a little bit of land, of something yours, Harold. Because *stake* is what makes us, what binds our presence as men in this social fabric. As guideposts and providers, versus some likeness of chattel, of skins who grow and die without resonance. I tell you what, Harold. Protestantism and yeomanry can be damned. There are only two things on this planet that matter, that you either have, or you take: earth, and birth."

# 5

Sylvia sat on the edge of the cotton-tick mattress in the lamplight. She'd sponged out the scrapes and blackberry spines on both she and the boy's skin, and dabbed them with a tincture of iodine. Sonny now slept in the front room, in the breeze through the porch door. Syl wished to sleep, was as exhausted as the boy, but she couldn't stop worrying over her husband, and what would become of his meeting with Mr. Wallis. Her fingernails drifted the topography of her skin, her shoulders, her forearms, her thighs.

From the Hills to the Delta, to the Piney Woods and back again, she and Hare had traveled, had scrapped, had fallen further and further behind. Their marriage was an odyssey of erosive, gentle collapse, a dissolution from the self-sufficiency that each had been taught and raised by. Their forebears, all from the hill country, north Mississippi, had been owners of small plots of corn, mostly, alongside just enough cotton for clothes, drapes . . . necessity. The lifestyle that Syl and Hare had been raised by was an ethos, an earnestness as was wrought from maybe seventy-five acres and a couple of dogtrot cabins. Their people were never croppers, nor tenants, but landowners. And though she and Hare's families had been large—especially during their grandparents' and great-grandparents' eras—the clans were a world removed from any nabob plantation dynasty. They had owned no slaves, nor wanted to. Rather, their modest size was their sustainability; it was their community, their love, and their labor force at once. Everyone pitched in, their collective efforts in both the field and at home resulting in a shared family yield. The commune's only real ties to consumerism were the tools they had bought, since they could not always forge. The rest, whether spokeshaved chair or chest of drawers, and from clothing to cookware to coffin, had been produced by hand and sweat of brow, as God intended.

*The love of Christ*, Syl thought. *The many children, the work. The crop. The lives of our grandfathers and their small parcels. The land, my god. The owning of land. Oh, and the stories of old Carolina, passed on. The richness of legacy and . . .*

*But this? Now? Hare and I have become such sorry people. Strangled in a home we can't never own, on a farm whose yield knows neither border nor ambition. Our foundation is gone*, she thought. *Our fathers, our families. The land. My husband, twisted up by the spiral of it all. Gone.*

She knew Hare wouldn't be able to resist whatever Mr. Wallis wanted. Her husband was desperate with guilt over his non-providing, and he'd do what he was instructed. Beyond even economics or ownership, Hare needed to matter, to feel valuable again. She knew the Wallis cohort would take advantage of this desire. They would lead her husband to rupture, ruin. To violence.

She thought of Gabe.

*I can go away. I could.*

Syl envisioned him in the meadow, sculpted and godlike, a poise so intrinsic to her own father, her grandfather. She sat on the tick mattress, her sweat trickling, her print dress risen just above the knees. The heat passed through her but she shivered as if frozen. She took the washrag from the chipped enamel basin, squeezed off the warm excess and watched it streak down her wrist, and she caressed herself at the neck and shoulders and arms.

*He's the only one 'round here like they was. My daddy. My grandy. Moving through time, in command. Gabe's the only one on this farm can't be broken.*

She had watched Gabe for years, since they had moved onto Wallis Farm. Watched him more than she should, she knows. (Syl had once suffered a single, hard slap from Hare for this brazenness, having asked too many questions about Gabe at one sitting: How had a Black man come to own his land on a cropper farm? How was it that one season Gabe had refused to accept the price per pound that Mr. Wallis had offered? That he'd even threatened to take his yield to a neighboring outfit if he wasn't paid right? And where was the man's wife at, any-way?) Gabe's family had gone on and his land was secure—two factors that exempted him from the relentless pressure to produce. He was the only one around them who didn't kowtow or submit to the underlying current of instability. Everyone had to make ends, of course. Yet Gabe's ownership transmitted a security like none other.

Most of all, Gabe could leave. Though he had chosen not to, he *could*.

This liberty was all that mattered to her. Not even Syl's prayers could constrict the idea of flight. On the mattress, she raised onto the balls of her bare feet, her knees cocking higher, her buttocks bearing down. She held it all inside, this fear, this fondness. *Owns his land*, she thought. *Damn him*. She whispered the scripture but couldn't tamp the idea of what she wanted. *Owns himself.* The scrapes on her skin and the heaving rush of blood; she was molten with life as the washrag caressed.

*I will go*, she thought, though she did not know when. *He's the only one*.

She heard the dead thunk of Hare's boots on the porch boards, then jumped up and smoothed herself. The cabin door opened just as she entered the front room. In the darkened corner, the boy lay asleep on his cot.

"What's wrong with you?" Hare asked.

"Nothin'," Syl replied, kneading her neck. "Just a little scraped up from berry-pickin' with Sonny. So hot out there."

"Yeah." Hare walked to the kitchen and began to rummage, palm-ing a tin of tobacco while taking a seat at the small table. "Cornbread?"

"Just here." She moved in behind him, and took a skillet off the small iron stove. She could tell he was drunk. She cut him a thick slab of cornbread, then took the buttermilk from the icebox and poured him a glass.

Hare nodded when she set the meal before him. He crumbled the bread into the buttermilk, then used a fork to stab and stir the clotty mixture. He downed most of it in one gulp, gasped, and exhaled loudly, his breath of whiskey and sour dairy.

"They want me to be their man," he said. "Say they's trouble fixin' to spread on the farm."

"Oh?"

"Coloreds."

Syl had known this was coming. She could not have lived on Wallis Farm and not known. She'd heard rumors of visitors to the coloreds' cabins at night, and snips of clandestine sermons from the mouths of those who knew no church.

She didn't care. *Nor*, she thought, *does my husband*.

"What trouble?" she asked.

"Organizing. Subversion. Mr. Wallis and his band is scared." He scoffed. "All that money, this land, and they're scared of a few colored niggers. I swear."

"They ain't no trouble, is there?" Syl asked. "I mean, no real trouble, right?"

"I don't guess so. Not here, anyway."

"Well then, what are they—"

"But they may be trouble. Especially if Wallis and them say they is."

"Well, what on earth does that mean?"

Hare's eyes flashed intolerance. Syl looked away.

"What it means," he said, "Is that they need someone in charge on the property. What it means is, well. It means that if Mr. Wallis and them say they's trouble, then they's trouble. Period."

He drank the last slick of buttermilk, and nodded for her to get more. She did.

"But what is it they want with you?" she asked.

"They want me to be what they can't. To be their eyes, ears. Fists."

"But they's not any *real* concern, Hare. You know this."

"Not much of anything, really. Just a little bit of talk. Couple of those young agitators."

"So why—"

"I'm 'bout done with these questions." He stood up and stepped toward her, backing her into the small cabinet. "Here's how it works," he said. "They say, and I do. And then *I* say, and *you* do. Ain't no way around it. No way, lest you want to get up and move on again. Get to god knows where. Is that what you want? 'Cause they ain't but a handful of farms still left to work on shares. Nobody needs a man anymore. Nobody needs anything but money and machines."

"But——"

"May be there's more farms like this, left for us to rot on. Maybe over in Alabama. So I ask you, are you wantin' to move?"

"No. But——"

"No's all you need to say."

"But the boy?" she whispered.

"What do you think's gonna happen to him if we start draggin' him all over creation, lookin' for some new version of this same shit life? Huh?"

With this, she snapped. "What do *you* think is gonna happen if we don't? How you think Sonny's gonna turn out? You think he'll grow into some big shot? Some kinda Wallis if we——"

Hare smacked the cabinet beside her head. Syl shrieked, so he covered her mouth with his hand, pinning her against the cupboard. Hare then leaned in close to hear ear, his whispers adrift on a violence that, no matter how many times she'd encountered it, still thrived with new terror.

"Now, I don't know where it gone wrong for us," he said. "But it did. And so you need to listen . . . and then stop goddamned talkin'. You hear me?"

"Mmm-hmm." She nodded.

"Okay," he said, and took his hand from her mouth. "Mr. Wallis says we can either be with them, or move on. Says that if we stay around, if I can prove myself to them, then maybe we——that is *you* and *me* and *Sonny*——can finally get aholt of some land of our own, some . . . I have got to get us ahead. Get us back to the way it was supposed to turn out. And I *will* do this. I am going to do this."

He stepped away from her, shook his head a little, and scoffed. "Besides. The thing is, Mr. Wallis says they're gonna change all this land up. They gonna close the whole damned farm down, turn it into somethin' else. So we gotta act now, before it all disappears."

Sylvia breathed slowly. "Turn it into what?"

"Somethin' else entirely. Not even a farm."

"But you know the coloreds won't be put back again. That old life is too far gone. It has been, don't you think?"

He picked up the dishware and handed it to her, turned and walked into the center of the main room, and sat down in his rocker. Opened his tin, rolled a cigarette, and stared into the black, empty fireplace.

"You're not gettin' it," Hare said, uncaring whether she heard him or not. "I said, this ain't even gonna be a farm no more. There's not even gonna be a Wallis Farm to be 'put back' on. The coloreds are gonna be put off this land, whether they want to go or not. This life? This prison of the past? This life is over."

Sylvia stepped over to the sink basin, poured some water onto a rag, then cleaned and wiped the glass and fork. She closed her eyes as she did so.

*The crop*, she thought. *The love of Christ, gone. And now Hare. Gelded by men he cain't equal, but who he'll never stop measurin' against. The storm of his insufficiency will destroy us.*

The mules were all but gone. The Negroes would no longer submit. Syl wiped her hands on a dish towel, and considered what she now knew: her husband would fashion himself into a suicide of sorts, a Wallis expendable. She understood now that if she stayed on this farm, she and the boy would go down with him.

Hare kicked off his boots, dragged his cigarette, and a moment later threw the butt into the fireplace. He moved the ladder-back chair out on to the porch, to catch the breeze. Dug in his pockets for his pint.

She knew he would be asleep, fast, precisely where he sat. It was a strange thing, his ability to sleep upright, all night, in that rocking chair on the porch. He was a corpse of toil and sweat and whiskey, and the only thing that might rouse him now was the need to piss, or to curse the world God provided.

*I'll go to Gabe*, she thought. *We will leave this place forever.*

# 6

Gabe lay awake on his stitched canvas mattress, and stared at the photo of his daughter. He smiled at her smile. Waved at her mitten-handed wave. Took in a vision of Chicago, its rising scaffold of flat rooftops in the distance, and the low ceiling of clouds above that. He wondered how Jessamine's feet stayed warm in all that snow.

He would go to them, sometime, when the time came to sell. Or perhaps they would just come home, if he asked. If he ended up buying more land instead.

His bare feet caught the drift of breeze through the house, and his nose took in the scent of leftover rabbit and pepper stew in the kettle. He'd been unable to take ample care of his wife, and, worse, to tolerate his own infant. Now his only family left were either the aged uncles and aunts, people who shared some long-ago shuffle of kinship, or the tight-knit families, Junior Bates's and the like. None of these relations brought him comfort at night. Over these hours, it was only himself and his small farm—his father's land, his grandfather's stake—as surrounded by the virtual continent of Wallis.

It troubled Gabe that over the past season, Miss Beverly had become just a bit too withdrawn, a bit too patient with her husband's antics. Gabe believed she was too worn down. Partnered to this, Mr. Wallis had abandoned any firm interest in whether or not this year's crop was even being farmed to full yield. He hadn't brought on anyone new, save a few hands too old or too young or too stupid to claim work elsewhere. Not once had Wallis even come by to check on folks, to inquire about their health and children. The bossman hadn't even given his yearly visit to waste breath on the terms of anybody's arrangement, or the details of their effort versus his expectation.

Gabe had known off years, and he understood the way a farm's collective temperament could waver, or quibble, or howl. Yet this was different. From the ill-stocked farm store to ill-tended rows, the very ethos of production seemed to have soured in the Wallises. (Had it also in himself? Was some epidemic infecting them all?)

And now this: young activists in from elsewhere, up North, their ideals meshing with those of work and Providence.

*I could*, Gabe thought. *Could just go on, at last. Take right back up with Mina, and with my Jessamine. Find work there, in the snow. Brick and rooftops. Be a daddy to her, like mine was to me. Hell, the patches of my own rooftop ain't no more than scrap flashing anyway. I could leave and be done with this place forever. Nobody would ever even know I'd been here.*

He wondered what would become of the land if he left. He did not plan on dying anytime soon. In fact, he planned to live as long as his grandfather, the first Gabriel, who spat vinegar and wormed shine, and worked the animals well into his nineties, a pack of spotted feists in his wake. Because this was what was done. It was their communion with posterity.

Yet for whom was Gabe keeping the little plot? Unlike his grandfather, or his father, there was nobody to pass down to, nor interest from siblings strewn elsewhere. Who was going to learn of the mules? Who could he teach about the peanut vines? Who would learn to slaughter, scrape, and boil the hogs? To prepare the salt box? To cure?

*Maybe she would*, he thought. *Little Jessamine.*

Maybe if he held out, maybe if it turned out Wallis was gonna sell off his acreage, his daughter would come back to Mississippi when grown. To live and inherit and carry on this land. Build a new, fancy house, and care about TV and movies, magazines, and the like. Maybe her mother would tire of the ice, and grow weary of calling on Gabe to abandon post. All the renting, the winter, the exhaustion of city uncertainty. Hell, he thought, all this time and they still needed assistance—who could sustain that?

His family had fought so hard to keep the farm. *If Jessamine were a boy she would be here*, he thought. *Maybe.* Maybe if he just asked Mina to come home . . .

The only thing Gabe knew for certain was that right now the mission was to hold the land: for his family before, and, mostly, for Jessamine. This space had shaped the fact that they could not be removed—whether by work or weather, sickness or violence. Nobody had taken it from them, and nobody could. How on earth could he let it go now?

*Jessamine won't never come back*, he thought. *Mina won't come back. Not even for a season. People's only being tugged away from this place.*

Gabe then considered leaving his lot to the church. Or, hell, maybe even to those boys who'd come down to change things, the Snicks and Kings and COFOs and Riders. He could provide them a place to gather, a base camp of sorts, like cover fire for their fight. Bless 'em.

*I could hand it all over*, he thought. *Leave this spoilt Mississippi, so lonely.*

Yet they were too close to something. To something on the farm that he just had to figure out. The Wallises' neglect was a marker of a process: either Gabe would sell out because they coveted his land, or he would buy in, in full, because they were done with this backward-ass stewardship. In either case, it would soon be clear.

In the photo, in the snowdrift, Jessamine's cheekbones were high and shiny, like those of her mother and grandmother, a legacy of the family's Chickasaw bondage. The child's overcoat, her smile. Her toboggan. The rooftops in the distance, the pointed spires of a church like those he'd seen only while shoving through Europe during the war. Through Chartres with the Red Ball Express. Hammer Down, the experience only strengthened his resolve on the farm.

Hammer Down, in theater, Europe, where Gabe had throttled his deuce-and-a-half transport truck through hail and snow and mortar fire, through exhaustive hallucination and corporeal agony. Back and forth over supply lines, again, again, his palms rubbed as raw as a strawberry on the gearshift, and, later, as rough as a cracked heel, a hoof. Trucking back and forth, slapping himself awake, cigarette after cigarette, anything to keep the Red Ball operational.

If D-Day was the heart of the invasion, the Red Ball Express was the

blood. Oil, water, food, meds, the Red Ball trucked in every mandatory supply for an Army to move, to live, and to win. Without them,
without this back-and-forth transport, D-Day was spectacle, and
Europe was lost.

Gabe and the rest—the majority of them Black men—sucked it
up and drove on, the nights smearing into daybreak, to Chartres and
back, again, again. Got so tired they flicked lighters on their skin to
stay awake. So tired that at times even a Luftwaffe assault became mere
aggravation, a rousing annoyance.

The roadsides were a slick mix of snow and mud, a splatter of
stacked fieldstone wall and scorched farmhouse. The gored-out car-
casses of livestock and soldier were almost Permian, near-reptilian in
the wake of the artillery.

Still, the trucks drove on, drove past, drove through, again.

(Though once, they'd been forced to make an extended roadside
stop—at which point they watched a Frenchman kick a dead horse. The
lot of Gabe's convoy, five deuce-and-a-half trucks, two jeeps, had been
made to halt while the lead vehicle crew repaired a crankshaft. The
boys were freezing and starved, vibrating from both the frigid temp and
amphetamine jimjams . . . and they were skillet-shot kills for the Ger-
mans. Yet they exited the trucks anyway, their eyes scouring the gray
sky, their ears cued for the rev and sputter of aircraft. They had huddled
up to smoke, to share a belt from a bottle, and then cracked up as the
old Frenchman implored the dead horse: to move from the roadside,
to hide from the soldiers, as if Gabe and the boys were there to steal it,
or, more pressingly, to eat it. As if Gabe's company cared about anything save fixing the fucking crankshaft before being strafed by Messer-
schmitt. Anyhow, when the old man first kicked the horse, its eyes half
open and its spine sticking up through its croup like a daisy, they had
tried to stop him. *Arret, monsieur! Ça va! Hey, man!* Yet he had kicked the
horse again, while his swollen, pawlike hands yanked the bridle rope,
and his eyes darted from the carcass to gathering squad. The man was
frenzied. Starving. Beyond all laws of humanity.

The soldiers had muttered to themselves, and they lit second
smokes, standing close to their engine blocks to catch the flush of radi-

ant warmth. *My lord, the flush of that warmth.* Gabe had shaken his head at the Frenchie, had then giggled. The old *fermier* had laid into the horse relentlessly, his boot into its neck, his tugs on the bridle, until the bit raked the animal's teeth out and the man had slipped in the mud. It was pure slapstick.)

Deployment had ripped Gabe, them, from the structured fabric of existence; it had revealed the truth of the anemic White South. Upon his return to Mississippi, having lived mission critical, Gabe would no longer tolerate the way things had been. There was victory in Europe. There would be victory at home. Hammer Down.

So he had worked the land, and held firm the land. And he knew that the land would outlast any code, and he swore that he would never, ever cede it—lest he got a proper price, or acquired a larger plot. Gabe drove on, he drove forward, mule to milestone, his resolve like a diesel engine, slow and grinding, his objective clear and getable. For himself and his forefathers, and most of all for his child, he would steward this place at all costs, until his enemies had exhausted themselves, had ground themselves to bone dust.

*We built this place*, Gabe thought. *All of it for the others—save these here little farm plots of our own, speckled like pepper 'round the hills. My father, my grandfather. My own. This little spot is ours. We built this whole goddamned South, and I* will *keep what's mine.*

He rubbed the photo with his thumb, then lay it facedown on his chest. The breeze slinked over his skin, and the amber late summer sunset smudged into the cabin's waxy windows.

Gabe had just drifted into a nap when a small battery of knocks hit his door.

# 7

*S*he don't know nothin', Hare thought. *Never will. Her jitters ruling her body. Her backhanded suggestions. That woman moves 'round me like a specter, like some haint, dodging this way and that, bent from my gaze. Thinkin' she knows better than me—as if. Her cowardice. I sit in this chair and make like I'm asleep. Sit here silent, arms on rests, my breath a slow brook of water, while she muddles about in the kitchen, in the bedroom. Her knees creaking. Her thoughts racin' like she knows anythin' at all.*

*Sit in this chair and feel my feet on the porch boards, and the whiskey warm inside me. This chair, what my grandfather built. It has sat both him and my father. I have carried it from farm to farm. It is my final piece of their stake; it is the hand that clasps my father's hand, and my grandy's—though I got no memory of chair-buildin'. No memory of workin' the spokeshave, or the lathe.*

*Goddamn it, I love her. But her insolence? She thinks me a failure, a lesser man. But what would she have me do? What else is left?*

*This chair under me, so smooth and reliable. Ain't even a drop of glue in these joints. Drug farm to farm, field to field; it is the only thing I have left. It has sat my father and grandy. Has even rocked a Bird Clan Chickasaw woman.*

*Syl thinks she knows, thinks to influence my actions. Thinks she knows best, her body and thoughts ruled by tremors, her existence some living testament of Jeremiah. Goddamn her, I love her. I hear her in the trickle of water from the basin. I hear her thoughts of judgment, or perhaps of some damned fantasy. She thinks I'm asleep; thinks she knows the future.*

*I love her. She don't know nothin'.*

*"An example," they said to me. Mr. Wallis and the rest. Their whiskey. Smiles. Promises of what's to come on this farm. Christian ethic and community, my ass. These groups they count on ain't nothin' more than alphabet letters: Klan to SCV,*

Citizens' Council to LMA——or whatever all that other terror business is. The heads on the wall of their lodge, black bear and buck . . . ain't nothin' but heads. Symbols, like me.

They want me to be the eyes, the ears, the fists. "Find an example," they ordered. "Make an example of someone." A symbol, to send the rest of the blacks packing.

There ain't no time left for Delta and Providence Farm. Ain't no time left for mules, or men. So cast down that markin' knife and chisel. Cast down your lathe, and your steam-bent wood. At last, this land will move into the future. And I will be a part of it. I have to.

Syl don't understand this. Her thoughts are too distracted by sorrow and sin. She don't get that Mr. Wallis and them's finished with this old-timey soil business.

"You make an example" Wallis said. Our example. "And the rest of them coloreds'll run off for Chicago." They say if I do what they ask, they'd surely be a small piece of homeplace for me. Some dirt I can own. With decent schooling for Sonny, if I just do what they ask.

Maybe more important was what they ain't said. What they didn't have to lay out was what happens to me if I don't participate: I'll be thrown off with the rest of the croppers. Forced to confront an even greater ruin. A greater span of distance from security. Stability. Respect.

But Syl don't know this. She can't foresee anythin', save the ruination of the memories she lugs around, farm to farm, year to year. Her fossil thoughts of handmade chairs and cast iron. A dowry of linen from somewheres, Carolina. Of family land, of commune.

Curse all that history. Cast it all off. This here, now, is about the driving of the exodus, about the deliverance of this farm to the future. To a place beyond the clear-cutting of land by Allis-Chalmers and International Harvester. Hell, Mr. Wallis even swears they'll move the whole goddamned big house into town! Make a monument of it in Pitchlynn proper, then build a country club out here on the land.

A club?

A club. Fancy housing in the footprint of tenant shack. A whole new community, like some limp jeremiad. A castrate place, producing nothin' at all, and with no ability to further legacy.

*Hell,* Hare thought. *I'll take it.*

*Syl thinks I don't know, that I cain't hear her footfalls so quiet across them boards. That I'm sound asleep, imaginin' the creak and bow of the floor to be some dreamlike drift, some vessel on water. As if the puff of breeze from her sneaking by me on the porch was some sea gust. As if I don't know where she's off to. As if I was asleep, unaware.*

*I love her, goddamn her.*

# 8

Gabe opened his cabin door and beckoned her inside. Syl looked around nervously and said nothing. The purple evening light was dimming into navy, and the smell of stew put a sumptuous undercurrent on the cabin air. She paced the room and stood near the dying fire, her eyes avoiding her host. Gabe stepped over to the cabinet and produced a glass of tart, blackbird wine.

The orange light of mellowed embers. The now-and-again crack of splitting hickory. Syl could visualize their exodus with everything she had: her boy in tow; the three of them on the Illinois Central, toward Chicago. Away from the coming purge. She felt the future burning in her abdomen; movement had been happening all around them, all their lives. She could not and would not bear the idea of abandoning her life to the failure of expectation, or in this case, kindred hate.

She believed that Gabe could save her. That they could change each other's stories. The boy's, too. Forever.

"Chicago," she whispered. "Can't we go? Shouldn't we both be born again?"

The wine, having fermented for no more than a month, scratched her throat, flushing through her like dye in water. Like blood in water, billowing into diffusion. *We can leave this place together*, she thought. *We've been pushed towards this all our lives.*

"Help me," she whispered.

Gabe sat down beside her, his dark skin shiny in the firelight.

"You're the only one who can take us," Syl continued. "Me and the boy. There's nobody else on this farm who can help. Nobody free of the obligation to Wallis, or of the violence that's 'bout to boil up all around this place."

She reached over, slowly, and put her hand on his. "We have got to leave this farm, *now*. I must save my child. And I swear, you will find restoration in yours."

Gabe stared at her, and nodded, but he didn't say a word.

"Chicago," she said. "Help us all."

# 9

The next morning, Junior Bates and his SNCC compatriots stood on the small, splintered porch in front of Gabe's cabin. They called to him, and knocked. When no answer came, they knocked again.

Unsatisfied with the turnout at their meeting the night before, the activists had come to realize how vital local folks like Gabe really were to their success. In particular, they had come to understand their tactical soft spot, their ambitious near-novelty without the involvement of community leaders. They had discussed this late into the night, discussed the local people while camped out in the pastorium in back of the single-room church, the Wallis Farm A.M.E. On military cots, in the stuffed air of the rectory, their bodies went unwashed and their fingers clasped cigarettes. They whispered of tactical strategy, and felt powerful, felt adult. They were guerrillas, freedom fighters. They were out to reshape a nation.

They could only glimpse the magnitude of history around them. Yet because they knew this, they knew to trust only facts: it was August 1964, the end of Freedom Summer. It was gaspingly hot as they lay on creaking canvas cots. They knew Wallis Farm was nowhere near the coast, yet one of them had brought up Gilbert Mason anyway, a kindred example of civil disobedience in that it had not gone right the first time. This, too, was a fact—this history was truth—and so they smiled upon hearing the man's name: *Mason*. They imagined him down on the coast, in Biloxi, huddled with his community in their own clandestine meeting, 1959. The boys pictured their predecessors, the budding activists, all of whom had pledged to walk together onto the Whites Only beach, arm in arm, before wading into the Gulf waters, unstoppable.

"Whoo," Junior Bates had said with a chuckle. "Can y'all even imagine?"

On their cots, in the dark, the young men recounted how things had *actually* unfolded after that first Biloxi meeting: Dr. Mason had shown up to that initial beach protest, that "Wade In" as it would be known . . . only to find that he was alone. Not a single one of his comrades had shown up.

This was the first-ever direct-action protest in Mississippi.

"Nineteen fifty-nine," one of the young men had whispered. "I was only thirteen!" They had giggled at this, and then took turns recalling the story: how Dr. Mason had walked out onto that beach anyway, alone, onto the white Gulf Coast sand . . . whereupon he was hassled, and shackled, and lugged off by the cops.

"Persistence," another had stated, the word as packed as a prayer.

A week after Dr. Mason's arrest, he had marched right back out onto that same strip of beach. This time he'd been joined by eight others. And a week after *that* arrest, he'd been joined by over a hundred men, women, and children. The lot of them were beaten with pipes and pool cues.

"Bloody Sunday," one of the young men had whispered in the chapel.

No matter. Dr. Mason and the others had returned to the beach the following week. And then they went again. And again, and again.

The young men knew these facts, at least. "Tomorrow," one said, tamping out his smoke. "We go to Gabe again."

Yet Gabe wasn't at home. They figured that maybe he'd ridden into Pitchlynn, for the colored half of Saturday. They did not note the absence of his feist, June, who should have terrorized them from the shade beneath the raised cabin floor. They stepped off of the porch and then walked off of Gabe's property, and back onto Wallis Farm, and the fight. They would try again later. Call on him again, and again, for however long it took.

In the cabin, in the bedroom, in a ribbon of honeyed light, Gabe lay naked on the lumpy tick mattress. His body was chiseled by years of task and diet. His skin a smooth contradiction to the decades of sun.

Gabe's face and skull were collapsed like some caldera, having been battered beyond identity. Blood and serous fluid now coagulated in the heat, and a swarm of humming black flies skittered in and out of the wound. The tap stick club, bloodied, lay on the floor by the bed.

The only other claim made on his body were his genitals, which were now shorn and littered in a far corner of the room. The serrations around their absence made his skin appear petaled. The laceration itself wept into the soak beneath his legs.

# SOME GO HOME

# 1

Colleen came to at daybreak, in the driver's seat. One eye was swollen shut, and her jaw thrummed from being struck. A swarm of pain was massed around the exposed nerves of her bottom teeth, teeth that had punctured her lower lip before chipping off against the steering wheel.

This was in the time before Derby, but just after the war. Four, maybe five years before she got pregnant.

The sunlight was gentle through the haze of humidity. She looked out, at the vast field of green corn she'd swerved into the night before, and the massive sprinkler truss she had hit head-on. The hood of her car was wrinkled against the pivot irrigator tower.

She held her breath, and twisted the keys in the ignition. Felt a gust of relief when the motor somehow cranked. The tires rubbed the battered wheel wells as she drove in reverse, doubling back in her ruts until she reached the county road.

She passed boll buggy and row crop, farmhouse and hamlet, past clutters of country folk on warped wooden porches, their hair wild, their Quikrete carports attached to long-rooted double-wides. She passed buttoned-up single-family homes on modest acreages, houses that were clones, somewhat, of the one she'd grown up in (and the one she would one day wind up in with Derby).

She followed the yellow line between Highways 7 and 15, toward Pitchlynn proper. At a stop sign just in town, the car's engine light lit up; the vehicle shuddered as its power seeped away. She managed to turn toward a three-store strip mall before the engine was starved and the steering wheel locked. Colleen listened to the change in the asphalt grade as the Cavalier rolled dead in a beauty parlor parking spot.

She lumbered out of the car in her miniskirt and desert combat boots. Her white blouse and pink tank top were marbled by blood. She had to steady herself against the vehicle before wobbling into the salon, and posting up against the reception desk.

The air was frigid from industrial AC and fouled by the tang of hair dye. The room was loud with the yikyak of middle- and old-aged ladies, and the young and middle-aged women who primped them.

Colleen stared around the room, the white of her open eye flared by a ruptured blood vessel.

"What in the world?" a woman in foil strips hollered.

"Lord have mercy," another gasped.

"Who is *that*?"

The braid of mostly elder voices rose into a high-toned, full cackle, their comments spanning fear and fascination. Of course, nobody *did* anything, save lower their glamour mags and shake their heads in fascination, or disbelief.

"Land sakes, she's bleedin'!"

"She shore is."

"Well, how do you think she——"

"Jesus, y'all," a young beautician finally barked. "Somebody get up and give her a chair." This woman did not wait for a volunteer, but instead cocked the hood back on a commercial hair dryer chair and yanked a client out from underneath. She then helped the broken stranger into the seat.

"You're okay, gal," she said. "You're okay."

Colleen tingled from the beautician's touch. She sat down slowly, her contused back in spasm. Looking up at the young woman, she could not help but smile——which reopened the splits beneath her bottom lip.

"Bitch!" she yelled, as the pain knocked her semiconscious.

"Call the ambulance!" someone shouted. Though half of the room had been immobilized by profanity, the other half dug through large vinyl purses, clutching for clunky, pay-go cell phones on which their grandkids had preprogrammed 911.

"Huh-uh," Colleen mustered. "My folks can't afford the bill."

The beautician spied the ball chain around Colleen's neck and pulled the dog tags out from her tank top. "Scratch that, y'all. Somebody call the VA, quick!"

"*Hell*, no." Colleen shook her head violently. She tried to stand but doubled over, falling back into the chair.

Again, the woman put her hand on Colleen. "VA clinic's just up the road, girl," she said. "We'll drive you."

"No friggin' way. That place wasn't built for my body." Colleen straightened up, even managed a tiny grin. "Anyhow, I swear, this is only as bad as it looks. I just need to get home. Please."

The beautician took a deep breath and glanced around the room. She shook her head, then called out, "Okay, y'all. Somebody get a damp towel. And some Goody's powder. And grab that little first-aid kit in the reception desk. Pronto!"

"Ice her dang face!" another woman ordered.

"They's a tube of Orajel in my purse somewhere!" yelled the most aged of the bunch.

Colleen sat in a daze, reeking of bourbon and body oil, as the squad applied a hodgepodge of remedies. The ladies doted on her, and did their best to patch her up, before the young beautician announced that she was driving the stranger home.

"I'm Deana," she said, helping Colleen to her feet. The two ambled out the glass door, arm in arm.

Colleen stopped in her tracks when they approached the totaled Cavalier. (She did not know whose farmland she had plowed through the night before, nor could she explain why, exactly, she'd swerved into the field at full throttle.) Deana said to keep moving, that they'd worry about the car later.

"Just straight home, right?" Colleen asked as she sank into Deana's passenger seat. "No VA. Promise, Deana?"

"I promise," Deana answered, patting the patient's bare knee.

Colleen muttered her address, and passed out.

# 2

She had redeployed a few months earlier, from formation at Fort Bragg to a picnic at her parents' house, their porch banister and clothesline T draped in red, white, and blue bunting. A proliferation of plastic decor was brought in from Walmart, as were the red-checked tablecloths, blue plasticware, and plates. A posterboard sign boosted a hand-scrawled WELCOME HOME!

It was glorious, Colleen thought. Really was.

Her mother, Jeanette, would not let her lift a finger to prepare for the picnic, ordering Colleen to stay inside, where she sat impatiently, watching *Extra* and *TMZ*. Her friends and former coworkers had been invited, as had her mother's friends and her father's cohort, the latter mostly clad in coveralls with brass buckles, in work boots and net-backed ball caps. A hunk of the church group was on hand to rejoice.

The card tables on the lawn showcased a brigade of ceramic and Tupperware potluck. A large cooler was full of Miller Lite, Milo's tea, and Co-Cola. A Boston cream pie seemed to sigh from the heat, then collapsed onto its foil crust container. When at last Colleen ventured outside, people hugged her and shook her hand. They asked her how it had been, and she said, "Not too bad," and they smiled and they nodded and thanked God, their enriched hamburger buns stuffed with the pulled pork that her father, Brice, had spent all night tending.

"So glad to have you home," folks said, and they meant it. They then moved on to speak of Sunday school or stormcasts, or to swap Pitchlynn gossip.

Colleen did her best to be thankful for the fact that things had carried on without her. She told herself this was a good thing, that she didn't need them to have needed her, and that wanting them to have needed her was not only unrealistic but selfish. As the picnic wore on, she tamped down all that needing, that wanting, and she instead smiled, and answered questions about her well-being and her plans.

Ultimately, it was the clothes that unspooled her. The women at the picnic wore jeans whose back pockets featured button-down flaps with elaborate stitching. Silver thread loops and jags drew great attention to their asses. They were so odd and luxurious: these asses, these jeans. Colleen wondered when on earth people had moved to wear such embellishments. She was curious as to how folks had come to envy the flashiness of the gesture, the frivolity of it during a time of deployment, and devastation.

Only a hiccup of culture had transpired without her. But those jean pockets? After she noticed them, she had noticed that the women's hair was shorter and more angular. From there, it hit her like a slap: she didn't know the songs on the radio, the new sitcoms or celebs, the gossip, the recently deceased, or, somehow, even those living in the spotlight. She was being lauded as exceptional, plated up as a hero with a heaping side of sacrifice, though not even a crumb of disposable culture had pause to mark her, their, absence.

Brice, her daddy, had ordered the hog pre-gutted at the processing store, having long grown tired of using his own gambrel hooks, likewise of hair-scraping and blood collection. Colleen went with him to pick the pig up—a castrated male, not a gilt—and helped him sling the paper-wrapped cadaver in the truck bed. At the house, they had positioned the hog on the expanded metal grate atop his pit, then lit the rick of hickory that was to be tended all night long, its smoke seeking him with every wind shift, his sweat pouring as he swabbed the steaming carcass with a newly bought floor mop, its yarn tendrils sopped in vinegary sauce. Hour after hour Brice had smoothed sauce onto flesh, while stoking or subduing the coals beneath the hog's exposed, gutted belly. Colleen knew this ritual. It was familiar and homelike. In fact, the only real difference between this so-named "pig pickin'" and the many her daddy had put on before she deployed was that Brice now sipped Pepsi instead of Budweiser. (He'd experienced what was referred to as "an episode" while she was away, something her folks had not wanted to bother her about. The term worried Colleen sick—an "episode"—though her parents were dismissive if not defiant whenever the subject came up.)

She blushed when the picnic guests toasted her service. Struck down beer after beer, eating neither pig nor pie, though patting her belly whenever Brice looked in her direction. She drank and she grinned until the visitors had peeled off, to better parties, or to relieve sitters, or to go over the next morning's Sunday school lesson. When the party was over, only head and hooves left on the grate, Colleen started to help clean up, and was again banished by Jeanette. So she grabbed a couple more beers and walked into her old bedroom. Stretched out on her bed, turned on the television, and shot the remote, again, again.

# 3

Over weeks, into months, the beers became a rope for Colleen. That is, they were utility versus celebratory, pulling her from one place to the next. At just about any joint in town, a new Miller hit the bar top before the swill of the last passed her lips. The barkeeps knew she was good for a tab. Most nights, anyway. And even if she wasn't, the dude hovering around her would be. Roughneck to frat boy, country-clubber to queen; for Colleen, they, too, were utility.

Unlike her benign allegiance to alcohol, the powder became the Cause. It was not snorted. Not shot. Not even snowcapped on a weed bowl. Not plugged. No, for Colleen, it was all about the way the stuff glazed her teeth. The way the burn of it coated her cracked enamel chips, shoving the pain down her throat to make way for numbness. She couldn't tell if she was truly high or not. (At least, she liked to tell herself she couldn't tell.) Instead, she focused only on the quasi-clinical process: rub powder over broken teeth, harbor pain, swallow pain, repeat. Call Sarge and ask for more, or find someone who'd already found Sarge (and ask that person for more). Repeat. She could take or leave the meth or weed. But that singe of exposed dental root? She grew desperate for the combat of Pain vs. Powder. At times, it seemed to be the only marker of her existence.

She wore fatigue pants and tank tops. Her hair was shorn to a buzz, and her dog tags hung backward, the bead chain cutting into her trachea. Her under-eyes were purple. The bartenders knew her well enough to serve her without a smile, but they forgave her the shitty tips because she was a hero, and, despite her efforts to the contrary, real good-looking. She showed up, stayed all night, drank, snuck in and out of the men's room, and rubbed powder on her gums with her gun finger. The regulars toasted her service and waited for her to die on a back road. (It hadn't happened yet, but it would, they knew. One way or the other—whether she was walking, or driving, or riding with some drunk—there was zero doubt about it. That girl was a ghost-to-be.)

In these bars, Colleen knew everything that would unfold, night after night. She appreciated the nonthreatening uniformity of it all.

Until one Thursday evening, when Deana showed up. She had a female friend in tow, and they took up a red vinyl booth. Sat across from each other and cut up over beers.

Deana did a double-take when she saw Colleen at the bar, then leaned in to her girlfriend and whispered, and laughed. A minute later, the beautician walked over to order another pitcher. She wore tight jeans with fancy embroidering on the ass pockets, alongside a yellow knit blouse and white tennies. Her hair was still damp and smelled citrusy clean—even through the smoke. She cleared her throat and spoke up:

"G.I. Jane! How you, girlfriend?"

Colleen glanced over, nodded hello, then sipped from her bottle. Her cheeks got hot.

"I ain't gonna lie," Deana said. "You don't look a hell of a lot better than when I last saw you. How are those chompers, anyway?"

Colleen flashed her brittle grin. "Nothin' I can't handle."

"I bet," Deana said. "Say, how about you come drink a few with us?"

"Well."

"We don't bite, girl. Plus, I'm buyin' the pitcher. You in?"

Colleen sniffed, and her throat muscles tightened in anticipation of the powder drain. "Oh, why not?"

Over the course of that pitcher, and a few more to follow, the girls talked about girls, and about boys they all knew; they talked about cell phone plans and television, and watching video clips on either device. Deana and her pal asked Colleen about the war and earned stock, optimistic replies; the pal—Colleen hadn't caught the girl's name, and was too far into conversation to ask it again—spoke of work at the beauty parlor, and of looking for better work, and how she wished Pitchlynn was big enough to bring in a ride-share service, so she could put together enough bucks to do . . . well . . . do *something*. When Deana had then asked her colleague, "Like, do what?" the young woman had drawn a blank. All three had laughed over the fact that, hell, they were already doing pretty much want they wanted to do: having pitchers of beer in a bar, on a Thursday, late.

For a blip they were nothing more twenty-three-year-old women, not a care in the world, burning up a random summer night, talking bullshit.

At some point the friend said she had better hit the road, in order to keep her car between the ditches. Deana and Colleen chastised her a bit—not too much—then bade her farewell, and ordered another pitcher.

The two felt like they were just getting started when the bartender rang a cowbell and yelled for everyone to get out.

"Aw, man," Colleen said, her eyes gleamy from booze.

"I hear you girl," Deana replied. "I hadn't hooted up like this in forever. And boy, do I need it. I gotta get your phone number."

Colleen looked away for a moment, then stifled a sudden giggle. "Say, Deana. Let's get hitched."

"That's it, soldier gal. You're cut off!"

"Really. Let's tie the knot," Colleen insisted. "Keep this night goin'."

"What kinda woman do you think I am?" Deana asked, gulping the last swallow of beer.

"I didn't mean it *that* way," Colleen blurted. "I don't think!"

"Sorry, troop, but I'm already taken." Deana held up her ring finger, wiggling it for

effect. Only, there wasn't a wedding band. "Oops. Separated, I mean. The ring's in my purse. But still."

"Son of a bitch." Colleen winked and slapped the tabletop, then stood up and marched to the bathroom. She rubbed the last of her powder stash over her gums, then split without saying goodbye.

Having weeks before sold the Cavalier for scrap, she started the long slog home, her combat boots kicking into the gravel at the road shoulder. At some point, a headlight cone stretched out in front of her. She lit a cigarette and listened as the vehicle drove up behind, idling down to a roll.

"Hey, girl?" a man called out. "It's too dark out here to be walkin' by your—"

Colleen glanced back, to a man in a pickup truck cab. She kept marching.

"Whoa, now," he slurred. "Hold up. I's just offerin' you a ride. And maybe a little taste? I'm headed over to Sarge's. You're welcome to tag along."

She knew the guy. She thought she remembered him, anyway. Her pace ticked up as she walked back into darkness, until the creep of his headlights prevented this.

"Aw, come on," he whined. He put the truck in neutral and revved the engine a couple of times.

Colleen flicked her cigarette into the cab, and then crossed the road as he cursed her. She didn't so much care about drunk men in trucks, but she knew better than to show up at Sarge's house. Not that she didn't love the guy—hell, they were bonded by deployment, after all—but everybody knew that there was a telltale, critical diff between making the powder come to you, and you chasing down the powder. Even Sarge had told her to never want to come over; he said his house was infested with addicts, a real vector of anxiety and anguish (which was a surprising hazard of the gig, he added, more taxing, even, than ducking the law).

Having recovered the lost, lit cig, the driver revved his engine once more, then peeled away. Colleen marched into the night, a crisp motion in her step as she thought of her new friend, Deana.

SHE WOKE to the sound of her father home for lunch. She heard Brice's truck door shut, and smelled the grub on the table. Wincing against the semi-brightness of her bedroom window, she turned to stare at her pale pink walls: at the Basic Training and AIT, Army certificates and the high school diploma, a grad tassel dangling from its frame. She thought about the night before, and the night before that. She got up and cracked the window, lit a Misty. Dragged it a few times, then punched it into a Pepsi bottle that floated a reservoir of butts in the backwash. She threw on a robe, stepped into the bathroom to pee and brush her teeth, and to stare herself down in the mirror. She stepped back into the hallway, her socks whispering on the beige carpet as she walked to the dining room.

"Hey," she said, joining her folks at the table.

"Well," Jeanette started to respond, but dropped off against a look from Brice.

After her daddy had offered a quick edit of grace, they ate green beans with hock and pepper, instant mashed potatoes, and cuts from a ham slab with slices of Roman Meal. Colleen fiddled at the food with the fork tines, and gulped her extra-sweet tea.

"Colleen," Jeanette spoke up. "We was thinkin' it might be nice to take Dave up on gettin' your old job back."

"Uh-huh." She poked at the ham.

Brice joined in, "Or I could always talk with the Dunlaps. See about whether they might need an extra hand 'round the gin. If you'd like."

"Thanks, Daddy." Colleen nodded. "Maybe."

Jeanette continued, "Because, really, it's time. It is past time."

"Yeah, loud and clear," Colleen replied. She stood up, tea in hand, and walked back down the hall and into her room. She didn't slam the door.

Midday news was on the television on her dresser. Colleen lay on her bed, lifted her shirt, and patted her tummy, her fingers moving across the taut, creamy skin. Colleen liked the feel and shape of her stomach. She liked to thump it, to rub it or drum it with tender slaps, and sometimes to show it off in a tank top or bathing suit. It was perfect, it was young. Smooth, yet powerful, somehow. She'd never been much of an athlete, yet during Basic at Fort Jackson she'd led her platoon in sit-ups. There, where the females perform modified, women-only-type push-ups; where the march back from bivouac was twelve miles long for females, versus the men's twenty (as if the women couldn't handle it); where clandestine liaisons with fellow troops first began to seek out space, to formulate beyond the NO ENTRY doorways or behind the plastic drop cloths of barracks under renovation; where lovers learned to deviate from the well-used paths on Tank Hill and into the sand-floored woods; where they had wriggled into bathroom stalls, at once as banished and as resilient as queers in a tiny redneck town—Colleen had been amazed at her physical ability, at the strength and sculpt of her stomach. Once, when pitted in an informal, off-duty sit-ups competition, she had even outdone her male counterparts.

The very best thing about coming home from war was that the shape or size of her stomach hadn't changed. Though all else had betrayed her, from fashion to her faith to her father's phantom "episode" and the unspoken, looming prognosis, Colleen's midriff was the one thing she still understood.

She stretched out on the bed and pushed her tummy up and down, grabbed the glass of tea, and held it there, watching it rise, and fall. As the watery coolness centralized on her navel, she thought once more about hanging out with Deana.

# 4

## MY DAMN RULES

- No powder
- No more than three late nights a week
- No strange dudes in the house
- Must stick close when my husband visits OR Must get lost for a
    couple hours. Or more.
- Grow your hair out and try to look pretty
- Don't mope
- Remember that you kick ass
- Clean up and pay a little rent
- Really No Powder . . . Zero!!

Deana proved to be a bitch taskmaster of a landlord. Colleen loved every bit of it.

When the former had suggested she could use a roommate, a little company to help cruise her over the choppy waves of her separation, Colleen showed up at the apartment the next morning—before a by-then-sober Deana had a chance to change her mind.

The place was a two-bedroom garden apartment in an old brick Queen Anne. A converted fourplex close enough to town square that they could walk into the Pitchlynn bustle if they wanted, but with an isolated back deck that faced a vacant lot of wild kudzu. The latter allowed Colleen to roll out of bed, grab her coffee and smokes, then sit outside amid a jungle-like tangle of vines.

They talked about places where they'd like to travel.

They drank Miller Lite and went out.

They spoke about high school and work life, and about the politics of the war, and once or twice Colleen rambled about women at war . . . though the topic was generally muted. They watched *Meet the Press* in their pajamas, and/or a string of old action flicks on TBS and WGN. *Predator. Independence Day. You've Got Mail. Dances with Wolves.*

Deana fussed at her, and fussed over her. She forced Colleen to don a plastic smock, and subjected her to kitchen-chair haircuts. (Okay, maybe not *forced* her. After all, Colleen could have refused.) She daubed Colleen with makeup now and again (cue: Colleen acts disgusted), then wiped it off at the end of the night, the remover's acrid scent a near-aphrodisiac. Colleen, in turn, tried to mind her appearance, and her ways. She kept Deana's rules close in mind, and, except for having to make way for Deana's husband once or twice a week—an aggravation, for sure—she prided herself on following them to the letter. She still moped sometimes, and she pushed the late-night thing now and again. But Deana's authority was easier than the Army's, or certainly that of her parents. After a few weeks, Colleen even cracked a few beers with Deana's hubby, who was, admittedly, a nice enough guy who needed to grow up.

# 5

On the night she met Derby, all Colleen wanted was chocolate pudding pizza. She and Deana were posted up at the Pizza Hatch, where Colleen had treated them both to the all-you-can-eat buffet, a token-of-gratitude dinner in lieu of proper rent. Both women were fine with this symbolic remuneration; Deana did not yet expect more from Colleen than companionship, a pitch-in on chores, and news of a job-lead here or there.

Colleen had piled up a boneyard of crusts, drunk four Cokes, and then, to Deana's disgust, made her move for the "dessert pizza." Derby had appeared at the buffet table at the same time. Their eyes locked for an instant, and smiled at each other. He found him very cute, until he nabbed the last slice.

"Whoa, dude," Colleen said, staring in disbelief as the stranger walked back to his two-top. He was tall, and wore his Levi's tucked into his work boots. Had a deep farmer's tan and a real good butt. She shook her head at the latter attribute, grabbed another pepperoni, and slumped back into her booth.

"What?" Deana asked.

"Some guy just——"

Derby stepped in and cut her off. "My bad." He snickered, then set the dessert slice down at the edge of their table. He nodded at Deana. "Hey."

"Derby," Deana replied. "Been a while. How you?"

"Better than ever. Now." He smiled at Colleen, paused, and walked off.

Colleen attempted to sustain her indignation.

"Jesus," Deana said. "You're blushing."

"Bullshit."

"Denial only makes it worse." Deana shook her head. "I'm guessing you don't know Derby?"

"Who knows? Cares?"

"He's six-seven years older than you," Deana explained. "Though age don't mean a thing, you know? He's a real good guy. So good-lookin', mmm. But a real messed-up family. Hobbs?"

Colleen shrugged.

"I swear, Colleen. It's like you'd been raised in the woods. Sit tight. I'll go grab him."

Colleen clenched Deana's arm. "Don't even."

Deana stared at Colleen's hand until it was removed.

"Sorry," Colleen said, "but—"

Deana nodded an okay, then pushed Derby's plate across the table. "I'll leave you be, this time. I'm just happy to see your blood up. I tell you, I *knew* there was a little spot of titillation in there somewhere! Now eat your chocolate pizza. Which is disgusting."

Colleen dragged her finger through the pudding sauce, and sucked it clean.

# 6

"Do it, Colleen!"

"Oh, you're gonna do it. She's gonna do it, y'all!"

"You gotta do it for us, Colleen. Come on!"

"Don't be selfish, girl. It'll be great. We got your back."

"It's about time you pulled it together, Colleen. Let's do this thing!"

Colleen hadn't been hot-box recruited since the Army pressured her signature at the high school job fair. She was visibly frustrated by the nagging, the coercion, the henpecking, the pleads (though a part of her took to the doting).

"You gotta do it," Shirley State said, hand cocked on her ample hip. "When are we ever gonna get a veteran to showcase?"

Emma Crowther drew her blow dryer like a .45, boasting, "We're gonna take the competition down."

Echoes erupted from the ladies on the floor. Appeals that Colleen must, in fact, register to participate in the pageant.

She was hungover again, and her resolve was flimsy. She wished to condemn the idea of entering a beauty contest. Yet she, like them, had grown up here. At one point or another they had all dreamed of being the Strawberry Maiden. And though their bodies, ambitions, or politics might have developed in stark contrast, some girlhood part of these women still coveted the sash—in particular, if they could redefine what type of woman got to wear it. They wanted to fuck things up a little bit, as it were.

"Come on, Colleen," Deana said. "Just give in and let's get you fixed up. The deadline's here and we gotta file your paperwork."

Beyond any girlhood entrancement, there was the lure of the prize money. Five thousand bucks could go a L-O-N-G way for Colleen. She'd give $1,000 to her folks, $1,000 to Deana for rent and bills and beers, and keep $3,000 for future rent, bills, and beers.

Still. Colleen thought of the spectacle. "Y'all, just let me alone. Not it."

Deana stepped behind the salon chair in which Colleen sat and rubbed her friend's neck. "Don't fret, girl. We got you covered. You need this. Besides, *we* need it. The shop needs the business, the exposure. I hate to be greedy, Colleen, but it's really more about helpin' us."

"Then *you* do it," Colleen said.

"I'd be all over it if I looked like you!"

"I repeat," Colleen stated. "Not it."

Deana exhaled, paced away, and let the other beauticians and patrons jump back into recruitment. Colleen kept refusing, squirming, denying them—until an idea hit. She walked across the room and pulled Deana aside.

"If I take that crown, then I wanna get the hell out of Dodge for a few days."

"Christ," Deana said. "Go anywhere you want, you'll have five thousand bucks!"

"No, I mean *us*. Like, a girl's trip somewhere."

Deana thought for a second. "Sure. Whatever. Deal. How about the coast? You been down there lately?"

"I've never been at all."

"What? To the Gulf? It's only, like, six hours away! But okay, whatever, yes. *Yes*. After you win we're headed to the coast. A girls' trip. Yeah?"

Colleen nodded.

Deana turned to the room, announcing, "We've got ourselves a beauty queen!"

The hair and makeup strategy sessions had commenced within minutes. Colleen let Deana shampoo her, the kneading fingers and organic herbal scent shooing away the hangover. The parlor crew buzzed with talk of the sponsorship, ball gown to makeup, posture to proper manners. They called Colleen "our hero," and claimed she'd be a beacon to all women in Pitchlynn. They ordered her to get her teeth capped at the VA—something she had to do anyway, as she could no longer bear the post-powder pain—and to sustain a training ritual of diet, exercise, and beauty pageant binge-watching. From there, she was instructed to get out of their way, to let them do their job on her body.

"Sergeant Strawberry!" one of the women exclaimed.

"Corporal Cuteness!" said another.

The door chimes jingled, breaking up the bull session. A collective gasp hit the room. Deana stopped kneading Colleen's scalp and called out, "Hey, Derby."

He was out of place, fidgety. He nodded at Deana, then bit back a smile when Colleen leaned up from the washbasin. A few ladies scrambled to cover their roller-dense hair, and the stylists stopped snipping and gawked.

"Hey, uh, well," Derby said. "I think I need something for the sun. You know?"

"How's that?" Deana asked.

"You know? Like, I'm in the sun all day. A lot."

Colleen cut in, "They call it suntan lotion, dude. You get it at the Walgreens."

Deana pinched Colleen's neck. "Good for you, Derby. You're right, you *do* need somethin' to protect that face. But suntan oil's too perfumy for a man like you." She described some men's botanical product; they didn't carry it at the salon, but the Sally Beauty store over in Batesville stocked it.

"Thanks, Deana." He looked to Colleen. "And, um. Would you maybe wanna—"

"Huh-uh. Nope," she said. Deana pinched her neck harder. "Ow! Shit. I mean, no, thanks."

"But maybe we could just—"

"Hey, I appreciate it." Colleen cleared her throat. "But how 'bout you just get on now? Find your *lotion*."

The room cracked up. To his credit, Derby did, too. He shrugged his shoulders, winked, and looked at Deana. "Can't say I didn't try."

"That you did, bud," Deana replied. "And extra credit for doin' it in here."

"Ladies," Derby said, and walked out.

Colleen whipped around and glared at her friend.

"Save it," Deana ordered, and moved on to conditioner.

# 7

The summer sun slapped her. Belted her, bronzed her, blazed. She was bloated. She was on her period, and felt like a bloated maraschino under a cafeteria lamp. A buffed-up, pickled cherry atop a box pudding pie. The Corvette she rode in on, a '67 convertible, 427 cubic with Rally Red paint, did not have a backseat, so Colleen's ass was plopped on the metal of the trunk, her high heels dimpling a folded dish towel on the shotgun seat leather. It was oven-hot June. Her pantyhose constricted, and the sash sawed at her neck.

There were American flags of various sizes, in hands and on lampposts and picketed into the ground. Colleen waved at the crowd and they all waved back. Lap after lap, the 'Vette cruised around town square, the aroma of cotton candy and hot funnel cake wafting. Deana had ordered Colleen not to touch her face, her makeup. Rather, Colleen had to fan it with only her fingertips. Her dress was short and shiny, made of spangles. Felt shrink-wrapped. Laps and laps around the courthouse square, past strawberry kiosks and strawberry hats, and white paper plates of real strawberries dolloped with Cool Whip. The banner above was the same from years past, proclaiming the annual Strawberry Festival. Colleen had no idea if they even grew strawberries on a commercial level in Pitchlynn, Miss'ippi, but she was positive that these berries had come from somewhere else, given that nobody's garden ever produced any after April.

There were Mexicans in town now. Maybe not Mexicans, but Colleen believed them to be Mexicans. Their children spoke with redneck accents. They were nice enough folks. Save for the church or the store, they pretty much kept to themselves, though here they loitered in groups at the edge of the crowd; 'round and 'round they came, in jean shorts and T-shirts with their own American flags. Whenever the car idled, the hot exhaust caked up in the still air. The driver had to keep the 'Vette moving, Colleen thought, crawling along, *He has got to keep up the breeze.* At every lap of the square she looked for Deana. Deana, who chatted folks up, bragging, probably, on behalf of the beauty shop's ringer-contestant. Now and again Deana looked back and smiled, thumbs-up. For Colleen, this made it all okay.

Susan George Wallis and a few others, in fine linen and seersucker, had congregated in the half shade of the crepe myrtles by the court-house. (Between pageant grins, Colleen couldn't help but glare at them. These people were just too smug, too at ease, too . . . established.) She circled the white-pillared courthouse at the center of the square. Folks were gathered by the Confederate statue, the white marble soldier who stood at attention with rifle, facing south. She had seen him all her life. They all had.

Colleen figured she'd won the pageant because she was a veteran. She hated that she was a veteran. She was proud and guilty and confused by being a veteran. She so wanted these folks to understand what it was like. Yet knowing they never would, and that maybe *she* never would, she wished she had signed up to extend her tour, had at least re-upped to Germany or Korea, or anywhere else, forever.

'Round came Deana again, thank god. She and Colleen would hit the coast soon enough. Drink boat drinks and sleep late, embalmed in suntan oil and frigid motel air-conditioning. Salty ocean skin and sand in carpet. Colleen would at last see the shore!

That guy came around, too, the cute guy, Derby Whatever. (Deana said it'd been Hobbs but was now something else). Grinning. She saw him cut to the front of the crowd. She looked away from him, the Cor-vette exhaust clogging her nose, the sun swallowing her.

A veteran. A woman. A southerner. High school grad. A num-ber of things, and now the Strawberry Maiden of Pitchlynn, Missis-sippi. A PA system announced her name again, then fitted the breadth of her deployment into a half sentence. Strawberries and melted whipped cream dripped from white paper plates. She was sustained by the fact of money for her parents, her father, and for a motel room at the Gulf.

Only three more laps under the banner and sun, past that stupid, cute Derby, and to Deana again. Only . . . Deana was now talking to her soon-to-be-ex-husband. She laughed with him, her arm swatting his shoulder. Volunteers in red T-shirts handed out paper plates of strawberry goo to visitor, old townie, and new Mexican alike, and mostly to the children of all of these groups, kiddos clumped up in a pack, their faces a smear of cream and delight. The PA announced the lineup of tonight's free music on the square. Funnel cake fryer and sweat congealed in the aroma. Colleen's ass seared against the hot metal hood of the 'Vette. She was desperate for a beer.

When the parade was over, the Corvette's driver helped Colleen out and into a designated "Cool Zone"—a signing booth at the back of Tudor's Hardware Store. A few townsfolk followed her in and made phone-photos with her, against the backdrop of copper and PVC pipe. Someone brought her bottled water. She asked for a Miller instead, and everyone laughed and nobody got her one.

Deana came in. Hugged her. Really held her tight and went on about how proud she was. Deana's husband stood behind them, offering a dopey wave and a congrats.

"We did it, Dean," Colleen said. "You had better get packed and get ready for—"

Deana cut her off. "I found a lost tomcat on the street. Maybe you recognize him?" She stepped back from the well-wishers and dragged Derby over by the hand. He was tall and musky, and he wore that charged grin. Colleen lilted, sank, and lilted again. Where in the heck was that beer?

"Hey," Derby said. He held out his hand. Colleen shook it, but it was awkward, more like holding a rag. She looked at him cross—*What, you can't shake a woman's hand like a man's?*—then turned back to Deana, who was framed by mousetrap and rat trap and spider trap and d-Con, and she started yapping on about the pageant, the heat, and, most importantly, their trip. A minute later, Derby got a word in edgewise. He just had to.

"I'm afraid I've gotta get on," he said. "But I just wanted to revisit our, my, question about maybe getting a bite or something? Like . . . *lunch*."

"Nice try," Colleen said. "I mean, thanks, but . . . naw. I don't do lunch, man."

Deana shook her head and put her hand on Derby's back. "The heat and high heels have wilted her brain." She ushered him toward the door, whispering, "I'll work on her."

Derby exited via the pest control aisle, chuckling to himself about this being the third time he'd laid eyes on his future wife.

# 8

Colleen tugged at the camouflage miniskirt and white satin sash, and insisted, again, that she wasn't going to make it. Back at the beauty shop she had thrown up repeatedly, with Deana on hand to hold back her perfect hair. The two of them now sat in Deana's car in a parking lot.

"I can't," Colleen repeated, her face leached of color.

But she had to. That was the deal: a Strawberry Maiden made public appearances, promoting Pitchlynn, the region, and the people. To ditch an event was to ditch the crown—and she didn't even have the prize money yet.

"Suck it up, troop," Deana said. "You're tougher than this. You have to be."

Colleen listened, and nodded as she stared out of the car windows.

"Besides," Deana added, "this is your turf. You own this."

As if striking out a light, Colleen tried to relocate her drone mode, a mindset she hadn't occupied since deployment. She yanked on her white hose, stepped into ruby heels, and donned the bedazzled dress blue service cap (lightly, so as not to crush her lifted 'do).

"Go," she ordered herself, her eyes gelled and lifeless. She threw the car door open and marched toward the building.

The National Guard armory was a construction of beige paint, tan bricks, and polished cement flooring. At the back of the building was a motor pool of sand-colored vehicles, Humvees and Emergency Comms, artifacts now, stationed behind chain link and razor wire.

On that day, however, news trucks littered the fire lane and parking lot, their color-pop logos and satellite feed antennas stabbing the sky.

Colleen got sick on the asphalt, then cursed her civilian weakness.

"Okay, so you're ready," Deana assured, rubbing her back. "If things get that bad, I'll pull you out myself. Now charge, girl. Charge!"

Minutes later, Colleen took the makeshift stage in front of nearly two hundred battle-dress-clad former comrades. The majority lofted cell-phone cameras, egging her into the spotlight. Others sat and stared, wondering why in hell they'd been assembled for this bullshit.

Colleen was introduced by the local pageant chair, and then by her former CO. When the latter handed her the microphone, the soldiers went wild, dog-barking, whooping, their fists ramming the air.

The fluorescent lights sheening her nylons, the title sash mapping the valley of her breasts, Colleen gazed out at them, these troops she had camped with, slept beside, showered near, or shat among in DIY plywood latrines. Suddenly it was as if she could see *inside* those who didn't care about her, and those who resented her presence; inside the fatherly types who had sat with her at chow, offering advice or witticism, as was generally coupled to Bible verse.

Frozen onstage in ruby heels and short skirt, Colleen saw inside those who still wouldn't think twice about a little grab, or a too-deep tickle, or who could peg her to a wall with their own bodies. She could see inside those who had done so.

She locked eyes with Van Dorn, her minder from the Bradley vehicle on the night of that close-quarters op. He smirked with disdain, and then spat on the floor.

The formation's barks grew louder, their fists pumping like pistons. There was further onstage introduction, and then Colleen read flatly from a prepared statement: an appreciation to all for their service and their heroism, alongside a promise that neither she nor the rest of the community would ever forget the unit's sacrifice for our nation. She rolled her eyes and took a few steps, then turned and twirled, as per the appearance instructions. The boys went ballistic.

Then, as quickly as it had started, the event was finished. She had survived the battle, again. Colleen pageant-waved a goodbye and turned to walk off the stage. She paused, and gutted out a passing tsunami of shame, then hurled her own fist upward, and started to bark.

Because this, too, was a part of her. These gestures were a part of their insiders-only ritual. She sneered at the troops as she marched down the stage steps, flicked them a double-bird, and hollered out, "Fuck-all y'all, my dogs!"

Offstage, she signed a headshot for her old CO. She saluted him, walked outside, lit a smoke, and ordered Deana to get her the hell gone. It was the last time Colleen would ever see her old unit, or anything formal of the United States Army.

Fifteen minutes of back road later, not a word between them, Deana and Colleen pulled into a cinder-block diner north of Coahoma. The gravel parking lot was packed with trucks and beater cars. A yellow message-board sign promised both the BEST SOUTHERN BREAKFAST and the FRESHEST CABBAGE ROLLS.

"I shouldn'ta done it," Deana said.

"It's okay, girl," Colleen replied. "In a way, I needed to see those guys. Needed to say goodbye."

"Good on that," Deana said, patting Colleen's thigh. "But that's not what I'm talkin' about." She cut the motor and motioned to the front of the diner, where Derby sat alone on an old wooden bench.

"Jesus, Deana. You kiddin' me?"

"He's a good dude. I just thought—"

"I don't care what kinda *dude* he is. It's not your place. It's just not." Colleen cursed as she threw open the car door and kicked her legs out onto the gravel parking lot. "*Good dude,*" she huffed, walking into the restaurant.

She spoke nearly six words to Derby while they waited on a table, then gave a grunt or two more when they were seated.

"I need kibbe," Deana offered the silence. "I mean, I *need* it."

"Fried chicken for me," Derby replied. "Though I'll trade you a drumstick for a grape leaf."

"Maybe."

The place was packed with all hues of country folk, and the servers drew from a bottomless well of sweet tea. Thanks to the generations-old Lebanese legacy in Mississippi, the trio ate chilled tabbouleh with warm pita strips, wrapped grape leaves and kibbe balls (both baked and fried), a bulger crust with a core of molten minced lamb, pine nut and cinnamon and pepper and chopped onions . . . and, for Derby, that side of expertly fried chicken.

Despite Colleen's protest, Derby had paid for all before she even asked for the bill. As the trio loitered in the parking lot, Deana said she had to call her husband. She winked at Colleen and paced away, phone to ear.

The gray afternoon clouds hung heavy with rain. Colleen kicked at the gravel.

"So how 'bout this, Colleen?" Derby began.

"Not interested."

"How about in a couple weeks, soon as I finish my renewables course, we take a drive up to Oxford? Hit the best restaurant in town— on me."

"Nope," she replied.

"Dutch treat?"

"No way."

"Okay, got it. Screw Oxford. Too fancy-pants. Instead, how about we pick up a couple of beers, then go eat some . . ." He cocked his eyebrows, inviting her to finish the sentence. "We go eat some . . ."

She glared at him. "Thai."

"*Thai?*" he echoed. "Sure, yeah. I know the perfect spot. Thai works for me."

"Then deal," Colleen said. "But a one-time-only deal."

Derby nodded his compliance. He had no idea of where to find Thai food, let alone what the Thai ate. But he couldn't kill his grin. "It'll be the fourth and final time I ever bug you."

# 9

A couple of nights later, a few beers in, Deana and Colleen were splayed out on the apartment sofa, watching a PBS doc on Gertrude Bell. Deana was rapt, her empty ice-cream bowl on the side table. Colleen was stretched out in full, her feet propped up on her best friend's thighs.

"Hey," Colleen said at the conclusion.

"Hey, back, girlfriend."

"You know, I'm almost mad about it."

Deana raised her eyebrows. " 'Bout what 'it,' exactly?"

"You know," Colleen teased. "About your setting me up with Derby and all."

"Well, you weren't gonna do it for yourself."

"And?"

"Were you?" Deana pinched Colleen above the knee, eliciting a jerk. "Are you?"

"No." She replied. "I guess not. But Dean, what if I don't want a boyfriend? What if I don't want anything to change? What if I have better plans than that?"

"Better plans? Like watchin' this tube all day and night? Drinkin' beer?"

"Like, you know what. Like, hey, let's plan our trip. You've spent more energy fixin' me up than you have on the beach party. We're supposed to celebrate, and I need to move forward!"

Deana looked to the television. "Listen, we gotta speak about that for a second. So focus in, okay? I need you to really listen. Please?"

"Oh shit," Colleen said, sitting upright.

"Now, first . . ." Deana exhaled. "Where to start? First, you are gonna be able to drive to the coast, or anywhere, anytime you want. Because I am giving you my car."

"What?"

"More practically, I'm givin' it to you so you can get to these Strawberry Tour trips without having to wait around on me. Or me wait on you!"

"I don't need a car, Deana. So skip that, and what's really up?"

"You do need one. Well, you will need a car, anyway. For the Strawberry appearances, at least."

"Spit it out."

"And far more important than that," Deana continued, "far more important if I'm being greedy, anyway—which I am—is that you'll need the car to come visit me."

Colleen knew what was coming. She looked back to the television.

"Hon?" Deana spoke. "I have to go home. I'm going home. Giving my marriage another try. Me and old what's-his-name have been having some good times again, and. Well." She leaned over to embrace Colleen, issuing a run-on string of: everything-will-be-okay / nothing-will-really-change / you'll-see-me-every-day, I-swear / we'll-tool-around-and-flop-around-and-watch-teevee / you-come-over-and-we'll-still-do-the-pageant-stuff / and-I'll-help-cover-the-rent for a couple of months, and . . .

"Dammit," Deana continued. "Just be happy for me." She grabbed Colleen's hand and placed it on her abdomen. "You're gonna be, like, a second mama, you know?"

Colleen flinched, then stared at Deana's lap.

"Please," Deana said. "Just be happy. I don't want to do this without you."

Colleen slid her hand off of Deana's body. "Sure, okay, Dean," she said, then stood up and went to her room.

An hour or so later, Deana knocked on Colleen's bedroom door.

"It's all good, D.," Colleen called out. "I'm just tired. Lots to process."

"I gotcha," Deana replied. "Good night, then."

"Night."

Through the particle-board door Colleen heard Deana's footsteps fade down the hallway. "Night," she repeated, but to herself.

*Is this all you have to say? The best and only syllable? The single word offered instead of any other possible word?*

*What about a name? A beckoning? Why not a one-word question: "Deana?" Even this would have brought a reply, a reconsideration. Or how about, "Dean, I'm lonely, and I'm scared, and I'm lost," or "Dean, I'm not strong enough to fig-ure out why you're the only person I find love for"? Or, heaven forbid, what about a paragraph? A chapter? A novel of conflicted thoughts, needs, or collapses that tether your homeplace to the away place? An epic of confusion about where you've been, and who you were? How about a "Dean, who am I now? What the hell do I want?"*

*Or what of a testament to the new complications? To the . . . the . . . cru-cible. The crucible of who you might want to be, and, good lord, the questions about how to get there——as can be spoken aloud, to the only soul you've found who not only accepts your ragged-ass state of being, but who'll drop everythin' she can to help you work through your lack?*

*What about that? All those words, or thoughts. Or anything more, really. You don't even have to know what you want to know right now. You don't have to offer her anything, save an admission that you need to feel . . . what? Close? Safe? Trusted? On orders? You don't even need to know what you need. Who you are, what you want. You don't even really need to know. You just need to start speaking.*

*So given all that, given now, what do you really have to offer?*

"Night?" Colleen whispered. She lay in silence, the crescent moon's light casting through the off-white mini-blinds.

When she was convinced that Deana was soundly asleep, Colleen threw what she needed into her old Army duffel, and headed out.

# 10

She chain-smoked while staring through the break in the blackout curtains—as did many others inside Sarge's house. Yet instead of their concocted scenario of raid or bust, of FBI, MBI, ATF, or even UFO, Colleen knew that no one was coming to get them. She only wanted to watch the street.

She saw the passersby in front of the little brick house, the house that looked just like the other houses beside it. It was a little brick house in a hood of little brick houses, a formation of post-WWII ambition turned post–*Brown v. Board* erasure. These were squares, plots, tracts, cells. She watched the neighborly parade of rickety old folks and distracted young. The body-compromised, and the cops. Nobody on those blocks walked for leisure or exercise; they did so out of necessity, to the convenient store for groceries, or perhaps to the bus stop, and on to hour-wage work. Colleen watched and she waited for repair to resume on an old Monte Carlo up on blocks by the curb. She watched the others come and go from this very house, their nervous to-and-fros spread across all hours and weather, across race and age and class. She watched the unmarked cruisers idle in wait at the stop sign, or peel away in response to an in-progress down the block. Mostly, though, Colleen watched the elderly woman across the street, who sat alone in a metal glider behind a rusted screen porch hour upon hour, every day, back-and-forth rocking, waiting to die.

The rest of Colleen's congregation griped for her to be careful, to get back from the window. They picked at their skin—their scabs like chicken pox—then peeked over her shoulder and asked if she'd seen it:

*Did you see it? Do you see 'em? Oh man, they's out there, they's coming, and, like, I'm not sure, but I think I saw them in the back I can't tell but I'm telling you they're coming and, like . . . I don't know——ha ha——I'm so fuckin' high, you know, but I mean . . . do you see 'em, did you see it?*

"Nothin's out there," she'd reply, and perhaps pat a knee. She'd then turn back to the window and try her goddamned best to not go hit that powder.

It was her ability to transcend the stuff that made Sarge offer it for free. She'd go hang in his bedroom for hours at a clip; he'd let her in through the triple locks, to the mother-in-law add-on that insulated him from the rest of them, the "fleas." She would dump out his ashtrays and they would fill 'em back up together, watching ESPN Classic and the SEC Network, reruns of the football games they had missed while deployed. They watched so many games that they even spoke of betting on them——a laughable analogy, since Sarge's life and livelihood was already a wager on reruns. He bet that people would come back to him, come back harder, giving more of themselves . . . until they wiggled down the drain.

Only, not Colleen. Not yet, anyway.

She and Sarge both knew that soon, she'd give him whatever part of her he wanted, however he wanted it, as often as he allowed. For now, though, theirs was a kick-ass sort of camaraderie. They were a squad of two, against the fleas who beat on his metal door every five seconds, who machine-gunned his phone with texts, calls, and voice mails, Jesus Christ. He swore that these people were needier than the fuckin' orphans he and Colleen had seen during deployment. Nits. Lice. Fleas. Skin-pickers. Reruns, every one of them.

She and Sarge chattered about player positions and three-four defense packages, and after a while he'd offer her a taste, and she'd pause and say, "Naw, thanks, Sarge, not tonight." Now and again, at halftime mostly, they'd surf the cable channels, pausing to consider shards of the outside world.

At daybreak, she would split from Sarge's room and return to her front window perch, wondering how long she could hold out, and why in the hell she even tried.

One night, during some halftime, out of some sense of deference,

Sarge let the clicker loiter on this twenty-four-hour-news package about the Women's Trauma Recovery Program at the VA center in Menlo Park, California. The lady reporter noted that it was the only space of its kind. B-roll footage showcased female vets in session and in dormitories. Sarge and Colleen watched a woman who sat alone in a library, then a crew of females who strode the orchard-like grounds that cradled the stucco-and-Spanish-tile facility. With vine-topped trellis and bougainvillea blossom, the place was a dreamscape, an otherworld.

"Menlo Park," Sarge uttered, a frail hint of optimism in his tone. "Sounds like a cigarette brand, but it looks *way* cool. I wonder how hard it is to get in there. Like, if you could—"

"Game's back on," Colleen said. "Turn it."

The two weeks she spent there dragged out like an era, cig after cig ripping her lungs like silicosis, tarring her hair, stinking up everything. She finally moved upstairs in search of proper sleep, to be away from the powder fleas and introduce herself to the ones who never woke: the slugs. She crashed on a pallet of cheap blankets constellated by burn holes, and kept a diet of days-old coffee and maybe raw ramen. She shat water, and her tummy burned. But she slept.

The landscape of that little upstairs—a converted attic, a couple of rooms and dormers—was littered with baggie corners and ashes and blood-blotted cotton balls. Empty pill bottles lay everywhere, their orange plastic smeared by dry saliva, the biorecord of tongues that had licked out all residue. Ripped-open soda cans sprouted used syringes like lily blossom bouquets, with cig butts as infill and ashes spackling everything. Ashes and blood-spotted makeup remover pads. Carpet stains. Cut lengths of electrical cord. Mirrors, and a flat-screen. Dead lighters everywhere. Blanket nests in every nook.

This space was where Colleen had finally arrived at the truth: She was never a powder flea to begin with. She had once more mustered into the wrong goddamned army!

She told Sarge of her revelation as if witnessing to him, speaking gospel. She then issued him her orders: Dilaudid, or no, better yet, Opana.

"That is *wild*," he replied. "I never would've pegged you for a slug."

"Hell, Sarge." She grinned. "Me, either!"

He hitched an old rifle sling around her bicep. Used his thumbnail to slice up a sliver of the tiniest pill, then cooked it down in the shorn-off bottom of an empty beer can, dissolving the time-release casing. While doing so, he brought up the tag football games they'd played in the compound, back in-country. He and Colleen went on about how rad it was to be able to ignore small-arms fire while executing the perfect button-hook out-pattern.

"Now, that there's a skill," Sarge said, fixing her. "They shoulda covered *us* on ESPN Classic!"

She began to agree, but her mouth fell slack. She glanced over to the crook of her arm, then went limp. And he cradled her.

* * *

Deana's car squealed to a stop against the curb, and she launched out as quick as a missile. She double-timed over the concrete walkway, bolting to the front door of the little brick house. She lifted her fist to the door. Then she paused.

This had to be the place. Just had to. Colleen had described it to her late one night, the postwar brick bunker that she had ridden by—one-time-only. The trafficked, side-street home with blackout curtains on the downstairs windows and aluminum foil over panes at the top. (You could either score at Sarge's, Colleen had explained, or you wound up in some rando cracker lab lodged in a vacant double-wide in the country. *So this*, Deana thought, *had better goddamned well be the place. I am* not *headin' out to the country*.) She took a deep breath, and delivered a trio of punches on the weathered door.

"Colleen?" she yelled. "You'd better get your bony ass outside! *Now!*"

The fleas fled the perceived invasion, hiding in bathrooms and closets. Deana kept on screaming, until one of the others, the upstairs slugs, finally open the door just a crack. Deana pushed through him and into the house. Her flood of curses was as fouled as the Ganges; she marched room to room, downstairs then up, her hand over mouth and nose (as if this would kill the smell of the place), until she found Colleen heaped and high in a blanket-nest.

"Get up," Deana ordered. "Get up!"

Colleen winked. "It's okay, babe. I am so, *so* good."

Deana continued her tirade, reminding Colleen that she had a crown to uphold. That the beauty shop had put their asses on the line for her. "For chrissakes, you're a veteran."

"Yeehaw," Colleen mumbled.

Deana yanked her friend up by the arm, then stared hell into some gaunt twerp who questioned the aggression. Deana then dragged Colleen down the stairs and out the door, into the air, hot, clammy, drenched July air, in front of the old woman on the rocker who stared back at them.

"I can't believe I'm doin' this bullshit," Deana continued. "For heaven's sake, Colleen. I am countin' on you to help raise this baby!"

Colleen stopped and stared at Deana's abdomen for a few seconds, before glancing up to meet her eyes. "Give it up."

"*Give it up*," Deana mocked, yanking her friend the rest of the way to the car. "Boo-hoo. I swear. You've got more goin' on than anybody I know. And look what you're doin' with it."

She buckled Colleen into the passenger seat, slammed the door, and walked around the hood of the car. Got in and cranked the motor. "Now, here's the deal. I can either take you back to my place, or the VA, or the police station. Your call."

Colleen rolled her eyes.

"What I thought. But I tell you what, Colleen. If you try to split my guest bedroom again—hell, if you even look outside the window longingly—we're done. I won't have anything more to do with you. You hear? Colleen? Do you hear me?"

"I hear."

"You'd better," Deana insisted, peeling down the street. "I swear, you *will* make this up to me, girlfriend. I mean, you had better get cleaned up fast. 'Cause this ain't *about* you, Colleen. It's about me, and your folks, and the gals at the shop, and—"

"Okay. Just . . . shhh."

"It's about a crew of good people who have lined up to help you. The whole town, really." Deana stomped the brakes, bucking Colleen forward. "So how long is it gonna take you to get squared away, anyway?"

"Huh?"

"How long? How goddang long till you're cleaned up?"

Colleen stared through the front windshield, down the street and into the tree line on the far horizon. "Few days?"

"Better be," Deana huffed. "Lest you forget, Colleen. You've also got a date."

# 11

He had promised her Thai, said he knew the perfect spot. Having been backed into a soft and compelling corner, Colleen had agreed to that first date with Derby, providing he could meet her requirement.

This had been four, maybe five years before she was pregnant.

Yet after Derby picked her up for the date, when they were already on the road, just far enough away from her place to feel committed, he had announced that Thai was off. He told Colleen that he'd thought about it, "thought a lot, truth be told," and that he'd even found a candidate place, up near Memphis. A dishwater joint that got okay online reviews but nothing great.

"But I just couldn't risk any 'okay' anything," he explained. "I refuse to take you to any sort of 'nothing great,' you know? Especially since it's the only date we'll ever have."

She huffed.

He continued. "Then I figured that I had rather take you straight to Thailand. Take *me* there, too, since it'd be my introduction to the cuisine."

"So you're drivin' us to Thailand?"

"Oh hell no," he said. "This old truck would never make it. But I found the next best thing." He went on to explain that, having done some demographic research on the library computer, really parsing out the who, where, and why of American Thai enclaves, he had instead set his sights on someplace a bit more getable than Phuket.

"The West Coast has good Thai," he said. "*Great* Thai, it seems. So do D.C. and New York, of course. But the two biggest, closest spots are . . . well, can you guess where?"

"How 'bout I don't?"

"That's correct: Chicago, and Dallas."

Colleen didn't care about Chicago, though she had perked up over Texas. "We're headed to Dallas?"

He stared at her. Grinned. "Yes."

"Really?"

"Well. We are *technically* drivin' in that direction. Southwest, sorta. So here's the plan. We're gonna make a stop, right up here, on a nothin' patch of land outside of our beloved Pitchlynn, Miss. We're gonna talk for a while, and have a snack or whatever. Watch the sun fall. And after that, if you want to drive on to Dallas, then, dammit, we're drivin' to Dallas, okay?"

*Okay*, she thought. *Okay, someone is taking care. Taking charge. Trusting me to trust them to take the wheel on my behalf, but for once with my interests invested, and without settling for whatever comes along as default.* This was good. It had felt so damned good to be thought about, and in this case to be thought about as movement, as open possibility, as exception. Why was this? Why now?

A few miles later they snuck onto the FOR SALE property that would at some point become her house. Their house. It was a small hunk of land like the hunk of land she'd grown up on. The generic brand of place she had never envisioned returning to, precisely because it was the type of place she didn't want to die on—until that moment, on that day, with that man. Somehow. Why?

Though she couldn't verbalize it at the time, let alone think straight about *any* facet of her life, truth be told, Colleen knew she'd been rudderless, unsatisfied, and without clear objective. She kept a beauty queen sash in the trunk of her car, draped atop the gas mask she'd snatched from battalion supply. Neither had brought her comfort, and their collision didn't fit. (In fact, she had mucked herself up pretty good trying to make either of them function.) So as the sunlight began to honey, and with Derby walking them around, explaining what he was gonna do to the place, step by step, the mission convicted and defined, at once familiar and yet somehow transformative, she felt compelled to join his vision.

He was charismatic, and commanding, and she believed he'd take care of her. Listening to him orchestrate plans, she knew that he believed them, too.

She sure as hell needed some saving.

Most of all, despite the bruised-up, banged-up state of her being, she knew that somehow she also needed to save. And from what Deana had told her about Derby's family, she would likely have her chance. She understood that it often took scarred-up people to soothe other scarred-up people. She could co-contribute to his redemption.

He offered her some venison jerky, stuff he had made on his own. The cooler in his truck bed held an iced-down twelve of Miller; he palmed a pair of them down into foam koozies, then proposed a toast to this first-last date. Derby then lowered the tailgate and they sat on it and listened, considering the contours of the rolling land and the flinching of tree leaves in the wind. It was a real lovely cliché.

"You'd better put a bank of windows in the back of that little house," she said. "Catch every bit of this late afternoon sunset."

"You're right. A bay window would—"

"I didn't say bay window," Colleen corrected him. "You can't open a bay window, so you won't enjoy this breeze."

He tipped his beer at her, nodded his agreement. They chitchatted for another fifteen minutes or so, the low sun smudging over the familiar. At some point, Derby got ramped up to take her deep onto the property, to show her the spot he'd picked out for the pond. "I think it's perfect. Real secluded," he said. "Though of course I'd love to get your take on the placement."

She looked down her nose at him, shaking her head. "Not tonight, cowboy."

He blushed. "I didn't mean it like *that*," he said. "Not that I wouldn't mean it that way. But, I mean . . ."

"Don't flatter yourself. What I'm sayin' is, I don't fish."

Derby nooded, and took another gulp of beer.

"Though I do eat," she added. "So get me to Dallas, or—"

"Love it," he replied. "Let's go."

They drove southwest for another forty minutes, talking and story-telling, and for a mile or two sitting silent as the first stars prickled the evening, with each of them wishing that the other would give in, would suggest just pulling over at a diner, or even for fast food. They both understood that nobody was going to Dallas that night. They did not know what would happen if they got any farther from home.

Colleen thought about Deana, but not so much. Mostly, she thought about sharing this feeling with Deana, about wanting to admit that the date hadn't been so bad. That it was kind of fun, really. Real fun, actually. She wanted to explain that, like herself, Derby was also on a mission to redefine himself. He was seeking something new from the future.

Yet she decided to keep all the flush energy bundled up for herself, at least for another date or two. Or three, or more. She didn't want to give away the privacy of the joy, or try to describe things to someone uninvolved. (Plus, given all the pressure Deana had piled on about Derby, it would take some time for Colleen to offer thanks, to admit that she was in fact happy about the hookup.)

In the semi-silence of the truck cab, sitting high behind the headlights, and with the razz of his compound Kevlar tires on the highway, Derby had at some point asked a burning question: "Do you ever want to talk about . . . the war or whatever?"

She looked out the side window for a few seconds. "I don't guess so," she replied.

He did not feel rejected. Nor was she mad that he'd brought it up. "Gotcha," he said. "Just didn't want to not ask, you know?"

"Copy that," Colleen said.

They wound up in a booth in a Waffle House, not too far from the interstate at Grenada, Mississippi, after Derby finally admitted that he wasn't prepped for Texas. Colleen had pretended to take him to task, but then let him off the hook, care of the promise of an All Star Special. She was impressed when he slid the server ten bucks at the onset, and asked for two large Styrofoam cups (into which he poured their contraband beer).

Derb had then proposed a second toast, "To the Thai next time."

Colleen rolled her eyes, and took a deep, uninterested breath.

"To the Thai that shall bind?" he proposed.

She turned to look out the window.

"Okay, okay." He laughed. "How 'bout, 'They say that the road to Phuket is paved with . . . ' " He cleared his throat and waited. " 'Paved with . . . ?' "

"What?" she scowled. "Is 'paved with *waffles*'? Is that what you want me to say?"

"Pave it with whatever you want. I don't care. I'm just trying to loosen you up, so I can work my way to the other side of the booth."

She didn't respond to this, meaning that she didn't shut him down. Derby got up from his seat, then stepped over and slid in beside her.

They were all lit up by yellow logo signs and fluorescence, framed out by massive windows, a perhaps-love story for any passerby on the state highway. The booth was a bit cramped, but it felt right.

# THEN BACK, AGAIN

# 1

U P opened his eyes, and looked to the light-break between curtain panels. Early morning, maybe six-fifteen. The bedroom was softened by late winter gray.

This was during his last season in Chicago, right before Dru died. Just a few months shy of his move down to Mississippi, when the idea of Pitchlynn was still folly, a lie.

It was a routine season of deprivation, when the damp ashen atmosphere lopped the skyscrapers. By all measures it was a stock interval of ice. A time that everybody dealt with, had dealt with, *would* deal with, and which would fast enough fade to memory, then concept, after the sun and spring did their job. Chicago was, after all, the most glorious so-called "sky's out" space in America. Its springtime was so very much worth the wait.

He'd spent his life between near northwest Chicago and his folks' North Shore home. So he knew that in this city, at this time, you slogged, you bundled, you warmed indoors. You made complaint, or you complained about people who complained about weather, and you fought from points A to B, your head bowed against the wind, your boot soles flicking icy drips inside every double doorway. Hats and scarves and coats sagged from brass hooks at the end of the bar booth. Quivers of muddy icicles clumped up at the back of wheel wells, while ridges of frozen, fouled snow encrusted the curbs.

Most importantly, however, there was this, too: the flush. You extracted potent hints of it while standing by the radiator and staring out the window at night, watching the snow cascade in a streetlight cone. You snatched heat-by-association from the aroma of a passing bakery, whether that heat implied *piekarnia* or *panederia* or some hipster take on *patisserie*. You were even made flush by memory, by the ubiquitous tales of walking on frozen Lake Michigan back in high school, and the burning whiskey shots you and your crew had consumed in the shelter of a creaking ice ridge (you fearless, jubilant dummies). And perhaps flushest of all, as JP had insisted to Dru during their first winter together, was the tucking-in to the heat of the dryer exhaust vent outside of a coin-op Laundromat, your coat tented open to catch the hot, scented gust.

Yes, for JP the ice remained quite typical. You endured it, you abided, until one morning you woke to the sun. You then caught the swimming-pool-blue-sky-through-kitchen-window, and, moments later, went outside, giddily, greedily, for the first time in months. And though it was still twenty-seven degrees, though the streets were still soiled by salt crust, you stripped down to a thin sweater or thermal undershirt, your armpits ripe from cloister, and you eyeballed the city, the absence of fog, and the steppe of squared rooftops returned to the horizon—"sky's out" was the phrase, is the phrase—and your chest opened. Your pulse throttled. You knew that this city would soon become incomparable.

Thus, JP looked for sunlight through the curtain break.

Dru no longer followed his story line. No matter the overpriced ricks of firewood he brought home, the three-day weekends South, or the fact that he now drove her to work, downtown at Wabash, into the clotty throng of traffic, she refused to believe that the winter would end. At home, she bundled, she huddled, she curled up silently on the couch and watched television. Made her obsessive lists on Post-it notes and paper scraps, a long-established habit that seemed to have drifted from reminder to documentation, to relentless complaint.

Their days were often an exercise in not touching. They dodged each other in the kitchen, their limbs never glancing. If JP leaned in to kiss her—a semi-forced effort on his part—she bickered about his abrasive stubble. Her back pats, or the occasional high five, seemed the last markers of her ambition for intimacy. By early March, he'd given up on either offering or winning affection. He, they, had grown metronomic.

But they still said *I love you*, in bed at night. They said it and they meant it, and Dru would broker a smile, and they would grin at each other, and then turn to their respective books, respective bedside lamps. Soon after, those lights would be extinguished and JP would silently pray, something he hadn't done since being confirmed in the presbytery at thirteen.

Dru was sick. A part of him knew this, anyway. Something was wrong that went well beyond mood swings. Something biochemical, neurological. Something triggered. Yet JP couldn't bring it up. What was more, he didn't want to, and neither did she. The idea of giving the topic a name was more terrorizing to them than ignoring the symptoms, enduring the silence. Besides, she'd recover soon enough. When the baby arrived. And the sunlight.

So, lying on his side in bed, turned away from Dru, JP would pray while staring at the part in the heavy curtains. He would fall asleep facing them, then wake to do the same.

On this morning, the sun was missing again. JP eased out of bed and stole into the kitchen, then prepared hot white tea in a burnt-orange kettle. He brought a half sleeve of saltines and a litter of vitamins to her bedside, vitamin D in the lead. Waking, Dru smiled politely as she crept out of bed, patting his leg while ignoring the tea, and then she shivered (dramatically?), running her hands up and down her arms. She hauled the burden of herself to the bathroom, her pregnancy fully pronounced, and she peed, and then hoisted up and looked for anything strange in the bowl water.

"All good?" JP called through the door.

"Uh-huh," she replied, exhausted by the question and the surrender of privacy.

They dressed for work to the din of NPR on the Bose Wave radio in the kitchen. Dru made a list on a Post-it note, stuck it into her pocket, then pocketed the pad.

He was bundled in Patagonia, she in Pendleton wool. JP went down to the secure parking area to warm the car, while Dru gathered her slim plastic binders of printed data: spreadsheets and market graphics and slogans to present to City of Chicago housing official and private northside donors, all marketable and conceptually vibrant ideas, in hopes of garnering even more funds for even more low- and mixed-income neighborhood revitalization. To Dru, Chicago remained a wreck. She was addicted to fixing it.

JP marched back upstairs to hurry her. She rolled her eyes at his offer to carry her bag. Before walking out, they peered into the small nursery, a mostly-IKEA affair, light gray and white with a flourish of tangerine, executed with semi-precision. Though the aesthetic achievement no longer kicked up the pulse, the IKEA now conjuring a private college dorm room, they couldn't help but pay homage to the space every time they left the house.

They drove from their Bucktown worker's cottage toward that cloud-chopped downtown skyline. Dru needed to pee, again, and she jostled in the heated leather seat. She ate crackers and chewed a couple of mint-flavored Tums. There was more NPR. She clicked a pen open and scratched on a Post-it, then stuffed the missive into her coat pocket. JP reached over to stroke her hand. She let him, and even reciprocated, squeezing his fingers.

Snow or no snow, they were thrilled about Lucinda. The child would be named after Lucy George Wallis, Dru's sister-close cousin. Nothing could take the shine off of that.

NPR national pitched over to local, WBEZ. South Side traffic was clogged, on account of "another dog trapped on the Eisenhower Expressway." A shepherd of some sort, the female news announcer noted. It was caught, as per the usual, between the concrete barriers.

"It'll be okay," JP said preemptively.

"It won't," Dru replied.

# 2

They'd met at a party in a loft with a rooftop deck, a couple of years before. It had been a brisk October evening, at the home of a respected activist-poet——a board member of Dru's nonprofit——who was life-partnered to a celebrated architect from JP's extended circle. There were drinks. Handshakes. Qualifications. Charcuterie. Their flirtatious parry over social responsibility and mixed affordable housing, versus the fact that JP owned a rehab-slash-house-flipping outfit. There was the way Dru spoke of Mississippi, and the way he began to make fun of this.

"You've been there?" she asked, eyebrows arched.

"No, ma'am," JP replied in a soap-opera southern drawl. He'd grinned wide as a melon slice, until she stared him into submission. "Hey, no offense," he offered. "Promise."

Dru sucked her drink through the cocktail straw, then, "You'd better watch it, man. And you had better stay cute. I tell you, if you ever lose that cute, your comments'll have your ass in a sling."

Her wink.

His craftsman's hands.

The authority she wielded while discussing Chicago building codes. Her interrupting an adjacent academic conversation made of classist snark to assert, gently, that if humanities scholars would only mix a bit more Virginia Pugh with their Virginia Woolf——the former being the birth name of Tammy Wynette, Itawamba County, Miss'ippi, of course——well, academics might not seem like such one-dimensional snoot-holes. " 'Cause, I mean, nobody wants that, right, y'all? Don't you guys want to talk to the very people who need talkin' to?"

JP, embarrassed at this, but even more so enraptured, branded the declarative nature of Dru's interruption as Pure midwestern. "Not one hint of southern passive-aggressiveness, yet not rude enough for New York," he explained. "A sure sign that you have embraced the nuance of my region."

"Dammit," she replied. "You're right."

Following a half hour of their own kinetic, rambling conversation, the two had snuck up to that rooftop deck, where they encountered a gaggle of young poets, tattooed and oily-haired, and desperate to be, well, poetic . . . and who were sparking a joint.

A *joint*, JP thought. How silly. And lovely. And panic-y. And, *I will if she does.*

As their footsteps crackled into the tar-and-gravel rooftop, its décor of container gardens and pitched skylights and clean aluminum heating exhausts, he did. Because she did.

When the poetic stoners had filed back downstairs to the party to drink free designer beer and dissect the elites (who would never, no fucking way ever, resemble their own future selves), JP asked Dru to please stay behind. He mumbled and shuffled in that decorative gravel, stared out at the miles-long city, and told her she made him, well, *comfortable*. He'd then mumbled more, said that he was sorry to be forward, but, well, truth was he hadn't smoked weed in a long, long time . . . and why in the hell had he done so anyway? . . . But whatever, he wasn't going to worry about it because you just have to cut loose sometimes, maybe . . . though still, he felt like it would be a bit weird to go back inside and try to do the social thing . . . not that he couldn't, but, you know, so, um, yes, "Would you mind staying with me for a few more minutes?" he asked. "Oh, and I don't know if you caught it the first time, but I'm JP."

"I caught it," Dru had replied. Then she kissed him.

After, his head had tilted sideways, like a puppy's. She giggled and turned away. Neither of them knew whether to kiss again, or to ignore the first peck altogether. So they just stood there, hands in pockets while staring out at the city, bumping shoulders like teenage crushers. A minute later Dru had pulled out a Post-it note and a pen, writing:

*JP. Weed. Night. Chi-skyline windows like glitter: October rooftop northside party. Winter so close it's a bit cold I smooched him. Jesus!*

"What's up with that?" JP asked.

"Habit." She had folded the note and jammed it into her pocket. "Don't let it get to you. I just can't trust my memory."

"You telling me you'd forget all this?"

She shrugged. "I only know that I don't want to. Though in a way, half the remembering is up to you, right?"

"Me forget *you*? Not a chance."

Dru retrieved the note from her pocket, then put it into his. She tugged on his jacket lapel a couple of times. "Make sure you don't."

# 3

Over that first year, they sat at sidewalk cafés in Wicker Park, in late May, drinking straw-colored Kölsch in the sun. They chased rumors of otherworldly *gaeng garee* in Skokie, and found *cochinita pibil* sandwiches on a side street in western Humbolt Park. They moved into a rickety loft near that same sandwich shop . . . before Dru gave up some frame of her guarded independence, her defiant autonomy, and agreed to relocate to one of JP's past flips, a design-website-profiled, gut rehab in Bucktown.

All the while, she'd made known that these stops were only temporary; she was moving home to Mississippi, period. All the while there were her little bouts of sadness.

At least, *little bouts* was how JP thought of them then. The offline, off-radar, curtains-drawn-for-a-day-or-maybe-two-type moods. Hyphenations. They were just a part of the deal with her, but still.

The upside was so much stronger. An eclipse, it seemed, that made everything okay. Because for JP, the upbeat Dru smothered any sense of the down. And whenever it couldn't, when she couldn't quite claw back up, they would hit the road. Outrun her condition, so it seemed. To the Brat Stop in Kenosha, Wisconsin (his idea). To Club Ebony in Indianola, Mississipi (hers).

Now and again Dru would mention the years-before death of her cousin Lucy George. These memories might be triggered care of a travel write-up of Mississippi in the Sunday *Times*, or conjured by the B-roll in a cable movie rerun. No matter the prompt, the facts JP collected were forever the same: Lucy had fallen from a tree as a girl, and she died. Dru had witnessed the event, and left Pitchlynn soon after.

No. Not left. She was sent away from home.

Now and again, Dru's memory was struck by Lucy out of the seeming blue, if not in stark contrast or clash with the setting or moment. Such was the case after a date night to Little Italy, an evening of *tagliata* with rosemary and sage, and triangle-shaped *fazzoletti* stuffed with *funghi porcini*, as had been sailed in across a virtual Mediterranean of *vino rosso*. Dru and JP had come home in a state that limned love to agitation, a.k.a., they were slobbered by wine. Dru had thrown open one of the huge double-pane windows, then straddled the sill while smoking a cig. (She forever refused to tell JP where she'd hidden the pack.) Unable to scold her, or to carry on at all, JP had fought out of his clothes, then collapsed into bed. Dru had joined him there soon after.

He was all but passed out when he heard the click of her pen, and grumbled into his pillow.

"What?" Dru had whispered, sitting upright beside him.

He turned toward her. "Why?"

"Why am I writing?"

"Crying."

She fidgeted for a moment, put a brake on her thoughts. "Did I tell you that I called her 'Sissy'? That we were—"

"Yah, yah, like sisters. You told me. I'm sorry you're sad again."

"Not again. Always."

He'd issued a grunt of support.

"Dying is the easy part," she said.

His hand slid onto to her thigh, and he patted it. He knew the story: she'd been conditioned to carry the guilt. Made to believe she was the cause of Sissy's death. By her aunt and her parents; by her friends and Pitchlynn families—or so she detailed for him again and again. Following a brief, blurred period of anguish, of shame, of . . . well, he wasn't quite sure, Dru's folks had sent her off to school. From there, semester after semester she'd come home for a portion of the holiday break, though most often she spent holidays with her parents in holiday destinations. Summers were for camp or family travel, or, later, for part-time clerkish jobs in exclusive, second-home locales. Positions procured care of her family's social networks, and which removed Dru from confrontation with either kin or hometown.

No matter where she was placed, nobody had ever talked about Lucy George. Over the years, Dru had rarely been home long enough to ask.

"Sorry, babe," JP whispered. "So sorry."

"Why?" She nudged him. "Why, exactly, are you sorry?"

He mumbled something and passed out.

# 4

On a hot Saturday morning in June, Dru told him she was going with him to scout properties with flip potential. She didn't ask. Didn't suggest. She told.

JP did not welcome the intrusion. Yet he also knew which hill to die on, and this wasn't it. So he stepped into the bathroom and groused in the mirror, then called out, "Wear jeans and a T-shirt. These homes are nasty. Trash, animal waste. *Human* waste, even. No water, so you can't wash your hands."

Dru put on a short yellow skirt, white tee, and sneakers. He huffed at her, then grabbed his tool belt and clipboard and a couple of high-powered Maglites.

"Let's go, then, tough stuff."

They drove west on Monroe toward Garfield Park, past dishwater catfish joints and bilingual title loans, liquor stores and old brick churches. The cloudless sky was chalked by airplane contrails. JP turned onto a side street lined by moldered historic homes, mansions-turned-multi-units with spires and sagged roofs, their slipped shingles like lost teeth. The lots were large and overgrown, and the porches and curbs overflowed with people. Young and old paused to stare at JP's vehicle, an alien craft that would bring nothing good.

The Queen Anne on his docket was a brick construction, circa 1890. Plywood covered the downstairs windows, and the intricate masonry was eroded. JP cut the car engine and glanced at Dru's skirt. "Don't worry about the neighbors," he said. "Ignore them and you'll be fine, promise."

She stepped out and slammed the car door. "Hey, y'all!" she called to the onlookers. They paused, and some waved, and then went back to their lives.

JP stomped to the rear of the SUV, then lifted the gate and threw his leather tool apron over his shoulder. "Point made," he huffed. "Now let's go."

When she began chewing him out in front of the others, JP had dropped his gear and wrapped his arms around his wife, lifting her high in the air. He carried her into the shade of the crumbling front porch, all but crushing her words. There, the damp aroma of wood rot hit Dru's sinuses. When he placed her down, she shut her eyes and steadied herself against the banister.

"You okay?" JP asked. "Dru? Christ, babe, you okay? I'm sorry, I—"

"Two seconds," she huffed. "Don't freak out, okay?"

"I was just nervous. Embarrassed. I didn't mean to grip you so hard, I—"

"Shh. Really. It's okay." She put a hand on his shoulder. "I'm not *that* pregnant. You just squeezed my lungs out, turkey."

# 5

And many months later, in winter, the NPR droned as they drove downtown. Dru stared out the passenger window, to the ice-crust lots and the bundled throng who trudged toward the 'L' station or bus stop, their bodies bent against the wind.

"It's not the dog on the highway," she said, turning down the volume. "It's the kids, Jayp. The kids."

"I don't get it," he said.

"You sure as shit don't."

That remark almost caught him. His jaw clenched as he imagined pulling to the side of the road, ordering her out. Despite himself, he could all but feel the rush of frigid air into the car cabin as she marched away in the snow——and he liked it. For a breath, anyway.

"Can you even still call them that? Kids?" she asked. "It's a gang initiation, where these kids . . . These . . . The new thing is that they have to steal a dog. Like, *someone's dog*, Jayp. To jump into the gang, they have to throw the dog over the retaining wall. At rush hour, between barriers, they just chuck it into traffic. After that, the older members bet on how long the thing will live."

"This is why Animal Control exists, babe. They'll——"

"No. They won't. They won't shut the interstate down to save one goddamned dog." She kicked the underside of the dash. "Don't you get it? This will come back to them. If the kids grow up a bit, and get wise, then what they've done is gonna wear them down. The memory will tear 'em apart."

They sat in silence, in gridlock.

"It's time for me to go home, Jayp," she stated. "You'll like it down there. I promise. And I'll be so much better. You'll love me again. You will—"

"Okay," he said, his eyes on the street ahead.

"Okay?" she perked. "Like, for real 'okay'?"

His smile had carried them over a few more miles. He then turned the radio back up, though not loud enough to be abrasive, calculating that, as she had before, Dru would calm down with the wearing of the day. She would realize that life was in fact pretty fair and wonderful here. He wagered that upon his picking her up after work she would admit that she'd just lost it a bit; she would confess that she was simply, extraordinarily uncomfortable and emotional, was worried about carrying to term. That she was sorry for this weakness, and that things would be fine.

He swore on all that she only needed a little bit of sun. A little Vitamin D, B12, and 'Sky's out!' And, oh yeah, to *not* be pregnant.

JP tapped the accelerator as he anticipated yet another description of the buttery warmth of Mississippi. He knew that later that night, Dru would describe, again, how at the first hint of Spring—*like, sometimes as early as February, Jayp!*—daffodils would thrust up on every length of sidewalk and side yard. How the spectacle of saucer-sized, pink and white dogwood blossoms would follow suit, as did redbud and white azalea, blue hydrangea and pink crepe myrtle. Dru would surely make a case for the clean perspiration of July and August, and the late-summer rows of small green cotton shanks. And after he balked at this last claim—he had been there in summer, and there was no such thing as refreshing Mississippi sweat—he knew she would swat him, and admit that, *Okay, well, summer's kinda awful!* That she would in turn make him admit that summer in Chicago was no picnic, either. She would insist he agree that the lack of airplanes overhead, anytime, sounded fantastic. Make him commit to a dream lacking air brakes and smog, and to the laze and the core of cordiality. He would be made to pledge allegiance to pulled pork sandwiches and hot tamales, and to having to stock up on beer every Saturday, since Sundays were legally reserved for the sole purchase of the Lord.

"Lovely, right?" she'd insist. "And those trance blues?" With this question, she would nudge him. "You know you love 'em. So you can't wait, right?"

He would answer Yes, and Yes, again, and he would tell her he couldn't wait to get down South (knowing full well that the proposed move would be compartmentalized into yet another long weekend trip, or two, or three). He'd nudge her back and smile, and pat her tummy. "Can't wait."

As he pulled up to her building, JP knew that Dru would produce a Post-it note pad, make a record of his promise, and stuff it in her coat pocket. She did exactly that.

# 6

er Braxton Hicks contractions rolled in like the front surf of a hurricane. The birthing process was co-directed by their hippie doula and their golf-ball-swatting ob-gyn in a reserved, decoratable hospital room on a fiercely clinical ward. The machine readouts were offset by JP's playlist and Dru's dimmed lights.

As the crowning drew close, she shoved and pushed and pained for endless hours, the doula offering deep tissue rubs and position adjustments . . . until at last the birth mother announced, "Fuck this. Bring on the goods," and a nurse anesthetist was enlisted.

Childbirth was a hybrid, as were the parents. For a time, they were unified by awe.

\* \* \*

Dru called JP on the morning of her death; she called him more than once. He didn't answer. The phone records would reflect that she had then dialed her old house phone in Pitchlynn, though that line had been disconnected after her mother passed. (The Wallis Farm manor had been empty for quite some time.)

While JP didn't know about the letter mailed to Susan George, he rushed home to find a Post-it note on the kitchen table. It was a print version of the text she had sent him a half hour earlier: *Fed Lucy. Going out. Back later.* She'd drawn a circle around the words.

Beside the table, the infant snoozed beneath thick blankets in a Moses-like bassinet. He gathered Lucy up and held her. He waited and waited and waited.

The *North Mississippi Cardinal* ran as many details as they could muster, though this was for the most part a cobbling of wire feed: the deceased had climbed up onto a concrete jersey barrier on the opposite side of the gang initiates, and the dog. She had for a moment watched the latter lope back and forth along the shoulder. Car after car throttled past the event, their Doppler honks driving the dog from lane to lane. Et cetera.

The *Tribune* and *Sun-Times* ran this same basic feed. The *Reader* ran a piece about socially conscious blunders, while the ASPCA released a statement that one's own self-interest must take precedence over the interests of an animal.

### NEW MOTHER DIES WHILE SAVING DOG
### TRAPPED ON INTERSTATE

JP gave no comment. Arrangements were "not yet complete."

# 7

Oh, but that first-ever trip South had been a miracle. It had proven to be one of so many visits to come: O'Hare to Memphis or Hattiesburg, Midway to Jackson or Gulfport . . . then back again. Weekends built of getaway fares and frequent flyer payouts, which Dru had booked with increasing, near-habitual frequency. These journeys were the idyll. The stuff. The flush. Whatever the label, they were also abiding: as history, as sensory, as, well . . . *Dru.*

Which was why JP had refused to let them go, as he tried to plow forward, in Chicago, alone.

He couldn't do it. He recognized soon enough that their relationship was fading, that the fine etchings of memory were eroding with time. When the feel of Mississippi sun through car window became conceptual-only, as did the aroma of alluvial or blackland soil, or the thump of the music, or even the maddening vision of hateful iconography—he decided, at last, to move down to Pitchlynn.

This had been his promise to Dru, sure. Yet more so, it was the only way to keep her alive. It was the only way to recall a guitar lick on a rental car stereo on the way to a goat roast, to a house-party-picnic, the one to which Dru had taken him on that first-ever trip South. It was the only sure reminder that the composition had consisted of two parts: a slippery jangle on the tenor guitar strings and a *chukka-chukka-boom* on the bass.

JP refused to lose control of this detail. He could not risk not remembering.

He moved to Pitchlynn to recall the slink of this Hill-Country-not-Delta blues, a blues as is thrust forward by a lean setup of snare drum, of cymbal and kick that slashes into the background of the guitar, chugging in circles, constantly repeating, revolving, again and again.

No. No matter what. No matter what codes he'd have to violate, or how abrasive he'd have to live, JP would *not* let these details go. He would not relinquish the beat, the drawl, revolving, again. This music, its prolonged, rounded crests whose feminine thrum pulses into rhapsody, revolves onto itself. Is memorized. Over and again, it revolves, alive. Is living forever.

They had driven north on Highway 7, toward some turnoff Dru swore she would recognize, another sub-county road near an old A.M.E. church—or so she thought she remembered.

She had turned down the music. "Best!"

"Best?" JP asked.

"Best! Best catfish. Heat. Music. People. Natural world. The best of us is here, I promise."

He looked over and was crushed by her brown-with-gold-flecked irises, and by the caramel-brown hair fanned in the open window wind. "If you say so," he said. "I'll——"

"Turn! Turn here, turn, turn!"

The tires squealed when JP whipped it onto the thin, potholed stretch of road, and into some lost country interior. The fields beside them were even more desolate and weedy, yet somehow also teeming and wild, marred now and again by gutted structures of tarpaper and scrap. The sun now struck them from a near-horizontal hover, its butter-yellow smoldering into rose. Twenty or so miles later, they came upon a community cast in the thinnest green of new evening, and a cluster of small farm homes un-choked by stoplight or grocery or gas station. In front of the homes was a hum of activity, from barbecue pit smoke to basketball games to folks who simply hung around porches rocking, or folks who hung around yards with neighbors, their forearms at rest on defunct cars, the hulls of which were installed on the property like sculpture.

At last, as promised, they reached the site of the best celebration they would ever attend (including the one on that Chicago rooftop deck, and the exultant dinner that followed their City Hall wedding). A stretch of dated vehicles parked on either side of the road. Partygoers milled about, or were plunked down on open tail gates, laughing, and sipping beers. The brunt of the pilgrims walked toward a small, leaning farmhouse, as was surrounded by scrapwood outbuildings.

"Aw hell yes," Dru said, reaching over to drum JP's thigh. They got out of the car, stretched, and took in the surroundings. She exchanged a *Hey, y'all* with a cluster of revelers, then pulled him on, toward the sound of live music.

Fifteen minutes later, the piping-hot catfish crumbled over his tongue and white bread coated his teeth. Peppered batter and Louisiana hot sauce made his nostrils drip. He mouthed a *Holy shit*, and whistled the heat away.

"My word," he exclaimed.

"Told you, Jayp," Dru replied. "What'd I tell you?"

He wagged his napkin-wrapped sandwich as if he were a pastor with a Bible, then turned to the large woman behind the plywood food counter. "You're an angel."

The woman bellowed, "Not yet! I'll see you for seconds, man."

The catfish and goat sandwiches were a buck apiece, as were the Budweisers pulled from the ice in a metal trough. The food stand was a makeshift setup beneath a tilted carport of old flashing and warped four-by-four posts. The crowd of locals, ages nineteen to ninety, were clad in jeans or overalls or coveralls, alongside a few who had dudded up in slashes of color. Intermingled with the African American community at heart were gritty White hipsters from Memphis, soused university Greeks from Oxford, and a flock of bespectacled folklorists with mounted cameras and mics. As the last jade traces of dusk seeped away, a talc-fine dirt drifted into the halo of yellow floodlights.

A single speaker PA and mic were set up in the yard. A guitar, dissonantly tuned, blared straight through a beater Peavey amp, while a nearby mismatched drum kit went without amplification. Songs were built around that same *boom-chukka-boom* heard in the rental car, and the glistened bodies of young and old wriggled and writhed together in trancelike stupor.

Dru asked JP to dance, but he was too shy, or perhaps too afraid. She mocked him gently for this, then left him standing alone as she swayed into the crowd. Partners quickly clustered around her, their hips and torsos swaying into the precise curves of her own. From the margin of the crowd JP sipped beer and bobbed his head, wishing he had the guts to get in there.

With the turnover of the performers, Dru walked back to him, one hand holding her hair up while the other fanned her neck.

"You gotta get over yourself and get out there, Jayp."

"I'm workin' on it."

They moved to a wooden picnic table at the shadowy edge of the crowd, then sat on the top with their feet on the bench. JP pointed out the slice of moon, which hung just above the roofline of the farm shack.

"A sentimentalist," Dru said. "How refreshing." She dipped her head onto his shoulder, then put her hand on his knee to still his tapping foot. "You okay?"

"Perfect," JP answered. "Best."

She kissed him, and nothing else had existed. Nothing else ever would.

Over the next couple of hours they talked, they kissed. They drank more beer, and kissed. At some point, Dru made clear that though she hated the idea of leaving, and "in particular of leaving off of all this kissing," it was a long drive back to Pitchlynn. She also noted that the party would soon turn into a smear of too much moonshine and too many boisterous country teenagers. Thumping break beats would soon smother the blues licks, and while this, too, made for a hell of a soundtrack, the kids would also sneak too many beers, trying to act like adults, while the old men would surely act like brazen youngsters, firing their sidearms at the moon.

JP never wanted to leave. He only agreed to do so on the condition that she first let him have a dance. She obliged.

The next morning, a Sunday, she shook him awake with particular vim. "Get your bony midwestern ass out of bed, babe!"

"Shh." He turned away. "Just . . . *shhh*."

"Nope. Now. We're late for church!"

"Oh come on," he whined. "Don't tell me you get all churchy when you get home. I am *not* in." He drew the blanket over his head.

"Now!" She laughed as she yanked it right back off of him.

Fifteen minutes later, their teeth half brushed and with water bottles in hand, they drove west. Warming late morning air rushed through the open car windows, and hanging boughs of hardwood shaded the ash-gray asphalt. The two-lane road both lifted and lolled over the ridges and hillocks of north Mississippi, past the strip malls alongside I-55, and into the Delta landmass of cotton and soy acreage, of wire-walled boll buggies, and here or there a teethy row-plow, rusted dead in a curve of alluvial dirt off the turnrow.

The road at Moon Lake ran the contour of the banks. Now and again, a short dock or boat ramp broke up the cypress groves in the shallows. It was breezy out, so the greenish slate lake was dimpled by waves. JP and Dru at last drove up on a cleared embankment and to a string of parked cars. At lakeside, a congregation of twenty or so had gathered, in church suit and jogging suit, in fly-screen lace hat and ball cap alike.

Dru parked, and JP followed her down to the service. The congregation was wrapping up a verse of "New Burying Ground," as was followed by a chorus of *Amen* and *Hallelujah*. Three pastors stood together in waist-high water, wearing black robes with gray stripes on the sleeves. Beside them were a handful of individuals in white robes: the people who were waiting to be reborn.

The preachers took turns delivering brief, inspired sermons, buildups to the climactic, familiar phrase of, "In the name of the Father, the Son . . ." The novitiates were then ushered beneath the water in unison, "and the Holy Ghost" being the last words they heard before transition.

The white robes of the new flock floated on the lake's surface like lily blossoms. The bankside community launched back into song:

*"Jesus on the mainline. Tell him what you want!"*

The baptized emerged with slick faces, obvious wonderment. They wiped their eyes in anticipation of new clarity.

A soloist belted out a proposal to those who remained uninitiated: *If you want your body healed . . .*

*Then tell him what you want!* the congregation replied.

Dru sang along. She sang loud.

Standing beside her, JP could only smile and clap, as he didn't yet know the words.

# VERDICT

# 1

While on one outskirt of Pitchlynn, Mississippi, a young couple was bowled over by the presence of twin newborns, on another, distal side, an overdetermined man—a DOC guard, grade Correctional Officer II, puller-down of $24,420 per annum, pre-tax—clipped his ID badge to his pocket and holstered his state-issued Glock.

Doc wasn't on duty, but he was in uniform. Though not assigned to the security detail in Jackson, he told Jessica he was driving down there anyway. Period.

Her response was to argue with him from bedroom to kitchen to driveway, and even step into the street as he drove around her and away. She lectured, then implored, and even cried out that Doc had given enough time and life to that old man. Besides, Christ, didn't Doc understand? Hare Hobbs didn't need any additional protection—let alone any provided without so much as a day's pay.

"I will *not* forget this, Doc," Jess stated, her eyes welling. "Last chance to stop and think. To make sense of yourself. Please."

He couldn't. Didn't. Doc only mouthed an apology, then threw his truck into gear.

Besides, his mission had nothing to do with protection.

He gunned it over the north Mississippi blacktop, the breeze gushing in through the open windows of his pickup. It remained hot, though the September air now seemed to yawn more than strike. The sunlight radiated on his midnight-blue polyester shirt, and that ID badge reflected on the windshield. Pulling onto I-55 at Grenada, he poked at the scan button on his factory radio in hopes of catching commentary about the trial. He rolled up those windows and hit the cabin AC.

A couple of hours later, Doc cruised into downtown Jackson. At a stoplight, a cluster of young White women stepped into the crosswalk with pink posterboard signs: WE SHALL STILL OVERCOME.

Doc drove amid state and federal buildings, taking in the media trucks, the tourists, the activists and gawkers. The cell phones in everyone's hand capturing every instant. He found a parking spot half a mile from the Hinds County Courthouse. Got out, straightened the tuck of his blouse, and grabbed his Glock 22 off the bench seat. He started marching, fast.

Doc reached the swarm on Pascagoula Street within seconds of the highly publicized perp walk. Television producers shouted, "This is it!" and "Shot on that van!" Microphones were thrust up on booms; video and still cameras mobbed the steps of the large deco building, wrenching into a phalanx on either side of the white passenger van. A double line of U.S. marshals in Kevlar vests and ballistic shades joined a Jackson PD detail to form an alleyway between the vehicle and courthouse entrance. Doc stepped in to join them.

Faces and lenses reflected in the tinted van windows, as did thrusting placards and fists. Shutter clicks flitted as its doors swung open. Two marshals climbed out, looked around, then removed Hare Hobbs. His blaze orange coveralls were at least two sizes too big, making the old man appear infantile, frail. His hair was gray and oily. His skin paled to near blue. His wrists and ankles were shackled, so the marshals helped him limp along.

Activists shoved against the double line of officers. Hare's face was dogged by fear, and he blinked like a bird as he staggered through the drift of stale breath and sweat. He took in the strands of commentary over the live feed.

The old man felt in tune with every muscle and movement. His focus was to display great exhaustion. Brittleness. He was proud to have thought to shit himself earlier, elated to have been granted the clean, oversized jumpsuit, because he knew the on-camera image it provided. The world would now witness a weak, washed-up elder, all but swallowed by the coveralls while plodding in agony, his fetters scraping the sidewalk. This was their chance for redemption.

Hare wondered why none of the officers on call had noticed that they'd been infiltrated, that Doc wore a completely different uniform than all assigned. Beyond the throng, Hare then caught a glimpse his daughter and Ladybug, on camera with a reporter: some upscale Black female, surely in from somewhere else. He looked around for Derby, and, mostly, for his firstborn, for Sonny. Hare still had faith that Sonny would get there, would save him. Despite the mangled plane and ICU hospitalization, he scanned face after face for any glimpse of kinship, of empathy, still believing Sonny might show up to protest, to testify, to . . .

He flinched when a gob of spit hit his jaw. Biting back a tirade, Hare nestled his head against his shoulder, gentle as a lamb, and tried to wipe it away.

* * *

DOC THOUGHT of Jessica again, and of the loose but resilient tribe of family and friends who had shepherded her childhood. Detroit to Pitchlynn to Chicago to Clarksdale, to Memphis to Pitchlynn to Chicago to Pitchlynn to . . . to the outskirts of Pitchlynn, and to the fenced modular home, tidy, on a cinder-block slab, with him. Gabe's murder had terrorized her people off of their land, unmooring them from both future and past.

* * *

DESPITE HIS efforts, no one saw Hare as anything more than hate. His teeth ground as he accepted this old truth, then let go and let it roll over and through him like a spiritual, like gospel.

He wished to Christ he had a fistful of soap lye. He envisioned slinging a cloud of it into the eyes of protester, reporter, and cop. They would fall over each other, screaming, their fingernails clawing the meat of their own faces, scraping eye socket and lip. He pictured the flailing cameramen, blind, shoving lenses in what they assumed to be his direction.

He shook off a chill of pleasure, bowed his head, and paused as if to topple. The marshals reached in to steady him, while the crowd held their breath. Shutter snaps filled the silence. Hare coughed hard and doubled over, his vision emblazoned with dancing white stars. A few of the onlookers gasped at his fragility.

* * *

CLUBHOUSES, DOC thought. He thought of the clubhouses in most Mississippi towns. The inns, the B&Bs. The clubs built on former plantation land, or in former plantation fashion. The old Wallis Farm, where his people, where his wife's people, and where Gabe had spent so many years building a legacy. Their lives and backs and pennies invested—for nothing, no return whatsoever.

Doc was enraged by his desire to shower at the Pitchlynn Country Club (est. 1966). To sauna there, even, despite the Mississippi heat. To drink a beer you could sign for with your membership number. And the food, he thought now: a communion. And the Friday evening dances and Easter buffets? The weddings now and again? What if he had married Jessica there? What would the caliber of this ceremony have implied?

Doc wanted to tip well. He wanted a garage-parked golf cart in his home in the adjoined PCC gated community. He wanted the clubhouse, its high white columns and wide rocking porch, as was modeled, somewhat, on the original Wallis House, as was reconstructed on the same footprint of earth, after they'd trucked the haggard old mansion into town. Doc wanted to play a round of golf (he'd never even swung a club), and wanted afterward to join the guys at the clubhouse bar for a whatever the fuck a "*Cutty Shark*" was. He wanted the Egg Bowl on an overhead flat-screen, Ole Miss whipping Mississippi State; he wanted Jessica to show up an hour or so later, fresh off of her tennis lesson, or her aquatic aerobics lesson, or her *yoga*, or her whatever; he wanted the two of them to have a couple more drinks (would Jessica still drink her same wine in that type of place?), and to watch the other members come and go, in and out of the clubhouse dining room, or the add-on ballroom, or the small pro shop, all waving to each other, everyone saying, *Hey, y'all*, and cracking risqué jokes, all of them passing and greeting, all members; he wanted Jessica to be full, to be drunk, to nibble at club sandwich, to stab at crisp fries with a frilled toothpick pulled from the toast; he wanted at some point in the early evening, sunset lingering, for him and Jessica to get back in that golf cart and giggle at each other, and bellow a few more greetings at members while on the cart path home, Doc swerving now and again into the elaborate grass for kicks, into the Bermuda, the Zoysia, the bent grass, the rye, Jess swatting at him and being embarrassed about his buzz, and he thus swerving farther onto the fairway, to push things and poke a little fun; he wanted them to hit the automatic garage door opener and pull the cart in and kick off their shoes and walk through a utility room and into the foyer and through the kitchen and to the bar, to mix another drink, and finally to glide out onto the large back deck and patio pool area, to the banded lounge chairs beside the stainless-steel gas grill, where they'd watch the last light fade over the angular rooflines, the rooflines on houses so thoughtfully spaced by lawn; he wanted to watch the color bleed onto the decorative cotton field behind their house, its blossoms white as a blizzard, its antiquated prop combine forever parked and rusting, its turnrows manicured by crews of Mexican migrants in green rubber boots, before sometime later (an hour? two? Doc must've nodded off), standing up and all but floating into their California king-sized bed, the AC pounding through the vents in the cathedral ceiling. Doc wanted a benign but worthy gripe session about dealing with their kids' college fund, and about how Jessica had had to pay off her own damned loans—and not just her associates', either, but in this case her BSN, or her RN (or, my word, maybe even her MD?)—alongside a sidebar complaint about taxes and NASDAQ; he wanted a legit gripe session about insurance premiums and a primary care physician; he wanted to bask in eighteen-hundred-thread-count hemstitch sheets, and to joke about the country-ass ways of their parents and their grandparents—but with respect, and with longing, and while wishing so badly that their folks were still around to witness and to share; *Your mama, in Detroit?* he'd ask Jessica, or *Auntie Jeanes and Gramma Mina, in Chicago?—right here on this*

*Mississippi spot! Can you imagine it, Jess?*; *Can you imagine them coming back home to see us like this?——My god, they would have loved it . . . though they would have kicked our leisure asses into shape! Would've had a thing or two or three to say about this domesticated bland we're rockin'!*; Doc wanted to fall asleep next to his wife, his Jessica, both of them sated and spoiled and retired, having never once left the gates of the Pitchlynn Country Club Estates all weekend; he wanted Jessica to sleep, my god, to sleep like a rock so secure, for once, just to sleep through the night.

Or sometimes he wanted to hate all of that stuff. Or maybe just to roll his eyes at it, and dream of some wildly different version of purchase. Truth was, Doc didn't really know if he wanted that crap or not. Having glimpsed it firsthand, he just wanted a shot at figuring it out.

"If we'd only been given our stake," he muttered. "If Gabe's land had been passed down, as was intended."

Doc could breathe this other history. It seared his lungs like an asphyxiant. Now, however, at best, at the *very* best, he knew it would be their kids who might grasp at or refute such dreams. If their schooling went exceptionally well. If their kids grew strong enough to move out of state.

*Stare into him*, Doc thought, as Hare staggered close. He opened the thumb break on his holster. *Stare into him, and make him know denial. And finish him.*

\* \* \*

*FOLD AND FALL*, Hare thought. He was within ten paces of Doc. *I will collapse as I near him. Faint almost, onto myself. And they'll all reach out to assist me. Gently, so gingerly. Of their own free will. Neither Doc nor they will be able to help themselves.*

Hare knew this, his eyes glancing to his state-issued flip-flops. He gauged the gentle grasp of the marshals on his biceps, and knew that when the time came to collapse, to go slack and fold, he'd slip right through their fingers.

Hare refused to look at Doc. He did not know what the young man intended, and he did not care. He knew only that the long blade of his thumbnail would slice through artery, or gouge out eyes.

The lens shutters clacked at the speed of automatic weapons. The crowd screamed out for vengeance. And it began.

Hare let his body cascade forward. As anticipated, because of the troopers' feather-light touch, the old man was let free to collapse onto the sidewalk. As expected, and despite Doc's having released the thumb brake on his holster, he was first and foremost a victim of instinct: he darted out of the security line and dropped to his knees, to catch Hare.

The crowd lurched forward like a farrow of piglets on a sow. They looked on as the two men collided, and then met the pavement in a tangle.

While flailing to right himself, Doc felt something stab at his neck. It seared like a hornet sting, maybe worse. Though distracted, he pushed the old man up and off, and then scrambled to get to his feet.

Hare was faster. Doc watched from one knee as the old man snatched his Glock, then fired off a clinic of rounds. The first shots leveled the guards who had held him, and the next volley kept all others at bay. As if on swivel, Hare ripped the pistol in perfect interval, at perimeter, the arc of bullets dropping men indiscriminately while clear-cutting the crowd.

Bystanders sprinted or froze, cowered and collapsed. They muttered, or screeched like crows. Insulated by shock, Doc stood bolt upright and wiped his palm on his neck, and considered the thick curtain of blood on his hand. He wondered what on earth . . .

It was Hare's thumbnail, of course. Given the bleed-out, Doc understood that the old man had nicked an artery. He looked from his hand, and back to Hare. He felt his own pistol peck his chest.

"They just couldn't let it lie," Hare muttered. "They couldn't see past what they wanted to see."

Despite everything, Doc shrugged.

Hare's eyes bulged with disbelief, with fury, yet Doc refused to look away. In protest, the old man fired four more quick rounds—two on either side of Doc's ears—dropping another quartet of officers.

Doc's eardrums split into tonal roar, and his body erupted with pain. Still, somehow, he focused only on Hare. Though the Glock muzzle again jabbed into his chest, Doc resisted the urge to look down. As the blood sopped his shirt belly, he began to consider the moment as a potential, well . . . *end*. He thought of Jessica, their children, and their welfare to come, and . . .

*If only they had found any record of the transaction*, Doc thought. Jessica's family had sworn there was one, a title or financial note of some kind, in the bank right there on the square in downtown Pitchlynn. Gabe had spoken of it with his sisters, and with Jessica's aunt, Jeanes. Yet after the trial, the first one back in '65, just before the Wallises broke ground on the country club, no record was found: of the deposit box, or the quitclaim deed, let alone any evidence that the former slave Gabriel had been a customer.

Nobody had known anything, save what they were told by Mr. Wallis. In response to the formal inquiry made by Jessica's family, both public and legal, Wallis had challenged *anyone* to question an upstanding woman like Miss Beverly. Fact was, he noted, Gabe's family were only tenants, having been croppers before, and in bondage before that. While the farm's history was rudimentary at times, Wallis admitted, a living experiment in historic preservation, a museum, really, its ownership was nonetheless clear: the land was and had always been in Miss Beverly's family. She had kept it, and she had served it, and, most importantly, she had served the people who farmed it with kindness and consideration. More so, Wallis added, his wife had done this for far longer than any operator in the state, what given the farm's unprofitable and, sadly, unsustainable status. He had explained to press, police, and clergy how, truth be told, Gabe's family had benefitted more than most from her benevolence. It was such a shame, Wallis decried, that in the wake of the murder Gabe's own clan would scramble to ruin his memory, and the memory of that place, and now Miss Beverly's reputation. Ingrates and upstarts, he derided . . . though he said he still pitied them, scrambled as they were by childlike pain.

A new truth had been forged in the spirit, letter, and tone of the old.

The Wallis land project had gone forward soon after. The house was trucked to town, while the club took up the land.

Doc's eyes locked on Hare.

"They wouldn't let me, Doc," the old man said. "Just wouldn't let me die invisible. I told you I weren't no more than a mascot. I ain't never been nothing more." Hare shivered, and jabbed the Glock into Doc's chest. "I got a daughter who sold me out, and my son changed his name. I got a wife who run off and left me like trash, and . . ."

Somehow, Hare's face brightened. "But I *do* have an alibi, Doc. Did you know that? I got an alibi, come down here in a plane. Sonny was comin' down to save me. He was comin' with the truth. At last."

Hare fired another volley of shots at the crowd. "Only, he ain't made it, Doc. And he ain't gonna make it, either. So guess what? You the last one who can save me. This here is the very last chance. *Your* last chance. Now, please, tell me, Doc. How do I get out of being me?"

Doc didn't reply. For one thing, he'd heard only the sustained, roaring tone from the gunshots. For another, he didn't care to listen. Eyesight was all that mattered here. He refused to look away.

In fact, it was Hare who had finally glanced elsewhere, surveying the crowd, to see if anyone else might assist him. Those who weren't sprinting off were either crouched or crawling, or balled like pill bugs in the dirt. The only person still standing was Winnie.

# 2

"You loved him, though? Gabe?"

This was the last conversation Sonny would have with his mother. He'd been trying to get at it for years.

He had wanted so badly to be in love, for so long. Wanted so badly for someone to come and unravel him, and to understand what had been left there, on the porch of the cabin on the farm, with the chair. He wanted to understand how to share this loss: of faith, of trust, of adoration, of past. Of story, really.

Sylvia had been bathed in fluorescent hospital light when he asked her. She was propped up in an adjustable bed, and for once could not evade his inquisition. (Of all the things to land one in the hospital, she'd stepped on a sewing needle. The No. 19 fabric spike had driven deep into her foot, point to scarf to shank, curling a cut nerve in the process, and prompting wildfire infection.) There was a tube in her arm and a daytime movie on, above. She sucked watery juice through a straw and said nothing.

Sonny had pushed her. "It took me forever to figure it out. As a kid, I thought Daddy had told you to leave the farm for our own well-being. I thought he would soon come after and join us. That he'd hired Gabe to drive us to the train station, you know? Took me years to understand that you and Gabe were—"

"Gabe had a wife," she all but spat, clutching the plastic cup, her hands mackled by age spots.

"But his wife had left him. Before."

"Correct."

"And then you and he . . . I know now that you and he were—"

"You don't know nothin', Sonny," she'd snapped. "And you don't need this. Now look here. Gabe had him a wife. He drove you and me to the train station because he was a good person. That's it, that's all." She had glared at the television. "Don't invent."

"But—"

"But makin' things up isn't fair to the truth. You're addin' drama where it doesn't exist. This ain't some love movie. Some exotic black-white romance or whatever. My *word*, Sonny, the honest-to-Christ reality is that Gabe understood things. He'd been on that farm longer than ever'body, and he understood the gravity of the place, the time. He didn't answer to anyone, in particular to Wallis—whereas your daddy and every other man's livelihood meant that they did whatever the bossman wanted. So *that* was my attraction to Gabe. That, and the fact that he lived in the battle over whether or not to move on, for his family. He could go, but he hadn't. I was desperate to go, but I couldn't."

"If there wasn't any romance, then why are you so angry?"

"Because I *knew*, Sonny. I knew what'd happen to him before I ever asked him to take us."

"What do you mean? Like, you knew he was going to die?"

She shut her eyes. She had at least known it was possible, known what it would mean for Gabe to take her and Sonny away from Hare, then return to the farm.

Sonny pressed her. "But you asked him anyway? *You asked him anyway?*"

What could she have done? What? Could she have asked Hare for permission to go?

"Sonny," she muttered. "It's okay that you don't get it. You was a boy, and Hare was your dad. And I'm sorry that it has hurt you this bad for this long. But don't you see? We had to leave, fast. There weren't no other way but to—"

"Of course there was a way. There's always another way."

"And your daddy wasn't goin' anywhere. He was already bunkered up with Wallis and . . . So I had to go to Gabe. I told myself that I had to protect you. And me. And even Gabe—or so I hoped, anyhow. 'Cause Mr. Wallis and them? They was done with that farm. They needed everybody off, and only violence was gonna make that happen. Your daddy told me this, and then I told it to Gabe. And knowin' that, I figured he'd come with us. To Chicago, his family. Figured he didn't have no other choice."

"No," Sonny replied. "No, you didn't."

She stared at him for a moment, until a tear traced her cheek. "No. But I told myself that he would. Because I *needed* to believe it, you know? I needed to believe he would come with us. I sat right in his cabin, and I asked him to help you and me, and I needed to believe that when he said yes to us, he understood what he was committin' to. I *had* to believe that he knew there was no way back. And that therefore we wasn't responsible. No way he could help us, then go home like nothin' happened."

"And Gabe knew this, too, didn't he?"

"He did."

"So you both understood. But then you let him take us *anyway*? Even after he said he wasn't coming with us to Chicago?"

"Yeah," she whispered.

"So you're a part of it, huh? That makes us both a part of what happened to him?"

"Yeah," she repeated. She wiped away another tear, but then her face grew stern. Because, versus any reason or belief, any right or wrong, more than anything she had needed Gabe's goddamned truck. She would have done whatever was necessary to get it.

Sonny looked away from her, and to the ivory hospital wall. His thoughts cycled through all the reading and research he'd done about Hare: the old paper clippings and legal dockets, the magazine profiles and on-camera interviews. Online and in the library, care of textbooks and law journals, in search of the complete story. New coverage of the retrial had arrived every day.

He had never known that he was an accessory. He understood then that he would have to leave immediately for Mississippi.

"Daddy was passed out cold when we left that night," Sonny said. "In his chair. Drunk. He could not have killed Gabe."

"I remember every bit," she replied. "Now stop. You been hung up on this for way too long."

"You're not hearing me, though. He didn't do it."

"What do you really know?" she groused, sitting up. "Or better still, what is that you *want* to know? What are you trying to fix here, Sonny? All this business, all this time you've spent hung up on Hare. For what? What's it gonna do?"

"But I saw him, Mama. I saw Daddy passed out in the chair. We both saw—"

"For one thing, you don't know if Hare was really asleep or if he'd just shut his damned eyes. For another, even if he didn't do it, well . . . don't it matter that he forged a whole new life from the accusation? Does it mean anything to you that he reaped benefit off of Gabe's death?"

"He has always maintained his innocence."

"But he never condemned the act! Sonny, *come on*. Your daddy wore that murder like a medal."

"I—I think it was the Wallises. It was Mr. Wallis who—"

"And I promise you this, son. The accusation that Hare done it weren't much of a stretch to begin with. Your father could barely live in his own skin."

Strangely enough, despite himself, Sonny started to mutter those old Ferlin Husky lyrics: *When troubles surround us / when evils come / the body grows weak / the spirit grows numb.*

He had heard the song so many times growing up that it had become a sort of de facto soundtrack of Sylvia's denial. Year after year, his mother would hum if not sing it to repulse any question or comment involving Hare, or Wallis Farm. *When these things beset us / He does not forget us / He sends down his love / On the wings of a dove.*

"Hey?" she groused. "You know the one thing a man like that can't stand? A man like Hare?"

Resigned, Sonny sighed. "What's that, Mama?"

"He can't stand being disposable. He can't stand not being needed."

"But this is about the trial. It's about delivering the truth."

"Especially a white man," she continued. "I swear. All my life people raised me to be terrified of a black. But you take a white man who figures out he's just as sorry as the rest of us? That the world can go on without him? Now, that, Sonny, is a *dangerous* man. And that's exactly the type of man you trying to redeem."

# 3

On the courthouse lawn, Winnie's hands were held out in front of her, palms up and fingers fanned wide, as if this pose would stop any munition. She stared at her father, shaking her head in disbelief. Positioned behind her, the object of concern, was Ladybug. The child sobbed as she huddled beside the crouched reporter and her cameraman.

Hare started to call out to them, but couldn't. Instead, he pivoted back to Doc, as if on appeal. He dropped the gun and held his arms out, glancing to Doc's neck and to the gushing carotid. Hare's lips parted as if to speak, and his eyes filled with tears, and he slumped.

For the rest of Doc's life, he would wonder what had moved the man to cry. Was it because Hare's rage had decimated his own family? Did he weep for his grandchild, to whom he had just delivered lifelong trauma? Or was there something more?

Doc would pull this apart through extended recovery and rehab, and through the outstretch of sensorineural hearing loss, this being the lasting physical impression of the moment. He would ponder it as the criminal charges piled up against him. (He had, after all, infiltrated the courthouse security detail. Bringing a weapon had pushed a tenuous police impersonation charge straight into a felony-class offense.) He thought about it when he was relieved of duty, likewise of his pension, and as he became a flash point of blame for any and all who needed a target.

He thought about it while witnessing the impact of his actions on Jessica. Good lord, how he had added to her lot, having transformed her theoretically elective job into a must-keep position, complete with must-have health insurance; having fractured her daydreams of further education, of double retirement pay, or of travel; having even soiled her social standing, if only tacitly, whether in book club or church group, let alone her secret little dream of someday running for alderman, or . . . None of this had crossed his mind beforehand.

Doc considered Hare's tears when interviewers had asked him to describe the moment, though he never gave detail of his antagonist's face. With the blanket of probation draped over him, and then, years after, the liberated rousing of a counternarrative, a folk-hero type of label that brought young people by Doc's house now and again, graduate students and the like, and which later found him on the receiving end of boosted charitable collections, sometimes even care of Jessica's same church group, or as a sort of honorarium or speaking fee provided by various community colleges or universities, or, many, *many* years later, as supplied by progressive, candidate-sanctioned events—though not even these factions considered Jessica's role in things, no matter how hard Doc had pushed the impact of her narrative—he would think about Hare, and those tears.

He would spend endless months, then years, operating a zero-turn riding mower across the football field at the county high school, a job he was afforded despite the known red flag on his background check, and one which he would pilot well past any reasonable age of retirement. Alongside a mastery of relevant landscape machinery, now and again Doc could experiment with the nap of the turfgrass, or perhaps the turfgrass hybrid itself, and even tinker with the paint types, aerosol or latex, employed as both regulatory field marker and school-themed aesthetic. He could ride back and forth on the zero-turn and consider, and reconsider, the moment of his survival; he did the same in the fieldhouse, or even while standing at the sidelines, watching his children both cheer on and compete in regional 3A competition.

Doc once thought about Hare while he was lost in the belly of Vaught-Hemingway Stadium, University of Mississippi, Oxford. He'd been on hand to watch the Gridiron Classic, where his oldest, an undersized tight end who was athlete enough to serve as utility, played in his final high school playoff game, before taking up a scholarship and a commission, care of the Air Force Academy in Colorado Springs. Specifically, Doc got lost while looking for the men's room—and, truth be told, while just tooling around the massive hull of space—and then, despite himself, had snuck into the Rebel Club, the university's elite donor level. Perhaps his entry had been granted because Doc had his coveralls on. (He'd long since taken to wearing them, his lawn-care uniform, even on weekends.) As in, the very concept of Doc on site was chalked up to maintenance.

Jessica was not on hand because she could not get off shift.

The opulence of the club, the controlled climate and aromatic drift of succulent foodstuffs, and, of course, the clientele on hand, reminded him exactly of that first job, at the Pitchlynn CC. Yet the vacancy of it all, the echo and sterility, also reminded him of an empty prison corridor. Of a body left alone with its own sense of worth, or a body made desperate to make worth of itself.

Beyond the field view and robust concession, the spiked Cokes and Patek Phillipes, and the wash of Ole Miss propaganda, what had moved Doc the most was the floor-to-ceiling stockpile of cottony toilet tissue, stacked high in an open double-door supply closet inside the Rebel Club men's room. The rolls alone were the type of fixture he and Jessica would never afford (their budget being, at best, good for another Angel Soft eight-pack). He was reminded of those PCC members who pilfered rolls of similar into their gym bags, and who skimmed from the clubhouse stores of soap, shampoo, combs, towels, Barbasol, and Bic disposables.

Doc wondered for the hundredth time if looting was what had made the men successful, or if success itself had persuaded them of the privilege and right to steal. Staring into the closet, the barrier of tissue, this rampart flanked by rows of glass-bottled lavender hand soap, likewise wrapped stacks of folded, linen-like, air-laid paper towels and foil-wrapped chocolate mints, he considered what would happen if he snatched just one little . . .

He didn't. Couldn't. For one thing, he didn't believe in theft. For another, he didn't believe he could get away with it. There were eyes on him, everywhere. Always had been.

Besides, what was it Hare had claimed about Doc and rich people? "You obviously ain't one of them! And you ain't never gonna be."

"Are you?" Doc had asked himself, staring at a cache of ass paper worth more than he made in a month.

Nope.

He thought about this truth, and he thought about Hare, and he was furious. What on earth had made Hare Hobbs weep? Given all, had the man even deserved to cry? Though Doc could never, ever bring his considerations up to Jessica, he could not get over his belief that Hare had felt sorrow. That even a wretch could grieve.

In any event, the facts were only this: with his final breath, Hare had fallen forward, not a word, toward the gray granite steps in front of the art deco Hinds County Courthouse, with its rooftop statues of Moses and Pharaoh and Socrates. He'd fallen toward the checkerboard pedigree of the government quarter of Jackson, Mississippi, as if plunging, somehow, through history: to a time before the snarl of contemporary infrastructure and industry, before the laying of asphalt and application of public utility, and even before the original platted plots of dirt road development.

Hare Hobbs had collapsed at the factual apex of Mississippi's geographic, Jeffersonian democracy, a location proposed in 1802 by Thomas Jefferson himself. He fell dead as a stone into the representative center of the center of the state, a land site designed to grant equal access to government by any and all Mississippians who might seek justice.

(Tribal land that was ceded by the Choctaw under extreme duress, of course.)

The old man fell forward, with fissure vents of bullet holes in his back.

Doc had caught him again, and they went down together.

# 4

Sonny's eyelids clenched tight against the beam of the hospital lamp. "You there?" a woman asked, her tone welcoming. "For real this time? Hello?"

Through the gauzy light he made out her berry-colored scrubs . . . and then sank back into the hallucinatory murk.

"Huh-uh, no," the nurse aide insisted, shaking his shoulder. "Don't want to lose you again, friend."

Primed by opiate, his consciousness ebbed, though the nurse aide would not let him drift off. Waking, he swallowed over and again, flinching and then panicked by the tube in his throat. The tubes in his arm, in his penis. He could barely lift his head, but he saw the apparatuses on his legs, made of stainless steel rings, held by pins, rods, and wires.

"We gotta get your body back in order, fast," she said. "You hear me?"

He squinted.

"Yeah," she said. "You hear me. Now, no doctor's gonna tell you this outright, but we need you to start workin', hon. We need you to do it fast. Your insides has shut down. It's been too long now. Too many days."

He flexed the corner of his mouth. The nurse nodded in response, and began to sponge him. "Just tell your body to come back online. I mean it, okay?"

He blinked, his throat still fighting the tube. His eyes welled.

"Hey, hey, it's all right. Look here. You're famous, man. Which is funny, 'cause nobody knows who you are! There's lots of people waiting to talk to you. All kinds of reporters, calling day after day to see if you're awake. Wanting to know where you were heading 'fore you smacked into those trees!"

Her chuckle was as warm as a quilt, and he was desperate for her to put him back under. Instead, she stepped to the Formica bedside stand, then displayed for him the remains of the aeronautical map: stained by watermark, its shape chewed away like a moth-eaten fabric. He recognized the hatches, and the dials of yellow, purple, green: Tupelo Regional.

"How 'bout that?" she said. "Like a treasure map, am I right?"

He considered the little blank spot of his birth, a green void just outside the printed word *Pitchlynn*. He remembered, for the thousandth time, his final night on the farm. How the cloud-veiled moon had shone through glimmer-glass windows. How his mother had awakened him with her hand over his mouth. She'd demanded his silence while rushing him out of the cabin, before they sprinted down the dirt farm road and into the cab of Gabe's waiting pickup truck. Her frantic reassurances as they sped over gravel, then asphalt. Sonny remembered Gabe driving them off the farm, not a word, and he remembered wanting so badly to ask about the mules: What would happen to them? What were the secrets Gabe told to make them calm?

When they reached the train depot in Clarksdale, the three had stood silent beside the pickup truck. Sonny watched Syl and Gabe stare at each other. A minute or so later, she had turned away, not even offering her thanks. She'd snatched Sonny's hand back up and had run them through the station and to the platform. Northward, to Chicago.

He recalled, again and again, how the two had then traveled for what seemed like days: drowsed, starving, stopping every little bit, every small-town depot rousing him into the ripe smell of his mother, to the reek of her arms over him, unwashed. Upward, fleeing Hare and home, and flying through space—though Sonny had never understood why. He'd been given no map to follow. What of his clothes, his school? His arrowheads and toys? What of the soap figurines, and his squad of tin soldiers? His View-Master viewer? All were left behind. The only totem he retained was the Indian Head knife in his pocket.

He had turned this night over nearly every night since he left it. Details coming and gone. Questions formed, or answered, or lost.

No matter. The last time he saw his daddy was forever the driving force, the through line: Hare had been passed out cold in the chair, the one that his great-grandfather had built. The man had been splayed out like death, only snoring, Sonny believed. He believes. His mama had dragged him right past, over those creaky porch boards. Hare hadn't so much as twitched, stone-drunk as he was.

The old man was innocent. Scout's honor.

The Plane Man hated to think of all the wasted energy, time, attention, breath, disgrace. His own time line, even, the decades of his life kept in suspension. He'd been sick, sort of. Forever stuck, until the buildup to the trial had provided a shot, a starter pistol fired in order to hurtle him into some . . . *relevance?* . . . Some *magnitude?* . . . Some . . .

He'd been lured by a Big Fix, and had flown down to confess: on the night of Gabe's death, Hare had been near-comatose, dead drunk. And Gabe? Gabe was with him and Sylvia, his mother, at the station. This truth was, and always had been, the only thing he could tell.

The nurse aide dabbed his cheeks with a tissue. "Just gotta will your body back to action, right? I believe you can do it. So do it now." She picked up his chart and notated her round. "Want me to turn the teevee on before I go?"

He blinked.

She lifted the remote and clicked it. "I guess you don't care what you watch, so I'm just gonna leave it goin'. Keep you company, all right?" She wrapped his limp fingers around the call button handle. "Now, don't fret, pet. Think positive. Start with tiny good thoughts. Good little tiny thoughts. Doable things. Looking-forward-to type of things. And blessings, okay?"

He dozed in and out of the white light, his lips daubing the tube. The afternoon newscast promoted ongoing updates of his very situation, something he could tell was just that, an update, versus any pressing or late-breaking news. (How long had he been in the hospital, anyway?) And Eddie, Ed, Sonny, Hobbs, now the Plane Man, was astounded to see the still photography of the crash: a slim white fuselage that hung like a piñata in the pines. A blink of B-roll that captured a sheriff and volunteers milling below the trees.

The follow-up news teaser focused on a legion of first responders amid a downtown Jackson crowd. Onlookers wept as paramedics hoisted body bags onto gurneys.

## NEW INFORMATION AT SIX ABOUT THE HARE HOBBS MASSACRE. WHAT WENT WRONG, AND WHY.

For so long he had drafted it: the book-close of his return. As if he could script himself back in time. Before the ceaseless Chicago schoolyard taunts over his Mississippi drawl, when his back-asswardness was a conduit for bullying at school (a relentless affair that had only tapered with the onset of free weights, and bulk, and football); before the girls he could never connect with there, or the few women with whom he'd sputtered out later on; before the growth of his menial labor into paper-based work, or the abandonment of paper-based process for a stock computer terminal. Before the loss of Wallis Farm defined the lack in himself.

Only . . . the crash. The crash had prompted the recovery of a new, earlier truth. As if born again, and for the first time in memory, he now recalled a distant afternoon *before* the night of the chair. A string of afternoons, even. Times spent hiking deep into the gut of the Wallis Farm land with his father. Little-bitty-type days, when the two of them would go hunting arrowheads:

"Go ahead and squint a bit," his daddy had suggested. "Squint, and you can almost see 'em." Hare smiled as the boy tried to fashion his eyes the right way. "That's right," his old man continued, his hand soft on Sonny's back. "Just look out over the cotton field. Or, no, better yet, turn your eyes to that tree line on the far horizon. To that old growth, way back there, the big tree line. And *then* squint."

Sonny had done so. In the haze of bright light between open and closed eyes, the boy had believed he could see them, far in the distance, across the field. In the splinters of shadows and the blurred light flickers through his lashes, they were alive.

"Yeah." Hare spoke softly. "Before all this farm mess, they was here. Ever'where. Before these fields was clear-cut and planted. Before the land turned to profit, and the people to slaves. Chickasaw and them was like a whole other planet before our family was settled, that's for sure."

The boy had then held open his palm full of arrowheads. "Is that why there's so many?"

Hare nodded. "They was clans all over creation. Chickasaw, Choctaw, or Creek or whatever. I tell you, Sonny, if you was to have flown up above us, flown all around this state, this South, you would have seen forest, and mound, and people all through here, moving. Tribes. Thousands and thousands, maybe more. Cities-like in some places, while camplike in others. Wouldn't look like no quilt of cleared fields. There weren't no tenant shacks, or mansions. No mules or combines, industrial crop."

"What'd they do then?" the boy asked, his eyes squinting against the far horizon of trees. "How'd they go about?"

"I don't know much, Sonny. Just what my daddy and mamaw told me."

"They *saw* 'em?"

"Daddy's daddy did, for sure. Hell, I guess one of your great-grams was even a Chickasaw woman. Bird Clan!"

"What?"

"Don't you dare say nothin'. Nobody likes to tell that kind of thing." Hare had lingered in silence long enough to make his point, then mussed the child's hair. "But it's almost like we can still touch 'em. Bird Clan, Sonny. I guess my grandparents, or maybe great-grands, was the last folks to live in the same space as these others."

Sonny had squinted harder as he gazed into the tree line.

HE SQUINTED against the fluorescent hospital light, and to the close of his story: a migration of sorts, a lovely death. A deliverance. He had been removed from the land, and for decades had dreamed of being returned to it, with his father.

Only, Sonny's return was never about Hare Hobbs at all. He could see this now. The relocation? The return? The compulsive strands of narrative: about a chair, or as carved into the handle of an Indian Head pocketknife?

It was a hallucination, an appropriation at best.

There were facts to be had, and perhaps he could start with these. He believed, and had perhaps read, that the Indians had been seasonal. Migratory. A synthesis of homeplace and roaming. He had read this along the way, perhaps, but then discarded it when the narrative didn't suit him. Their kinship ties? In some cases, they'd been mutable—and quite normal. The families were fixed, yet they flowed, their leaving in full embrace with coming home. (Sonny decided again to forget their removal, a fact that made things way too messy.) He had learned this someplace, likely in those library texts. Yet he'd discarded the things that didn't adapt to his story.

But now? The truth of that last night? The chair? None of it mattered. It had never mattered at all.

*All that goddamned time*, he thought. *That lost yardage.*

Besides, Hare was guilty enough. He was not worth saving. Never had been.

*I am going to let go now*, Sonny thought, though he did not understand exactly what letting go meant. To drift? To fall? To go straight home to his mother and forget this place? To re-immerse with her into rerun cable flicks on Sundays? Or to instead put his body in the bucket seat of a rental sedan, setting out to cruise the Mississippi hills for lost siblings? To . . .

Funnily enough, he might return himself to an old, crumpled-up daydream of coaching peewee football in Chicago.

Because there were so many little things to live out. The biggest little things imaginable. A sheer winter hike to the local chain grocery. Bacon smoke. A baseball game.

At the end, it was Sonny's *inability* to save Hare that had proved the greatest reward of his efforts. The gift of his burden was the failure of his cause.

*I am letting go now.*

He drifted then, he fell. He soared into the white light, and the past molted away. His body seized up and his breath gusted out, and Sonny was the one who was saved.

# LIFE RAFT

# 1

A revolution. A homecoming. A devastation by love.

For Colleen and Derby, it was as if the past had been obliterated by baby Sarah's yawn, while the future unfolded on Junior's
cat-sized sighs. The twins were at once an existential backflip and real-
world front somersault. The debut parents felt godlike yet humbled,
infinite yet insignificant . . .

They were elated. Astonished. And goodness gracious, *concerned*:
first-timer, clichéd, new-parent-concerned. When the twins dropped a
little weight, Colleen's response was to feed them when they cried, and
to wake and feed them when they didn't. The infants responded with
spit-up and drool, and smiles, sort of. The pair mushed their faces up
against her very sore breasts, and then slept for no more than a hyphen.
Both Junior and baby Sarah also soiled themselves relentlessly (which
Colleen was told was a "good thing"). They bawled like beasts. They
loomed like terrorists, in that they drove Derby and Colleen away from
security or self-confidence, and into the truth of their inadequacy to
protect. With the slightest rasp or sneeze, the pediatrician was called,
as were nurses-on-call, as were parent-friends, and semi-friends, and
JP, and Colleen's parents, and . . .

On the family's fourth day home from the hospital, having reached
a summit of waked exhaustion, Colleen barked at Derby to please
dear god keep the well-wishers away from the house! (Except Deana,
of course.)

Praise be, though, at that time the couple's awe blanked their help-
lessness. Among other things, the twins provided them a source of
great entertainment. The parents could pull Junior's clef-bowed legs as

straight as bars, watch those rubbery little limbs bow right back up . . . and laugh into tears on the living room carpet. Because Sarah somehow favored the actor Joe Pesci, they took turns calling up the Yankee *paisan*'s movie quotes while ventriloquizing the infant. They took photo after photo after photo.

During one of Derby's endless runs between convenient store and country market, in-town grocery, Walmart, or Walgreens, he picked up the Pitchlynn daily *Cardinal*, and saw the write-up: a photo of the twins in their knit hospital caps, pink for Sarah and blue for Junior, alongside a stand-alone pic of the "former Strawberry Maiden" in her dress greens. He presented it to Colleen with a "Guess who made the Talk of the Town?" She soaked up every printed syllable. To Derby's surprise, however, she put the clipping in a drawer instead of up on the fridge.

At some point, a producer from the NBC affiliate in Tupelo even phoned the house, asking for Colleen and citing the joyful *Cardinal* story. He told her that the station was interested in a segment on her. A vet-turned-beauty-queen-awarded-two-more-blessings type of thing.

"Actually, I don't think that'll work," she replied. "I've had my coverage, you know?"

The producer, taken aback, began to question this position, until Colleen cut him off: "But if you wanted do a little somethin' on just the twins?" she added. "Like, maybe somethin' about how special *they* are? That'd be great. We can do a picnic, or you can watch and see how they——"

It was the producer's turn to cut Colleen short. He agreed that this sounded like a fine idea, and said he looked forward to running her pitch by his assignment editor. If things went well, he and the crew would soon be out to see her——or out to see those babies, anyway.

She hung up, and looked down at the toddlers, two dollops of euphoria on a padded green play mat. Just then, Derby came in from the carport-workshop, sweated to hell. Colleen made a sour face and told him to keep his filthy hands away from everybody.

He rolled his eyes and went to wash up in the kitchen sink.

"Boy, you had better slap some Speed Stick on, too!"

"Go easy, it's blistering outside. I'm workin' on a rockin' horse, but I have to finish two."

"I don't care if you make a stable," Colleen said with a laugh. "You stink!"

Derby dried his hands on a dish towel and leaned up against the adjoining doorframe. "Did I ever tell you about the first time I saw you?"

"Oh no, not now." Colleen grinned. "Nobody wants to hear some old—"

"The thing is," Derby said, "I can't even remember. I swear I can't recall anything before this very second. Right now, you are the most beautiful woman I have ever seen."

Colleen walked over, into Derby's embrace.

"Love you, Derb," she whispered—then wriggled from his grasp. "But please go rinse."

"Enough. I gotta finish with the jigsaw. Then I'll cook us somethin', and then I guess I can—"

"Derby?"

"What?"

"Somewhere in there a nap? Please?"

"Lord, yes."

Elation, exhaustion. Beauty, and baby shit. As the afternoon closed, Derby produced the twin rocking horses, forgot the nap, and moved on to a pair of gourd rattles. He then cut a team of teddy bear footballers out of plywood, alongside bunny rabbit cheerleaders, each of which was sanded, painted, and mounted across the top of the nursery wall. He finished off the evening by assembling a pair of mobiles made of coat hangers and ping-pong balls and toy airplanes hung by fishing wire.

Colleen daydreamed about the TV segment. She engaged the twins in imaginary on-camera interviews that affirmed their first impressions: of their renowned parents, and, in particular, the blessings of such a dynamic mother. She nibbled their inchwormy fingers, pinched their rolled-dough thighs, and swooned to the whisper-thin echolalia of sounds they made when she sang to them. Her pulse lilted when their eyes strayed to follow the flares of light.

A WEEK later, with the infants having been fed and put down again, and with Derby in the shade of the carport, his jigsaw whizzing again, Colleen called the Tupelo affiliate to find out when to expect the news crew. The receptionist took her name, put her on hold, then sent her to voice mail. She spoke until the recording cut off, offering details about Sarah's new taste for her own toes—gag!—and how Junior's eyes were, like, really starting to *see*. Best of all, Colleen was pretty sure the twins could already tell who she was . . . and wasn't that, like, super-early for babies? "I swear," she went on, "these kids are really, really special."

Neither the network nor Derby would reveal that the segment was never going to happen. It had been a package deal, a nasty bid by the producer—of the same crew that had confronted Derby in the driveway—to get an on-camera interview with her husband. Nobody cared about Colleen or the twins. They only wanted to expand on the gothic stage play of Derb's childhood, of what it had been like to come up a Hobbs. The wanted new angles on the massacre, new wind to keep their ratings aloft. When Derby had refused the interview, the offer to profile his newborns was dropped.

Derby came in from the carport and wiped his brow with his T-shirt tail. Colleen glanced up from the television, announced, "Hungry."

He rolled his eyes, then pivoted toward the kitchen, en route to throw yet another fistful of hot dogs into another saucepot of water. A minute later, he drifted back into the den and walked over to the cribs.

"I think I'm gonna go back to work tomorrow," he said, and baby-talked the twins.

"Not yet, hon, okay?" she replied, her eyes still on the screen. "JP said you could take whatever time you wanted."

"Well . . . yeah. But I'm just not sure he meant it."

"Ask him. Or maybe just take him at his word. Believe me, he'll be fine for a little longer. But Derb? I am out of it. The no-sleep, nonstop? The not knowing what's normal? Christ, I worry so damned much that I'm . . . I'm consumed, babe. I'm *out*."

He leaned down and kissed her forehead. "Don't I know it. I am terrified I'll fall asleep on that scaffold!"

"This isn't about me. I'm worried about them, you know?" she motioned to the cribs. "I can't sleep. Can't relax. Can't afford to make a mistake. So I need you here, to help me figure out how to . . . I'm not sure what. Keep me from myself, maybe. Stay focused on the twins, okay?"

Derby nodded. "You're overtired. Spent, of course. I promise you'll feel okay with a little bit of rest. We both will. You ain't gonna mess anything up."

"I don't know that. You don't know that." Colleen stood and went to pick Sarah up, then held the infant to her chest. "I'm telling you, something's building. And it's already too much."

Derby reached over and caressed her arm. "I do know," he whispered. "And I'm not trying to deny that your worry makes sense. But this isn't, well . . . *that*."

He didn't need to mention the story about the Iraqi woman, as this was a lens through which he now saw her. The revelation had enabled a cop-out of sorts, something Derby could use to police her trauma, her worry, or the appropriateness of her mood.

"That's got nothin' to do with it," she said.

"It wasn't your fault."

"You're not hearing me."

"Was years ago now, babe, it——"

"You're not listening!" She clutched Sarah closer.

Veteran. Strawberry Maiden. PTSD. Mom. Small-town redneck Mississippi girl turned small-town redneck Mississippi woman. Everybody had to slap a label on you, it seemed. And once they'd done so, well, that was just who you were—whether you liked it or not. Whether the claim even fit. You became theirs, sort of. Defined and put away.

Only, Colleen knew better. She had traversed the planet, after all. Upended a regime, a country, even took aim at a religion . . . all while being globalized and conglomerized, both media fluffed and media saturated. She was one of the one percent of her countrymen, whether billionaire or academic, senator or stay-at-home, who had actually taken part in this process. Consequently, as if she were windswept by a gale of anti-culture and anti-identity, the experience had ripped Colleen from the very idea of herself.

She'd been born again. Factory-reset, pulled offline. And this removal had revealed to her—to all involved—that there was no morality, no biology, no geographic allegiance, no law. There was no 4 July or 11 September, no courthouse memorial or 4A football anthems. Truth be told, you didn't have to be, become, or believe in anything at all. You sure as hell didn't have to settle for anyone else's prejudgment.

"I loved the war, Derby. Despite everything, I loved it."

Case in point: They weren't liberators, but beasts. Not heroes, but a gang. Their Cause was never really a cause at all. Christ, even physicality had been shown to be a hoax. One instant your body was a thousandfold bundle of name, relationship, ritual, and association; the next, you were a post-blast of blood vapor and skin. (They had witnessed this ballistic transmogrification of a body, and they had made jokes about it. What else could you do?) At times, they had even turned in on themselves. The males had certainly turned on Colleen a time or more.

The only true perversion of deployment was learning that in their absence, during the very apex of their so-revered, so-called Service . . . nobody back home had missed a ball game, a rerun, or a beer.

"I'm worried," Derby said. "I know it's just the baby blues, but . . ."

The kicker was that Colleen had finally accepted all of this, the hypocritical, unmovable, stratification of home. Granted, it had taken her four, maybe five years now, with her pregnancy a sort of symbolic last stand. Yet at the end of the day she'd even accepted it with Derby, a relegation to nothing special. To a label or two, at best.

The problem was her children. She had never loved anything so much. She hadn't even been able to *conceive* of a love so torrential. And so this, then, was the rub. Colleen knew that not even this love could save them from becoming what they were predestined to become: small-town redneck Mississippi kids, who'd turn small-town redneck Mississippi done. At best, she believed, they'd work themselves up to the ranks of not quites. Not quite pretty enough, or not quite rich. Not quite smart or sophisticated, or settled in with themselves. If they left home, she knew, they'd be not quite un-southern. If they stayed here, even prospered, they'd be not quite proper South.

To stop her chin from quaking, she grinned. "This ain't the 'baby blues,' Derb. This is the rage of having zero control. My own children are the reminders that I'll fail to protect them. And that failure, *my* inevitable failure to liberate 'em—not some dime-store war story—is why I don't want you to leave us alone."

Derby leaned against the wall by the doorframe, then slid onto the floor. The silence was ticked by the pinging pot on the burner.

# 2

Susan George sat on the manicured grass, her legs cocked beneath the spread of her long skirt. Her fingers piddled absently with the petals of a lily that had loosened from the wreath. The pallor of sunlight was now and again blotted by islands of white cumulus, and continental winds cut the baked morning air.

"I wish you wouldn't make me question myself," she said to nobody.

Her eyes traced the cuts of black lettering in the gray-white headstone; she took in the peppery specks of the composite and the rough-hewn edges of the base. Though distinct in its relative newness, the stone's aesthetic dovetailed with the existing graves and monuments, tucking in among austere marker, neoclassical laurel, and weathered CSA imagery.

She thought about Dru's letter, its admission and implication. She had never discussed with anyone her own consuming guilt, nor the anger born of her belief that Dru had caused Lucy's death.

As is, everyone involved or of age had settled on the agreed-upon narrative: the girl fell, and died. *Her* girl, her daughter. Lucinda. Lucy George. It was an accident, everyone knew.

It wasn't enough. There had to be more. A resolution, or, as it happened, an implication. An accusation. For Susan George, there were no facts involved in an accident or mishap. You needed lies to make memory. Lies that helped you hold on.

Without that drama, here was life: Susan George would visit this little plot twice a year, every year. She would place lilies in a cement vase adjacent the stone, then sit and snap waxy grass blades between her fingers. There would forever be a pile of small detritus, leaves and loose bullshit gathered beside her daughter's grave. Susan George would clench this up when she left, then throw it in one of the green metal trash bins hidden within clumps of boxwood along the main drive. She would then go home and spend the rest of the day and night on her back porch, drinking. If she stayed awake long enough, she'd take a short walk over to the old Wallis Farm house, to stare up at the branches of Bel Arbre. Year after year after year. Never enough.

"I'll try one more option," she said. "One more approach on that house, in hopes of saving a relationship to that child. By the way, did you know that Dru's child was named after you?" She smiled. "How wonderful."

She reflected on this for a moment, then continued. "Failing that, I'll send Dru's letter to our attorneys. I just have to. Our tree, our town, won't be put under threat. There's still so much more work to do. To update without loss. To renew without replacement. We can . . ."

She paused to contain herself. "I won't let this town go," she repeated. "No one will take you from me."

# 3

Colleen went to Dallas once, to compete in the Southeastern Regional beauty pageant. Nearly all of Pitchlynn, from church groups to the beauty shop, Tudor's Hardware to Cothron's Filling Station, had donated to fund the Strawberry Maiden's attempt.

From the instant she had looked around the capacious hotel lobby, she knew that she wouldn't win. The contestants in Texas were women, so incredibly . . . *women*. They were checking in beside her along with their costume assistants, and hair and makeup pros, pageant coaches clad in undergarment endorsement logos, and, above all, astonishing outfits. They were clad in the stuff of couture legend. Hell, even the hotel receptionist was more sophisticated than Colleen.

This realization had bruised her, but not too deep. In the end, she felt more overjoyed than overwhelmed. The design of the massive atrium of the Hyatt Regency proved reward enough, as had the step-staggered buildings of the hotel-office complex. While on the pageant itinerary tour, she took in the Dallas Reunion Tower, a glass-walled sphere striking skyward amid the skyline, a visual victory of sorts.

She was astounded by space and architecture. Even the obstructed view of downtown from her hotel room felt like a lesson, a new lens. Though bodies came and went, and could be molded to represent any manner of things—beauty, honor, horror, loss, heroism, hedonism, whatever—these structures were transcendent. Beyond decay or interpretation, they were, she thought, her future. At least they were some unfamiliar, ascertainable version of possibility.

This wasn't some country-mouse-goes-city moment. It was a newfound attraction to perpendicularity, to the possibility of horizontal *and* vertical vision.

The concierge had told Colleen she could see Las Colinas from the observation roof, that she could even see Fort Worth. Yet moments later, standing on the upper deck of the hotel, Colleen had been most drawn to the stream of cars that cruised I-35 below. To the mute parade across the mirrored windows of the buildings beside the interstate. She watched a spectrum of vehicles lurch onto a cloverleaf like cells through veins. Watched the stratus clouds feather both in sky and on window.

In reality and in reflection, everyone was going everywhere: above, below, amid the architectural indifference. Colleen was ecstatic to exist among all of it. Was enlightened by the newfound manipulation of space. She wanted so much more of this education, anyplace she could find it, as often as she could.

"DALLAS," COLLEEN muttered to herself years later, sitting on the edge of her roof. Her legs dangled over, her feet kicked at the air. She took a large gulp of beer while scanning the north Mississippi treescape. She didn't hear the vehicle come up the long dirt drive, let alone hear the mewling of her twins inside the house.

"Hey, girl?" Susan George called up from the yard.

"And . . . my god, there is so much to consider, to . . ."

"Hey!" Susan George yelled. "Your babies are cryin'!"

Colleen stared down at her well-dressed counterpart, surprised that she hadn't even heard the vehicle pull up. She hadn't seen Susan George since the baby shower. "How's that?"

"Get down here, now, and tend to your children," Susan George ordered. "C'mon, I'll help." Her heels spiked the earth as she held the aluminum ladder. Colleen climbed down without a word, then led Susan George through the carport and kitchen door.

Inside, Colleen reached into the fridge. "Beer?" she asked.

"Thank you, no. Just a minute of your attention."

They went into the living room and sat. Colleen lifted the twins up one at a time and rocked them until they quieted. Their skin was splotchy. Their dark hair, slicked. Despite the ceiling fan at full blast and the box fan in the window, the room was ablaze.

"Make yourself comfy," Colleen said, motioning to the uphol-stered rocker.

Susan George sat, then watched Colleen lay each baby on the couch, before strapping on her nursing pillow. A moment later, her blouse unbuttoned and the babies fixed on nipples, Colleen exhaled and looked to her guest. "Sorry."

"Again, I'll just take a moment," Susan George said. She fanned her-self with her hand. "My lord, it's hot in here. I don't see how you stand it. No air?"

"It isn't that Derby can't fix HVAC. He knows how. It's just that both the compressor and exchange went out on the one we've got now. So it's a catch-22, you know? The old AC's not worth fixin', but we can't quite afford a new system. Yet."

"My word." Susan George shook her head.

"Well," Colleen said. "Tough titty."

"I see. So, let me be blunt. I'm here because I'd like you to get your man back on script."

Colleen winced as Junior tugged at her. "How's that?"

"Derby and JP are a couple of mules." Susan George smirked. "Am I right? They are stubborn and kicking. And they simply won't give up this fool's errand of a task—no matter what the outcome is to the town, to themselves, to any of it."

"I wouldn't fret too much," Colleen said. "When Derby gets into something, he *gets into* it. Sooner or later, though, no warning, he'll drop-kick a project just as quick as he picked it up. The process'll make you crazy if you know him long enough."

"I'm afraid I don't have any more time to give him." Susan George straightened up in the chair. "Your husband assured me that he would handle things. Yet he hasn't so much as called. He's fallen straight off the map."

Colleen stared at her, said nothing.

"My goodness." Susan George smirked. "He never told you? Never mentioned that he was going to work with us? Well, Colleen, if it helps, he was acting on *your* behalf far more than ours. Besides, it wasn't a big affair. No conspiracy, but rather a . . ."

Colleen looked to the ceiling fan while the woman prattled on. She then snickered to herself. "Rich man's war, poor man's fight. Same as always, huh?"

"This isn't about class," Susan George said. "It's about community, and history. And moving forward without selling out. So, please, spare me your platitudes."

"You're in my house, now. Remember that."

"I am," Susan George replied. "I'm in your house because I believe that, like me, you get the big picture. See the future, so to speak. So consider this. You get Derby back on script, and we will be forever in your service. As I told your husband, I don't care what it takes. He can call in sick. Mis-order materials, or misdirect the whole she-bang. Violate a code or three. Whatever grinds the project down. The point here is that JP doesn't have the moral right to do what he's doin', whether he's got the legal right or not. Besides, that man doesn't even *care* about the place. He's here out of sorrow, and indulgence. Petulance."

"He is."

"But for us? That house represents the future of our town. The ability to grow, to move forward. It's our—"

"Hold up," Colleen said. "What's this 'our' biz? It isn't my space. Never was."

"Which gets us to the point. It *can* be. In fact, please imagine it that way, Colleen. Imagine raising your babies on that property while living in that back bungalow. You, your children, right there in town, on that land. I beg you to think of Derby as caretaker, paid well enough, benefits and all. Picture strolling the sidewalk to Pitchlynn city schools, a child in each hand, instead of them busing out to county. Think of these little ones playin' ball, or of her taking ballet, or having their friends come over—having friends *walk* over, that is—from their own homes down the street. Down the line, think of Ole Miss or Millsaps, or wherever else they might want to go to college. Of *college*—just think. Of study abroad? Of the jobs they'll find after? You'll be endowing your babies a whole new past. As I told your husband, Colleen, we'll help y'all get there, too. Babysitting to summer camp. School recs, or what have you. Swimming lessons at the PCC. Your children certainly won't have to join the service to get by, or . . ."

Colleen rubbed one thumb in the opposite palm, as if working out a cramp. A few seconds later, she switched to the other hand, her thumb kneading ever deeper. "I am so tired of being mustered for other people's bullshit."

"Pardon?"

Colleen stared out the windows. "I mean, what really changes for *me* if you get that house back?"

"What do you want to hear, girl?" Susan George asked. "You want to be an astronaut? Too late. A debutante? The President? Ditto, too late. You want a birthright? Not gonna happen. And yes, you're correct, whether you help us or not, you may still feel . . . in service. But this isn't about you. This is about your twins. They'll sprout from either space, whether in town or out. Just like I did, or just like you. That's the only truth I know to tell." She huffed, and shook her head. "But you already get this. You're just pickin' a fight for sport. So why don't you come out with it? What do you want? Who do you really want to be?"

Colleen jabbed her thumb deeper into her palm, scraping at last into a tender, familiar pain. One that reminded her she was alive.

When she'd yanked the sow into the tree, the carcass hadn't so much as jiggled, despite the violence of her every hoist. The rip of the rope had left her hands so raw. Not marked, or scabbed, but raw and vital at the marrow.

She'd been focused that night on operation alone, from the pick-up at the meat processor, to dragging the hog over JP's lawn on a litter made of plastic tarp and ratchet strap. Even Colleen's pregnancy had been no more than a tac nav, a bullshit variable to overcome.

From the idea of the pig, to the plan, and through the breadth of execution, the action had burst with life, with promise. Colleen had felt mission critical at last. She'd been exceptional, again.

The experience had also reconfirmed her convictions, the truths she'd picked up while away. First and foremost, Colleen knew that no blossom or tree, no estate manor or land held any real value. As such, she understood that neither JP nor the LMA were any better than conscriptors: each of them, all of them, always, the same. Folks like Colleen suffered the blows of their campaigns. Always had, always would. Rich man's war, poor man's fight. Her twins would be the next ones put to service.

Still. Her target that night hadn't been JP, or Susan George. It was Derby. It had to be. The Wallis House was a quagmire, and she believed that the pig would either scare him off site altogether or radicalize him to confrontation. With his father, or the LMA, or . . . whomever he needed to move past in order to move free.

Fight, or flight, the sow would shove Derby off track. (This was, after all, how terrorism functioned. Whether hung from a rope or put on a pike, or a cross.) It would spurn his independence. He would liberate himself.

She had only compromised him. Versus an awakening or a reckoning, he'd instead followed his daddy's example: Derby threw his lot in with Susan George and the rest, and the promise of their domestic mundanity. And hell, he'd even wavered on that.

"An insurgent," Colleen stated, her babies at breast. "I can be the destroyer."

"I'm sorry, what?" Susan George asked.

Colleen's squad had learned foco theory while killing endless downtime in their barracks. Trapped between boredom and anxiety, and with small-arms pop on the periphery, they had battled insecurity care of discussions of the *Brigate Rosse*, the Red Brigades, or the ELF. In the chow line, they were emboldened by talk about the Free State of Jones County, Mississippi. About AIM and Pine Ridge and the occupation of Wounded Knee. They watched *The Battle of Algiers* in the rec tent. Streamed AQI kill vids on their smartphones in the Humvees.

Power. Procedure. All it ever came down to was land. Was people wanting, taking, or using land, and the throwaway bodies that were needed to secure it. From Sykes-Picot to Wallis Farm, federal redlines or shock and awe, Colleen and the rest of the squad had slung example after example of this history at each other, while flopped out on a rack, say, or while huddled up to smoke. One troop would tell of a wiki-borne factoid, while another cited a newswire or documentary, an op-ed or conspiracy site. No matter the source or the era, the cause was always the same: another fucking land war.

"Here's the deal," Colleen said. "You're the regime. JP's the invader. So we *gotta* have us an insurrection, right?" She grinned. "Somebody's gotta put a little squeal in the pigs."

Truth be told, Colleen had also hung the sow for herself. It was a protest. A lash out. A slap to the face of her domestic reconscription. From the moment Derby had taken the Wallis House job, she knew she'd been dragged into a fight without benefit. A battle based on everyone's development but her own.

Susan George stood up to leave. "As I said, I can do without the platitudes. Now, listen, *please*. This is the last time I'll offer."

Colleen nodded her understanding. "Then I guess you should get back to Pitchlynn."

Susan George sighed, then gazed over at the infants. "They're beautiful. Just like their mama. But Colleen, I'd say it's best if you hide your drinkin'. Better not let anyone catch you up on that roof with your twins left alone in this heat. Word would spread like fire that you're an unfit mother." She tapped on the crib. "Someone'll call CPS. They will steal your children away."

# 4

The windows of Wallis House were removed. The empty sashes had been tacked over with plastic sheeting that pulsed ghostlike in the breeze and snapped like pennant flags at a car lot. The exterior paint had been stripped from the substrate, and scaffolding crawled up the walls. To an extent, the home now resembled one of those mansions-turned-scabs back in Chicago. Only in this case, wind depending, the putrid scent of the pig wafted well beyond the property, into the streets.

On the back lawn, JP and Derby worked beneath a pair of maroon tailgate tents, heat-stripping the old window frames, the muntin and casement, metal turnbuckles and hand cranks, while ever-mindful not to crack the leaden glass. Their faces bore sweated galaxies of paint fleck and splinter, and their eyes were hatched red behind plastic safety glasses. The canvas drop cloth they stepped on was littered with worm-like strips of old paint. Their voices muffled by resp masks, they still cut up quite a bit, generally at the expense of one another.

Though their formal relationship remained employer-employee, truth be told they were partners, and they both knew it. JP took the lead on capital and contract (and again, on the caustic visual strategy of this project). Derby set the pace for how the work was to be executed, illustrating and educating about the craft-based processes employed.

Day after hour at the back of the house, the sun blazing onto the maroon tent fabric above them like a diffuse, bloodlike ball. They drank Gatorade and water, and dragged themselves to the meat 'n' three counter at Cothron's Filling Station for lunch, or, more frequently, they went home for the break (JP to dote on Lucinda; Derby to take in the twins), never gone long enough for work-weariness to set in . . .

before coming back to slog through the hellish afternoons. Gatorade and water, Gatorade and water.

They were heat-stripping the last of the wooden window frames when a tan SUV pulled around the back drive and parked. Susan George stepped out, as did a man in a khaki poplin suit, and a cop.

"I don't know who you continue to think you are," she barked. "But I know who *I* am, as does this town. And as of eight o'clock this morning, the LMA and Historic Pres District have filed for statutory authority of this house—alongside every other damn injunction my attorney here could file."

The man in the suit issued JP a thick envelope. "It's all inside. Why don't you come on by my office to discuss? Or send representation. Or both."

JP flung the envelope on the workbench. "Sure thing," he said, wiping the grit from his neck. He motioned as if to resume work.

Susan George threw her finger in his face. "Listen here. You may be able to shove yourself into any neighborhood in Chicago, anyplace just black enough to gobble up yet white enough to flip. But this house won't be made into your spite-born spectacle. You are to desist, immediately." She gauged the blizzard of paint and wood scrap, likewise the plastic-covered windows and the scraped house itself. "My lord. Don't touch anything else."

Susan George marched toward the front of the house, calling her men to follow suit. The cop tromped off on command, though the lawyer lingered for a moment.

"JP," he said calmly. "I don't want you to take this as any sort of threat, but this thing can turn real ugly, real fast. I knew your wife as a kid, and . . ." He held a hand out to try and calm JP's glare. "Please. Her parents were good people, which is why I hope you'll hear me out." He went on to detail the letter from Dru, the notion and threat of her compromised capacity, and how that would impact any judicial proceeding, let alone mark his wife's memory, both to the town and to Lucy, when the child got old enough to wonder about it.

"Are you implying that my wife was too sick to have a will?" JP said. "Or that I took advantage of her state?"

"A judge will determine that. I'm only telling you this out of courtesy. To Dru."

JP scoffed and turned away. "Derby? A favor?"

"Okay," Derby answered.

"Show these people off of my property?"

After Derby nodded his confirmation, JP walked off, past willow and oak, cedar and magnolia, then stepped inside his bungalow and snapped the dead bolt. He drew the curtains, kicked off his boots, grabbed a beer, and stretched out the couch.

The sitter had taken Lucy for toddler play at the local Y, so the silence was marked only by the humming refrigerator coils and the kick-on of central air. JP's mind reeled so fast it exhausted him. He put the beer on a coffee table and shut his eyes for a moment. He heard the smack of the SUV doors before the car pulled out of the drive. He drifted.

His catnap was broken by the distant rev of a power tool. He took in the ribbons of sunlight through the part in the curtains, and he smiled. Sitting upright, he listened to the whine of the small engine and tried to match its identity. A mower? Weed Eater?

It was a gas-powered pole pruner. JP bolted up and out the door, screaming for Derby to stop. Rounding the front corner of Wallis House, he saw the massed magnolia branch smack the walkway. From atop the adjacent ladder, Derby killed the pruner motor and made his way down.

"Sorry, JP. The cop ordered me to—"

"Bullshit. Nobody forced you. They can't."

"But what did you want me to do?" Derby asked. "Or please, better yet, what are *you* doing? Why are you trying to—"

"Like I told you, this isn't about me. And all you had to do was let them live with this. See it. Breathe it. Let them stew in their own rot. But you just couldn't. You just couldn't help but help them. Could you?" He turned back toward the bungalow. "It's like you're on command. Installed, and in their service. So pack your gear. You're done."

"Huh-uh, no. Hold up." Derby marched behind JP, peppering him with requests to reconsider, to understand.

"You're done," JP repeated, then stepped inside and shut the door.

Derby loitered for a moment, expecting a chance to talk it out as the adrenaline ebbed. Didn't matter, didn't happen. So he walked back to his truck, grabbed a square-point shovel and a blue plastic tarp. He spread the latter out beside the carcass and started scooping. Somehow, he believed this was the right thing to do.

Working the sow with the shovel, black flies nettling his skin, Derby cursed the bullshit notion of right and wrong anyway, then drove deep into the country to dump the body.

# 5

*D*amp *black cotton. Buttery croquettes and raw shrimp in a crystal bowl on crushed ice. This is the last memory you left me of her.*

*Do you recall what you asked me, Susan George? After the funeral, before I was sent off to school? Before I began cutting my home my family my state out of myself, gutting myself from the shame? Can you remember?*

*You and I stood amidst all of them: the LMA, and the folks of note, all gathered in your dining room. I wore black fabric. The window light lacquered your long oak table. Folks had brought crystal and porcelain bowls of shrimp on ice and croquette and fruit salad and crackers. Oyster crackers and all manner of whiskey.*

*"Couldn't you have saved her?" you whispered to me, your fingers like talons on my arms.*

*My shoulders and back stuck to damp black cotton. I had wandered so long in the heat outside, bawling behind the house. Praying to see her, to be allowed to see her one last time. Bawling and sifting as the fact faded to memory. Even then I tried to understand how she fell. I was just a girl. What had I done? What was I capable of?*

*"Did you even try?" you demanded, your nails carving crescents into my shoulder. "Did you even want to?" The cotton stuck to skin. My bangs slick against my forehead. When I didn't answer you told me I was a mess and to go clean myself up. You turned away and ordered someone to refresh the veined shrimp.*

*White skin blotched red. Engraved. I am writing in circles in the grey winter light. The gust of dry heat falls from ceiling vent. Snow gently thumps on the windows. My child: nursing, taking my nourishment, my memory, my lie. Save save save: I am not well after all.*

*Oh but remember taking Lucy and me to the Gulf that first time, Susan George? Our "History Trip," you called it? Even now: in frozen Chicago I still remember you cruising the two of us on Highway 90, by the coast. <u>We</u> remember, as she is right here with me. Lucy and I were what? Nine? Like twins, like sisters: riding along and staring at the water. The two of us in the back seat our bare legs stuck to seat vinyl. The car windows rolled down the hot salty gusts. Astonished by the sea birds to the right. Cruising just over the water, the steel-blue-brown-green-water.*

*Only, you made us look <u>away</u> from the shore, and to the houses: "Now look at that one, girls. A beauty. Girls? Pay attention." You made us look at the houses, so pillared and colossal. You educated us about spiral double front stairways. Ionic column or Creole porches. You stopped the car to order our attention away from the salt on skin, from the pelican dives. You ripped our fascination from the winglike double-rigs of shrimp boats, and to the houses, the monuments of power on earth. "Land Markers" you called them, prepping us for the family take: the Pitchlynn CC and the tracts of development, the commercial in-town holdings. My very own house: a candidate for development to come.*

*How much do we even own? How much is enough and what have we done to get it? To keep it? Could it really be that the land was all that mattered to you? You said it was the birthright we'd been given. The earth that made us Wallises.*

*I lost track of what is important. Sitting in Chicago, the fat snowflakes against the window, the patting of audible fact: Lucy and I try to remember. We are lost to the process.*

*Do you always dress the body? Wipe it clean? Right the neck? Reposition patella and hip? Or did you just leave her on display, to make a point? Tell me: is the sewn skin covered? I am asking you now since you kept me from seeing her. Do you ever question this: shutting me out? The sending away? Do you question the effect on me, or the rift that arose within my family? Tell me: do you display cracked teeth or torn lips? What shade of wax was puttied into her forehead? Please tell me how you tended to our pulped, broken Lucy?*

*No more revisions: I am furious with you. I am furious that I could not see her or say goodbye. Despite the child at my breast I remain so enraged. You cut me you cored me you left me in loop: suspended: she and I are still in the tree. We still sit together, our legs dangling from the branch. And then: a flinch of time. A nothing touch, so goddamn quick. Wasn't it? A little shove, I,*

*I watch her fall: now so slow, until her head hits the lower limb. Her neck cracks backwards. Eyes open. Shard teeth.*

*Susan George I have saved: my god I have amended. I have cut clean through to my spine to find facts. Still: she is here again, now. Have I not done enough?*

*I have not. So I am coming to you with my final amend: I will bring you my daughter. We will reconstruct without lies. The shame the love, the brutality of it all: for your Lucy George, and for my girl, named Lucinda.*


*For you for all of us,*
*Dru*

# 6

The pine panel walls of Colleen's living room gave off a buttery glaze from the sun. Deana's daughters—Ruby, three, and Emma, five—darted in and out of the room, ever involved with a proliferation of strewn toys. Her son, Forrest, was out "runnin' chores" with his daddy, meaning that the two were holed up in some smudgy BBQ joint, watching SEC football analysis and devouring pulled pork.

"I just can't get over these babies." Deana beamed. "I wanna eat y'all up!"

Colleen sat on the couch, the nursing pillow around her waist. She winced as Derby Jr. and Sara nursed.

"Sore?" Deana asked.

"Oh my f'in' god." Colleen's eyes welled just to acknowledge the pain. "I'm a failure."

Deana knelt down to examine, putting a hand on Colleen's shoulder as she peered close to the breast. "No wonder! They're not latchin' right! They're gettin' ahold of it, sort of, but they're just *off*. Look here." As if examining an under-sink leak, she guided her hand down to Junior's chin, using one finger to pull it down. The result was a more fully open mouth, which accepted the whole of Colleen's nipple.

"Better?" Deana asked.

"Maybe? I think?" Colleen replied. "But still. *Ouch*."

"I know it, girl. I remember. But it's not about failing, okay? It's just about knowing what to do. Give it a couple more minutes, and when they're done we'll fix you up. Meanwhile, I just want to stare at this scene. You're like a painting or somethin'. All sunlight and twins, hallelujah!"

A decent breeze coasted through the open windows. The room was a soundscape of suckles, of ice splitting in tea, and of the small brass ball chain clacking the globe light of the ceiling fan. Within minutes, Colleen draped Sarah on the towel over her shoulder, while Junior continued to nurse. Deana got up and grabbed a second towel, softly removed the boy, baby-talking him about his pudginess, and laid him across her own chest and shoulder. The women couldn't help but giggle while each one burped a baby, rag-towels draped over their shoulders, back pats in unison.

"Thanks, Dean," Colleen said. "Derby told me I should just lay one down while I take care of the other."

"Well, that's just silly. Did you tell him that was silly? That whoever was lyin' on their back was gonna get fluxed?"

"I did——but using different words! Anyhow, I figure it's best just to let one keep feeding while I burp the other, you know?"

Sarah let out a hatchling's worth of gas. "Did I just hear a dry burp?" Colleen asked, looking to the towel. "Yes. A gift from my sweet girl!"

Junior, however, soiled both the towel and Deana's shoulder. The beautician shrugged, stood up, and put him down in his crib. She cooed and covered him, then cleaned herself off.

Colleen began to fasten her blouse, wincing with every button.

"Whoa, hold up," Deana said. "You've gotta leave 'em out for a second. Those whales must surface!" She reached over and swatted Colleen's hands from the shirt, then unfastened a button. "You open the rest."

Colleen did so, exposing her swollen breasts to the breeze. Though her nipples felt shredded, the air was, somehow, gentle.

"Do this every time you feed at home," Deana said.

"As in, *always*?" Colleen replied.

"They'll get better after a few days. You'll see. Oh, and use your own milk. It's the best thing there is for the rawness."

"Like, get it from . . ." Colleen motioned to her breasts.

Deana giggled. "Where *else* are you gonna get it?" She reached out a cupped hand as a gesture of encouragement. Colleen stared at her, then grasped herself, lightly kneading her own breast and nipple, her jaw clenched against the pain.

"There you go," Deana said. "Just get some milk out, a little bit. Rub it on there."

Colleen did, her hands trembling.

"It'll get better," Deana said. "And if Derby gives you any 'cover yourself' man-bullshit, then shut him up or send him to me."

Colleen nodded again. She focused on the sound of the girls playing in the other room, and on the sunlight, and the hint of Deana's cinnamon gum.

"Dean?" she asked. "Hey, Dean?"

"Yup?"

"What say you and me load the kids up and get the hell out of Pitchlynn?"

Deana scoffed at the question, though she grinned. Seconds later, they heard Derby's truck barrel into the carport.

"I mean it," Colleen said. "Dean?"

Deana patted Colleen's knee. They heard the kitchen door open and Derby's work boots pound the linoleum.

# 7

She gunned the remote in search of anything of value: travel, leisure, or local gossip. (And, yes, though she knew better she spent
the most time taking in that Tupelo affiliate, looking for any mention of an upcoming segment about twin newborns.) All she saw was
another Hare Hobbs package, recycled B-roll with at best a trace of
new, local info.

Derby was outside, again, avoiding everything, again . . . save the
string of endless projects on behalf of the twins. Colleen turned up the
television volume, to try and deprive him of this escape.

The so-called "Hare Hobbs Massacre" had inspired a brief spray of
national network segments (average two minutes one second). A voy-
euristic American peek at the South, the event provided the nation both
reassurance and a reminder that caste and cultural stereotype remained
firmly locked in place: us, them. Next.

Far more than any export, however, the shoot-out itself (one minute
twenty-two seconds real time) was bespoken for local news. Though
the story had come and gone within a wink of national attention, the
narrative and its tangents would color the state for a generation.

Colleen clicked through the coverage day after day, a de facto col-
lage of security cam footage, news crew, and phone clips. Time and
again, she watched the Glock poke Doc's chest, while Hare's lips
engaged in what appeared to be questioning. She saw the young guard
stare back at her father-in-law, saying nothing, and without the need
to respond.

*The guard wasn't even scared.* She recognized the adrenaline of Doc's
related, real-time trauma. His hand was clapped at the side of his neck,

the blood flowing between his fingers. Yet he was collected. He was at one with the exceptionalism of the moment.

Though the Hobbs children would not attend their father's state-paid funeral—itself a flash point of protest and media, though by relative measures a fizzle—care of legal proxies they closed out the old man's physical holdings, acceded to the reclamation of his estate by the state, and the unceremonious decommission of his Platz. Without a single in-person meeting, they took up an offer of service from an upstart, profile-hungry Pitchlynn attorney, who would help them draft a statement of remorse and sorrow, editing out tones of guilt (or legal culpability); for a defined time, per the attorney's suggestion, they even offered to meet privately with any victim of Hare's crimes. To assist? To listen? To speak? To confess? Neither Derby nor Winnie would ever be sure of the function, though in the end it wouldn't matter. Nobody took them up on it.

Yet before then, there, *now*, for Colleen, the only thing to consider were clips. They were a puzzle, a fixation. A triptych of violence, at once intimate, pop spectacle, and removed from time or place. She could consider its profundity on these terms. She was desperate to be moved by it.

So she watched, and watched, with the Bresties' Nursing Pillow for Twins around her waist. (Deana had christened it the "Life Raft," a name Colleen did *not* find affirming.) At some point, she spotted the guard's wedding band, and wondered if his wife had been in on the attack, or if the man had abandoned her interests to his own. Or hell, Colleen thought, maybe his wife had already up and left him.

The twins nursed in unison, their bulged bodies wrapped in mock–football jumpers. The zippered sound of the hacksaw rose from the workspace set up in the backyard. Derby was cutting pipe length for a set of monkey bars. He'd first mentioned the project while they were in bed that morning, his body still scented by the shellac from the pull-wagon he'd finished the night before. Despite her appeal that he spend more time with the babies, or, better, with *her*, he had instead started cutting the pipe that morning. She knew he'd be up well past midnight, again.

Since being fired Derby had, as always, sedated himself with task after task: mundane and profound, practical and ridiculous. A wire-hanger mobile now hung for *each* baby, and he'd built new cribs to go underneath each mobile. A locomotive and boxcars had been jigsawed out of plywood. A tire swing now swayed, as did a rope swing, just in case. He'd made a soccer goal, a beanbag toss, and a pair of miniature cane fishing poles.

"We get the work done now so we don't have to later," he kept saying. "I don't ever want my kids to want."

*Monkey bars for twins who can't even crawl*, Colleen thought.

Her husband all but trotted in and out of the house, back, forth, his hands fouled by grease and blister, pausing only to give Colleen a cheek-peck as she sat in the Life Raft, or to fix her tuna fish sandwiches, or grilled cheeses, or, for some reason, my goodness, her demand for hot dog after hot dog, and, perhaps, to pick up and swaddle the twins.

Smiling, smiling, Derby Friar. Good ole boy, the best ole boy. To his credit, he was quick to launder the soiled nursing pillow, and the soiled towels, and the soiled fucking everything. He took the trash out without prompt, and did the dishes before she'd had a chance to digest the meal (a.k.a. hot dogs). If you gave him a job, then the job would get done. The catch, of course, was that he had to be jobbing. He was fidgety when talking, or sitting, or touching. When Colleen dozed off, or turned on the television, Derby bolted for the carport-workshop, not a word.

He cooked, he cleaned, he built, he rebuilt. He went shopping, he dropped off, he picked up, he returned.

Late one afternoon he stopped long enough to answer the phone, his mood primed to thrash yet another insistent reporter. Colleen sat on the couch listening, as he had instead issued a series of grunt-like responses: "Uh-huh," "Yeah," "Yeah," "Okay," then hung up.

"It was Winnie," he announced. "I guess we . . . we're gonna get together, soon." For the first time in some time, he beamed. He even loitered for a sec, before darting back out to the workshop.

\* \* \*

GROOVING HACKSAW into metal, the sun nearly dipped, Derby pictured the scene: monkey bars in the yard behind the house, catching the web of afternoon shade cast through the cluster of pink crepe myrtle. He knew that some years later there would be a deep impression of dead grass and disuse; he foresaw the dust-thin rust on the painted metal bars, and the wistful day he'd have to dismantle the unit, the twins having long since moved on. He smiled at this coming history.

Before that, however, before he and Colleen knew it, they'd be staring out the window as Junior and Sarah invaded the structure, laughing and shrieking and falling off, crying. He figured one twin would prefer the swing, perhaps to sit and ponder, while the other would make chin-ups and build muscle. In fact, he *knew* this to be true. He would *make it* so. He even pictured their cousin Ladybug tempting the twins off of the monkey bars, so she could teach them to play football.

\* \* \*

WHEN THE hacksaw ceased, Colleen took advantage of the silence. "Hungry!" she yelled out, then whispered to the twins, "I know we're not really that hungry. But how else can we get Daddy's attention? If we don't catch him now, he'll start in to welding. Then we won't see him for hours. And twilight's already coming on." She called for him again, to no avail. "By the way," she said to Sarah, " 'welding joins pieces of metal by the use of heat, pressure, or both.' Did you know that?"

This description was, verbatim, that provided by the American Federation of State, County, and Municipal Employees (AFSCME). Colleen cited another passage to Junior: " 'Brazing or soldering involves a filler metal or alloy'—don't forget."

A year or so back, she'd helped Derby study for his welding qualification, the first qualification he wanted to master before pursuing a contractor's license. In preparation for the exam, he'd bought a series of damned expensive training manuals. After reading each section,

he'd ask her to quiz him. They had drilled every night for weeks, sac-
rificing dinner, date, and intimacy (though to be fair the process was
somewhat intimate, in that it was shared). All said and done, she knew
the text as well as he did. Though the tedium of his dreams could be
grueling, Colleen had clipped her complaint, fighting off boredom,
hope, and her own budding interests in favor of the promise of his
advancement. Alongside the challenge of the test itself, she knew he
could take his skill set anywhere. Set up shop all across the country, if
not beyond its borders.

"What's up, babe?" he asked through the open windows.

"Hungry," she repeated.

He had never even taken the welding exam. Satisfied with passing
the practice tests, he instead moved on to other projects—namely, to
working with JP. For all his good ole boy stability, Derby Friar was also
a man forged by abandonment. As was applied to a new trade or skill
set, or even to the breaking-in of 501 jeans, he committed to things in
full, stuck with a vision for a while . . . then pivoted sideways, toward a
new, lateral vision.

It had taken Colleen a while to understand that he wasn't bored or
inattentive. Rather, Derby was at his core riven by some broken legacy
of tradesmanship, a vague, craftsman's ideal of his grandfather's that he
was desperate to recover, and which would divorce him from his own
father's past. A generational skip, she supposed. A patch.

"Okay, hot dog," he said through the window screen. "But this time
I'm using the grill, to char mine beyond recognition. I am so sick of
tube steak."

She rolled her eyes, so he turned away, frustrated. "Proper venti-
lation," Colleen whispered to the twins. "Oxygen mixture, acetylene
safety information. Can you believe I still remember that stuff? What
a waste."

She sighed, and her breath hit Junior's neck. When he wriggled in
response, Colleen blew on him again. Once more, he wiggled—only
this time he smiled. His eyes scrunched up just like Derb's.

She had just given Junior his first-ever tickle. She was elated.
Astonished. Obliterated by joy. And she knew that there was only one

other person on the planet, and that there would only ever *be* one other person on the planet, who would fully immerse in this significance with her.

"Derb!" she called out.

"Two seconds, babe," he called back, exasperated.

"Derby!" she called louder, looking to the bloodlike, crepuscular evening. She fumbled with the thick pillow that held the babies as if on a tray. "Derb, check this out!"

He turned the grill tank on, then stomped back over to the window and snapped at her. "*What?*"

Colleen stared back at him.

"What?" he groused again.

"Nothin'. Just, nothin'."

He held her gaze for a second, then swiveled back to his task.

"Minimum of twenty feet between tank and project," she muttered, and positioned the twins back to nursing. "Above all, you have to clean the lines. Have to check and inspect them before every single use. Must make sure the lines are . . ."

She looked through the window and saw Derby's posture sag, and knew that he already regretted barking at her. His hands on his hips, he stared down at his chest. Took a deep breath, coughed, then waved off the propane fumes. He turned the grill ignitor, *click click click click . . .*

"DERB, BABY, PLEA—"

*Whomp!* The explosion sucked the scream from her throat. Colleen smothered the children as the windowpanes shattered into the room, her body absorbing the shards and splinters. The heat of the blast seared the back of her neck.

Colleen didn't lift her head for several minutes. Rather, she breathed in the scent of her babies, who were scrunched into the soft folds of her breasts and tummy, bawling.

Emergency crews soon arrived on scene. Paramedics took the children—all but yanking the infants from Colleen—and rushed the whole family to County. In response to the EMT's questions, Colleen offered only name, rank, DOB, branch of service.

# 8

A couple of months after Dru walked onto Chicago's Dan Ryan Expressway, producing a violence akin to that which mangles the strays on county road Mississippi, the Labrador and pit bull mixes, bait dogs and/or gun-shy runts, their rubbery tongues and dangled teats . . . or, perhaps more appropriately, after Dru was crushed like the armadillos that now litter these same Deep South blacktops, like the despised and out-of-place vermin that only recently arrived-in-region (so say the old men in Tudor's Hardware, on the square), nine-banded immigrants from Texas that have decimated the quail population (the old men say you can try to bring a covey of Wisconsin bobwhite or gambel or Georgia giants, but they'll guarantee you not one bird will last a generation; heck, nobody has seen decent quail coveys since way back on the old Wallis Farm), scaly, scuted pests that have burrowed up the farmland, boring holes into field and meadow, holes the perfect size for snapping a horse's metacarpal, holes so perfect as to cripple the handful of for-show-only mules that still roam on leisured legacy farmland, yes, after Dru was killed just like *that*, like some dumb *thing*, some regional liaison of snuff, well, JP had decided to give her away.

Sitting on the hardwood floor of the empty house in Pitchlynn, unloading box after box of her clothes, his infant stretched out on the padded play mat beside him, he'd decided it was time: to consider Dru's clothes, and to remember their drape; to recall the mood and season of each item as she had worn it; to reaffirm (or reimagine) any and all related memory; and to plunge into near-panic over what to save for himself, and more so what to save for Lucy. A Hermès scarf? That pair of red handmade cowboy boots? Perhaps Dru's father's old oversized, masculine Timex? Yes, these token items were to be saved for the child. The rest was to be stuffed into white plastic garbage bags. JP would then take them, her, *Dru*, to the Goodwill. Goodbye.

Only, damn it all, there wasn't a Goodwill in Pitchlynn. There was a Salvation Army, and a place called Annie's Re-Do. JP scouted both a few times, to gauge which outlet would be the best final resting place.

The Salvation Army staff was friendly and dependency-recovered and had no shortage of donations from individuals and, as was evident by the crest-marked passenger vans in the parking lot, protestant churches. JP had therefore decided on Annie's Re-Do, a musty repository in a corrugated structure next to a string of corrugated structures out by the beauty shop. The register at Annie's was tended by an old man whose forehead was bubbled by tumors, a feature that reminded JP of the burls on an ancient oak. The clothing was hung onto bowed chrome racks by a redneck teen queen, whose hammy appraisals of new stock was idealistic and immature, and at home in the space.

JP had gone to Annie's often since moving to Pitchlynn, leaving his wife there one bag at a time. The man with the tumors was gracious enough to let JP present a labored, often meandering backstory with every single drop. He would smile at JP and wiggle a finger at Lucy (in the harness on her father's chest), learning that Dru's dirty, court-worn tennis shoes were *not* court-worn tennis shoes. Rather, they were documents of her ability to suspend a game, in order to indulge any bored kid who happened to wander onto the City of Chicago's public courts looking to whack a tennis ball like a baseball over the fence and into traffic . . . thus deflating all competition. ("Infuriating!" JP had exclaimed, earning a nod of sympathy from the clerk.) It was important to note that Dru's thick woolen scarves, Scottish and knotted and useless in Mississippi, were the last, best carriers of her scent.

"Am I weirding you out with this?" JP had once asked the man.

"Naw. I'm tickled to hear it," was the reply.

On this day, the day JP was headed home to Chicago, the old man greeted him with a kin-like grin.

"Last one from me," JP announced, plopping the garbage bag onto an old ladder-back rocking chair by the entryway door.

"No stories today?" the clerk asked. The teenager paused his perusal of newly racked clothes.

"Baby's in the car, so I'd better keep moving. You two take good care." JP wavered at the door. "I mean, y'all. Y'all take care."

Outside, he put the car in gear and cruised to the edge of the parking lot. A shoebox of Dru's recovered Post-it notes rode shotgun. He was poised to drive straight to I-55, to head north and never look back. He figured his life would end up on the northside of Chicago, in Bucktown or Wrigleyville, Lincoln Park, or, hell, maybe even all the way up to Evansville. (He could glimpse, perhaps, maybe, moving into some huge ruin, South Side or southwest, before filling his days with ethical property restoration . . . if such a concept even existed.) He had to get back to the weather, to the familiar obstacles.

Pulling to the lip of the parking lot, his blinker on for a right turn toward the interstate, JP stopped. He looked around, considered his own unfinished business, then turned left instead, toward Derby and Colleen's house.

Behind the sagged perimeter of yellow police tape, the small house was tranquil. The yard had been rutted by emergency and media vehicle tires, and the grass in between now grew stitch-like and wild. JP parked, and looked back to find Lucy conked out. He left the AC and motor running as he stepped outside.

He walked around back, to the blast site. The house had been sprayed with a white extinguishing agent, and the window frames held only fanged glass. The yard was littered by particleboard and plastic toys, and the metal poles of the monkey bars. The grill had been removed, leaving a charred stretch of fescue.

After checking on Lucy, he stepped into the carport, and peered through the diamond window of the kitchen door. He knocked out of habit, but of course no one answered. He considered the workshop Derby had set up against one wall, the hand tools hung on pegboard, the trade manuals and mason jars of loose hardware. The paint scrapers, and the barrel of wooden dowels and scrap molding. Items that were amassed for restoration, or rebuilding . . . but which instead now served as markers of hurt.

JP had never cared about Pitchlynn, though he'd done untold damage to a man who did. Under the guise of redemption, or penance, or some one-liner, aggrieved widower act, he had only come South with the agenda to hurt *back*.

He understood this now. He admitted it to himself.

Still, his pain was cavernous. How could Dru's family, her people, have treated her so poorly? Laid such guilt at her feet before shoving her off? While he now acknowledged without question that his wife had been clinically ill, he couldn't get over the idea that this place had fired the condition. If Pitchlynn had not abandoned her, she, in turn, would not have abandoned *him*.

Stepping to the workbench, JP inspected a glass jar packed with bolts and nuts, washers and grommets. He slung it down against the concrete, and a hail of glass and shrapnel skittered everywhere. He stepped over to the pole pruner in the corner, then picked it up and hurled it into the drive. He did the same with the Weed Eater and the square-point shovel; the rakes, the hoe, the post hole digger, and little Poulan chain saw. At last, he hoisted the big Husqvarna, but he was too gassed to chunk it.

JP WAS a third of the way through Bel Arbre before anyone noticed. He chain-sawed from within the cavern of thick lower limbs. The scream of the Husqvarna was all but deafening, and the skin of his palms had been split from vibration. His arms trembled to work the big saw, so he leaned his body into the cut, rocking the blade back and forth by shoving one hand onto the orange plastic casing. In reply, the blade bucked back now and again, jolting him to a stop. Splattered in sweat and sawdust, he then pushed it even harder.

Folks soon gathered on his lawn in a pack, yelling for him to quit. More than one neighbor dialed 911, though operators refused to acknowledge a "tree killing," or a "You've gotta stop him!," instead transferring the call to the non-emergency center. Behind the audience, the sitter held Lucy on her chest, pacing around at safe distance from the racket. (She had not known what to make of JP's flip-out, and hoped only to receive a sweet bonus and good rec.)

After exhaust from the chain saw motor had fogged up the streets, a pair of police cruisers pulled onto the property, followed by the fire department's first responder vehicle. Swirling colored lights blurred into the billow of smoke in the dusk. The cops called to JP over the patrol car PA, though they could only request that he stop, given the legality of his mission. At best he could be issued a citation for noise.

As if drawn by extrasensory distress, Susan George raced onto the scene. She, too, screamed at JP, then hurled her shoes toward the tree, one by one. She marched from cop to fireman to the growing crowd of townsfolk, demanding for anyone to stop him, to stop him *now*. No one did.

"Don't y'all get it?" she yelled. "This fool is gonna *kill himself*! And he's got a little girl. Now come on, help! Who are we?"

When no one reacted, she stormed straight toward the tree, but was arrested by the piercing crack.

Everyone scattered, fast as children.

# 9

olleen slung her old Army duffel bag into the car trunk, then slammed the lid. On the back floorboard of the vehicle was a small cooler stuffed with snacks. Riding shotgun was a spill of scratched CDs, a road map, her phone charger, an open pack of Mistys . . . and an *un*opened e-cig kit.

Her mother paced the front porch, bobbing Junior in her arms, while Little Sarah wriggled on a quilt beneath a catalpa on the lawn. Colleen's father paced around the old Celica chattering to himself. Having checked every fluid, Brice now stared at the tires as if to threaten them. Though the car had been good to go for a dozen years, the farthest her parents had driven it was to a vacation rental in the Smoky Mountains. Colleen would surpass that distance in a day.

Derby hobbled out onto the porch and into the yard. Leaned hard on his cane as he limped over and handed Colleen a blue porcelain urn.

"I put packing tape on the top," he said. "Otherwise it was gonna clack every time you hit a bump."

He had cycled through a winter of pigskin grafts, then cadaver grafts; through traction and rehab—and now, more rehab. He still wore a heavy plastic boot, and his eyes were glassy from pills. He hated having to rely on the latter, especially now that spring was at full throttle, but his body could not yet incorporate straight pain.

The urn was a gag of sorts, a morbid joke to anyone beyond the couple themselves. While not as pronounced or indulgent as a proper living wake, it served the same essential purpose: to recap the narrative that had bound him all his life, and as reminder that there were other stories to be told. At least, he figured, there could be different perspectives on the telling.

Derby and Colleen had collaborated on the idea that they, or in this case she, could help to fill the vessel with a hodgepodge of her own influence. Instead of the contents representing the life he had lived, or even the one he had insisted upon with her, in a sense they could represent things he hoped she would invest in him, show him, teach him, in the future. He scooped a few initial handfuls of backyard dirt into the urn, and told her that he didn't care what else might end up in there: sand, rocks, a pop top, or chopsticks.

"But if you can help it," he added. "How 'bout—"

"No ashes," she interrupted. "Or cig butts. I get it."

He kissed her forehead. "Now take this thing as far as you want to," he said. "Do what you will with it, and then come on home. Please."

"Roger that, babe."

Jeanette had barked the loudest over her daughter's decision to bolt. In a preemptive effort to keep Colleen in place, the mother-now-grandmother had both babysat and hired sitters, had cleaned and cooked and shopped. She had listened without judgment, and had researched trauma treatments from psychoanalysis to psychotropics, sharing all of her findings with anyone in the house. Having redecorated Colleen's old bedroom, updating the decor to suit independent adulthood, Jeanette even turned her own crafts room into a first-rate nursery. Between Derby's rehab, Colleen's shock, and the twins' relentless needs, the woman was exasperated. And terrified. And pissed.

Derby was mad, too—except when he wasn't. He had alternately or concurrently felt abandoned, betrayed, agitated, furious . . . and, goddammit, forever in love with Colleen. Though the meds worked pretty well to dull the blade of his emotions, any interaction with her, whether co-spooning baby food or squeezing side by side to brush teeth in the tiny half bath, still provoked him to snap, or bark, or brood.

Mostly, he begged her to stay. Her response was to touch him gently, nod in understanding, and say nothing. Though she was shrouded by guilt, her decision to leave was not about him, or them. At least, it wasn't about them *yet*. And Colleen knew, and her family knew, that nobody needed to push for a referendum on her marriage or her motherhood. If they had, or did, she'd be out the door forever.

So the household had resigned to the fact of Colleen's bug-out exactly as her folks had to the military deployment: spare any protest, and pray hard for safe return. Colleen seemed to be suffocating right in front of their eyes, and nobody knew how to revive her.

In the wake of the propane blast, Colleen had fallen into a clinical sort of calm, one kindred to her experience of four or five years before, in the days before Derby, but just after the war. She no longer groused or growled or giggled. Rather, she grew machinelike, insensate, even nursing her children as if on orders. And while this iteration was preferable to any seeking out of powder, or some other mode of her active ruination, it was toxic nonetheless.

Her decision to leave was only set into motion after Derby's medical bed was installed in her old bedroom. Having helped her husband situate on the adjustable, rubber-coated mattress, Colleen had then run to the bathroom to puke.

Her proximity to trauma, to a literal bed made by trauma, was just too much to stomach. Looking after Derby, tending his opioid mutters, smelling him and not finding the scent of his 3-in-One oil or cut lumber or earth, but rather only the fragrance of urine and plastic tubing, she'd been strafed by failure. It was, after all, the lack of her attention to detail—in this case, informing him of a commonplace propane hose leak—that had shattered things.

The only idea that could cut her emotions was the notion of physical distance. She believed that she would have to run, in order to return.

So she had flushed her puke, brushed her teeth, and gathered herself up in that little half bath. Walked outside to consider her surroundings. Her parents were sitting in their glider rockers on the porch, fussing with each other and holding her babies. The quartet swayed back and forth, happy as larks. Sarah was asleep on Brice's shoulder, while plump Derby Jr. fidgeted in Jeanette's lap. On a tile-topped end table sat a glass of Pepsi for Daddy, and a sweet tea for Mom. Colleen saw the perfection of the moment. She needed to rediscover how to *feel* it.

So she went back to her room, climbed onto that medical bed, and sat alongside snoozing Derby. She unfolded a highway map, letting it drape across his body. Now and again, if he grunted or seemed out of sorts, she patted him, and hummed a little bit, to soothe. "Sorry, babe," she whispered. "Hang in there."

He had *already* hung in there, of course. His reward would now be to live mostly alone: no wife and partner, let alone a confidante, friend, or anyone but his in-laws to putter around with. (Colleen was incensed that JP had left without a word, never even mailing a card to the hospital, let alone visiting, or calling, or sending a goodbye text.) (It would be some time before she and Derby found out about the 529 fund he'd set up for the twins, established after JP had sold the house to the LMA. It would take even longer before the chasm of frustration, or anger, or just plain old hurt, shrank down to a pothole's worth of abandonment when JP came to mind.) (They would never, ever know that JP had driven into the regional hospital parking lot on the morning after the tree fell, his last day in town. That while idling there, Lucy napping in the booster in the backseat, he had considered the drift of folks from the building entryway, and their radiated waves of anxiety. That he'd watched patient and volunteer and service provider flow in and out of the sliding glass doors, often slung up or limping, or just tacking toward the huddle by a cement ashtray on the periphery. That he had wanted to go in and visit, but had no idea of what he'd say to Derby, or Colleen. No idea of how to . . . apologize, or even attend? That instead, putting his car into gear, JP had decided to figure it out over the long drive home, certain—as certain as people are who talk themselves into taking care of things down the road, but then don't—that he would reconnect with them soon, yes, just as soon as things felt settled.)

One scrap of solace was that Winnie and Ladybug were back in orbit. In a sense, now that Hare was gone, Derby could turn the corner and realize the person he'd wanted to be: a seeming one-liner punch line, Mississippi local with a little house on his own plot of land. He'd tend a small stocked pond and wield a yeoman's work ethic. Most of all, he would at last live different, only in the exact same place, rehabbing family.

Good ole boy, the best ole boy. He wanted these things with her, and on behalf of the twins.

*Maybe*, Colleen thought, sitting beside him on the bed. She traced the highways on the unfolded map of America, St. Petersburg to Cincinnati, Boston to the Bay Area. Her heart began to skitter when she saw the name Menlo Park.

\* \* \*

SHE HAD a vision of what would come next. A reincarnation of a scene she had cobbled together over years of watching movies, or flipping through mags, or from the images of adventure born in that very childhood bedroom. Though the daydream had taken on new wrinkles over the years (a dream wasn't any good if it couldn't run adjacent to reality), swapping out professions or partners, if not the plot altogether, it had always begun with her driving away from Pitchlynn, and ended with a variation of her eventual return home.

In this case, on that day, the dream involved a reckoning with the desert:

On some afternoon hour on I-40 east, in Arizona or New Mexico, she would crest a great hill at great speed, her stomach lilting and plummeting, as if flying through turbulence. The hilltop would overlook an epic expanse, hemmed in by craggy cliff and populated by red desert mesas. Astounded by the openness, by the painted rust and amber shades of earth, the white rock formations here and there, Colleen would pull the car onto the shoulder and park. She would throw a sweatshirt over the scalding hood, then sit on it and smoke a joint—a habit picked up in the Northwest, the effect of which she could handle, could manage without abuse, and which whisked her to the elating but secure border of paranoia, like leaning over the edge of a metro tower as the wind lashed. She would sit for more than an hour, watching a dense storm system at the far edge of the void. Miles and miles away, the cloud cell would drift over the red, oxidized valley, so clearly defined against the surrounding blue sky. She would stare into and around but never *through* the storm, an opaque, shifting mass whose shadow crawled up and down the sides of outcrop and spur, across flattop and arroyo, blotting the far horizon, but never reaching her.

A day or so later she would pull back into that Mississippi driveway, in that same beater car. Her body would be less elastic, though still naturally fit, mostly young. She would have West Coast hair. In the yellow grass beside the driveway, her now three-year-old twins would be playing with plastic trucks. Junior would be a bit larger than Sarah, it would seem. The boy would be just a bit more *something*.

Her mother would now sit alone on the porch, watching over the toddlers, a glass of tea beside her. At the edge of the field that stretched out behind the house, Derby would guide a three-plow behind her daddy's old Allis-Chalmers D17, a handsome throwback tractor, misfitted and overambitious given the size of the plot—and as such, perfect for Derby. Catching sight of him, she would shiver against the seat belt.

It would be time to come clean. To offer him, at last, the full scope of her war stories, from deployment to Sarge, to the pig in the tree. After that, he could choose to take or leave the crush of her history. No matter his decision, it would be the only way forward.

The twins would stare at Colleen as she emerged from the car, their eyes sparked by concern, perhaps excitement, as they tinkered with memory.

* * *

So there was the compulsion to run, and the vision of coming home. Yet it was the actual, real-world drive *away* from Mississippi that defined her. Because the wildest thing happened: she couldn't leave.

Instead of turning north to Memphis, breaking free of the state in an hour before shooting west to California, Colleen decided to take the long way out. She drove through Oxford and Batesville, and to the far edge of Clarksdale, before turning south on Highway 61. She wanted to see the Delta one more time, with the fuzzy plan to end up in some motel in Louisiana, en route to Texas or maybe just New Orleans, having cut west on I-20 in Vicksburg. This route added only an hour or so to the schedule. She figured it no more than a long goodbye.

The signs read Bobo, and Alligator, and New Africa Road. She drove past sprinkles of small, weary buildings and businesses. Past shuttered doors and title loans and mural-clad nightclubs and reinvented work farms; she drove past manors and stately courthouses, the signifying tendrils of a lost identity, the totems of opulence, both dead and relentless. Flat blankets of cotton and soy fields unfolded for miles, as did corn, Mississippi corn, its acreage radiating outward on all sides, the seeming thickets of it broken at times by the mirrored ponds of a catfish farm. Outpost to outpost, field to field, there seemed so much time to think, or maybe even outrun thought.

She saw a sign announcing a small state park, and turned westward to enter it. Hers was the only car in sight, save the park ranger truck that sat outside a double-wide office. She pulled up in front of a large observation tower, an open-air, framework structure that was several stories tall, and with a zigzag staircase leading to a visitors' deck.

She got out, stretched, and started climbing the tower steps. The ascent reminded her of scaling the Victory Tower, a Basic Training structure back at Fort Jackson, South Carolina. She had aced that obstacle, beating out all in her company, all those years ago. Here, she sweated immensely with the ascent, pausing to gasp, though she didn't stop until she reached the upper platform. Her reward was a sweeping view of the Mississippi River, its statesmanlike width and vast alluvial plain. This was the superior vena cava of American identity.

It wasn't enough. Nowhere near it. So she climbed down and drove on, drove southward, deviating again. Colleen made use of the unfamiliar county roads, gaining a better handle on the Delta before hitting the interstate. She passed sign after sign, blue, brown, and green, reading Fannie Lou Hamer and James O. Eastland; B. B. King, Willie Morris, and Chief Greenwood LeFlore . . .

"Jesus Christ!" she shouted out upon seeing a Jim Henson Museum billboard. She swerved onto the road shoulder to take in the image of Kermit the Frog. Who knew that the amphibian was from deep in Mississippi?

Turning back onto Highway 1, she passed the small state parks around the Indian mounds. She thought to pull in and consider the grassy, lovely hillocks—but didn't.

In Vicksburg, she stopped at a Wendy's. Over a value meal with Biggie iced tea, it came to her that she had to see the coast. Deana had once described the phosphorus in the ocean, and how at night, every now and again, it sparked from your body as you swam. Or no. Actually, Colleen couldn't remember if Dean had been talking about the Gulf waters, or maybe the Florida Atlantic, or . . .

"Oh hell, Deana," she said way too loud, and then apologized to the family in the next booth.

Sitting and chewing her value meal burger, Colleen adjusted her exit strategy for the last time. Realizing that the only way to see the Mississippi coastline was to head east, not west, she decided to drive back toward Jackson, then Meridian, and to damn near Alabama, before cutting down the back roads to explore the breadth of the state's far boundary, and toward its tiny heel of shoreline.

She arrived at Pascagoula on fumes of exhaust, and exhaustion, and she vowed to hit the road west the next morning. At the very least, she knew the coastline interstate would chug her back through Texas (which could be doubly interesting, she thought, if it went anywhere near Dallas.) (It did not.)

She cruised Highway 90 along the shore, the dipping sun a cascade over steely water and white beaches. Tall columns of starlings twisted up like tornado spires. She cruised past antebellum mansions and post-modern high-rises, by weather-razed bungalows and post-Katrina condo boxes—side by side, mismatched, erected hodgepodge according to which structures had or had not survived the last hurricane. Now and again, she was distracted by the gloss and fire of neon from a massive casino hotel, and the draped vinyl banners that advertised three-for-one drinks and sluttish payouts. She looked left, to the water, and to the waning sunlight in the grainy hydrosphere. A mile or more out was a staggering wall of clouds, clouds like a continent, like some great looming Dover. These, too, were subject to the changing light, though they never moved closer to shore. She followed the silhouettes of brown pelicans in formation, gliding just above the surface of the amber tide, toward a stray pile or buoy or nearby marsh, to nest until daybreak.

The cars parked by the beach were rusted beaters, by and large, and/or beaters disguised by bright paint jobs. Their owners slung all manner of fishing accoutrement, plastic bucket, tackle box, and cooler.

Sea rods flung from the sides of a wooden pier like conductor's batons. The water transformed in spectrum, orange-lit to amber, crimson to purple, steel to blue, to bluer still.

A roadside marker proclaimed the drag to be the Gilbert Mason Memorial Highway. Colleen had no idea of who Dr. Mason was, nor did she care to find out. She was, however, tempted by the promise of a roadside seafood joint and the crowd gathered inside, communal under stark fluorescence.

She spotted a wooden sign that noted VACANCY and WATER VIEWS, then hit the brakes and pulled into the cluster of rental cottages adjacent to the highway. She noted the newness of the construction: new hedges, new asphalt lot, new bright yellow parking lines.

No history. No problem. She booked a room for the night, then unloaded the car. She left the urn in place, covering it with an old T-shirt. As she walked toward the cottage door, her shoulders and back burned and her knees felt like sopped sponges.

Inside, she threw the air conditioner on high, splashed her face with cold water, then paced over to the mini-fridge. Kneeling in front of it, she whispered, "Come on, now, please," then mouthed a silent hallelujah when she found it contained service. Grabbing two light beers, she went out the screen door of the bungalow and onto the small wooden deck. She closed the blackout curtains behind her, and sat in a banded patio chair.

The coastal wind was salted and thick. The deck was ringed by tall shrubs, so she couldn't see the ocean while sitting. Above her, just off the cusp of fingernail moon, was a large star. A planet, she supposed, though she really didn't know. She could look it up, sometime.

Colleen listened to the semi-regular flow of cars along the beachfront road, and the crumbling lull of the waves. She pulled a second chair over and put her bare feet in the seat, and she wished, and for a streaking instant *felt*, that she was out in the dark water, blind to all beneath, treading alongside Derby.

She downed the first beer in two huge gulps. When the wind shifted in a certain direction, she could hear a small party in the distance. She wondered if sometime her whole family, whatever that might look like, could gather here over a holiday.

The lamplight of the room seeped through the cracks in the curtains. She opened the second cold beer, took a sip, and wiped her lips with the back of her hand. Colleen understood at that instant that she did not know many things, and that she would only ever uncover a filament of truth. She knew that she loved the twins, even if she couldn't stay with them right now. She knew that of all the things or places that might unfold, whether Menlo Park or Mars, she would for damn sure take her children to the Jim Henson Museum in Leland, Mississippi. Sometime. She knew that a version of her husband was in an urn in the car, but did not know how long she would carry him. She knew that this broken state, her homeplace, was at once somehow beautiful, though she could not yet explain her relationship to it. She knew the feel of the salt air collecting on her skin, matting her hair. She knew the sound of the surf crushing sand in the distance.

She knew that she wished to do better, to be better. This, at least, she knew.

# ACKNOWLEDGMENTS

To my family, Lindsey and Whiting and De Masi and DeLoca. Thank you, love you.

To Bill Clegg and Jill Bialosky, with reverence for your belief, your insight, and your relentless coaching-up. (No small tasks, these.) To Drew Weitman, without whom this book would not be.

To my writer-reader-feedbacker pals: Kyle Beachy, Margaret Patton Chapman, Kelly*Luce, Robert Rea. To Chris Bower, forever on deck.

To Nancy Russell.

To Alice Randall, Mary Miller, Mihaela Moscaliuc, and Michael Waters. To Kate Daniels, Ted Ownby, Allan Hunt, Sara Levine. To Justin Quarry, George Livingston, Doreen Oliver.

To Lee Eastman, for insight into art-making. To Stephen Hendee, for art-making, and insight into propane grill catastrophe. To Amy Martin, a mold cracker among moldy crackers.

To Vince Springer, the only person other than my dad whose Happy Veterans' Day hits home. To Mary Gauthier, a comrade in the combat that is art.

To the Center for Medicine, Health, and Society at Vanderbilt University, the Center for the Study of Southern Culture at the University of Mississippi, and the MFA in writing at the School of the Art Institute of Chicago. To the Virginia Center for the Creative Arts, whose partnership with the NEA in support of veteran artists was pivotal to this book, and to the creative work of so many.

To Nashville, Austin, Oxford, Chicago, and the friends I long to see. Whether we are an hour or years removed, missing you keeps my pulse up. Per tutti i miei amici a San Terenziano, Comune di Gualdo Cattaneo, Umbria.

To the crew at W. W. Norton, editorial to design, sales to social media, and to the folks on the clock at National Book Co., Throop, PA.

To the booksellers. I miss being one of you, and won't forget what you do.

To the soldiers. I don't miss being one of you, and won't forget what you do.

# A NOTE ABOUT REFERENCES

This novel holds dialogue with a years-long blur of reading, listening, watching, reflecting. A few sources of note:

*The Mississippi Encyclopedia*, eds. Ted Ownby, Charles Reagan Wilson, Ann Abadie, Odie Lindsey, James G. Thomas Jr. (University Press of Mississippi, 2017).

*Dixie's Daughters* by Karen L. Cox (University Press of Florida, 2003).

*Making War at Fort Hood* by Kenneth T. MacLeish (Princeton University Press, 2013).

*Creek Country: The Creek Indians and Their World* by Robbie Ethridge (UNC Press, 2004).

"Some Go Home" by Jerry Jeff Walker, *Bein' Free* (ATCO Records, 1970).